FRANK MUIR was born in Glasgow, Scotland, and plagued from a young age with the urge to see more of the world than the rain sodden slopes of the Campsie Fells. By the time he graduated from University he'd had more jobs than the Clyde has bends. Short stints as a lumberjack in the Scottish Highlands and a moulder's labourer in the local foundry convinced Frank to seek a less laborious profession. Frank is currently overseas where he is working on the next novel in the Andy Gilchrist series. He visits St Andrews from time to time to carry out some serious research in the old grey town's local bars and restaurants.

By the same author

Eye for an Eye

Hand for a Hand

FRANK MUIR

Luath Press Limited

EDINBURGH

www.luath.co.uk

To all women betrayed by those they trusted.

First published 2009

ISBN: 978-1-906307-51-6

The author's right to be identified as author of this book under the
Copyright, Designs and Patents Act 1988 has been asserted.

The paper used in this book is recyclable. It is made from
low-chlorine pulps produced in a low-energy, low-emissions manner
from renewable forests.

Printed in the UK by
CPI William Clowes, Beccles NR34 7TL

Typeset in 10.5 point Sabon by
3btype.com

Three lawyers' tongues, turn'd inside out,
Wi' lies seamed like a beggar's clout.

A couplet from Robert Burns' original
manuscript of his epic poem, *Tam O'Shanter*,
which he was persuaded to leave out.

ACKNOWLEDGEMENTS

WRITING IS INDEED a lonely affair, but this book could not have been published without the help of the following: Gayle Richardson and Kenny Cameron of Fife Constabulary for police procedure. Forensic pathologist Doctor Marjorie Black for keeping me straight on the gruesome stuff. Everyone at the Strathkelvin Writers' Group for their continued support, despite my lengthy absence (I promise to return). Gavin MacDougall for taking a chance on publishing me, and Leila Cruickshank, Alice Jacobs, and Chani McBain, for thoughtful and exacting editorial input. Other readers and friends, too many to mention, whose encouragement and words of support inspired me to continue. Many thanks to each and every one of you, especially Anne.

And finally, this book is fiction. Those readers familiar with St Andrews and the East Neuk may notice that I have taken creative license with respect to some local geography.

Any and all mistakes are mine.

CHAPTER ONE

Seventeenth Hole, Old Course
St Andrews, Scotland

TAM DUNN WATCHED the golf ball take a hard kick left and slip into the infamous Road Hole Bunker, a sandy-bottomed pothole cut into a steep slope that fronted the seventeenth green.

Bud Amherst, one of an American four-ball that teed off at seven o'clock that morning, first on the ballot, threw his five-iron to the ground and turned to Tam. 'Goddammit,' he shouted. 'Course's nuthin but sand traps. Why the hell didn't you tell me it was there?'

The way Bud played golf it would have made no difference if Tam had first led him by the hand and stood him in the bunker. But Tam the caddy, always hopeful of an American-sized tip, bit his tongue. 'My mistake, sir.'

Close to the green, the bunker looked like a hole in the ground, its face a vertical wall of divot bricks that even the pros struggled to overcome.

'Whaddaya think?' Bud asked Tam.

'Sand-iron, sir.'

'I know that, goddammit. Which way's it gonna break?'

'About three feet from the left.'

'As much as that?'

'At least, sir.'

Tam kept tight-lipped as Bud took a few clumsy practice swings. The only way Bud was going to get the ball onto that green, he thought, was to lift it and place it. Bud turned to the bunker, prepared to step down into it, then stumbled backwards.

'Aw God, aw God.'

'Sir?'

Bud slumped to his knees. The sand-iron slipped from his grip. Hands pressed the grass to take his weight. One of the Americans, the tall one called JD, trotted across the green.

'Hey, Bud, you okay?'

Bud stretched an arm out and flapped it at the bunker.

Tam stepped to its lip and stared down at the hand, at skin as white as porcelain, bony fingers clawed like talons. Even from where he stood he could tell it was a woman's hand, a fine hand, he thought, except the wrist looked butchered and bloodied, like a cut of meat hacked, not sliced, the bone glistening like a white disc smeared with blood.

And all of Tam's hopes for an American-sized tip evaporated in the cold Scottish air.

CHAPTER TWO

'YOU'D BETTER GET down here, Andy.'

'Where's *here*, Nance?'

'Seventeenth green on the Old Course. Next to the Jigger Inn.'

Gilchrist drew his Mercedes SLK Roadster to the side of the road and pressed his mobile phone hard to his ear. It had been a while since he had heard DS Nancy Wilson as breathless. Not since they had run the length of the West Sands chasing what's-his-name. Blake. That was it. Murray Blake. Rapist, serial shagger, petty thief. How some people thought they could get away with it never failed to amaze him.

'What's got you fired up?' he tried.

'Severed hand in a bunker. Chopped off at the wrist. Victim's in her early twenties, late teens—'

'*Her* early twenties?'

'Sorry. Yes. It's a woman's hand.'

Gilchrist tugged the steering wheel hard right, floored the pedal, felt the tail-end throw out as the Merc spun in a tight circle. 'Any rings?' he asked. 'Moles? Scars?'

'Nothing obvious. Fingernails are short. Not varnished. Skin on the palm's a bit rough.'

'As in manual labour?'

'As in someone who didn't use hand lotion.'

'Or couldn't afford to.'

'Maybe.'

'It couldn't have come from the mortuary or been cut from—?'

'Not a chance, Andy. She's been murdered.'

'Get on to the university, Nance. Ask if any students have gone missing, called in sick, not turned up, whatever.'

'Got it.'

'Has Mackie seen it yet?'

'Just arrived. Along with the SOCOs.'

'Get the fingerprints through the AFR system as soon as.'

'Got it.'

If the victim had no criminal record, the Automatic Fingerprint Registration System would draw a blank. But it was worth a shot. 'Estimated time of...' He wanted to say *death*, then chose, '...amputation?'

'Too early to say.'

'How about the other bunkers?'

'We've got a team walking the course.'

'Has the course been closed?'

'Can we do that?'

'Yes, Nance, we can. Get on with it.' He listened to Nance call out an order, then knew from the fumbling on the mouthpiece that she was back. 'Who found the hand?' he asked.

'The day's first four-ball. All Americans.'

'Statements?'

'As we speak.'

'Any thoughts?'

'Nothing definite. The sand was smooth, which might suggest the hand was placed in the bunker.'

'As opposed to thrown in?'

'Odd, don't you think?'

'Maybe.' Gilchrist listened to the shudder of Nance's breath and was again struck by the undercurrent of excitement in her voice. He thought back to her statement – *Not a chance. She's been murdered* – and knew from the firmness of her response that there had to be more.

'What're you not telling me, Nance?'

'She, I mean… the hand, was holding a note.' A pause, then, 'Addressed to you.'

A frisson of ice touched the nape of Gilchrist's neck. He booted the Merc to seventy. 'What's it say?'

'Murder.'

'*Murder*? Is that it?'

'That's it.'

'So,' Gilchrist said, 'whoever severed the hand is sending me a message.'

'Looks that way.'

'How was the note addressed?'

'Printed on the outside of the envelope. Your name. DCI Andrew Gilchrist.'

Andrew. Not Andy. Was that significant? 'Typed? Or hand-printed?'

'Looks like a computer printer. The ink hasn't run. So maybe a laser printer.'

Gilchrist eyed the road ahead and eased back. Something tugged at his mind. 'I thought you said *note*.'

'I did.'

'*Inside* the envelope?'

'Yes.'

'Someone opened the envelope?'

'It wasn't sealed.'

Although the envelope was addressed to him, found in the clutches of a severed hand, it somehow niggled him that it had been opened and read. He supposed it really made no difference, but it irritated him nonetheless. 'Why use an envelope to put a note inside?' he asked. 'I don't get it. Why not just the note? Why the envelope, *then* the note?'

'To keep the note dry?'

'Maybe.'

'Greaves wants to assign you as SIO.'

Senior Investigating Officer. Gilchrist laughed. 'I would have thought a severed hand clutching a note addressed to me would make it obvious that I should be SIO.'

Hearing those words made something slump to the pit of his stomach. He had always dreaded this moment, the day when he would be targeted by some sick pervert. And the pervert who severed the hand had asked for Gilchrist to be involved. No, more than that, *wanted* Gilchrist to be involved. But why? Was the woman someone he knew? And at that thought, a surge of fear jolted his system. He struggled to keep his voice level. 'Describe the hand to me again, Nance.'

'Left hand. Skin's flawless, except for the fingernails. They're cracked.'

'Split, you mean?'

'No. Cracked.'

'Not bitten?'

'No.'

Gilchrist felt relief power through him. It was every policeman's fear that their family would be the victim of revenge, their lives threatened by some criminal bent on getting even for some long-forgotten score. The thought that the hand could have been his daughter, Maureen's, had hit him with the force of a kick to the gut. Maureen lived seventy miles away in Glasgow, but bit her nails and picked the skin. Although he nagged her to death about it, she had never been able to kick the habit, thank God, and despite the gruesome task ahead he almost smiled.

'The nails look as if they've been trimmed,' Nance went on. 'But the cracks still show.'

'Meaning?'

'I'm not sure. But it might help ID her.'

Ahead, Gilchrist saw he was fast approaching traffic. He eased his foot off the pedal. 'Listen, Nance, I'll be with you in ten minutes,' he said, and hung up.

Dear God. What a way to make a living. Would it ever end, the muggings, the rapes, the killings? And now this. A young woman's hand. What had happened? Had her hand been severed in the course of torture? Was she still alive? No, he thought. She was already dead. But where was the rest of the body?

He gripped the steering wheel, floored the pedal, overtook three cars.

And why a hand? Why leave it where it was sure to be found?
Simple. Because the perpetrator *wanted* the hand to be found.
Hence the note. For him.

But who was this young woman?

At the age of forty-seven, Gilchrist did not know too many
young women. His daughter, Maureen, of course. But she had never
invited him to meet her flatmates or friends. Not that she hid them
from him, but she lived away from home, ever since Gail left him.
And then there was Chloe, his son's girlfriend. And that was about
it as far as *young* women were concerned.

Still, he needed to put his mind at rest.

He located Maureen's number and felt a flush of irritation as
her answering machine cut in. Leaving messages seemed to be his
way of communicating with her these days. He kept this one short,
ordered her to give him a call, then called Jack. It was a wild
thought. But better to be sure.

'Hello?' Jack's voice sounded tired, heavy.

'Did I wake you up?'

'What time's it?'

'Almost eleven. The day's nearly done.'

'Hey, Andy, it's you.'

'Who did you think it was?'

Jack coughed, a harsh sound that seemed to come from his
chest and make Gilchrist think he had started smoking again. 'And
to what do I owe this pleasure?'

'Isn't a father allowed to call his son and ask how he is every
now and then?'

'Come on, Andy. First thing in the morning?'

Gilchrist let out a laugh. Jack was a freelance artist whose
creative side seemed to flourish only on the other side of midnight
and sobriety. Midday could be an early start.

'How's Chloe,' Gilchrist asked.

'Fine why?'

Gilchrist thought Jack's answer was too quick. 'I'd like to talk
to her,' he said.

'Why? What's up?'

Because we've found a severed hand and I'm scared to death it might belong to Chloe.

'I might be interested in buying one of her paintings,' he said. 'Can I talk to her?'

'Yeah, sure. I'll get her to call when she gets back.'

'Out shopping, is she?'

'Something like that.'

Gilchrist pressed the mobile phone to his ear. Jack had a cavalier attitude about most things, but his voice sounded lifeless. 'Everything all right?' he tried.

'Sure.'

'Why don't I believe you?'

A sigh, then, 'We had a lovers' tiff.'

'And?'

'And she's stomped off to cool down.'

'Sounds serious.'

'She'll get over it.'

'Good.' And Gilchrist meant it. Chloe was the best thing that had happened to Jack. An artist too, she had a calming effect on his wild son, even assuring him that Jack no longer smoked cigarettes or any other substances. He almost hated to say it, but he trusted Chloe more than he did his own son. He held on, expecting Jack to continue, but it seemed as if the topic of Chloe was over.

Gilchrist decided to change tack and felt a flicker of annoyance that he had to bring the subject up. But he needed to know. 'How's Mum?' he asked, and grimaced as he listened to the slow intake of breath followed by a rush of release.

'Not good, Andy. Not good at all.'

'How long?'

'Couple of months. Maybe less.'

'Jesus.'

'They've got her on morphine.'

'Is she still at home?'

'You know Mum.'

Gilchrist pulled to a halt behind a traffic jam that trailed past the Strathtyrum golf course to his left and seemed to end at the town of St Andrews. Ahead, the grey silhouette of St Salvator's spire and those of the abbey ruins lined the dark skyline. By the university buildings, black rocks fell to a blacker sea. Gilchrist closed his eyes, dug in his thumb and forefinger.

Gail. Sometimes he felt as if he still loved her. Other times he was not sure if it was being betrayed that had given him the right to wallow in self pity. He never understood why he still cared for her. Was it his hurt over her infidelity? Or her utter rejection of him once she had left? Or was it jealousy at her having found someone else? And now she was dying and there—

'Andy?'

Gilchrist looked up. 'Sorry, Jack. Stuck in traffic. Is Maureen still helping out?'

'I guess.'

'Have you heard from her?'

'About a week ago.'

'I've left umpteen messages on her answering machine.'

'That's Mo for you.'

'It runs in the family.'

'Hey, we're talking. Right?'

Gilchrist chuckled. 'If you talk to her, Jack, could you tell her to check her messages and give me a call?'

Jack grunted, which Gilchrist took to mean yes. The Citroën in front of his Mercedes stalled then lurched forward with a burst of grey exhaust. Gilchrist followed. 'Listen, Jack. I'll catch you later.'

Gilchrist thought it odd how different his children had become. Maureen and Jack were growing apart, *had* grown apart, professionally, politically, socially and, even though he hated to say it, financially. Mo was self-reliant and careful with money, taking part-time jobs for extra cash, whereas Jack could go months without selling a sculpture or painting, and no commissioned work in sight. Gilchrist often wondered how Jack survived, then ditched that question for fear of the answer.

But Mo was different. A young woman with definite views on

how to run her own life, with no sympathy for those who struggled. If Gilchrist could barely handle his relationship with his daughter, what chance did Jack have?

He pulled onto the road that led to the Eden Course and the driving range, and powered towards the Old Course Hotel. He found a parking spot close to the Jigger Inn. Beyond the stone dyke that bounded the course, a white Transit van spilled Scenes of Crime Officers in white hooded coveralls. Six in total. The putting green was encircled with yellow tape that trailed to the walls at the side of the road for which the Old Course's Road Hole was infamous.

DS Nancy Wilson caught his eye as he cleared the dyke. Behind her, the stooped figure of old Bert Mackie, the police pathologist, was slipping into the bunker, his assistant, Dougie Banks, helping him down. Nance signalled to Gilchrist and stepped across the green, away from the bunker and the team of SOCOs.

Puzzled, he followed her.

They met as she stepped onto the tarmac road surface and gave a quick glance to the side. 'You look worried,' he said to her.

'Ronnie's here.'

'Ronnie?' Then the name slotted into the tumblers of his mind with a surge of disbelief. 'Ronnie *Watt?*'

Nance nodded.

Gilchrist faced the green, his gaze settling on the back of a broad-shouldered man in a dark blue suit. He felt his legs move as if of their own accord—

Something clamped his arm.

He froze, glared into Nance's eyes.

'Don't,' she said. 'He's not worth it.' She tightened her grip. 'He's the Crime Scene Manager.'

'Not on my shift, he's not.'

'Too late, Andy.'

'Jeff can take over.'

Nance shook her head. 'No he can't.'

'Why the hell not?'

'Greaves has assigned Ronnie.'

'Is Greaves out of his bloody mind?'

'Andy. Don't,' she said, then released her grip. 'It's in the past,' she tried.

But Gilchrist was already striding away.

CHAPTER THREE

'GREAVES SPEAKING.'

'It's Andy Gilchrist, Tom.'

'Andy. I was wondering when I'd hear from you.'

I bet you were, you blundering old maniac. 'I've got a complaint.'

'Certainly, Andy. Let's have it.'

Chief Superintendent Greaves' politeness threw him. So, rather than struggle with fake diplomacy, Gilchrist pulled the trigger. 'What the hell's Ronnie Watt doing here?'

'He's on temporary assignment from Strathclyde—'

'You do know about Ronnie and me?'

'Yes I do, Andy.'

'Well, surely you must appreciate—'

'Let me say this once, and once only. DS Watt is back with Fife Constabulary and assigned to the St Andrews Division of the Crime Management Department. As are you. That is fact number one. Fact number two. Part of my remit is to assign officers to solve crimes as I see fit, taking into account the abysmal shortage of manpower. Fact number three. I'm bloody grateful to have experienced overload relief, and if I had to shuffle teams on the whim of every individual who complained, where—'

'As Senior Investigating Officer I have a right to assign my own team. And the last man I—'

'You're not the SIO on this case.'

'What?'

'*I* am.'

For one confusing second, Gilchrist wondered if he had misunderstood. Then he recovered. 'They found a note with—'

'Yes yes, I know all about the note.'

'Whoever committed this crime wants me on it. I *need* to be involved.'

'I'm not pulling you off, Andy.'

Gilchrist's breath exhaled in a defeated rush. 'I don't understand, Tom.'

'*I'll* be sio on this investigation, Andy. But with the shortage of manpower on top of all the paperwork I've got at the moment I'm assigning you to take charge. Ronnie will be your assistant.'

'I thought he was Crime Scene Manager.'

'DC Jeff Bowers will take over.'

Gilchrist squeezed his mobile phone, wished it was Watt's neck. He had misjudged Greaves. Greaves had no intention of becoming involved in the case. Assigning Gilchrist as some temporary sio was like fiddling the books. Gilchrist glanced across the green. Watt was staring at him, teeth exposed in a smile like a snarl, jaw masticating with the childlike joy of chewing gum. Gilchrist turned as a helicopter flew in from the south, preparing to touch down at the back of the Old Course Hotel.

'Is that clear, Andy?'

Crystal. 'One final question,' he said. 'Why put Watt and me together?'

'Because in this Division I don't want anyone to harbour past grievances. We're a team, Andy. And I *insist* that we all get along. Does *that* make it any clearer?'

Gilchrist watched the helicopter hover beyond the hotel then sink from sight. He could almost smell the fuel from its exhausts, imagined he felt the downdraft from its rotors as it lifted off, taking him away for his connecting flight to somewhere exotic.

Now, wouldn't that be nice?

All he had to do was tell Greaves to shove it, he was resigning forthwith, and he would be out of there. Post-haste. Watt was still staring at him, still chewing, like some tough guy posing. And in that instant, Gilchrist made up his mind.

'Clear as mud,' he said, and clapped his mobile phone shut.

Nance caught up with him as he crossed the putting green. Watt widened his stance and smile. Gilchrist stepped down the slope on the other side of the green. Watt stood below him, by the front face of the bunker.

Only ten feet separated them.

Gilchrist closed the gap, then he stood before him.

At six-one, Gilchrist and Watt were identical in height. But where Gilchrist was long-limbed and lean, Watt was stocky and broad. And Gilchrist was a young forty-seven to Watt's ravaged thirty-three. Too many late nights drinking and bullying had aged Watt beyond his years.

Gilchrist eyeballed him.

As if unsure of the protocol, Watt thrust out his hand. 'Good to see you again, Andy.'

'Don't push it.' Gilchrist waited for Watt to lower his hand. 'And it's DCI *Gilchrist*,' he added, then turned to Mackie. 'What've you got, Bert?'

Watt stepped forward. 'This—'

'Is your name Bert?' Gilchrist snarled.

Watt flashed his teeth, worked his gum. '...Is addressed to you,' he said, and held out an envelope to Gilchrist.

The envelope had been flattened, but creased where it had been crushed between the dead woman's fingers. He noted his name printed on it. 'Tell me it's been dusted,' he said to Nance.

'It's been dusted,' she said.

'Anything?'

'Nothing.' Watt again. 'It's been wiped clean.'

Gilchrist eyed Watt. 'We seem to have a problem here.'

'We do?'

'You have a habit of answering questions not addressed to you.'

'Oh, yeah?'

'I don't like it.'

'I don't give a flying fuck what you like—'

'Let's get one thing clear—'

'Oh for goodness sake stop squabbling and lend me a hand.' Mackie clambered from the bunker, his face reddened from the effort, or frustration at having to listen to two grown men bickering. Gilchrist grasped Mackie by his gloved hand and pulled.

Out of the bunker, Mackie gave a stiff stretch, grimacing as he pulled his shoulders back. 'Oh to be young again,' he said, and peeled back the hood of his coveralls to reveal a bald pate as red as his face. Then he padded up the slope to the green.

Gilchrist struggled to ignore Watt's presence as he trailed Mackie. On the green, he asked the old man, 'What do you think?'

Mackie grimaced. 'That it's only a matter of time until the rest of the body turns up.'

'So it's murder. Not amputation.'

Mackie shook his head. 'Impossible to say. Whether or not it's murder,' he added. 'But whosoever's hand that is, was dead when it was hacked off.' He frowned. 'I'd be willing to bet she was murdered, though. The skin is unusually pale.'

'Meaning she'd lost a lot of blood?'

Mackie nodded.

'Are you suggesting her throat was slit?' Watt again.

'I'm suggesting nothing of the sort,' snapped Mackie. 'Don't be so bloody ridiculous.'

Gilchrist almost smiled. Old Bert Mackie had been Police Pathologist for Fife Constabulary for nigh on forty years. He had cut open more bodies, performed more post mortems, dealt with more ignorant individuals than Gilchrist had hot breakfasts. DS Ronnie Watt was no more an irritation to Mackie than a fly on his bald crown.

Mackie flapped a hand out to his side and caught Dougie Banks' eye. 'Bring it here,' he grumped.

Banks removed a plastic bag from the SOCO Transit van and carried it across the putting green. Banks was a doctor in his own right, but in the presence of Mackie seemed more like a student. Mackie grabbed the bag with a thankless lunge then turned his back as Banks returned to the Transit van. It pleased Gilchrist to watch Watt step in beside Banks, in forced conversation, a coward's way of not losing more face.

Mackie dangled the bag in front of Gilchrist, prodded the clawed fingers with a gloved hand. 'See here,' he said, 'the tips of the first three fingers are slightly flattened. And the base of the thumb, too. And what could be lividity at the heel of the palm. See?'

Gilchrist peered through the clear bag, thankful that it protected him from the smell of decomposing flesh. 'Meaning?'

'I'm guessing she was killed first, then placed on her back, probably on something hard while she was cut up. Maybe the floor.' He held out his left arm. 'Imagine this is her arm. If it was by her side,' he said, and bent his fingers into the shape of a claw, 'it would rest on the floor just like this. See?'

'She died without a struggle?'

Mackie lowered his arm. 'There appear to be no signs of distress in the fingernails, or the skin. No self-defence wounds. Nothing that would suggest she put up a struggle. But I'll be more definitive once I've had a closer look in the lab.'

'Any idea of age, size, anything that would help us pin her down?'

Mackie grimaced then let out a rush of air. 'Somewhere between fifteen and thirty, I'd say. Perhaps average height at five-four, five-eight. On the frail side, I'd say. Which could give the impression of being taller than she really was. And from what I can tell, I would say she was a natural blonde, too.'

Gilchrist made a mental note, then tried, 'Occupation?'

Mackie shook his head. 'The skin is fine, though a tad rough near the ends, the nails clean, so we can rule out any manual work. If she's from St Andrews, I would be looking at university records. A student, perhaps. But I couldn't say at this point.'

'You said there was no distress in the fingernails. Nance said they were cracked.'

'A little. My first guess would be not work-related, but poor maintenance, poor diet, that sort of thing. All in all the hand looks clean, almost delicate. Quite sad, really.'

'And were the fingernails trimmed?'

'They were.'

'Before or after death?'

Mackie shook his head. 'I've no clear way of telling. She could have trimmed them herself, you know. Women have a tendency to be more particular about their personal hygiene than men.' He frowned. 'But I'll look into that. If they were trimmed after death, maybe it was to clean them of incriminating evidence.'

'Like skin scrapings?'

'Yes. But that would suggest a struggle, and everything about this hand suggests otherwise.'

'How soon after death was the hand amputated?'

'Rigor mortis has set in. So, we're somewhere between twenty-four and forty-eight hours after death. I'd put us smack dab in the middle, say, at thirty-six hours.'

Gilchrist stared back along the fairway, at the green and brown undulating expanse, seeking out the distant figures of uniformed constables combing the bunkers. From behind the hotel, he could still hear the dying whine from the helicopter's engine. Groups of people looked out of opened windows. On the walkway below, a straggling line of spectators dotted the boundary wall. He returned to Mackie. 'Thirty-six hours places her time of death near midnight the night before last.'

'Precisely.'

'As good a time as any to kill someone?'

'Then hack them to pieces.'

Gilchrist shook his head. How someone could chop another human being into bits was beyond him. What went through their heads as they were doing that? What prompted someone to kill in the first place? Most murders were committed by someone who knew the victim. But in this case Gilchrist knew the murderer was someone who knew *him*. Did that mean the killer knew the victim? Or only that Gilchrist did? And why him? What was the connection?

He faced Mackie, struck by how clear the old man's eyes looked against the weathered grain of his face, like jewels set in blemished wood. A narrow line of white stubble ran under his chin where he had missed with the razor.

'Is there anything else you can tell me, Bert?'

Mackie held the plastic bag level with his eyes. 'The middle finger has a nick in the skin,' he said, and pointed at it. The bag twisted in his hand.

'A paper cut?'

'No. To the side of the nail. It's almost as if she's pulled the skin back to the cuticle. Not all the way back, mind you. The other fingers are quite tidy.'

'Not a nail-biter, then?' Gilchrist asked, worried by his need to seek further reassurance.

'This woman has never bitten her nails. But cuts and cracks and flaking skin and the like are all a natural process of everyday life. It looks as if this nick has healed. And maybe reopened.'

Gilchrist nodded, but he failed to see the significance of Mackie's comment. 'Reopened in a struggle?' he tried.

'No. That's not what I'm saying.' Mackie pulled the bag closer. The plastic almost touched his nose. 'There's some discolouration in the cut. Here.'

'Dried blood?'

'Not blood. No. It looks yellow.'

'Like an old bruise?'

'No.' Mackie swung the plastic bag towards Gilchrist and pointed at the middle finger. 'See here,' he said. 'It could be paint.'

'What kind of paint?'

'Couldn't say at this stage.'

Movement to the side caught Gilchrist's eye. Watt was stepping from the SOCO van. 'Listen, Bert, I'll leave you to it. As soon as you find out anything else, get back to me.' He turned and walked towards Nance.

'*Hey.*'

Gilchrist stopped on the edge of the green.

Watt was walking towards him like a lion with its eyes on a limping springbok. He waved a hand. 'We need to talk.'

Gilchrist turned, stepped down the slope, and stood at the edge of the bunker. One SOCO was on his hands and knees, brushing samples of sand from an indentation that Gilchrist assumed had been made by the hand. He heard Watt's breathing behind him.

'What's granddad saying?' Watt asked him.

'You'll read his report when he's finished.'

'Will he live that long?'

'You had something to say?'

'Yeah. I've been on the phone with Greaves.'

'Good for you.'

'And I don't like it any more than you do.'

Gilchrist barked a laugh. 'Don't flatter yourself.'

Watt twisted his head, spat out his gum. It flew over the tape and landed in the deep rough. 'Look,' he said. 'My life's changed. *I've* changed. I'm a different person.'

'What're you trying to tell me?'

'I want to put the past behind us.'

'Are you asking me to forget what happened?'

Watt seemed stumped by the question.

Gilchrist caught a faint whiff of stale alcohol and knew in that instant that nothing had changed. 'Greaves wants us to work together on this,' he said.

Watt chewed imaginary gum, gave a thoughtful nod.

'For the sake of the investigation,' Gilchrist went on, 'I'm prepared to do that. But the instant you screw up, I won't give a toss what Greaves wants. You're history.' Watt continued to nod, but Gilchrist caught a current of anger ripple across his jaw. 'Okay, so far?'

'Gotcha, Andy.'

Gilchrist shook his head. 'You're not listening.'

'Yeah, I got you.'

'No you haven't.'

Watt frowned. 'Oh, yeah, right. DCI Gilchrist. I got it. Yeah.'

Gilchrist turned to Nance as she approached him, notebook in hand.

'I need the two of you to talk to everyone who buys, sells, or uses paint,' he said. 'Ask if they remember seeing a woman, a natural blonde, in the last several days, maybe as far back as a week. Someone slender, tending towards frail. Might be worthwhile starting at the university, students who paint as a hobby, or know someone who does—'

'That's asking a lot.'

Gilchrist eyed Watt. 'Any other suggestions?'

'Yeah. Put out an appeal on the telly.'

'And ask what? Know anyone who's lost a hand? Get real. It's early days for that.' Something in Gilchrist softened at that moment. Maybe it was because they now stood at the start of a major investigation. Or maybe it was the thought of the massive task ahead of them. If he was to solve this crime, find the killer of the young woman, put to rest the grief of her family, he needed all the help he could muster. Maybe Greaves was right. Maybe he was going to have to bite the bullet of the past. 'We can try that later,' he said to Watt. 'When Mackie gives us a better fix on her ID.'

Watt nodded, and Gilchrist knew from the tightening of the jaw that his reluctant agreement had been noted. 'Any more questions?' he asked.

'Yes.' It was Nance. She had her notebook open and was scribbling in it. Without looking up, she said, 'Why paint?'

Despite Mackie's uncertainty, Gilchrist wanted to sound positive. 'Bert thinks he's found some traces of paint.'

'What kind of paint?' Nance asked.

'What kind of paint can you get?' Watt said.

'Oil. Watercolour,' said Nance, then gave Watt a smile that failed to reach her eyes.

'Maybe even printer ink,' Gilchrist added. 'But it's too soon to say. We need to start digging while Bert does his stuff in the lab. So get going.' He stepped away. 'Debriefing's in my office at six,' he said, and walked up the slope onto the green.

As he strode towards his car he shoved his hands deep into his pockets, felt his body give an involuntary shiver, and wondered if he was trying to shake off a chill or memories of the past? *For the sake of the investigation,* he heard his mind echo, *I'm prepared to do that.*

Work with Watt? As if the past did not exist? Could he really do that?

As a detective in charge of a murder investigation, perhaps.

But as a father, that was asking for the impossible.

CHAPTER FOUR

THE REMAINDER OF THE DAY consisted of a barrage of meetings and phone calls. After debriefing, which turned up a list of one hundred and twenty-seven names and addresses of students who had an interest in painting, or knew someone who had, Gilchrist put an end to the day. Without specifics from Mackie, they could be burning valuable man-hours and burying themselves in a mountain of needless information.

He reached Beth's flat just after eight-thirty and parked his Roadster next to her Rover. Despite leaving two messages on her answering machine, Beth had not called. The widening gap in their relationship troubled him, and he worried that they would not survive until the end of the week, let alone the end of the summer.

He let himself in and found Beth in the kitchen chopping tomatoes. She turned as he entered, and he smiled and stepped up to her, gave her a quick peck on the cheek. 'How are you feeling?' he asked. It seemed that he always asked that same question and always received the same lie for an answer.

'Fine,' she said.

'Any better?'

'I'm fine.'

'How was the shop today?'

Beth slid the wide blade of her butcher knife under the tomato slices, scooped them up, and dropped them into a fine-glass salad bowl half-filled with lettuce, cucumber, chives, carrots. On the black top of the cooker, two brown eggs rattled in a pot of boiling water.

Gilchrist tried, 'What are we having?'

'Tuna salad.'

'Sounds perfect,' he said, and saw in his comment that he, too, was becoming numbed to their existence. He longed to take her out for an Indian, a Chinese, even plain old steakpie, chips and beans at the Central, or a stand-up fish and chips at PM's for God's sake. But whenever he suggested they eat out, fear seemed to shift behind her eyes, and he changed the subject before the shaking started. It seemed as if the only food they could now eat had to be made with Beth's own hands. Something had to give. He knew that. But what, and when, were the two unanswerable questions.

'Beer's in the fridge.' Her voice livened. 'Could you pour me a wine while you're at it? Cindy bought some Cabernet Merlot. It's from Chile. I thought we might try it.'

'Sounds nice,' said Gilchrist, knowing the *we* meant Beth by herself. 'Small or large?'

'I'll start with a small, thank you.'

Gilchrist found his favourite corkscrew in the drawer in the utility room, the Cabernet Merlot in the small fridge. Beth liked her wine chilled. Or more to the point, Beth liked her wine. Her drinking was not at the out-of-control stage yet. In the meantime, Gilchrist kept a watchful eye.

He poured the red wine into a crystal glass, making sure he gave a good measure. He had come to learn that the bigger the measure, the slower Beth drank. When the glass looked as if it was nearing the bottom, she would gulp it down and look for a top-up. He flipped the top off a Budweiser, his feeble attempt to limit his intake of real ale, and carried the glass of wine through to Beth.

'There you go,' he said.

She pushed a tin of tuna to the side and lifted the glass to her lips.

'Delicious?' he ventured, and watched her eyes glitter back at him. 'Cheeky little wine with a taste of the Andes?'

She laughed and took another sip. 'Wonderful,' she said.

'So, how was the shop today?' he tried again.

'Okay.'

'Cindy still controlling the show?'

It was a joke of his. Beth ran her own business, an upmarket shop called *This and That*, which sold eclectic home accessories aimed at the American tourist market. But Cindy had proven so indispensable it seemed to Gilchrist as if she ran the business. And even more so since Beth's attack.

'She's thinking of leaving,' Beth replied.

Gilchrist reacted by taking a slow sip of his Budweiser. It tasted weak and gassy compared to an Eighty-Shilling. 'When?' was all he said.

'She didn't say.' Beth squeezed a long worm of mayonnaise into the tuna and chopped it with a fork.

'Why?' he asked.

'She wants to finish her education.'

'Go back to university?'

'Yes.'

'Courses don't start until September. That gives you plenty of time to find a replacement.'

Beth took another sip, longer this time, then eyed the bottom of the glass and threw it back. 'She's going to work in Majorca,' she said. 'Steve knows someone who runs a hotel. They're looking to staff up in the spring.'

Which gave Beth about one month.

Not good. Not good at all.

'Same again?' he asked.

'Sure.'

'Large one this time?'

'Why not?'

In the utility room, Gilchrist poured a hefty measure into her glass then tipped the bottle and poured most of it down the sink. 'What's the hotel called?' he shouted, his voice drowning the sound of running water.

'She told me the name, but I can't remember.'

Back in the kitchen, Gilchrist placed Beth's wine on the counter-top, then began to set the table, carrying plates and cutlery and bowls of food with one hand, finishing his Bud with the other.

Then they sat.

Neither spoke as Beth double-spooned the salad onto their plates, adding generous helpings of tuna, beetroot and rice. Gilchrist doused his salad with fat-free Italian dressing and peppered his tuna.

'I think I'll sell the shop.'

Gilchrist returned his knife and fork to the side of his plate. 'Beer,' he said, and rose.

When he returned, he asked, 'Why?'

'I told you. Cindy's leaving.'

Gilchrist took a slow sip of beer. His worst fears were being realised. Beth, once a successful businesswoman who ran her life and her shop with the drive and ambition of someone half her age, had been beaten into defeat. Not by poor management; her shop was a phenomenal success. Not by age; she had just turned forty. Not by illness. Not in any general sense of the word, that is. But by the mental after-effects of an attempted rape in her home last year.

'Cindy's not indispensable,' he offered. 'No one is.'

'I'm no longer happy.'

Gilchrist tried to keep the focus on Beth's shop. He had found to his detriment that whenever Beth mentioned not being happy, their discussion went one way. Downhill. 'You could put an ad in the newspaper,' he tried. 'I'm sure you'd be flooded with—'

'You're not listening to me.'

He took a mouthful of salad, and mumbled, 'Yes, I am.'

'What did I say?'

He swallowed. 'That you're no longer happy.'

'That's right.' Beth stabbed a forkful of salad at her mouth and crunched it with determination. She washed it down with a mouthful of wine, then stared at her food as if deciding what to kill next.

Gilchrist tried a forkful of his own, when all of a sudden Beth slapped her hands on the table. Her fork bounced off the wood and clattered to the floor.

She glared at him. 'I'm not happy, Andy. All right? I'm not happy with my shop. I'm not happy with my house. I'm not happy with the way I look, the way I feel. I'm not happy with my life. I'm not happy with us. I'm *just. Not. Happy.*'

Gilchrist let several seconds pass before saying, 'Anything to do with Buchanan?'

'Oh not this again.'

'You missed your last appoint—'

'*Fuck* Doctor Buchanan. I'm not going back.' She stood. Anger flushed her face. A tremor started at the tips of her fingers, worked its way up her arms.

Gilchrist pushed back from the table.

'Stay away, Andy. *Stay away from me. All right?*'

'Beth. I think—'

'I can't stand you *near* me anymore. I can't stand *anyone* near me.'

Gilchrist held out his hand to her, hoped she would take it, but knew deep within the heart of him that she would not. 'Beth,' he whispered, and stood. 'Let me help. Please. I can—'

'I don't want anyone's help,' she choked. Tears welled in her eyes. 'I just want to be alone.' She swept past him, through the doorway, along the hall, into the back bedroom.

Gilchrist slumped onto his seat. He placed his hands on the table, stared at his arms, surprised to see them tremble. He took several deep breaths, tried to still the pounding in his chest, then stood and walked through to the front bedroom, the one that used to be Beth's.

It was in this room, that queen-sized bed, wrists tied to that headboard, ankles to those footposts, where the attempted rape had taken place. After the incident, Beth had wanted to sell her flat, but Gilchrist talked her out of it, persuaded her to give herself time. *Six months. Even a year. You'll see things differently in time*, he told her. *Time is a great healer.* But he now worried that Beth was beyond healing.

Beth never entered that bedroom anymore. The door was always kept closed on a part of her life that she demanded be obliterated from existence. Nor the master bathroom, either. Not since the attack. But despite that, Gilchrist decided to take no risks. He'd had a carpenter friend install a proper lock on the cabinet and give him the only key.

Gilchrist unlocked the cabinet, removed a plastic bottle. In the kitchen, he half-filled a glass with bottled water from the fridge. Then he walked along the hallway, glass in one hand, valium pill in the other.

He opened the door to the back bedroom.

'Beth?'

Silence.

He stepped inside. Moonlight shone another window on the wall. Beth lay huddled under her continental quilt, her body folded in the foetal position. He sat on the edge of the bed.

'Take this,' he said.

Without a word, Beth turned, lifted her body on one arm, let Gilchrist place the pill in her mouth and give her a sip of water. She swallowed with an audible gulp and slumped back onto the pillow. Then she turned her back to him.

Gilchrist brushed his hand over the side of her face, tucking her hair behind her ear. 'Oh, Beth,' he whispered. 'Whatever's going to happen to us?'

But deep in the heart of him, he knew.

* * *

'Pint of Eighty, Eddy, and a couple of sausage rolls.'

'That fine woman of yours not looking after you?'

Gilchrist replied with a half-smile. After leaving Beth asleep, he had cleared the table, binned the salad, stuffed the dishes into the dishwasher, then stepped out for a pint and a bite in Lafferty's. He cocked an eye at the television set in the top corner of the bar and recognised the first and eighteenth double fairway of the Old Course. The hotel in the background swelled as the camera zoomed in on the seventeenth green, closer still until it slipped from view and the Road Bunker filled the screen.

35

'There you go, Andy. This one's on me.'

'Cheers, Eddy.'

Fast Eddy glanced up at the television. 'That one of yours, Andy?'

'Afraid so.'

'Was on earlier. And that plonker, the one you had the run in with years back, he was on. Chewing gum like some bigshot. You should've heard Marge.' Fast Eddy grinned, his green eyes glistening. 'Wetting her knickers for the guy. God knows what the women see—'

'Sausage rolls?'

'On their way.' Fast Eddy slipped out from behind the bar and headed to the kitchen in the back.

Gilchrist took a sip of his Eighty-Shilling, removed his mobile phone from his inside jacket pocket, and dialled Nance. It barely rang.

'Andy?'

'Where are you, Nance?'

'Just leaving the Office.'

'Alone?'

'At last.'

'Care to join me?'

'What for?'

'A pint.'

'I meant, for what reason?'

'Come and join me and find out.'

A pause, then, 'Let me guess. Lafferty's?'

Gilchrist chuckled. 'Sherlock Holmes the second.'

'Sherlock was a man. I'm not sure if that was an insult or a compliment.'

'I would never insult you, Nance. You know that.'

She chuckled in response, said, 'Give me ten,' then hung up.

By the time Nance arrived, Gilchrist had finished his plate of sausage rolls, which included two extra thrown in by Fast Eddy to make up for his poor service.

'Well well well,' said Fast Eddy, his eyes lighting up. 'My most favourite Detective Constable on the entire planet.'

'The answer's still no.' Nance pulled up a stool beside Gilchrist.

Fast Eddy placed a hand flat to his chest. 'You're breaking a lonely Irishman's heart, my lovely.'

'Give it up, Eddy. My knickers are handcuffed to my bra.'

Fast Eddy laughed, a staccato chuckle that had two women in the corner table frown his way. 'How do you know I'm not a Houdini in disguise?' he asked her.

'Houdini got out of tight places. Not into them.'

'Ah, but a man can live on dreams for only so long.'

Nance rolled her eyes to the ceiling. 'Your patter's getting raunchier, Eddy. Keep this up and I might have to charge you for indecent—'

'Exposure?'

Nance shook her head. 'Just give me the usual. And another one for Andy.'

'Ah, you've cut me to the core.' Fast Eddy pulled the first of two pints of Eighty, letting one settle as the other one swelled. 'And I'll never know how you manage to keep that lovely figure of yours looking so slim drinking all this real ale.'

'I get plenty of exercise running away from hard-ons like yours.'

Fast Eddy chuckled.

'Anyway, I'm far too young.'

'Not at all. I think we'd make a grand couple.'

'I think they should change your name to *Past* Eddy.'

Fast Eddy gave out another chuckle. 'And a wit as matchless as her eyes. How do you stand it, Andy?'

Gilchrist pulled out his wallet, removed a twenty.

'I'm getting these, Andy.'

'I owe you one, Nance.'

'Since when?'

'Since teaming you with Watt.'

Nance's face hardened. 'In that case, you owe me more than one.'

Gilchrist tried a smile, not sure he pulled it off. He pressed the twenty across the bar. 'One for yourself, Eddy.'

'Now that's what I call a true gentleman.' Fast Eddy pushed two pints across the bar, heads settling on a rising creamy base.

'There you go,' he said. 'That's one for the lady, and another for the gentleman.'

A woman sidled up to the end of the bar, and Fast Eddy flashed a faster smile. 'With you in a sec, love.'

Gilchrist raised his pint, tapped it against Nance's, and asked, 'How'd it go?'

'In what respect?'

Gilchrist smiled. He sensed Nance was playing it cagey, not sure how to take him, undecided whether to expect his wrath or his praise. 'With Watt,' he offered.

'One guess.'

'Don't tell me he tried it on.'

Nance screwed up her face. 'Not a chance.'

Gilchrist hoped she read the plea in his eyes. *Just let me know the instant he does*, he willed her. The man could not help himself. Like a leopard could not change its spots, Watt could not change his personality. It was as simple as that. Gilchrist looked to his pint. 'Well, keep me posted.'

'I can look after myself.'

Gilchrist smiled, took a sip of his beer. It tasted more bitter than the first one.

'Why did you ask me to come?' Nance asked.

Gilchrist twisted the pint in his hand. 'I can't explain it,' he said, 'but over the years I've come to rely on that gut feeling when things don't seem quite right, but you can't put a finger on it.' He took a long sip, loved the feel of the beer sliding back, and noticed, as if for the first time, how dark Nance's eyes were, almost black, how little make-up she wore, how attractive she was, and saw how Fast Eddy's patter might not just be patter, but a genuine attempt to find a date.

'And?' she said.

'And I call it my sixth sense.'

'I know all about that sixth sense of yours,' she said. 'It's not to be scoffed at.'

He tried a smile, but felt tired all of a sudden, tired of the endless pursuit of criminals, the pointless aim of it all, the charging, the sentencing, the jailing, then the early release so they could go out and do it again. The utter futility seemed overwhelming, like trying to stop the rising tide, a sea filled with barbarians, the rough and ready scum of the earth who would rather rob a ninety-year-old blind pensioner than do an honest hour's work.

'You're a bit of a local hero,' Nance said. 'Especially after that last case.'

'I got lucky.'

'Well, get lucky on this one.'

He felt a frown crease his brow, felt that familiar weight of failure shift through his being. 'I think that's why I asked you for a pint,' he said to her. 'I don't feel lucky on this one. I don't like it. I don't like it at all.'

'Because of Watt?'

'Among other things.'

'Such as?'

Gilchrist never understood how his sixth sense worked, only that he had come to depend on it. He struggled to ignore the sense of dread that swelled in his gut. 'I don't like my name being on an envelope. I don't like a hand being delivered to me. We're being toyed with.'

'You think we'll find the rest of the body?' she asked.

Bit by hacked off bit. 'I'm sure of it,' he said. 'We'll be given more clues. Why else write a single word on the note. *Murder.* What's that supposed to tell us? I don't know. But something tells me when we do work it out we're not going to like it.'

Nance sipped her beer.

'I think this case is going to be painful, Nance. I think that's what I'm trying to say.'

'Painful for you?'

He nodded and surprised himself by placing his hand on her shoulder. He flexed his fingers. 'And you watch yourself with Watt. Don't trust him.' He removed his hand, turned back to his pint. 'Just watch yourself, Nance. Okay?'

But he knew it was not just Nance he was worried about.

CHAPTER FIVE

GILCHRIST WAKENED WITH A START.

The ringing continued, an electronic melody that told him the call was coming through on his mobile phone, not his bedside phone. He threw back the bedsheets, slid his legs onto the floor. He stumbled against the wall, flicked on the wall-switch.

Light exploded into his brain.

He peered through half-opened eyes. Where the hell had he put it? He turned to the sound, saw his trousers, socks, shoes, shirt, strewn across the floor, his jacket dangling from the corner of the wicker laundry basket. A surge of nausea threatened to engulf him, then hung in the pit of his stomach. The ringing did not let up.

He reached his jacket and retrieved his phone. He cleared his throat, and choked, 'Gilchrist.'

'Christ. You sound rough.'

Gilchrist coughed. 'Who's this?'

'DS Watt. Sir.'

'What...' Then it hit him. 'Aw, shit. Don't tell me.'

'The Principal's Nose.'

'The *what?*'

'Another bunker on the Old Course. Sixteenth fairway.'

Gilchrist burst wide awake. 'Another body part?'

'Right first time.'

'The other hand?'

'Yes.'

Gilchrist felt his shoulders slump. He slid his hand down his face, felt the rough crunch of stubble on his chin and neck. His nightmare had started. 'Any notes?'

'Yes.'

Gilchrist clenched his jaw, felt the back of his eyes throb. A mental flash of Nance leaving Lafferty's after two pints, only ever two, blouse loose, a flash of cleavage like swollen flesh as she gave a quick peck. Then how many after that? Five? Six? More? Jesus. No wonder it hurt. 'And the hand?' he growled. 'Is that bagged and sealed, too?'

'Lying where it was found.'

Thank God for small mercies. 'What's the note say?'

'Massacre.'

Massacre? 'Handwritten? Printed?'

'Printed. Same as last one.'

'Spelled correctly?'

A pause, then, 'Yeah.'

Well, at least he could write. Or maybe he had spell-check on his computer. 'Who found the hand?' he asked.

Watt gave out a sigh, as if the demand of answering too many questions was tiring him. 'A man by the name of Charlie Blair while walking his dog,' he said. 'Would you like the dog's name?'

Gilchrist thought of hanging up, then glanced at his watch. 6:24. He walked to his bathroom, clicked on the light. 'Tell me we inspected the Principal's Nose yesterday,' he growled.

'Every bunker on the Old Course was looked at yesterday. And half the rough.'

'Who was in charge?'

'Constable Jack Murray.'

'Double check it.'

'Way ahead of you. Jack's already confirmed the bunker was clear.' A pause, then, 'We didn't miss it. The hand was placed there overnight.'

Gilchrist knew it was a long shot, but he asked anyway. 'Anyone see anything, report anything?'

'Not a thing.'

What had he expected? 'Stay there,' he ordered. 'I'll be with you in fifteen.'

Watt hung up before Gilchrist.

Shaved and showered and feeling shakier than a sea-legged sailor on dry land, Gilchrist looked in on Beth before setting off. She was sound asleep, her breathing as untroubled as a child's. He scribbled a short note, stuck it under a magnet on the fridge. Not that he thought Beth would call him, but as long as they were living together, he would do what he could for her.

He drove with the window down, the cold air blustering around his neck and face, blowing away the remnants of last night's beer. He should have had something more sustaining than sausage rolls, a couple of slices of bread at least, to soak up the alcohol. But in the end he had sat alone at the end of the bar, reviewing the list of names and addresses Nance and Watt had collected, making notes, scribbling thoughts, and returning home at the back of eleven none the wiser.

He drove into Pilmour Links, headed left towards the Old Course Hotel, and slid his Roadster into a parking spot close to the Jigger Inn again. He removed a set of white coveralls and gloves from the boot and fought off another wave of nausea that threatened to have him heaving over the stone dyke. But it passed, and he carried the protective clothing under his arm and walked along the side of the seventeenth fairway onto the sixteenth.

The Principal's Nose was not one bunker, but a cluster of three on the left side of the sixteenth fairway. In the distance, dragonlights lit the scene like a druid's party. As Gilchrist neared, he noticed the SOCO van on the fairway and realised he could have parked his Roadster closer. But the walk and fresh air was clearing his hangover. A pair of SOCOs shifted through the scene, white figures drifting in and out of the sphere of light like ghosts blown in from the sea.

As Gilchrist neared, the scene seemed to develop before him, as if dawn was approaching with each footstep. The stiff figure of Watt stood a short distance from the bunkers, on top of a hillock in the rough, talking into his mobile phone. His hand flapped out to his side, finger stabbing the air, voice lost on the cold breeze. Close by, a solitary figure in a yellow anorak and green Wellington boots looked seaward, as if oblivious to the animated discussion by his side. Something moved by the man's feet, a shape that manifested into a black labrador with doleful eyes that followed Gilchrist's step.

He reached the scene and donned his coveralls and shoe covers, then slipped on his gloves. The Crime Scene Manager, DC Jeff Bowers, ordered him to sign in. He scribbled his name then stepped into the lighted area, lifted the yellow tape and slipped under it. He half-expected to catch Mackie shoulder-deep in the bunker.

'Has Bert been called?' he shouted to Jeff.

'On his way, sir.'

Gilchrist stared into the bunker. The sides were steep, about two feet at the back face, rising to five at the front. The fairway fell towards the cluster of bunkers, a graded catchment for stray drives. Shadows danced around him as a SOCO grabbed one of the dragon-lights and shifted it several feet farther away. Gilchrist crouched.

The hand lay in the sand, close to the shallowest point of the back face, curled fingers up, a note clutched between thumb and forefinger. For a moment, he wondered how Watt had known what was written on it, until he leaned closer and saw the printing. He cocked his head to the side.

Massacre.

What did it mean? *Murder.* Now *Massacre.* And why those words? Was the killer trying to tell him something? Was some clue to be found in the words? Or in the location of the body parts? First the Road Bunker. Second the Principal's Nose. Was that significant? Or, first the seventeenth, and second the sixteenth. Should they now be focusing on the bunkers on the fifteenth? But that was too obvious. Was that what the killer wanted? To have them second guessing? Was it some twisted mind-game he was playing, just for a laugh, dropping clues that meant nothing at all?

Gilchrist stared off across the dunes towards the hidden sea, the wind as cold as ice against his face. It must have been colder when the hand was placed in the bunker. What had the killer worn? Something dark, so he could flit unseen through the night. And why no envelope this time? Why just a note? The ink had bled where the damp sea air and light morning dew had settled on the paper. Had the killer not worried that the printing might have become illegible, that his message might have been lost? Did that mean the message did not matter, that the word was meaningless?

He turned his attention back to the hand.

White skin was beaded in moisture as fine as condensation. Several hairs stood out, as if bristling with horripilation, or from the shock of being cut off from their source of life. And in that matter, he saw that the hand had been sliced from the forearm in a neat cut this time, several inches above the wrist, as if the killer had chopped it with a sharp blade and not quite hit his mark.

Gilchrist stood, squeezed his knees, tried to rub the stiffness away. The sand looked undisturbed, and he had the distinct impression the hand had been placed in the bunker with care. He looked to his feet. Had the killer stood on this same spot?

He moved back from the edge, stepped off to the side, and crouched again. The grass was thin and hard, worn bare from the harsh east winds and winter sun. His own prints were barely noticeable. Perhaps that was why the killer chose the bunker closest to the fairway, to avoid leaving evidence in the long grass. He faced the rough, saw the tell-tale trail of Watt's advance up the hillock, and that of the man and his dog. No, this killer was more careful. He knew what he was doing, and why he was doing it.

Gilchrist looked across the fairway, at the stone wall and the Eden Course beyond. On the other side of the wall lay a gravel path, all that was left of the abandoned railway line. That was how the killer had come, he thought, walked up the pathway that ran the length of the sixteenth, then leapt over the wall, crossed the fairway and placed the hand in the bunker. He would have returned the same way, he thought, maybe walked along the fairway a short distance. Or maybe he had it all wrong.

He turned to the hand again, intrigued by how unreal it looked, as if death had moved in and removed whatever vestige of life remained. He stared at it, haunted by a vague sense of familiarity. He had seen a hand like that once before, the hand of a wax dummy, years ago, as a child in Madame Tussauds in Blackpool while holidaying with his parents.

A cold breath brushed his neck. For one confusing moment he wondered if the dragonlights were playing tricks with his eyes, and he felt annoyed for not having noticed sooner. Perhaps he was wrong. He *had* to be wrong.

He leaned closer.

He was not mistaken.

The fingernails were longer on this hand.

He kneeled on the grass, felt the cold seep through his gloves and coveralls. He did not want to disturb the sand in the bunker, not until Mackie had a chance to inspect it. Bert could be a genius at times, an unassuming individual who had the uncanny ability to nail a case with the simplest of finds.

Gilchrist pressed forward as far as he could.

It was the thumbnail that settled it for him. The nail was long. Not too long. And not square, but rounded, flush with the curve of the tip, so that the nail looked white, a healthy solid white, as if it had been varnished. But the white tip, the white tip was...

Gilchrist felt his chest drain.

Dear God. Don't tell me.

His mind tried to tell him he was wrong. But he knew he was not. The underside of the nail was thick with paint.

White paint.

He now saw traces of paint in the cracks of the cuticles, a tiny spot embedded in the skin by the half-moon. Other marks, a touch of green, a hint of yellow, had him thinking that the killer must have scrubbed the first hand clean, trimmed the nails to make identification difficult. But now the second hand was out on display, as if the killer wanted them to know who the victim was. Or worse, wanted *Gilchrist* to make the identification. And Gilchrist saw that was why the first note had been addressed to him.

He stood as Watt approached him, shoes glistening black as he scuffled through the long grass. Either Watt had removed his coveralls, or never put them on. He stopped on the other side of the yellow tape.

'What d'you think?' Watt asked him.

Was it possible to recognise someone by their hands? If his own hands were found lying apart from his body, could Jack or Maureen identify them as his? He thought not. So why did he think he knew who these hands belonged to?

'You look rough,' Watt added.

Gilchrist remembered the first time he met her. *You don't wear rings*, he heard his mind say. *I don't like them*, she whispered. *I find them distracting.* He had thought it such an odd thing to say, that he had taken her hands in his and held them, looked down at fingers long and slim, at nails trim and clean, just the tiniest bit ragged from working the paints, scrubbing the canvases. Would he describe them as being cracked?

Dear God, tell me I'm wrong. Not this. Not this.

He stepped away then, pushed under the yellow tape, and stumbled through the long grass, to the peak of the hillock vacated by Watt. He faced the dark sea. His breath rushed in hard gasps, lungs filling and deflating as if seeking the last ounce of oxygen. He removed his mobile phone and on the sixth ring got Jack's answering machine.

'Damn.'

He hung up, tried again.

Six rings, then the answering machine.

He hung up. Tried again.

Come on, come on, I know you're home.

Shit. And again.

On the fifth attempt, Jack picked up, his voice heavy with sleep, or worse. 'This had better be good,' he slurred.

'Jack, it's me.'

'Aw, come on, Andy.' A deep breath then out with a tired yawn. 'It's not even seven o'clock yet.'

'I know, Jack, I'm sorry, but I need to speak to Chloe.'

'Chloe?'

'Is she there?'

'What for?'

Gilchrist felt his head slump. This was not good. Not good at all. 'If I can't speak to her,' he tried, 'just tell me she's okay.'

'What?'

'Tell me Chloe's okay.' Gilchrist tightened his grip on his phone, prayed Jack would simply pass his call to a sleeping Chloe and have her speak to him.

'What the hell is this, Andy?'

'Let me speak to her.'

A pause, then a defeated rush, 'She's not here.'

Gilchrist felt his breath leave him. There. He had it. He was right. He stared at the sea, felt the breeze squeeze tears from his eyes. Then a flicker of hope. Maybe he was wrong. 'She's left you,' he said. 'Hasn't she?'

'What the hell's that got—'

'Jack, listen—'

'No, Andy. You listen. What Chloe and I do with our lives has got eff all to do—'

'That's not why I'm calling.'

'Why, then?'

Because I think someone's murdered Chloe and feeding her to me in chunks. That's why. He took a deep breath, tried the soft approach once more. 'Jack, please, if you know, just tell me where she is.'

'Are you listening to me?'

Sometimes with Jack you had to take the direct approach. This was one of those times. 'Yes I am, Jack. Now you listen to me. This is not a personal call. I'm talking to you as Detective Chief Inspector Gilchrist of Fife Constabulary's Crime Management Department. Do you understand what I'm saying?'

Silence.

'I need to talk to Chloe,' he continued. He heard a hand brush the mouthpiece, and he caught an image of Jack pulling himself from bed, blonde hair tousled with bed-head, days-old fluff spiking his chin.

'You're serious?'

'Deadly.'

Jack's breath came hard and deep all of a sudden, as if his bedroom had flash-frozen. 'It's that hand thing,' he said. 'Isn't it? It's been on the news.'

'It's too early to say.'

'Don't lie to me, Andy.'

'I'm not lying, for crying out loud. We don't know.'

'Why call then?'

'To rule Chloe out.'

'I don't know where she is. We had a row. I told you that. She stomped off in one of her moods.'

'When did you last talk to her?'

'Three days ago. No. Four. Christ. I don't know.'

'Settle down,' Gilchrist said, struggling to keep his own voice steady.

'Jesus, Andy. What's happened to her?'

'Probably nothing, Jack.'

'Why're you calling, then?'

'To rule her out.'

'You know it's her.'

'For God's sake, Jack, will you just listen?'

'That's why you're asking to talk to her. You know it's her, don't you? The hand. It's hers. You know it is.'

Gilchrist felt his lips tighten as he listened to his son cry. He wanted to speak, but found his own voice had deserted him. He heard Jack say something, the words thick and unintelligible. He clung onto the phone, pressed it tight against his ear, and whispered, 'Jack,' then felt a puzzling sense of relief wash over him when Jack hung up.

He folded his mobile phone. His chest was heaving, his heart racing. He had handled it all wrong. Why the hell could he never get it right with Jack? Why did he always end up pushing him farther away? He felt the tight sting of tears in his eyes, the cold flush of ice in his lungs.

Christ. What if the hand was not Chloe's? What if all he had done was upset Jack? Dear God, he would love Jack to call him back and give him a right old reaming. Then Chloe would be safe and alive. He could stand that. In fact, he would welcome that. He stared off across the dunes, felt an odd reluctance to leave that spot, knowing that doing so would mean having to look at the hand again in the knowledge that if he was right, if his worst fears were realised, then the rest of Chloe would be presented to him piece by slaughtered piece.

Now he knew why his name had been on the envelope. What better way to hurt another human being, to *really* hurt them to the core, than to hurt their family?

But why? And why him?

He could think of a million reasons for someone wanting to even the score. *God Almighty.* He closed his eyes and prayed to God he was wrong on every one of them.

CHAPTER SIX

GILCHRIST DID THE NECESSARY.

He unfolded his mobile phone and dialled the number for DCI Peter 'Dainty' Small of Strathclyde Police Headquarters, Pitt Street, Glasgow, and asked him to put out a Lookout Request on a young woman, five-ten, twenty-two years old, a freelance artist by the name of Chloe Fullerton. He gave her last known address as Jack's tenement flat in Hillhead, Glasgow.

Dainty and Gilchrist had joined Fife Constabulary at the same time, and worked together on numerous early cases. Eight years later, Dainty married Margo Cunningham, a young PW, and moved to Glasgow the following year. They had kept in contact over the years, exchanging Christmas cards and information on relevant cases as the need arose. Gilchrist parted by saying he hoped he was wrong, hoped Chloe would turn up, then slipped his mobile phone into his inside jacket pocket.

From his hillock, the golf course was beginning to show signs of life. Behind the first tee, the Royal and Ancient Clubhouse stood like a misplaced mansion, alone in its stone splendour. People dotted Grannie Clark's Wynd, the asphalt footpath that crossed the eighteenth and first fairways and connected The Links to Bruce Embankment on the shoreline. To the east, the sky glowed crimson with a hint of white-blue through tattered clouds.

Gilchrist could not rid himself of his fear that he had lost Chloe. It seemed unimaginable to think she would never see another dawn sky, never feel another sea breeze, never feel the chill of life on her face and the warmth of love in her heart.

He searched the dunes, tried to find the spot where they had picnicked on the beach in January. It seemed absurd. But it had been Jack's idea. Freezing cold. Wind whipping in off the Eden Estuary. *At least we'll have the beach to ourselves.* Gilchrist almost smiled. They ended up sharing the West Sands with a string of people and dogs and couples in love, and sweating joggers and kids and fathers with swooping kites and teenagers with beach-bogeys that raced the length of the sands defying every gust of wind that threatened to topple them. They even watched some lunatic strip to his underwear and take a swim.

The chilled champagne heated their spirits and loosened their tongues and doused Gilchrist's dismay that Beth had not joined them. *This and That* had been busy; January a time for sales. But Gilchrist had known he and Beth were deep into the tunnel of her dark period.

He eyed the brightening horizon. How could he have guessed that parts of Chloe's body would turn up within a hundred yards of where they had laughed and joked and drunk champagne together?

Something gripped him at that thought.

They had yet to identify the victim. Which meant there was still hope. Slim hope. But hope nonetheless. And often that was all that was needed to survive. He forced himself to believe in hope, and prayed that Chloe would turn up in Glasgow, alive and well.

Something moved at his feet. The black labrador. He scratched behind its ears as its tail brushed the long grass.

'Her name's Biddy,' said the man in the yellow anorak.

Gilchrist scratched deeper. 'That's a rare old name.'

'That's what my father called my grandmother.'

'He must have thought she gossiped too much, then?'

'Among other things.' The man chuckled, held out his hand. 'Charlie Blair.'

The grip felt warm, hard, honest. 'DCI Gilchrist.'

Blair nodded. 'Nice to meet you at last. I've seen your face around.'

Gilchrist smiled. 'In the bars, no doubt.'

'On the telly.' Blair nodded over his shoulder. 'Quite gruesome,' he said. 'I don't think I would like your job. It must get to you.'

You get used to it, Gilchrist wanted to say, but he would be lying. Instead, he said, 'You found it? The hand, I mean.'

'Just passing.'

The significance of Blair's comment did not hit Gilchrist until Blair continued on his way and Biddy loped ahead, nose to the rough, tail like a black hand-brush sweeping the grass with canine pleasure. Gilchrist called out.

Blair turned.

They met halfway, and Gilchrist asked what he meant by *Just passing*.

'Exactly that. I saw Detective Watt standing at the bunker. At first I thought he was a drunk taking a leak, but then he called me over and asked me what I thought.'

'What you thought?'

Blair nodded. 'Of the hand.'

'I see,' said Gilchrist, and thanked him for his time.

'He's a strange one,' said Blair as he strode off.

Gilchrist found Watt standing at the edge of the fairway, and reached out and grabbed him by his coat lapels. 'Why are you here?' Gilchrist growled.

'What the fuck're you on about?'

'Why are you *here?*'

A steel claw gripped his wrist. 'Take your fucking hands off me.'

Gilchrist glanced to his side, saw the socos eye them with suspicion, as if undecided whether to step in and separate them, or stand back and enjoy the fight. Gilchrist tightened his grip. 'Not until you tell me why you were up bright as a lark way before dawn this morning.'

'I'm an early riser.'

'Who told you the hand was here?'

'No one.'

'Charlie Blair and his faithful mutt, Biddy, didn't find it. You did.'

'Is that what he told you?' Watt sneered. 'He doesn't want involved, does Charlie.'

'I warned you, Ronnie. One step out of line and I'll have you thrown from the Force.' Gilchrist gritted his teeth. 'Did somebody call you?'

'No.'

'I swear I'll have your phone records examined.'

Something went out of Watt's body at that moment, like a prisoner realising the futility of struggling against his shackles. Gilchrist responded by relaxing his grip.

Then he let go and lowered his arm.

Watt straightened his lapels, shuffled his shoulders, and smoothed down his jacket. He pushed his hand into his pocket, and said, 'I got this.' He pulled out a damp piece of paper that looked as if it had been ripped from an envelope.

Gilchrist read the pencilled words.

right hand — principal's nose.

Gilchrist looked at Watt. 'Who gave you this?'

'It was stuck underneath my windscreen wiper.' Watt's jaw was set as tight as rock. He widened his stance, and Gilchrist could almost taste the raw power of the guy.

'And you don't know who put it there?'

'No.'

'Were you going to show me this?'

'Of course,' Watt growled. 'I never got a chance.'

Gilchrist glared at him.

Watt shrugged. 'You looked busy. I was taking a call. When I spoke to you, you ignored me. What do you expect me to do? Get down on my knees and beg?' Watt sneered. 'Like fuck I will.'

Gilchrist narrowed his eyes. Watt was playing him for a fool. He held the damp scrap up. 'Whoever wrote this,' he said to Watt, 'is playing games with us. A note for me. A message for you. Did it not cross your mind that we're being set up?'

Watt tightened his lips.

'What about Blair and his dog?' asked Gilchrist.

Watt shrugged. 'What about them? He was walking down the fairway. I called him over, asked him to verify it.'

'Why?'

'Thought I could use a witness.'

'What for?'

'Protection.'

'From what?'

Watt chewed some imaginary gum. 'You're just itching to kick me out of it,' he said.

Somehow hearing the truth of his own vendetta against Watt shamed Gilchrist. He needed to rise above it all. But damn it, what the hell had Greaves expected? He took a step back. 'Any other messages I need to see?'

Watt shook his head. 'None.'

Gilchrist was prepared to bet a month's salary that Watt was lying. But what could he do? Tie him to a rack? Hammer bamboo shoots under his fingernails? He ran a hand through his hair. It felt damp. But the sea air had almost cleared his hangover. 'Another stunt like that,' he said, 'and I *will* kick you out of it. All the way back to Glasgow.'

Watt smiled.

Gilchrist should not have mentioned Glasgow. Indirectly, he had reminded Watt of the cause of their acrimony. That thought had him wanting to tear the smile from Watt's cocky face. 'After you removed the note from your windscreen,' Gilchrist growled, 'did you talk to anyone?'

'No.'

'Call anyone?'

'No.'

'You came straight here?'

'That's right.'

Watt could be lying, but how could he prove it? 'Get hold of Nance,' he said. 'Get her down here. With Bert. There's paint under the fingernails. I want Bert to tell us what it is. And if Brenda from the Procurator Fiscal's Office turns up, keep your hands off her. She's married.'

'What's that got to do with anything?'

'Everything.'

Watt worked his imaginary gum.

Gilchrist walked away. It was corny, he knew, but he counted seven steps then stopped and did a Columbo. 'Tell me this,' he said to Watt. 'Where's the Valley of Sin?'

Watt stopped chewing. 'The what?'

'The Valley of Sin.'

Watt gave an uncertain smile, and said, 'Between a pair of knockers?' He shrugged and chuckled. 'What kind of a question is that?'

Gilchrist smiled and wiggled his fingers in a toodle-doo wave. He had his answer. He strutted past the SOCO van, reached the boundary wall, and glanced back. Watt stood at the edge of the bunker, looking into it as if Gilchrist had not said a word. Beyond the dunes, a low sun pierced thinning clouds that stretched to the horizon. He leapt over the stone wall and put his head down for the walk back to his car.

His mind spun. He should send Watt packing. Get it over and done with. But he wondered if there might be something to be gained by not doing that. The killer was smart, cunning, and for some as yet unknown reason it seemed important for him to make sure Watt was one of the first on the scene.

Hence the note under the windscreen.

After finding the note, Watt said he had not spoken to anyone. But he was lying. Gilchrist suspected Watt had used his mobile phone. Why else had he crumbled at the mention of his phone records?

And then there was the Valley of Sin.

Not being a golfer and not raised in St Andrews, Watt's local knowledge was limited. The Valley of Sin was a grass swale that fronted the eighteenth green of the Old Course, a dip in the fairway that punished weak approach shots. To the golfing world, the Valley of Sin was infamous. But if Watt had never heard of the Valley of Sin he sure as hell had not heard of the Principal's Nose. So, how had he known that the Principal's Nose was a cluster of bunkers on the sixteenth fairway on the Old Course? It could have been the name of a pub, for all he knew. Had a fairy fluttered down and lit Watt's way with her magic wand?

Not a chance. Gilchrist did not believe in fairies.

But he did believe in phone calls and phone records.

He reached his Mercedes, clicked the remote, and opened the door. He was about to slip into the driving seat when he glanced over at the dunes, to the spot that had held so much promise for Jack and Chloe. He had seen in Chloe a woman who could settle the wild stallion of his son, who could pull in his reins and have him snorting with restive passion.

As Gilchrist stared seaward, he wondered what memories of St Andrews Chloe would have taken with her. Iced champagne on wind-chilled dunes? Shoeless strolls on sun-soaked sands? Jokes and hugs and kisses and beer?

And what of his own memories of Chloe?

He would remember her as a waif-like child with slender limbs and blonde hair, and eyes and teeth that sparkled with the promise of life.

And hands as fine as those of any model.

He slid behind the wheel and closed the door. He knew what he had to do.

For Chloe. And for Jack.

CHAPTER SEVEN

JACK STOOD OUTSIDE his tenement building. His breath evaporated in drizzle as fine as haar. To his side, water dripped from a broken drainpipe, as steady as a metronome. Runoff trickled along granite kerbs that edged North Gardner Street, both sides choked with parked cars. Jack blew into his hands, tried to take the chill from his body.

He had never owned a car, never wanted one, not even as a young boy growing up in St Andrews. Cars had never held any fascination for him, and as a consequence, he walked or took public transport. But at that moment, he wished he owned a car. Or had money, so he could at least call a taxi. He had spent the last of his dole cheque on a tab of speed to keep him awake for his latest work of art, a life-sized human figure sculpted from concrete and reinforcing steel rods finagled from a building site in Partick.

It was that sculpture that had set Chloe off. She had not liked it. But if he was being honest, it had not been the sculpture that upset her. It was the drugs. He saw that now. But five days ago he had taken her comments as a personal slight against his creative talents, and they had argued.

How could they? Chloe loved his sculptures. And he loved her paintings. Together, they were a creative team.

Apart, they were...

He took a deep breath.

He missed Chloe so much. He never should have gone back on speed. He never should have spent his dole money. And he never should have argued with her. What had he been thinking? But it had been the drugs. Now he was off them. By God, was he ever off them. He was through with all that shit. When Chloe came back he would tell her he was off them for good.

He looked down the hill towards Hyndland Road. Even from that distance, he heard the wet whisper of cars passing on the damp street. Overhead, the sky hung grey on grey. Maybe the rain would stay off. He pulled his combat jacket collar tight to his neck and hurried down the worn stone steps.

Chloe had been gone for four days now. *Four days.*

It seemed much longer since she had come home and found him on his studio floor passed out from exhaustion. Amphetamines were great to keep you awake, but when you came off them, watch out. He hadn't missed her the first two days. He'd been asleep most of the time. But it had now been four days since she told him if he didn't sort himself out she was through with him.

Look at your work. You're losing it, Jack.

You can do better than this. I've seen you do better.

They argued. Man, did they argue. And the following morning she rose from bed and left. Just like that. But she never took her paintings. Which was her way of telling him she would be back. On the second day, he called her mobile phone ten times, and each time got the recorded message, *It has not been possible to connect your call. Please try again later.* He even tried her parents' home then hung up when her mother said she was now living in Glasgow, and who is this speaking please?

Since starting their relationship about a year ago, they had never been apart this long without communicating, and when she finally called, he swore he would welcome her with open arms and tell her he was off the drugs for good.

He promised himself that.

If she called.

Of course she would call. Chloe wasn't dead. The hand wasn't hers. She was off on one of her sojourns, or staying with Jenny. That's where she was. With Jenny. Not that he had spoken to Jenny, just that he knew Chloe and Jenny were close. Not as close as they had been when Chloe had been dating Kevin. But close nonetheless.

Kevin's death had hurt Chloe, hurt her relationship with Jack, often came between them. Or it might be more accurate to say Kevin's *life* came between them. For Jack had always thought there was more to Kevin than met the eye. He had seen Chloe about town with Kevin, first caught her eye three years ago in the Ubiquitous Chip, fancied her even then. It was not Kevin that concerned Jack, but the company he kept. Jack was off drugs back then, and trouble was how he would have described Kevin's friends.

Nothing but trouble.

Jack reached the corner and turned into Hyndland Road. The wind stiffened, hard and cold against him. He tucked his head and braced himself as he waded into it.

By the time he reached Jenny's flat, his feet were soaked through. He stood outside her tenement building, not unlike his own. Not so rundown, perhaps. As he scanned the list of names on the doorframe, he realised with a mild surge of panic that he could not remember Jenny's surname. Roddie. That was her boyfriend, an Englishman with an English name and Scottish accent who worked in the city centre. They had dated for years. Chloe told him they'd split up.

He stopped at J. Colvin & R. Braithwaite.

That was it. Jenny Colvin and Roddie Braithwaite.

He rang the bell.

He turned his back to the door and blew into his hands. He felt chilled to the bone, gave out a cough. After what had to be a minute and a half, he pressed the doorbell again, this time held it down a bit longer.

Ten seconds later, a tinny voice crackled from the speaker. 'Who's this?'

'Jenny?'

A pause, then again, 'Who's this?'

'Jack Gilchrist.' He thought he heard a low curse, and added, 'I need to talk to you.'

'What about?'

'Can I come in?'

'D'you know what time it is?'

'It's about Chloe.'

'Chloe?'

He wanted to ask if Chloe was there, tell her he needed to talk to her. But he thought Jenny might lie for her, keep her hidden, so he said, 'It's freezing out here.'

The speaker buzzed, and Jenny said, 'Come on up.'

He was in.

Jack pushed open the heavy entrance door and fought off the feeling that Chloe was not there. He thought he detected something in Jenny's voice, which he had trouble interpreting, a lack of concern maybe. Chloe *was* there? Chloe was *not* there? He could not say.

He reached the top landing. The door to Jenny's flat lay ajar. He stepped into a narrow hallway that smelled of burned toast. Jenny's voice came at him from a doorway on the far right.

'In the kitchen.'

Jenny was dressed in a white baggy bathrobe that had to be Roddie's. It hung loose at the front and did little to hide the swell of her boobs. Her face looked tanned, as if she had returned from a winter holiday. She stiffened when she saw him.

'Jeezo, Jack. What happened to you?'

'Chloe,' he said.

'So you keep saying.'

'Is she here?'

Jenny frowned. 'I haven't seen Chloe in months.'

'Haven't you heard from her?'

'Not since before Christmas. Why? What's happened?'

Jack felt the power go out of his legs. He stumbled to the kitchen table and sat. He fought back the tears, but could not stop himself.

He buried his face in his hands and sobbed.

* * *

Bert Mackie called Gilchrist shortly before nine and confirmed he had found traces of oil paint under the nails of both hands and was waiting for results of a spectrographic analysis to determine the paint's chemical composition. That was all Gilchrist needed to hear to order Nance and Watt to continue their investigation of all things artsy.

Brenda McAllister from the Procurator Fiscal's Office instructed the examination of the second hand to be done under the supervision of two pathologists, which was required in a murder investigation. Alec Simpson, forensic pathologist with Ninewells Hospital in Dundee, was contracted to assist Bert Mackie.

Gilchrist assigned DS Stan Davidson to oversee a thorough search of the Old Course and environs and interview of the green-keeping staff. Then he sent one of the trainees out shopping with instructions not to return until she had a map of the Old Course that detailed all features. Next, he called the Town Council and ordered the West Sands closed, including cancelling the beach-cleaning tractor, in case the killer had not taken the pathway route, but come in over the dunes.

Unlikely, he thought, but it kept the scene quiet.

He called Martin Coyle on his mobile not long after nine with the intention of driving into Cupar to meet him. Coyle was in St Andrews checking out golf club sales, so they agreed to meet in the Jigger Inn.

By lunchtime, the investigation was no further forward. Gilchrist's hangover had returned with a vengeance, and after popping a couple of paracetemol he decided a hair of the dog was just what the doctor ordered. He arrived at the Jigger ten minutes early and ordered a pint of Guinness. Coyle walked into the lounge before he had a chance to take a sip.

They shook hands like long lost friends.

'Pint?' Gilchrist asked.

Coyle had one of those faces that always seemed to want to smile. When he spoke, his eyes creased and his lips parted in a gap-toothed grin. 'Just a soft drink,' he said. 'Tonic and lemon.'

'On a diet?' Gilchrist asked.

'Afraid not.'

'The wagon?'

Coyle smiled. 'Alkey.'

Gilchrist thought he managed to keep his surprise hidden. He and Coyle used to run cross-country marathons together when Gilchrist joined the Force and Coyle the Post Office as a telecommunications engineer. They would meet in the Whey Pat Tavern on a Saturday night at five, and stagger home this side of midnight after sampling the wares of most of the bars in town. Coyle in a bar without a beer was like a golfer on the course without his clubs.

Gilchrist sipped his beer. 'When did this happen?'

'Nine months ago. I woke up one morning with eyes like I had yellow fever. Doctor told me to give up the drink, or get measured for my coffin.' Coyle smiled. 'Well, I've got the grandkid to think of now. Not to mention Linda.'

At the mention of Coyle's wife, Gilchrist knew where the conversation was heading. But he was helpless to stop it.

'Do you still hear from Gail?'

Gilchrist grimaced. 'Indirectly.'

'How is she?'

Gilchrist took another sip of Guinness, then saw he was expected to answer. Defeated, he said, 'She's got cancer.'

'Christ, Andy, I'm sorry to hear that. I'm really sorry.' Coyle paused, then ventured, 'Is it..?'

'It is.'

Coyle smiled. 'That's dreadful. Just dreadful.'

'I'll tell her we've met.'

'Please do. And give her our regards.'

Gilchrist dreaded Coyle asking after Jack and Maureen and the conversation turning towards Chloe, so he said, 'Listen, Martin. I need a favour.'

'If I can.'

'Got a mobile phone number here. I'd like to see records from the start of the year. Including calls made today.'

Coyle whistled. 'That's a toughie,' he said. 'I might need to wait a few days before today's calls log on.'

Gilchrist nodded. A few days would be fine. As long as the wheels were turning. He handed the number over, and Coyle said, 'I take it no one is to know about this.'

Gilchrist put on his poker face. 'Know about what?'

It took a full two seconds for Coyle to catch on. He gave out a quick laugh, and said, 'I get it. I get it.'

'Get what?'

Coyle slapped his thigh and chuckled some more.

Gilchrist bought lunch, two chicken sandwiches and chips, and managed to keep the conversation off Gail and his children. Not that he did not want Coyle to know, he was not sure he could keep from showing his emotions. Despite being divorced for six years – or was it seven – Gail's leaving him for another man still hurt. And with his fears for Chloe, he felt emotionally raw, as if the vaguest whisper of either name would have him tightening his lips and swallowing the lump in his throat.

By two o'clock they were all talked out, having caught up mostly on Coyle's life, his mid-life crisis with his wife, and the underage pregnancy of their fifteen-year-old daughter who had given them a surprise grandchild. Gilchrist walked Coyle to his car, and Coyle drove off with assurances that he would call in a few days.

Gilchrist returned to the bar. Although he was driving, he ordered a second pint of Guinness. He could always call for a taxi and pick the Merc up later. He tried Maureen again, and this time she answered on the fourth ring with a curt, 'Hello?'

Gilchrist choked a laugh, felt a dead weight lift off his heart and soar skyward. He cleared his throat. 'Have you stopped returning calls?' he grumped.

'Oh, hi, Dad. I got your message.'

'All ten of them?'

'I've been meaning to call. Sorry.' She made a noise like a sponge being squidged. 'But you know I love you.'

And you've no idea how much I love you.

'I'll make a point of calling more often,' she added.

'Well, that's a start,' he said, then found himself asking the same question he always asked. 'Any chance of you making it up this way any time soon?' and expecting the same answer she always gave.

'I think that might be possible.'

What? He pressed the phone to his ear. 'Did I hear you right?' Maureen laughed, a soft rumble that cast up an image of dark eyes and white teeth and asked him how long it had been since they last met. Just after New Year? My God, was it that long? 'That's wonderful, Mo,' he said, and meant it. 'Any idea when this great event might take place?'

'Well, Chris and I are thinking—'

'Chris?'

'My boyfriend.'

'What happened to Larry?'

'That plonker?'

'I thought you and he were... you know?'

'Were what?'

'I thought you, eh, loved each other.'

'Correct, Dad. *Loved*. Past tense.'

Gilchrist felt his face flush. He and Maureen never talked about her personal life. His mild embarrassment seemed to remind him how far he had drifted from her life, and he made a mental note to try to sort things out when she came up.

'So, what's this Chris like?' he asked.

'You can find out for yourself next month.'

'So soon?'

'That's what I was trying to tell you, Dad, before you cut me off with the Larry crap.'

'Are you booked in anywhere?'

'Not yet.'

'Fisherman's Cottage isn't let,' he said, referring to his house in Crail, which had lain empty since he moved in with Beth after her attack. 'You're welcome to stay there.'

'Thanks, Dad. But Chris has friends up that way.'

'Of course. Right.'

As if sensing his disappointment, she added, 'But I'll run it past him. Okay?'

'Sure,' he said. 'I spoke to Jack.'

'Who?'

He struggled not to rise to the bait, Maureen's way of letting him know she seldom spoke to her brother. He blamed himself for that. If he had spent more time with his family instead of the case of the day, then maybe Gail would not have had an affair, and they would still be together as a family. And he thought of telling Maureen why he called Jack, of his fears for Chloe, of his concern for her own safety. But it was early days and he could be wrong. So rather than scare her, he said, 'Jack told me about Mum.'

A pause, then, 'Mum's not doing well,' she whispered.

'Is there anything I can do?'

'No, Dad. She's got Harry. I'm sorry,' she added, 'I know how you feel about him.'

Gilchrist eyed his pint. When he first met Gail, they would get drunk together, as if it was some rite of passage Scottish couples had to negotiate before sealing their love. Back then, Gail drank wine and the occasional beer, but after nineteen years of marriage had given up drink altogether and hated that Gilchrist continued. Dark beer especially riled her. He had never understood her rationale.

'By all accounts,' he said, 'Harry is a nice guy.'

He took a sip, waited for Maureen to speak. But her silence made him think she was no longer sure of Harry's congeniality, and he wondered if Gail's terminal illness had taken its toll on not just Gail, but Harry, too.

His phone beeped. 'Hang on, Mo. I've got another call.'

'That's okay, Dad. I've got to go. I'll tell Mum we spoke. Talk to you later.'

'Listen, Mo. Will you be careful?' But she had hung up. He switched lines, and said, 'Gilchrist speaking.'

'Andy, it's me.'

'Jack?'

'I'm at Leuchars station. Can you pick me up?'

Confused, Gilchrist felt his hopes rise, then stall. 'You have Chloe?'

'That's why I'm here.'
'I'm not sure I follow,' Gilchrist said, although he thought he did.
'I need to look at the hand.'

CHAPTER EIGHT

JACK'S FACE LOOKED as grey as the sky. His hair stood in untidy clumps that gave the impression he had not showered in days. His combat jacket hung from shoulders as thin as bone and sported greasy stains at the cuffs and neck.

They shook hands with nothing more than a nod, and Gilchrist tried to hide his concern with a quick smile. But he was fooling no one. He took Jack's holdall, led him to the Merc, and threw his bag into the boot. They had still not spoken by the time he veered left at the Guardbridge roundabout.

'You look as if you've lost weight,' he tried.

Jack shrugged.

'Are you managing to sell any work?'

'Some.'

'Keeping gainfully employed, are you?'

'You could say.'

Gilchrist accelerated up the slight incline, felt the car respond with a beefy spurt of energy. 'Talk to me,' he said.

Jack shrugged again. 'What do you want to hear?'

'Tell me what happened.'

'Chloe's gone. What can I say?'

'Define *gone*.'

Jack glanced at him with a grimace filled with contempt. 'What the hell do you mean by that?'

'Gone home? Gone away? Gone to Spain? What?'

'She's gone. All right?'

'As in, gone away from you?'

Jack tutted, then said, 'Don't treat me like an idiot, Andy. All right?'

Gilchrist swung out to pass a couple of cars, one of them a learner, and eased back once the road ahead was clear. It did not happen often, but when Jack behaved like this, he could be harder to reach than Maureen. Gilchrist tried again.

'You said you needed to look at the hand.'

'Yeah.'

'To ID it?'

'Yeah.'

'And put your mind at rest?'

From the corner of his eye, he watched Jack turn away and stare across the fields to the Eden Estuary. A solitary pig stood mud-stained and grumpy in a grassless sty. A pair of jets from RAF Leuchars raced into the sky like dark missiles then banked east and bulleted out across the North Sea.

'Why do you think you could ID Chloe from the hand?'

'Which hand is it?'

Gilchrist twisted his grip on the steering wheel. 'We have both hands now,' he said.

Jack sank deeper into his seat and stared out the window. It took Gilchrist a few seconds to realise he was crying. He reached across, was about to place his hand on his knee, when he pulled back. 'I'm not sure you're up for this, Jack.'

Jack sniffed, and said, 'I'll be all right.'

Gilchrist detected an undercurrent of anger, reminding him of how Jack used to behave as a child when scolded. He and Gail would wait it out, say nothing until Jack's mood evaporated. Silent, Gilchrist eyed the road ahead.

Jack ran the palm of his hand across his eyes. 'I loved Chloe,' he said.

Gilchrist felt his chest tighten. Jack was talking as if Chloe was already dead.

'She had this phenomenal talent as an artist. Like she had all this creative power within her just bubbling inside, waiting to erupt onto the canvas.' Jack shook his head. 'She made my sculptures look incomplete. She had this ability to make me feel humble as an artist, make me realise there was so much more I still have to learn, you know, without knowing she was doing it.' Jack stared off across the golf courses to the dunes beyond, and Gilchrist wondered if he was searching for their winter picnic spot, or remembering it was only January since they had all been together.

'That's why we argued,' Jack went on. 'Sometimes she would just go on at me, urging me to do better, like she knew I had it in me, but I couldn't get it out. It used to do my nut in. In the end we had this huge row. I just flipped.' He shook his head, and it took Gilchrist several seconds to realise Jack had said all he was going to say.

'I'm not sure if trying to ID the hands is a good idea.'

Jack turned to him. 'I need to know.'

'That's not what I meant.' Gilchrist felt Jack's eyes on him, and made a conscious effort to speak in the present tense. 'Does Chloe have any marks on her hands or fingers such as moles or freckles or anything that would provide conclusive identification?'

'Yes.'

Gilchrist felt his heart leap. He had seen no marks on either hand. In fact, both hands looked unblemished, almost perfect. Had he jumped to the wrong conclusion? Were the hands not Chloe's? For a fleeting moment, his mind nurtured that idea then thumped back at him with the question he could not answer. Why was his name on the note? The victim had to be someone he knew personally. He struggled to keep his eyes to the front, his voice level. 'Such as?' he asked.

'A scar at the base of her thumb.'

A scar? Mackie hadn't told him of any scars.

'Which hand?' he asked.

Jack seemed to think for a second. 'Right, I think.'

'You think?'

'No. Definitely the right hand.'

'How big a scar?'

'Half-inch.'

'Crooked? Straight? What?'

'Straight. She cut herself with a palette knife.' He almost smiled. 'Don't ask.'

'Any other marks?'

'On her hands?'

'Anywhere.'

Jack pulled up the front of his sweater. 'One of these.'

Gilchrist glanced to the side, but saw only white skin and felt a spurt of surprise flush through him at how thin Jack looked. Skinny verging on skeletal. 'One of what?' he asked.

Jack twisted in his seat and fingered a tattoo that stained his skin like a tiny ink blot an inch or so above his belly-button. 'It's a love-heart.'

'And Chloe had one, too?' Too late, he realised he had spoken as if she was no longer alive.

Jack seemed unaware of Gilchrist's blunder and lowered his sweater. 'Last Christmas,' he said. 'To seal our love. Kind of stupid, I suppose. It was Chloe's idea.'

Gilchrist stared at the road ahead. When he first met Gail, drunk and wild in the Whey Pat Tavern, up from Glasgow on her annual holiday, she had sworn at some American guy with a buzz-cut and two bared arms, blue with tattoos and taut with muscles. Gilchrist had escorted her from the pub after that, tried to calm her down. But something about the tattoos had her wound up.

My uncle had a tattoo, she told him. *An anchor with a silly rope wound around it.*

What's so bad about that? he had asked.

He hit my aunt.

It hurt to think that when he first met Gail he was taken by her vivacity, her pure uncut love of life. Nothing seemed too big to take on. The whole world, if they wanted. He had never been able to work out the exact moment Gail changed, the instant in time when something inside her died. He struggled to force his thoughts from Gail and focus on Jack.

'The scar on Chloe's hand,' he said to him. 'You said it was half an inch, straight, at the base of the thumb.'

'Yeah.'

'Why do you remember it so clearly?'

'Chloe had to have a couple of stitches. I took her to the hospital.'

'You and Chloe were dating?'

'Yeah.'

'So, the scar is recent?'

'Last summer.' He sniffed again, tugged a hand through clumped hair. 'Is that important?'

'Could be.' He dialled Mackie's mobile phone number. It was answered on the second ring. 'Bert. Gilchrist here. Have you completed your examination?'

'I'm still waiting for the results of the spectrographic analysis on the paint. But yes, I'm more or less finished.'

Gilchrist held his breath, as if not daring to ask the question, then said, 'Did you find any scars?'

'One. On the right hand.'

A bull butted him in the gut. 'Whereabouts?'

'Base of the thumb. It's fairly recent, I'd say.'

Last summer? Gilchrist pressed his phone hard to his ear as Mackie went on to confirm size and angle, then conclude with, 'It looks like a knife wound.'

'How about an artist's palette knife?'

'That's an interesting suggestion. But, yes, any kind of knife would make sense. Why do you ask?'

'Jack's with me. He might be able to make an ID.'

'Your son, Jack?'

'Yes.'

'Good lord, Andy. Are you saying...'

'Nothing definite, Bert. But we'd better take a look at it.' He hung up and glanced at Jack. 'I'm sorry, Jack,' he whispered. 'It's not looking good.'

'It's Chloe,' Jack said. 'I know it is.' His voice sounded steady, as if he was oblivious to the gruesome prospect of examining amputated extremities.

Gilchrist wondered how on earth he ever got into such a morbid job in the first place.

How cruel could it get? He felt his heart sink. He hated to admit it.

But Jack was right.

* * *

The mortuary at Bell Street was a drab affair with cruel looking surgical equipment lying on flat metal surfaces. The air hinted of decaying flesh and formaldehyde and left an aftertaste on the tongue. After Gilchrist introduced Mackie to Jack, Mackie led them to another room.

The air felt cold. Steel drawers glistened.

Mackie checked a log-book then shuffled towards the wall on his left. He halted halfway along, gripped a metal handle, and pulled out a sliding gurney on which sat two clear plastic bags. Through the plastic sheen, the amputated hands looked white, ghostlike, as if at any moment they could move of their own accord and crawl from their confines.

Gilchrist stood beside Jack. 'Ready?'

Tight-lipped, Jack nodded.

Gilchrist eyed Mackie.

Mackie opened one plastic bag, removed a hand, the left one, and placed it palm down on the gurney. Then he did the same with the right hand. He pushed the bags to the side and positioned the hands so they looked as if they were reaching out for Gilchrist.

Jack let out a rush of breath and took a step back.

Something clamped Gilchrist's chest. He stared at the hands, the claws, the lifeless things on the table. They had once belonged to a young woman, once touched and caressed and moved with life. An image of him holding those hands, looking down at those fingers, burst into his mind. He fought off an overpowering urge to take Jack by the arm and lead him from the room. But his pragmatic side kept him rooted. He had a victim to identify, a murder to solve, and he prayed to God that Jack would simply shake his head and tell him the hands could not be Chloe's, that they belonged to some other poor soul.

'The scar should be on the inside,' Jack whispered, and held his own hand out and pointed to the base of his right thumb. 'About here.'

Mackie eyed Gilchrist with an intensity he had not seen in the old man's eyes since he performed the post-mortem of his own sister-in-law. With grim-faced resignation, Mackie turned the right hand over and pointed a finger to a pink mark at the base of the thumb. 'This is the only scar I detected.'

Gilchrist felt his lungs deflate. He had his answer. His peripheral vision watched Jack's body sway as if buffeted by a wind. He grasped his arm, tightened his grip. 'Jack,' he said, 'I need you to be sure.'

'It's her,' Jack whispered. 'It's Chloe.'

Gilchrist stared at Jack's face. For his own benefit, he needed to hear more. 'No doubts?' he asked.

Jack opened his eyes. His cheeks glistened with tears. His breath shuddered as he stared at the hands, and he surprised Gilchrist by leaning closer and reaching out as if to lift the hand from the gurney. Instead, he tapped the back of his own hand. 'When Chloe was ten years old she crushed a knuckle on her left hand. Her pinkie knuckle. Compared to the others, it looked flat when she made a fist.'

Gilchrist glanced at Mackie. 'Did you take x-rays?'

Mackie nodded. He replaced the right hand, picked up the left, and pointed to the small knuckle. 'Fifth metacarpal shows evidence of having sustained a similar injury.' He looked at Jack. 'Did she say how it happened?'

'She'd been watching television. Some Korean expert on judo. She tried to punch her fist through a block of wood.' He gave a wan smile that died on his lips. 'She said that was a defining moment in her life, when she realised she would be an artist, not a martial arts expert.'

Mackie returned his attention to the hand, giving Gilchrist the impression he was leaving the hard part to him.

'That's all for now, Bert,' said Gilchrist, and tugged Jack's arm. He felt a moment's resistance, then Jack was by his side, out through the mortuary, and into a long corridor. They pushed through the double swinging door and into the grey light and cold air of a late winter afternoon. Together they walked past Gilchrist's Merc and over to the edge of the car park. Then stopped.

Jack breathed hard through his nostrils. 'I'm not mistaken,' he said. 'It's Chloe.'

Gilchrist said nothing. Christ, what would he give for a cigarette at that moment? Fourteen years since he last had a smoke, and the need still hit him like an unscratchable itch deep in his gut. 'Why don't you stay here for a couple of days?' he said.

Jack shrugged.

'I'll be instructing forensics to examine your flat.'

Jack turned at him, eyes burning. 'You don't think I had—'

'It's standard procedure. We need samples of clothing, hair from Chloe's hairbrush, stuff like that, to check her DNA.' He looked away, felt Jack's eyes on him. Jesus. He had the scar, the crushed knuckle, the paint under the fingernails. They would surely lift Chloe's fingerprints from Jack's flat. How *conclusive* did identification have to be? He gave Jack's shoulder a quick squeeze, not sure if he was trying to be strong for Jack or himself.

'I'm sorry,' he whispered. 'I'm truly sorry.'

Gilchrist watched his son walk to the car. Part of him was aching, too, for Chloe, for Jack, for Chloe's parents. But his own pain seemed smothered in dread. The killer was clever. They would not find the rest of the body intact, Gilchrist knew. He knew that with certainty. All he could do was dig harder, look deeper, maybe pull in a few favours, try to find some lead to work on. But in the heart of him he knew they were just waiting for the next body part to turn up.

And he was not sure he could take that.

* * *

Beth slipped her key into her front door and pushed.

She stepped inside, breathed in the familiar aroma of polish and potpourri. After last night, she realised she needed to make a change to her life. It had been a while since she'd brought fresh flowers home, and with them she sensed the renewed thrill of adventure.

That morning in the shop, she had talked to Cindy and discussed her departure. Three weeks this Friday. Which did not give Beth long to find a buyer. She was selling up, despite what Andy said. She was going to make a new life for herself, get away from St Andrews, move to Spain with Cindy and Steve, have a month's break from it all, then decide what she wanted to do with her future.

In the kitchen she picked up her phone, felt her heart stutter when it was answered.

She took a deep breath, let it out. 'We need to talk, Andy.'

'How are you feeling?'

She closed her eyes. He always asked her that. But if he truly cared he would give up his job. 'Fine,' she said.

'I can't talk right now. I'm tied up at the Office. But we could meet somewhere for a bite to eat, if you'd like.'

Resolve hit her as hard as a cattle-prod to the spine. 'I'm leaving,' she said.

'Leaving?'

'St Andrews.'

'I think you should talk to Dr Buchanan before—'

'My mind's made up, Andy. I'm putting the shop on the market.'

'Beth,' he said, 'you should give it some time—'

'I've given it enough time. I'm selling.' She listened to several seconds of silence, then added, 'I'm sorry, Andy. It's just not working out.'

'Beth,' he said.

'Please, Andy.'

'If we could just—'

'Don't. I need to do this.'

Another pause, then, 'Can I help?'

'Yes,' she said, and fought back the nip of tears. 'I'd like you to move out.'

CHAPTER NINE

FOR THE REST OF THE DAY, Gilchrist kept his failed relationship with Beth to himself, and buried himself in the investigation. He contacted Dainty Small with confirmation of Jack's ID, and asked if Dainty could have someone keep an eye on Maureen for him.

'Bloody hell, Andy. We're stretched thin as it is. But I'll see what I can do.'

Strathclyde Police visited Chloe's parents and informed them of their suspicions, always suspicions, nothing definite until they conclusively matched the DNA results or fingerprints. He drove to Glasgow and assisted Forensics with their search of Jack's flat. Three pairs of Chloe's knickers were removed from the laundry basket and samples of her hair from a hairbrush in the bathroom. They also took tubes of oils from her studio and lifted a perfect set of fingerprints from a coffee mug on a table by her easel.

By 10:45, back in St Andrews, Gilchrist had done as much as he could, and drew his day to a close. As he accelerated along North Street he knew he had lost Beth. Her decision to give up the shop had been building up for weeks, and he had feared it was only a matter of time. And now that time had arrived, the last thing Beth needed was to hear him try to persuade her to do otherwise. So he would do as she asked, and move out. Or rather, he would not return.

He drove straight to Fisherman's Cottage, arriving home this side of midnight to find Jack crashed out on the settee, the TV still on, and a half finished bottle of Glenfiddich standing upright on the coffee table. He decided to leave Jack as he found him, and went to bed, his heart torn for Chloe and hurting for Beth.

He slept in confusing fits and sweating starts, his mind firing images of Beth in tears, reaching out to him, only to morph into a waif-like Chloe who turned away from him to swirl paint onto an upright canvas with handless stumps. He pulled himself from bed at five and checked on Jack, pleased to see he had made it to the spare bedroom after all, and the bottle of Glenfiddich still at half-mast.

Two calls to Beth before eight o'clock were punted into her voice mail, and with reluctance Gilchrist decided that perhaps the best thing would be for him to stay out of her way for a few days at least, and focus all his efforts on the search for Chloe.

Forensics confirmed that the fingerprints from the coffee cup matched those of the amputated right hand, and an appeal for information on Chloe's whereabouts went out on the national and local news that day. Strathclyde Police had a young PW dress like Chloe; black woollen skirt, black sweater, shoes, jacket; and walk from Jack's flat down Byres Road onto Hyndland then left onto Great Western. Without knowing which route Chloe might have taken, they tried several walks, but by the end of the day no one had come forward. It seemed as if Chloe had stepped from Jack's flat mid-morning and vanished in broad daylight.

To make matters worse, Bertie McKinnon, a local hack with a pathological distrust of Fife Constabulary, and Gilchrist in partic-ular, stirred up local discontent with a passion. The incompetence of the Crime Management Department was spread across the front pages for all to see, with photographs of Gilchrist, the hapless SIO, in an assortment of unflattering poses. One inflammatory photo showed him standing alone on the sixteenth fairway, looking at his feet, scratching his head, under the headline *WHAT TO DO?* Another caught him stepping out of Lafferty's with the caption *MURDER'S THIRSTY WORK*. And an old one from McKinnon's archives of Gilchrist strolling along the beach with his ex-wife, so inflamed Gilchrist that he had to be held back from visiting the newspaper's office.

In support of Strathclyde's efforts, teams of plain-clothed detectives and uniformed police constables from Fife Constabulary were dispatched throughout the east coast area to hunt for Chloe's body. Farms on the outskirts of St Andrews were searched. Gardens, outhouses, sheds, huts, barns, stables, even pigsties and a child's tree-house were all turned over.

But they found nothing.

And nothing could be made of the notes recovered from both hands. It was impossible to find a sequence from only two words. No incriminating fingerprints were evident, as if the notes had been cleaned and slipped between lifeless digits. Only Watt's finger-prints were found on the scrap of paper pulled from under his windscreen wipers. Watt maintained his story that he removed it without thinking, believing it to be nothing more than an adver-tising flyer.

By the end of the third day, the investigation appeared to be stalling. All they seemed to have was a list of names and addresses of artists and students, parents and cousins, shop owners and paint suppliers.

But no suspects. Not even close.

That evening, Gilchrist called a press conference in the car park at the rear of the police station in North Street and confirmed they were now concentrating all their efforts in locating Chloe Fullerton, age twenty-two, last known address, Hillhead, Glasgow, who had been missing for eight days and was now presumed murdered.

Gilchrist hated to say it, but he was praying the killer would feed them another body part with another note, just so he had something to go on. So, when Greaves called him into his office, Gilchrist expected the worst.

Newspapers lay scattered across the surface of Greaves' desk.

Gilchrist closed the door with a firm click.

'What the hell's wrong with this bloody fool, Bertie McKinnon?' Greaves demanded, slapping the back of his hand across a front page photograph of the SOCO van on the sixteenth fairway. Three SOCOs, coverall hoods pulled back to reveal smiling faces, sipped tea from a silver flask and ate sandwiches. The caption *TEE BREAK* summed it up.

'He hates the local police,' Gilchrist said.

'He's got it in for you.'

'He's got it in for everybody.'

'But you in particular, Andy.' Greaves lowered his head, eyed Gilchrist over the rim of some imaginary specs. 'Does he know it's personal?'

'Don't think so. But it shouldn't take him long to work it out.'

Greaves returned a hard stare. 'Are you up for it, Andy? The investigation? You know we don't—'

'Kicking me off the case isn't going to help. McKinnon'll just say we're nothing but incompetent.' Gilchrist gave a tight smile.

Greaves seemed to let Gilchrist's logic work through his system, then said, 'Well, what have you done to the man, for God's sake?'

'Maybe I owe him a pint.'

'Well buy him one. Buy him a dozen. Get him off our backs.'

'Not as simple as that.'

'Quite.' Greaves picked up a newspaper folded open to the photograph of Gilchrist stepping from the Dunvegan Hotel, and smacked the image with the back of his hand, as if clipping Gilchrist around the ears. 'This does not present a good image of Fife Constabulary, Andy.'

At least he was still on the case. 'It was taken out of context.'

'I'm sure it was.'

'I was interviewing Tam Dunn again.'

'I'm sure you were.'

'And it was 11:30 at night.'

'That's not the point. The public doesn't expect to open their newspapers at the breakfast table and be confronted with glaring photographs of Senior Investigating Officers apparently out on the town when we've got such a gruesome bloody case to solve.'

'I wasn't exactly celebrating.'

'You're missing the point.'

Gilchrist raised his eyebrows. Greaves had a reputation of being unflappable. But something had him flapping at that moment.

'The whole thing's bloody scandalous. Makes us look like the Keystone Cops, for God's sake.'

'I really don't—'

Greaves held up his hand, as if stopping traffic head on. 'I don't want excuses, Andy. I want results. And I want results *now*.'

Gilchrist eyed Greaves. They were getting down to it, and he did not like where it was heading.

'And we can't have you and Watt bloody well squabbling in public.'

Gilchrist frowned. Greaves was referring to an incident at the university yesterday where he had grabbed Watt's arm and pulled him back from a heated interview with a student. The depth of Watt's anger had surprised Gilchrist. 'Define *squabbling*,' he said.

For a long second, Greaves glared at Gilchrist. Then he growled, 'Are you any further forward?'

'I would be lying if I said yes.'

'Bloody hell, Andy. McVicar's been on the phone twice today. The heat's been turned up and he's aiming the blowtorch in my direction. Bloody flame's turned from orange to blue, let me tell you.' Greaves leaned forward. 'Tell me something I want to hear, Andy. Give me something to calm the man down.'

Big Archie McVicar, Fife Constabulary's Assistant Chief Constable, was a staunch supporter of Gilchrist. But there had to be a limit to the man's patience. Gilchrist needed more than a pair of amputated hands and an army of police officers scouring the countryside. Like Greaves, he needed a result.

'Anything?' Greaves tried.

Gilchrist grimaced. Fabricating nonsense would help no one. 'Nothing,' he said.

'What the hell am I supposed to tell him, Andy?'

'That we're looking to increase manpower?'

'For God's sake. We've no one else to put on the bloody thing. We're stretched to the limit as it is.'

'Chloe Fullerton lived within the jurisdiction of Strathclyde Police. I would think a call from the ACC—'

'*Don't*,' shouted Greaves. 'The answer's an emphatic *No*.'

Gilchrist had anticipated no support from his superiors on the touchy subject of requesting assistance from outside sources, and had tried the back door himself. Even Dainty Small had given him a body-swerve, saying he was up to his oxters in alligators of his own. Gilchrist knew police units throughout the nation had their own tight budgets to meet, and financial constraints touched everyone in the food chain, from requests for additional manpower to the purchase of pens and paper. 'We're doing what we can,' Gilchrist continued, 'but without the rest of the body we can't expect much.'

'Well, do something, Andy. *Something*, for God's sake.'

It was on the tip of Gilchrist's tongue to ask for Watt to be replaced, but he thought better of it. 'We're widening our search,' he said, 'but the body's nowhere near here.'

'Where then?'

Where indeed? 'Glasgow,' he said.

'You have proof?'

Gilchrist shook his head. 'Just a hunch.'

'For God's sake, Andy. I need more than *just a hunch*. I need evidence. I need results. I need... oh for God's sake just get bloody well on with it, will you? I'll think of something to tell Archie.'

Gilchrist felt his face flush as Greaves reached for his phone.

The meeting was over.

Outside, the wind had risen, a cold easterly chill that swept in from the Eden Estuary and seemed to funnel its way up North Street. Overhead, gulls fought with the night storm, spread wings flashing white as they tumbled and swooped in the stiff gusts.

Gilchrist pulled his collar around his neck and walked towards College Street. The proverbial shit was piled at the fan and splattering through the system. First, ACC McVicar. Second, Chief Superintendent Greaves. Next, DCI Andy Gilchrist, acting SIO in a case stacked against him. His name was printed on a note, and the press were baying for results. Thoughts of having it out with

McKinnon surged through his mind. He glanced at his watch. Just after eight.

To hell with it. He needed a pint.

He reached the corner of College and Market Street and veered left into the Central Bar, promising to have greater willpower in matters of import. If McKinnon photographed him once more with a pint in his hand, well, that was just too damn bad.

The bar was redolent of cigarettes, beer, and warm food. The air swirled thick and blue under a high ceiling. Piped music competed with raucous laughter. High in the corner a television screen showed a muted football match. Rangers and Hibs, it looked like. A voice came at him from the side, and he stepped back as a barman weaved by carrying two ashets topped with flaked pastry and trailing a tantalising aroma of cooked meat that reminded Gilchrist he'd had nothing to eat since mid-morning.

He found a vacant spot at the bar, close to the till, and managed to catch the barmaid's eye. She mouthed, *With you in a moment.* While he waited, he dialled Beth's number and was again shunted to her voice mail. He left a short message, asking her to call if she needed to talk to him, and letting her know he was there for her. He glanced up to see Nance waving at him from the opposite end of the bar.

When he joined her, she said, 'Caught.'

'You or me?'

'Both of us.'

Gilchrist smiled. Nance was hard-working and thorough, and if she wanted to have a drink at the end of a long day's shift, then who was he to question her?

'Pint?' she asked.

'You talked me into it.'

She laughed, a staccato chuckle that almost took him by surprise, until he realised it had been some time since he had seen Nance happy. He had heard she had split from Greg, her partner of eighteen months.

Nance ordered two pints of Eighty-Shilling.

'On your second already,' Gilchrist said. 'Must've been a hard day.'

'A hard partner, more like.'

'How are you getting along with my favourite DS?'

'Sarcasm doesn't become you.'

Gilchrist scanned the faces around the bar. 'He's not here, is he?'

Nance shook her head. 'He's checking out a lead.'

'Taking the dog for a walk?'

Nance chuckled. 'I've stopped asking,' then tipped the remains of her first pint to her lips. 'Cheers.'

Gilchrist did likewise, loving the beer's smoothness as the first mouthful slid down his throat. He returned his glass to the counter, ran his fingers across his lips. 'Boy, was I ready for that.'

'Have you heard about the sweepstake?' Nance asked.

'Sweepstake?'

'Watt's started a sweepstake on when the next body part will turn up, and which part it will be.' She grimaced. 'He's one disturbed human being, let me tell you.'

Anger at Watt's callous disrespect of human life surged through Gilchrist with the force of an electric strike. He felt his teeth clench. Watt had to go. The man was a liability. He made a mental note to have it out with him first thing in the morning and have all bets forfeited and the monies deposited into the charity box. Then the slimmest of ideas shimmered before him.

'Did Watt put on any money?' he asked.

'He did.'

'Which body part?'

'Leg.'

'Left or right?'

Nance looked at him as if he had sprouted horns. 'I don't know.'

'And when does he bet this leg is going to turn up?'

'Tomorrow,' Nance said. 'You're not suggesting...'

'Not quite. But it's an interesting thought all the same.' Gilchrist lifted his pint. He had not heard from Martin Coyle about Watt's phone records. Maybe Coyle could turn an interesting thought into something worthwhile.

* * *

'Steady on there, big man,' said Wee Kenny. 'Watch what you're doing.'

Jimmy Reid grimaced a black-toothed smile. 'Just hold the fucker steady. Is that too much to ask?'

Wee Kenny scowled as Jimmy placed the red-hot poker flat against the skin. Black smoke curled into the air as he pressed down and rolled his wrist to ensure a deep brand.

'What's the matter, wee man? Never smelt burning meat before?'

Wee Kenny put a hand to his mouth. 'My the fuck. That's honking, so it is.'

Jimmy returned the poker to the brazier, slid grimy fingers across his forehead and licked the sweat from them. He seemed always to be sweating now. He had a touch of the flu. That was all. He hawked phlegm from the back of his throat and spat a gob of green into the brazier where it hit with a hard hiss then bubbled and popped. Then he removed a flat tin from his pocket and fingered tobacco onto a strip of Rizla paper. He evened it out, rolled the paper, ran his tongue along the edge. He pulled the poker from the fire and held it to his face. As he drew on his cigarette, acrid smoke forced his eyes to water, and he slapped the poker back onto the skin and pressed hard.

Wee Kenny startled, but kept his grip. 'What's it say?'

Jimmy held his cigarette in one hand, the poker in the brazier with the other. He stirred the coals and eyed the skin. Cigarette smoke shifted in the still air. He half-closed his eyes. The heat from the brazier felt as hot as the Spanish sun. Too fucking hot. He hated the sun. The sun was no place for a man to sit out in. He stabbed the poker at the coals, causing sparks to flicker and die in the night air. Urgency seemed to dictate his actions then, and he drew the tip of the poker across the skin, trying to brand a curve.

Curling fingers of black smoke rose into the darkness.

'What's it say, big man?'

Jimmy worked in silence for two more minutes, laying the poker on the skin, twisting and branding, Wee Kenny grimacing from the stench of burning skin and putrescent meat.

When it was done, Jimmy eyed his handiwork.

Wee Kenny squinted to read it. 'Blood-what?' he asked. But Jimmy had his eyes closed, his cheeks pulled in. Sweat glistened on a grey face flushed with heat. Wee Kenny tried again. 'Is that how you spell blood?'

'It's not blood.'

'I thought it said—'

'Don't be so fucking stupid.'

Wee Kenny looked to the coals. Reading had never been his strong suit. But Jimmy was different. Jimmy was smart. Jimmy could read. He even wrote letters to his brother in Barlinnie, and someone—

'Wrap the fucker up.'

Wee Kenny pulled the polythene wrapping from the box and did as he was ordered.

Jimmy took a final drag, the short stub crimped between the tips of his thumb and forefinger. His hollow cheeks sucked in with the effort, then he flicked the dowt into the brazier.

Wee Kenny glanced up at him, and in the passing of his dark eyes saw Jimmy for what he really was. He stared at the poker, at the handle sticking out of the red coals, at the tip glowing white-red. He had seen Jimmy in action and knew you could never tell with the man. You never knew the minute.

Wee Kenny tightened his grip, almost hugged his gruesome parcel to his chest. 'Is that us?'

Jimmy hawked another gob onto the brazier. 'Let's go, wee man.'

CHAPTER TEN

GILCHRIST PEERED AT the digital display on his radio alarm.

4:52. Bloody hell. He reached for his mobile phone and pressed *Connect*.

'Gilchrist,' he said, trying to sound awake, but his voice betrayed him.

'We've got another body part, sir. Report's just come in.'

Gilchrist slid his feet from under the quilt. 'Whereabouts?' he growled.

'Near the Golf Museum.'

Opposite the R&A clubhouse. Not a bunker in sight. 'On the Old Course?'

'No, sir. By Golf Place.'

'Who's at the scene?'

'PW Lambert, sir. She called it in about a minute ago.'

Dorothy Lambert. Dot to her friends and colleagues. 'Which part is it this time?'

'Leg, sir.'

Gilchrist narrowed his eyes as Nance's words came back at him. *Watt's started a sweepstake*. 'Have you called anyone else?' he asked.

'Not yet, sir.'

'Have Nance meet me at the scene,' he said. 'And don't call Watt until...' He glanced at his watch. '...5:45. On the button.'

'Sir?'

'And get Bert Mackie and his team down there right away. I'm on my way.'

He forced himself upright and stumbled to the bathroom. Rain battered hard against the frosted glass. He brushed his teeth, hard and vigorous, felt his stomach lurch as he poked too far back, and coughed into the sink. Why had he let Jack persuade him to have a half? Just the one. But one always led to two. He tried to convince himself that he'd had a few to keep Jack company, get his mind off Chloe. And at that thought he coughed again, this time spitting out a dribble of bile. Christ. Was he really about to see Chloe's hacked off leg?

He straightened himself and stared at the mirror, ran a hand over his face, felt the hard brush of stubble on his chin. Although his hair was dark, his beard was white around his chin and neck. Slivers of grey pressed by his ears. He tried a smile. It was a toss-up as to which was whiter. His teeth or his face. The bags under his eyes looked as dark as mascara. If he'd ever thought he was a looker, those days were long gone. Maybe it was just as well Gail had found Harry.

He shaved and showered, and as he stepped into a brisk east coast breeze he made a promise to himself that soon he would retire. He would take up photography again, be more serious about it this time, maybe turn the front room into a gallery, make a few bob selling framed photographs, just enough to supplement his pension. Much more sensible than running around town at all hours of the day and night looking at body parts.

Twenty minutes later, he pulled his Merc onto the expanse of asphalt at the side of the R&A Clubhouse. The rain had stopped, the air as fresh and cold as ice. He removed a set of coveralls and gloves from the boot, put his head down, and marched into the wind. Winter on the Fife coast could be freezing cold. That morning was making no exceptions.

Ahead, the lone figure of PW Dot Lambert stood as still as a silhouette by the dulled light from a streetlamp on the opposite side of the road. The area was devoid of police tape and cones.

Gilchrist reached her. 'Where is it?' he said.

'This way, sir.'

Gilchrist thought her voice possessed a hint of a shiver, from the cold or her gruesome find, he could not say. She pointed to a rolled sheet of plastic that lay just off the back of the footpath, then she stepped to the side, as if in deference to his seniority. The plastic had split open to reveal the knee joint and a length of white calf. Gilchrist slipped on his coveralls and gloves.

He eased back the polythene sheeting to reveal the painted toenails of a left foot. Rain dotted the plastic's grimy surface, but from the length of it, Gilchrist could tell it was a complete leg. He grimaced. *Left leg.*

Watt had won the sweepstake. A guess? Or had he known?

Gilchrist promised himself he would tear it out of him.

The package had been dumped on the grass next to the putting green, and by the way the sheeting had burst open Gilchrist would bet a month's wages that it had been thrown there.

Tossed from a passing car?

'How did you find it?' he asked Lambert.

'It was just lying there, sir.'

'Which way were you walking?'

She glanced over his shoulder, in the opposite direction of the beach, past the R&A Clubhouse. 'From that way, sir.'

'Did you walk along the Links Road?'

'Yes, sir.'

'From the pathway by the Jigger Inn?'

'Yes, sir.'

'So, from the Jigger it would take you what, five to ten minutes to walk from there to here?'

'About that, sir. Yes.'

'During which time this road...' He swept his arm from the seafront to Auchterlonies, and down past Tom Morris' to the house at the end of the terrace that overlooked the eighteenth tee. '... would have been in your view.'

'Yes, sir.'

It would have been dark, too. But still...

'Did you see anyone?' he asked.

'No, sir.'

'Any cars? Anything?'

'Sorry, sir. I was just walking past when I happened to look over and see it.'

Gilchrist nodded. At night, this was a quiet part of town. There was no reason for anyone to walk or drive down that way, unless they were heading to the beach. And who would do that in the pre-dawn hours of a winter morning? He turned to The Scores, the road that ran uphill at right angles to Golf Place. Hotels lined one side and overlooked an expanse of grass that fell away to rocks and the beach below. Martyrs' Monument stood dark and tall as a silent sentinel.

Gilchrist eyed the hotel windows. Most lay in blackness, but beyond The Scores Hotel a few rectangles of light spilled into the pre-dawn gloom. Had someone glanced out one of those windows? Had anyone heard anything, seen anything? Maybe a car driving past, someone walking? No, not walking. That was risky. Whoever dumped the amputated limb had to have done so from a car.

He studied the grass by the packaged leg, detected scuff marks, maybe two, a slither of mud, and saw that the car had to have been driving away from the beach.

He eyed the junction at the top of the hill. If you turned right at the Dunvegan, then through the mini-roundabout, that put you on the road out of St Andrews. And he saw in his mind's eye that the car had come from Glasgow. That was where Chloe and Jack lived. Why hide her body anywhere else? He would challenge Greaves again on working closer with Strathclyde Police.

From somewhere beyond the buildings that bordered the eigh-teenth fairway, he heard the unsteady rumble of a car's exhaust. He heard the sound again, a fading growl, eyed the road out of town and caught the shiver of parting headlights beyond the shrubs and hedgerows. But at that time in the morning it could be anyone.

He turned his attention back to the polythene package. Through the sheeting, the leg was long, slim, verging on the skinny. It lay at an angle, so the inner thigh lay exposed to him. A lump choked his throat. Had Jack's hand caressed that leg? Had his lips kissed that skin in moments of intimacy? Dear God, how could he let Jack see this? He was torturing himself. What the hell would it do to Jack?

He kneeled. The grass felt cold through his coveralls. The leg had been amputated at the top of the thigh, cut at an angle. He fingered a corner of the sheeting and eased it back to expose the top of the leg. The wind seemed to shift at that moment, and he thought he caught the smell of burning. He looked up, sniffed the air. Nothing. Maybe he imagined it.

He shifted the sheeting a touch more.

From the marks on the thigh bone and the roughness of the meat where the skin had been cut he guessed the leg had been amputated with a saw.

Mackie would be the one to make that call.

It struck Gilchrist all of a sudden that there was no note. Which was puzzling. Was that not what this was about? The killer taunting Gilchrist, torturing him, making him pay for the wrong some lunatic conceived had been done against him? And with that, he gripped the sheeting, pulled it back.

A rush of ice chilled his blood.

Dear God. There it was. His note.

He let go of the plastic, slipped on the wet grass, landed on his rump, and scrambled back, back with his elbows, away from the leg, away from the message that—

'Sir?'

He looked up at Lambert and forced a smile. But his lips jerked instead. 'Slipped,' he said. She helped him up. 'Stupid of me.' He brushed a hand over his coveralls and tried to convince himself that he had seen worse. The five-year-old girl they had pulled from the mud of the Kinness Burn four years ago. Even Mackie had gagged when the girl's head had slipped through his fingers leaving him holding her peeled off face as her skull bounced and skittered on the post mortem slab. But it had still not been as bad as this. This was personal. If the leg was indeed Chloe's, then she had been murdered for no other reason than to be hacked to pieces and sent to Gilchrist as some kind of morbid message.

Was that possible? Could someone be so heartless, so cruel?

Who was capable of even thinking of doing such a thing, then carrying it through?

He had to find out. And by God, when he did, he would nail the bastard to a brick wall.

He gritted his teeth and held his breath as he bent down to the amputated limb. Dear God, he thought. Just get on with it. He tugged at the plastic sheeting, lifted it up so that the leg could slide free. But it stuck for one tantalising second before rolling onto the grass to reveal a mass of blackened scars that ran from the top of the outer thigh to halfway down the calf.

His breath left him with a rush.

Christ. He had his note. Branded into the skin.

He stared at the ugly arrangement of disfigured letters, at first unable to make any sense of the mess, then deciphering the single word.

BLUDGEON.

The smell hit him again, a warm guff trapped by the polythene, which now rose from the blackened skin like a pall of invisible smoke that found its way into his mouth and lungs. The stench of the burned flesh of his son's girlfriend. He tried to force that thought away, but he was too late. He put his hand to his mouth, felt his stomach lurch. He stumbled to the side, bumped into a wooden fence, hung over it and dry-heaved onto the grass.

'Jesus,' he gasped.

Then Lambert was by his side. 'Sir?'

He straightened, dragged his hand across his mouth. 'Sorry,' he said, and closed his lips, faced the wind. He took a deep breath. The air smelled clear, cold, devoid of the stench of cooked meat that lay like a coating of filth on his tongue. He coughed, tried to clear his throat, but resisted spitting in front of Lambert.

'Sir?'

'I'm fine, Dot.'

'It's not that, sir.' Her eyes glistened in the cold, like those of a child reflecting her hidden fears. 'I think I remember seeing a car.'

'You *think* you remember?'

She nodded.

Gilchrist frowned. 'I don't follow.'

'It was parked on The Links Road. I remember seeing it as I walked past. It was there five or ten minutes ago, but it's not there now.'

Gilchrist followed her line of sight. 'Five or ten minutes ago?' he said. 'When I was looking at the...'

'Yes, sir. It was parked at the corner.'

'Did you get its registration number?'

'No, sir. But it was a Vauxhall. A Vauxhall Astra.'

'You sure?'

'Yes, sir. I've been thinking of buying one, and I—'

'Colour?'

'Dark-blue. Black, maybe.'

Gilchrist eyed the corner of The Links Road that ran parallel to the eighteenth fairway, and realised what the earlier sound of the engine had been. 'Facing downhill?'

She thought for a moment, then nodded. 'Yes.'

Gilchrist stripped off his gloves and coveralls, threw them to the ground, pulled out his mobile phone. 'Stay here,' he ordered. 'Nance is on her way.' He ran towards his car, had his keys in his hand and the number for the Office poked in by the time he opened the door.

'Crime Management.'

'Call Cupar Division,' he ordered. 'Tell them to set up a road block and stop all cars coming out of St Andrews.' He switched on his engine. 'We're looking for a Vauxhall Astra, dark-blue, black, or any other car that looks like it. All occupants are to be considered armed and dangerous.'

'I'm not sure I—'

'*Do it*,' he shouted.

He pulled into reverse, hit the pedal, tugged the wheel. The

Merc's tyres squealed as it raced up Golf Place. Cupar was about ten miles west of St Andrews on the A91, the main road to Stirling.

And Glasgow.

It was a long shot. Maybe his longest yet.

But if they were quick enough...

CHAPTER ELEVEN

GILCHRIST PASSED THE LINKS ROAD and noted the spot where the Vauxhall Astra had parked, a dry patch on the road, darkening by the second from a steady drizzle moving in from the sea.

He played out the scene in his mind's eye.

Car parked at the corner, its occupants peering through the windows to make sure their grisly package was found. Then releasing the handbrake and cruising downhill, into gear and the clutch out.

That was the sound he had heard, the Astra bump-starting.

He powered through the mini-roundabout and raced out of town. The clock on the dashboard read 5:43. Ahead, the Roadster's twin beams pierced the darkness. The rain had almost stopped, and the road glimmered with beads of water as bright as ice.

He roared past the Old Course Hotel to his right, its tan façade alight from an array of spotlights. Then the flat fairways of Balgove Golf Course, the undulating more demanding Strathtyrum, on to open countryside, all zipping past unseen in the pre-dawn dark, like night-time memories.

He caught the tail-lights of a vehicle ahead, gripped the steering wheel. But it could not be the Vauxhall. He glanced at the dashboard. 5:46. When had he heard the car bump-starting? He tried to calculate it, work back from that moment in time. How long had it been? Fifteen minutes? Ten? Less? At sixty miles an hour, fifteen minutes would put the Vauxhall fifteen miles away.

Through Cupar. And he would be too late.

Ten would be too late, too.

He grabbed his phone, hit Nance's number.

She answered with a snappy, 'Hold your horses, big boy. I'm already on my way.'

'Get onto the PNC and do a search for Vauxhall Astras,' he said. 'Dark-blue or black. I want names and addresses of all owners living in Glasgow.'

'Care to tell me what's going on?'

'Hang on.' Gilchrist glanced in his mirror, pulled the steering wheel, and overtook two slower cars, neither of them a Vauxhall. 'We have another body part down by the Golf Museum.'

'The Office already called,' she said. 'The left leg.'

'Yes,' he hissed. 'Surprise, surprise.' He felt his teeth grind. 'When Watt shows up, make sure you nail his feet to the ground until I get back. Got it?'

'Got it.'

Another glance at the dashboard. Almost ninety. If the Astra was doing sixty, he was making up a mile every two minutes. If it had a ten minute start on him, it would take him twenty minutes to catch up. By which time he could have reached Cupar and had a cup of tea and a sandwich. That thought settled him down. No need to kill himself hounding the rabbit into the snare.

He eased his foot from the pedal and dialled the Office. As soon as he was connected, he said, 'Has Cupar Division been called?'

'One minute, sir.'

'Don't put me on...' *Shit*. He tightened his grip on the phone and pulled out to overtake a van, caught a glimpse of an angry face as he shot past. What were these people doing up at this time? Back into the inside lane, dabbed the brake for the left-hand bend, through it and foot to the floor again. Seventy-plus. Still too fast.

He eased back.

'I have Cupar Division on the phone for you, sir.'

'That's not what—'

'DC Grant Neville. How can I help?'

Gilchrist felt his jaw clench. Nothing had been done about setting up the road block. Not a damn bloody thing. He should have called himself. *Shit*. And *damn it*. He felt his foot pressing to the floor again. 'This is DCI Gilchrist of St Andrews Division,' he said, struggling to keep his tone level. 'I asked for a road block to be set up on—'

'Yes, sir. We're taking care of that.'

Gilchrist felt a surge of regret at his flash of anger and misplaced assumption. Maybe he needed a refresher course on anger management. 'That's good,' was all he could think to say.

'The occupants are armed and dangerous,' continued DC Neville. 'What are we looking at here?'

All of a sudden, Gilchrist felt like the boy who cried wolf. What could he say? That it was a spur of the moment thing? That it was only a hunch? Greaves' voice came back at him, ingratiating as ever. *I need more than just a hunch. I need evidence. I need results.* Why the hell could he not keep his thoughts to himself?

'Sir?'

Gilchrist cleared his throat. 'I'm SIO on the body part investigation in St Andrews. A limb turned up half an hour ago. We believe the occupants of the Vauxhall can help in our investigation. We need to apprehend them for questioning.'

'Do you have the registration number?'

'No.'

'How many occupants?'

'Don't know.'

'Male or female?'

'Don't know.'

'Do you know if they're armed?'

Jesus. This was as bad as being cross-examined. 'We don't know for certain,' he said, 'but he, she, or they, should be approached with extreme caution. Is that clear enough?'

'Very good, sir. Anything else I need to know?'

Gilchrist's mind turned up a blank. 'I'll be with you in five minutes. Don't let any cars through until I get there.'

'Very good, sir.'

Gilchrist offered curt thanks and hung up.

He neared the Guardbridge roundabout, shot through it at sixty-plus, and up the hill towards Dairsie. He tried to rationalise his thought process, how he could have concluded that the car he was following had anything to do with the amputated limb. But that sixth sense of his, that niggling gut feeling, was doing its best to tell him to keep going, keep chasing, you've got them trapped.

Whoever *they* were.

At 5:54 he reached the roadblock, no more than twenty cars end to end in a line that stopped at a police car with blue twirling lights. Gilchrist pulled his Merc onto the pavement, switched off the engine, and stepped into the chilled morning air. The ground felt dry, the air fresh and crisp, and he realised the rain had some-how missed Cupar. He walked past the end car, a yellow Fiat, on past a white Lexus, then a tired-silver Jaguar xj-12 with an unfinished repair to the boot lid. Under the street-lights the red-oxide patch looked like blood, which had him thinking about Chloe, what her last thoughts had been as she watched her lifeblood leave her.

Christ, he was torturing himself. But images of Chloe's body lying in a pool of blood kept stirring in his mind. He thrust his hands into his jacket pockets and kept walking, past a decrepit pick-up with a ladder strapped to its roof, onto a Ford, past a Transit van, another Ford, and a—

The black Astra sat four cars from the front.

He forced himself to keep walking.

Exhaust fumes rose from idling engines like steam from panting horses. He ignored the vacant looks cast his way, felt his pulse quicken as he neared the Vauxhall. Almost on it. For one stupefying moment he toyed with the idea of walking around to the driver's door, pulling it open, and dragging whoever was inside onto the ground.

He drew level, threw a glance inside. The windows were misted. Then he was past it, fighting the urge to glance back. He had seen through the steamed glass.

Two passengers. Both male.

He kept walking until he reached the police car, its lights rotating in the night air, flickering like a surreal scene, confusing as a dream. Two uniformed constables stood with their backs to the car, and he stepped up to the taller of the two, a smooth-faced hulk of a man, about an inch or so taller than himself. He flashed his warrant card and introduced himself.

The tall constable was Mark Graham. The other, Vic Mackay.

'Where's DC Neville?' Gilchrist asked.

'On his way, sir,' Graham replied.

'Did he tell you what we're looking for?'

'Vauxhall Astra. Dark-blue or black.' Graham looked over Gilchrist's shoulder, and with all the stiff-lipped subtlety of a trainee ventriloquist, said, 'Like the Vauxhall four from the front, sir?'

Gilchrist smiled.

'We've already checked with PNC. It's registered to a James Fletcher.'

'Address?'

'Ardmore Street, Glasgow.'

Glasgow. Gilchrist felt a finger of ice brush the nape of his neck. Was his hunch right? Was his sixth sense doing the impossible again? He told Constables Graham and MacKay how he wanted to handle it. They nodded in understanding.

'Right,' Gilchrist said. 'Let's get on with it.'

He turned to the first car, a glistening black BMW 531, and stepped onto the road. He waited until the driver opened his window, then said, 'Sorry to keep you waiting, sir. You can drive on now.'

The driver frowned, as if undecided whether to be annoyed at the delay or relieved it was over, then spurted through the gap between the police cars with a squeal from the tyres.

Gilchrist did the same with the next vehicle, an ageing Ford Capri and a carefree farmer, then the next, a Landrover and a platinum blonde in her seventies, two dogs in her lap. She had to be violating some traffic law, but he waved her on.

The Astra pulled level and drew to a halt as he held up his hand.

Both constables stepped onto the road in front of it.

Gilchrist leaned forward as the window opened.

The driver tried a smile. 'Any problems?' he asked.

Even from those two words, Gilchrist detected the Glasgow accent, the street-wise manner. Not your upper-class citizen. He eyed the passenger, another man, his face to the front, as if he could not look the law in the eye. 'Pull off to the side of the road, sir.'

The driver grimaced, his swarthy features gaunt and rough from a couple of days' growth. 'What's this in aid of?'

'Routine check.'

'For what?'

'Pull in over there, sir.' Harder that time, leaving no doubt that he meant business.

The driver tugged the steering wheel and bumped the Astra onto the pavement with a squeal of rubber that had Constable MacKay reaching for his truncheon.

Gilchrist stood in the middle of the road, waved the remaining cars through while Graham and MacKay carried out preliminary checks. When the traffic cleared, he walked over to the police car and pushed his head through the open window.

MacKay was now seated, the driver's licence in one hand, his radio in the other.

'Does it check out?' Gilchrist asked.

'It checks,' he said. 'James Fletcher. The Vauxhall's registered in his name.'

'And the other guy?'

MacKay shook his head. 'Says his name is Joe Smith. I was thinking nothing out of ten for originality, then he hands me a passport.' He held the burgundy-coloured passport up and gave a wry smile. 'Joseph Smith.'

Gilchrist frowned. Who in their right mind carried their passport around with them? It was a long shot, but he asked anyway, 'Have you seen either of them before?'

MacKay shook his head.

'Right,' said Gilchrist, and walked over to the Astra. He nodded to DC Graham. Like a choreographed act, he and Graham gripped opposite door handles and opened the passenger and driver doors in unison.

'Could you please step out, sir,' Graham said.

Gilchrist smiled down at the upturned face, then stepped back, a silent invitation for Fletcher to slide out.

'Will someone tell me what the fuck's going on?'

'No need to use foul language, Mr Fletcher,' Gilchrist said, and watched a mixture of anger and surprise shift behind the man's dark eyes. He decided to take the direct approach. 'Where are you driving to?'

'Glasgow Airport.'

'From?'

'St Andrews.'

'Both of you?'

'Yeah. Me and my mate, Joe.'

'Why?'

'What do you mean *why?* Because I like him. That's why.'

'I meant, why are you driving to Glasgow Airport? Do you have a plane to catch?'

'Yeah,' growled Fletcher. 'We were going on our holidays until you lot stopped us.'

Hence the passport. 'Spain, is it?'

'Cyprus. Like to see the tickets?'

Gilchrist gave a short smile, doubt swelling in his mind. 'Not at the moment, Mr Fletcher,' he said, then added, 'Your car was spotted this morning parked adjacent to the Old Course.'

'So?'

'What was it doing there?'

'That's where I park it.'

'Overnight?'

'Yeah.'

And at that instant, Gilchrist saw his error. The dry patch on the road surface. The storm had lasted the best part of an hour. The Vauxhall must have been parked longer than that, and he felt the beginnings of a flush warm his neck and work its way to his cheeks.

'Your licence has your address in Glasgow,' he tried.

'We've just moved up here.'

'To do what?'

'Look for work.'

'As what?'

'Caddies.'

'Where are you staying?'

'At a friend's flat.'

'Student?'

'Yeah.'

'Address?'

'A dump in Howard Place.'

The Links was no more than a couple of hundred yards from Howard Place. 'Why park in The Links?' Gilchrist asked.

'Starter motor's shot. I park it at the top of the hill, so I can get a good run.'

'For a bump-start?'

'Is that against the law?'

'Not yet,' said Gilchrist, and tried another appeasing smile. *Shit*. How could he have been so blinkered? He had it wrong. Or was he missing something? But if he was, he failed to see it. He was about to buy Fletcher's story, when he frowned. 'How long are you staying in Cyprus?'

'Nine days.'

'Nicosia?'

'Limassol.'

'Where are your suitcases?'

'In the boot. Where'd you think?'

If Fletcher was telling the truth, then either Gilchrist or Lambert should have heard the boot being closed. 'This morning, did you?'

'Huh?'

'Put your suitcases in the boot this morning?'

'Last night. So we'd get a quick start.' Fletcher must have seen the despair in Gilchrist's face, for he said, 'Look, pal, we really do have a plane to catch. Do you mind?'

Gilchrist tried one final question. 'When you fly back from Cyprus,' he said, 'how are you going to start your car at the airport?'

'Jump leads.'

Touché. And check mate.

Fletcher looked at his watch. 'Why don't you look in the boot?' He held up his keys for the *coup de grâce*. 'Here,' he said. 'Let me show you.'

He raised the boot lid, pulled one of the cases out, and thudded it to the ground. Then he slipped his hands down the side of the other. 'Look,' he said, holding up a pair of jump leads. 'Believe me now?' He threw them back into the boot with a whispered curse, and said, 'Joe's got the tickets.'

Gilchrist nodded. What a fuck up. And what a blow to public relations. He tried a smile. 'Thank you for helping us with our enquiries, Mr Fletcher.' He stepped back. 'Have a good holiday.'

'Is that it?'

'It is.'

Fletcher grunted and heaved the suitcase into the boot.

Gilchrist returned to the police car, gave Graham a quick shake of his head, and heard the boot lid close with a force that made him think Fletcher imagined decapitating him.

Before the Astra drove off, Gilchrist called Nance. 'Forget the PNC,' he said. 'It's the wrong car.'

'There is a God after all.'

'Praying for a break, were you?'

'Something like that.'

'If you're going to pray for anything, Nance, pray that we find this guy. I think we're in for a rough ride.'

He hung up and watched the Astra pull to a halt at the traffic lights. Maybe it was something in the heat of the moment, some surge of adrenaline produced by the brain in the anticipation of making an arrest. Maybe it was the excitement that triggered his thought process. Or maybe not. Whatever it was, he had learned over the years to trust it.

MURDER.

MASSACRE.

Now *BLUDGEON.*

He whispered the words, rolled them around his mouth, not liking the feel of them, liking even less the dread rising within him like an incoming wave of despair. *Three.* That was the magic number, the minimum needed to create a sequence. More words helped, but less than three did not work. He thought he saw the beginnings of some sequence to the words, some reason for the order in which they were being fed to him.

But he could be wrong.

He dabbed a hand across his forehead. It felt sweaty and cold. Which told him he was worried. He was worried sick.

His hunch with the Astra had been wrong. So wrong.

And he prayed to God that the thoughts stirring and firing in his mind to reach their numbing conclusion were wrong, too.

But he could not rid himself of the fear that this time he was right.

* * *

'Next time I tell you to fill it up with petrol, you fill it up with petrol. *You got that?*'

'Yes, big man.'

A hand reached out and clipped Wee Kenny on the side of the head. He squealed, 'I hear you, big man, I hear you.'

The hand clipped again, once, twice, then balled into a fist that thudded the side of Wee Kenny's head with two quick hits. Wee Kenny howled. Tears nipped his eyes. But he did not retaliate. That would make it worse. He had fucked up.

Another punch caught him on the ear.

'Sorry, big man. Sorry. It'll no happen again.'

'You're fucking right it'll no happen again.'

Wee Kenny tucked his head down, took the next punch on the back of his head.

'You stupid wee fucker. That could have been us back there. Done and fucking dusted. D'you understand?'

Wee Kenny made the mistake of looking up and took a punch to the mouth that cracked his lips and cut short any thoughts he had of trying to explain what had happened.

But he was lucky to have found a garage open at that time in the morning. He should have filled the car up with enough petrol for the return journey, then they would not have had to stop on the way back and waste time, and would not have been stuck in that roadblock.

'And how often have I told you to get the boot painted?'

'A lot of times, big man.'

'That's right. A fucking lot of times.' Jimmy leaned across and punched Wee Kenny again, saw he had drawn blood at long last, then pushed himself back into his seat and gripped the steering wheel. The first thing he would do when he got back to Glasgow was organise a re-spray. Maybe change the colour. But he liked silver. The paint might look a bit dull. But it gave the Jaguar some class. Except that dent on the boot still needed doing.

And after the re-spray he would take care of Kenny.

The wee man was becoming a liability. Thicker than two short planks, so he was. He would talk to his brother, convince him Kenny was no longer fit for the job. Bill would understand, then give him the thumbs-up.

Or was it the thumbs-down?

He would slit the wee man's throat. Now, that would be a good way to do it. That's what he would do. Ear to fucking ear. He bet the wee man would bleed like a pig. Squeal like one, too. He smiled at that thought and reached over to Wee Kenny's shoulder.

'You all right, wee man?'

'I'm fine, Jimmy. I'm fine.'

'Sit up, then. I'm not going to hit you.'

'You sure?'

'Anyone can make a mistake.' Jimmy smiled. 'Don't worry about a thing, wee man. I'm going to look after you.'

CHAPTER TWELVE

GILCHRIST RETURNED TO THE SCENE of the crime. Yellow tape stretched the width of Golf Place, and a set of traffic cones arranged in a curve diverted beach-bound traffic onto The Scores. The SOCO tent was erected, the van parked in the centre of the road, doors open. The wind had died, and dawn was peeling back a cloudless sky, as if the early morning storm had been only a dream.

He parked his Mercedes next to Mackie's Volvo estate. He walked towards the tent where Jeff Bowers was talking to Lambert. He saw no sign of Watt. He caught up with Nance scribbling in her notebook.

'Have you seen Watt?' he asked her.

'Been and gone.'

'Did he say where?'

'Not to me.'

Gilchrist tightened his lips. Watt should not have left the crime scene without first checking with Gilchrist. It all added up to insubordination. Watt knew the rules, but chose to ignore them. All it did was stiffen Gilchrist's resolve to have it out with Greaves. But he needed to get moving with his investigation.

He nodded to the row of hotels and guest houses that ran along The Scores. 'Before anyone has a chance to check out,' he said to Nance, 'I want you and Lambert to go to every door along The Scores. Find out which guests occupy the seafront rooms and talk to them. Maybe somebody saw something.' He glanced at his watch.

'You don't have much time, so split up. You start with the Scores Hotel. Have Lambert take the one next to it. Then alternate after that. Get back to me by mid-morning.'

Nance stepped away as Mackie emerged from the SOCO tent peeling his coveralls from his head.

Gilchrist caught up with him by the uplifted boot of his Volvo. 'Initial thoughts, Bert?'

Mackie shook his head. 'I'm getting too old for this.' He unzipped his coveralls, stepped out of them, ran a liver-spotted hand over a balding pate. '*Bludgeon?*' He eyed Gilchrist, his sandy coloured eyes creasing against a brightening sky. 'Any idea what it means?'

Yes, Gilchrist wanted to say. *And it frightens me to death.* But he shook his head. 'Not yet.'

'Murder massacre bludgeon?' Mackie scratched his head. 'What's this sick bastard trying to tell us? Tell you?' His gaze fixed on Gilchrist with a directness that could unsettle judge-hardened prosecutors, and for one moment, Gilchrist felt certain old Mackie could see through his lie.

'The leg's a mess,' Mackie continued. 'The branding's uneven, probably as a result of the metal rod or whatever not being kept consistently hot or applied with even pressure. You know what I'm saying?'

'A DIY job?'

Mackie almost smiled, a quick tug of the lips, as if the effort of showing pleasure was too much to endure. 'The word starts off with the letters being over-branded,' he went on. 'Too deep. Too long. Running into each other. By the end, it seems as if he has it about right.'

'Practice makes perfect?'

'That's one way of looking at it.'

'And another way?'

'Anger.'

Gilchrist waited for Mackie to continue. But the old man stared over his shoulder. Gilchrist had come to understand Mackie's periods of silence, when he gave the impression of being inattentive, but in reality was deep in thought, mulling the intricacies of some case.

'It's as if he was angry to start with,' Mackie went on. 'Then calmed down as he branded the letters into the flesh.'

'Worked his anger out?'

'Precisely.'

'A sadist?'

'Definitely.' Mackie raised an eyebrow. 'Among other things.'

'Such as?'

Mackie exhaled a long puff of air, and Gilchrist was almost wishing he had never asked the question. 'I'm not a psychologist, of course. It's just a feeling. Nothing more.' Mackie's jowls jiggled as he shook his head. He stared off to the distance again, his eyes tired all of a sudden. 'It takes a certain kind of mental dysfunction to cope with cutting up a human body,' he said. 'And an even greater insanity to brand words onto it. I would say whoever did this had to be more than cruel. He had to be devoid of feeling. No sense of compassion, no sense of ethics, moral or otherwise, an abject failure to appreciate the difference between right and wrong.'

'Psychopath?' Gilchrist tried.

Mackie nodded. 'At a minimum.'

Jesus. Gilchrist took a deep breath. He had dealt with a number of psychopaths in his day, had seen enough MRI scans on the brains of an assortment of criminals to know that the neural activity in the pre-frontal lobe, that part of the brain that controlled impulsiveness, was lower in the brains of psychopaths than in normal humans. And without that ability to stop and think, to give consideration to the consequence of their actions, some psychopaths turned to murder. Although most of them could appear to lead the lives of normal citizens, behind that seemingly innocent façade lurked a manipulative and vindictive mind, a human animal with no conscience, remorse or compassion.

Mackie cleared his throat. 'This someone needs to be in control,' he said. 'The notes to you. The delay in the leg turning up. He's keeping you guessing, letting you know he's in control, or put another way, that you're *not* in control. And if I had to guess, I would say he's sexually deviant.'

'Why do you say that?'

Mackie shrugged. 'Another feeling.'

'Keep going.'

Mackie frowned, and Gilchrist thought he detected a hint of regret at his comment. 'This case is personal to you,' Mackie said.

'Let's have it, Bert.'

Mackie breathed out a defeated gush. 'Whoever's doing this gains little or no pleasure from normal sexual activity. At a guess I'd say he's into necrophilia.'

Necrophilia? Gilchrist felt his lips tighten. For God's sake. What the hell could he say to Jack? He closed his eyes and in his mind's eye saw Chloe naked, her eyes staring blind-sighted to the ceiling, her small breasts shuddering from rhythmic thudding...

Dear Jesus. He opened his eyes, gulped some air.

'Live bodies. Dead bodies.' Mackie's jowls shivered. 'I don't think it matters which to this demented creep.'

Gilchrist stared off to some point in the horizon. The sun was shooting pink streaks across the sky. How could the beauty of nature be spoiled by the rotten-to-the-core virus that was the creature known as *homo sapiens?* Because that's what man was, was he not? A creature. Nothing more than a living entity whose evolution had developed ahead of all other living entities and taken over, even killing its own species for... for...

For what..?

Pleasure? Sexual satisfaction? Dead or otherwise?

Gilchrist knew of no other species that killed for sexual pleasure. But maybe they were out there, hidden deep in some untouched tropical forest. Or at the microscopic level, where the struggle of life and death took on a different meaning. Maybe other creatures—

'I'm sorry, Andy. I shouldn't have...'

Gilchrist shook his head. 'I need to know your thoughts on this, Bert. No matter what.'

Mackie gave his words some consideration, then reached out for Gilchrist's shoulder. He squeezed. 'How's Jack?'

Gilchrist thought back to last night, at Jack's show of bravado, at the face that creased when he told a joke or held out his whisky for a drunken salutation, at eyes that lay dead behind the forced smile. 'He's having a tough time.'

'And you?' Mackie asked. 'You look as though you've been out on the binge.'

Gilchrist felt he could use a pint right there and then, but was not sure he could keep it down. 'I'm tired,' he said.

Mackie raised an eyebrow in disbelief.

'Get back to me with your report, Bert.'

Mackie gave Gilchrist one of his direct stares. 'Any suspects?' he asked. 'Any ideas?'

Gilchrist shrugged. 'Working on it.'

'The answer is in your past, Andy. That's where I would start. Someone you put away, someone vindictive enough to get even with you. Maybe someone recently released from prison.'

Gilchrist's own thoughts had already paralleled Mackie's. Whoever was doing this wanted to get even for some reason. And that reason was more than likely because Gilchrist's investigation had put him behind bars. He already knew that.

He had just not wanted to believe it.

'And cut back on the booze,' said Mackie.

Gilchrist walked towards the seafront, the breeze cold and refreshing on his face. He inhaled, tried to clear his thoughts, chase his fears away. *Cut back on the booze*. What was the point of that? So he could be stone-cold sober when he witnessed the sickest depravities of mankind?

He reached the seafront. Despite the road to the beach being cut off, several joggers were already on the West Sands. A pair of golden labradors loped and sniffed the sands while their owner walked the water's edge. A woman slipped onto the beach from the dunes and stepped across the sands with arm-swinging strides. He followed her progress, felt his mind pull him back to the cryptic notes, tried to fight against it, but failed.

Murder. Massacre. Bludgeon.

He saw a sequence. But it was too vague. Another note might confirm it for him. Or maybe not. He could be wrong.

Dear God. Tell me I'm wrong.

He closed his eyes, inhaled the sea breeze, found himself forcing his mind back to when Gail was still with him. Six years was a long time. Sometimes it seemed as if she had only just left.

Jack and Maureen, too.

He reached for his phone. He was wrong. He had to be.

He needed to hear her voice, needed to know she was all right. He dialled her number and eyed the black silhouette of a ship sliding over the horizon.

'Hello?'

Maureen's voice sounded tired and heavy, and he called up an image of her as a sleepy-headed toddler. He used to waken her with, *Wakey wakey let's get shaky*, and bounce her bed with a roughness that always pulled a smile to her face. Then she would reach up to him with tired little arms, and he would lift her from bed and carry her downstairs, the smell of sleep in her hair like her personal morning fragrance.

'Wakey wakey let's get shaky,' he whispered.

'Dad?'

'The one and only.'

A heavy sigh, then a rustling of covers, followed by a tired chuckle. 'It's been years since I've heard that.'

'I love you, Mo.'

A pause, then, 'Where are you?'

'Looking out over the West Sands. It's going to be a beautiful day. Cold. But beautiful. A lovely day for a walk along the beach. Care to join me?'

Another chuckle. 'Mum never said you were a romantic.'

Something turned over in his stomach at that comment. He used to send flowers to Gail, leave silly little love notes on her bedside table or pinned to the fridge when he was out on a case. And it struck him then that he could not remember when he had stopped doing that. Had he stopped because their relationship had run its course? Had he known something was wrong but made no effort to find out what? And Gail, too. When had she changed? When was the exact moment she stopped loving him? And why did he still struggle with her not being in his life? Was it because she had taken Jack and Maureen with her? Or was jealousy still smothering his emotions? And as a dark shadow worked its way through his mind he wondered how much longer Gail had to live.

'How's Mum?' he asked.

'I saw her last night.'

Gilchrist stared off across the water of the Eden Estuary, not trusting his voice.

'She's not well,' Maureen said. 'I mean, she's, she's desperately ill...'

'She's not in any...'

'She's on a morphine drip, Dad. It's only a matter of time.'

Only a matter of time. Jesus. When he and Gail married he would never have predicted this was how it would end. He had imagined they would grow old together, walk the beach with their grandchildren together. Not like this. Bitter and apart.

'Is there anything, I mean, can I do anything...'

'I don't think so, Dad. I'm sorry.'

He felt his head nod.

'Have you heard from Jack?' Maureen asked.

'He's up here at the moment. Staying at my cottage.'

A pause, then, 'Is it true about Chloe?'

'It's looking that way, Mo.'

'Oh, God,' she whispered. 'That's awful.'

It's worse than awful, he almost said. *Necrophilia?* Surely Mackie was wrong. 'Did you know Chloe?' he asked.

'I'd met her a few times.'

He thought he detected a shiver of regret at having raised the subject. 'Recently?' he tried.

'A few months back.'

'Before Christmas?'

'Yes.'

'At Jack's?'

'In town. How's Jack taking it?'

'You know Jack. Doesn't say much,' he said. 'Keeps it to

himself,' and felt a need to change the subject. 'Will you be seeing Mum again?'

'I see Mum every day now. But with the drugs and stuff she's mostly out of it.'

He hated asking, but the words were out before he could stop himself. 'Do you think she might, she might want to see me?'

'Oh, Dad.'

'Well then, if you can,' he whispered. 'If you get a chance, Mo, will you tell her I love her?' Maureen's silence only cut him deeper, made him feel the need to say more. 'Will you tell her I've always loved her?'

'Oh, Dad.'

The words were whispered, and in her whisper he heard the echo of his own pain. He watched the labradors splash into the sea and wondered why he had been so against buying a puppy for Jack. 'Listen, Mo,' he said, fighting to liven up. 'Why don't you come up to St Andrews this weekend? I could maybe wangle an early night, take you and what's his name—'

'Chris.'

'That's it. Take you and Chris out for an Indian—'

'I'd love to, Dad. But we've got stuff to do. You know. With Mum. And work and stuff.'

Her answer did not surprise him, but hearing her say it, say she had work to do, somehow settled his mind. 'Sure, Mo. Love you.'

'Love you, too, Dad.'

He did not know how to say it, but tried, 'Listen, Mo. Take care now.'

'Don't I always?'

He wanted to say more, wanted to tell her his fears. But how could he? 'Call me,' he said.

'Sure.'

'No. I mean it, Mo. Call me.'

'Dad?'

'More often. We should talk to each other more often.'

'Okay, Dad. But I've got to go. Love you,' and hung up before he could respond.

He felt that familiar need to fight off the dark feelings, heard his mind whisper, *Focus. Focus on work. It's how you've managed to cope over the years. Cut everything else out and focus. On work.* So he called Stan and asked him to track down anyone recently released from prison, and who had been put away by Gilchrist years ago. But only those who had killed before, on the theory that revenge by itself was not reason enough to kill for the first time.

Or was it?

Well, it was as good a place as any to start.

He walked from the seafront, back to DC Bowers. 'Who's checked in at the scene?' he asked.

Bowers nodded, opened his book. 'Right here.'

Gilchrist scanned the signatures. His own was not there because he had arrived before Bowers, although a note had been added by Lambert that DCI *Andy Gilchrist arrived at the scene at 5:27 and thereafter identified the body part as a left leg.* Gilchrist calculated that by the time he had donned his coveralls and carried out a preliminary inspection of the polythene package it had probably been close to 5:35, 5:40, when he left the scene. Nance's signature was first after Lambert's at 5:44, then Watt's at 5:48.

Gilchrist thanked Bowers and walked past the R&A Clubhouse.

He reached his Mercedes and punched in the number for the Office. 'When was DS Ronnie Watt informed of the body part at the Golf Museum?' he asked.

'That would be, ah, here it is. 5:46, sir. You asked that we didn't inform him before 5:45.'

Not quite, Gilchrist wanted to say, but chose not to get into it. 'Was it you who made the call?'

'It was.'

'How did he respond?'

'He just said that he would be on his way, sir.'

Gilchrist snapped his phone shut.

Watt had arrived at the scene only two minutes after the Office called, which meant that he must have been on his way when they rang. Why would he be out and about at that time in the morning?

He had guessed the correct body part. Did that mean he had known when it was coming? Had someone called him about it?

Gilchrist let that thought filter through his mind, work something out, come up with possibilities. But he seemed to generate more questions than answers. It seemed that Watt knew more about the body parts than he was letting on. Why? Who had called Watt before the Office had? And why was Greaves hell-bent on having Watt on Gilchrist's team when he knew about their past?

Too many questions. Too few answers.

Gilchrist promised himself he would change that.

CHAPTER THIRTEEN

'MARTIN. ANDY HERE. Any luck?'

'It's just come in. Like me to post it to you?'

Gilchrist accelerated out of Golf Place. 'Can I pick it up?'

'When?'

'Now.'

Martin Coyle laughed. 'You're still as pushy, Andy,' he said. 'But I won't be heading out for another hour or two. Why don't you swing by?'

Gilchrist confirmed Coyle's home address and assigned the directions to memory.

Twenty-five minutes later, after taking a wrong turn, he drove up to Coyle's home, a detached stone mansion that sat high on the outskirts of Cupar with a distant view of the sea. Coyle met him at the front door, wearing a short white dressing-gown that looked as if it should be binned. White legs as bare as sticks dangled to a pair of scuffed slippers. He smiled at Gilchrist. 'Stop in for a cuppa?'

Gilchrist found it impossible to resist Coyle's gormless charm. 'Why not?'

Inside, Coyle led him along a hallway with high-gloss doors that seemed out of character with the stone structure, and into a kitchen with grimy linoleum tiles centred by a beaten pine table. The sink stood heaped with a clutter of dishes. The room was redolent of coffee and toast, the cooked air tainted by a musty fragrance that seemed to come at him from the side.

He turned. Two ageing dogs, a clot-haired collie and a matted wire-haired terrier, looked up at him with hound-dog eyes, then rose from their battered wicker baskets and kowtowed towards him, their tails brushing the tiles. He leaned down, dug in his fingers behind the collie's ears, and said, 'Names?'

'Jack and Jill,' Coyle replied.

'Which is which?'

'*Basket.*'

Both dogs skulked to their baskets, leaving Gilchrist to wipe his fingers on his trousers. As they stepped up and over the wicker edges, he could not help but notice how both of them were hung.

He raised an eyebrow at Coyle. 'Jill?'

'It's only a name,' he said. 'They can't speak English.' He shrugged and chuckled. 'Linda's idea. Don't ask.' Then he reached for a large white envelope on the shelf by his head and held it out to Gilchrist. 'This is what you're after.'

Gilchrist thanked him and was about to open the envelope when the kitchen door swung open and Linda walked in wearing a threadbare bathrobe and sporting a thatch of witch-grey hair that looked as if it had not seen a brush for a month. She rushed over and put her arms around him. 'Andy, love. How nice to see you again.'

She felt soft and fat and smelled of bedclothes and dogs. The rounded shoulders of her robe were knitted with dog-hair. He responded with, 'Nice to see you, too,' and was squeezed with a big-breasted bear-hug.

'We're so sorry to hear about Gail,' Linda said, relaxing her grip. 'Aren't we, Martin?'

Coyle smiled and nodded.

'How are you coping, love?'

Gilchrist felt his face flush. 'Fine,' he said.

'And the kids? Jack and Maureen, isn't it?'

'They're fine, too.'

'Poor souls. I always think it's those that have to live on that suffer the most.' She placed her lips to his cheek and kissed him. 'God bless you, love.' Then she stepped back. 'Have you eaten?'

Gilchrist patted his stomach, 'Had something earlier,' he lied. 'Thank you.'

Linda scowled at the wicker baskets. 'Who's a pair of lovely wonders, then? Eh? Eh?'

Gilchrist smiled as both dogs' back-ends twitched with measured pleasure. Then he turned to Coyle and waved the envelope. 'If you don't mind, Martin, I'll skip the cuppa. I really should get going.'

Linda left Jack and Jill for a moment to kiss Gilchrist on the cheek again, then Coyle led him to the door.

They promised to keep in touch.

Gilchrist waited until he could no longer see the mansion in his rearview mirror before pulling off the road. He opened the envelope and removed fifteen pages of computer print-out that listed in columns, from left to right across the page, date, telephone number, time of call, duration, and cost.

He checked the last call.

To a mobile phone number he failed to recognise. Three days ago. At 22:54. Lasting two minutes. Which probably meant that the print-outs took him to midnight of that day, the day they found the hand in the Principal's Nose. He found the first call that day at 04:49, and felt his brow furrow.

One minute only.

Watt had said he had risen early. Why? To make a call? Who would he call at that time in the morning? And why only one minute? Gilchrist couldn't see it being a wake-up call to a friend. He eyed the number. It looked similar to the mobile phone number of the last call on the print-out, a two minute call. He double-checked and confirmed it was. So, the first and last calls of that day were both to the same mobile phone number. Which meant..?

Gilchrist flipped through the rest of the pages, checked the earliest dates, confirmed Coyle had acquired almost seven weeks' worth of records. He checked the first call.

Same mobile phone number. 07:51. Three minutes long.

And the last call that day.

Same mobile phone number. 23:03. Two minutes.

Gilchrist turned back to the most recent page, searched the lists for the same number, and found it. Three more calls to that mobile phone number had been made three days ago. He removed a pencil from the door pocket and circled each of the numbers. He ended up with five circles three days ago. And five again, the day before. He worked his way back.

Sometimes Watt's records had no less than a dozen calls on any given day, but always a minimum of three to that same mobile phone number, and almost always the first and last calls of the day. And the earliest of the morning calls was seven days ago, at 04:07.

Gilchrist opened his mobile phone and punched in one-four-one, which prevented the recipient from tracing the number of the incoming call, then the number. He pressed the phone to his ear, not wanting to miss the slightest sound.

Fifteen rings later, he hung up.

Had he dialled the wrong number?

He checked the number on Coyle's sheets and tried again, taking care to enter it correctly. He got through, counted twenty rings that time, then hung up, and stared off across the rolling hills at a herd of cows as small and brown as Jerseys.

Why was the call not answered? Maybe a sequence had to be followed before the person answered. Maybe he had to let it ring an agreed number of times, then hang up and try again. If that was the case, then he would have only one chance to try it without letting the person he was calling know someone was onto him. Which meant he had already blown it, and maybe Watt was being warned off at that moment.

Gilchrist thought for a moment then dialled the Office.

'Put me through to Dick,' he ordered.

Several seconds later, an upbeat voice chirped, 'Yep.'

'Andy Gilchrist here.'

'How's it going? Long time, long time.'

'Can you do a reverse number check for me?'

'Looking for a name and address?'

'Yes.'

'Need bank account details, driver's licence?'

'Give me what you can.'

'Residential or business?'

'It's a mobile phone number. So I'd guess it's personal, not business.'

Dick tutted. 'Could be a problem. Depends on which company. Some of these phone companies spring up out of nowhere, do the biz, then evaporate. Pow. Just like that. Sometimes you can't get a damn thing. But I'll give it a go. Shoot.'

Gilchrist recited the number, and said, 'As soon as.'

'You got it.'

Working back from the most recent date, Gilchrist fingered the columns, searching for numbers he recognised. On the third page, which listed Watt's outgoing calls the day before he returned to Fife Constabulary, Gilchrist came across a number that reverberated in the depths of his memory banks. He stared at it. He had seen it before, but could not recall whose number it was. He checked the memorised numbers on his own mobile phone.

Fifteen seconds later he had a name.

His lips moved in silence as he read the full telephone number, one digit after another, making sure he had it right, then failing to understand how it could be on Watt's records in the first place. He checked other pages, flipped the records over and over then back to the beginning to make sure the number on Watt's record, the number that should not be there, was the number he was reading.

But he was not mistaken. The number was right.

Starting with 0141, the code for Glasgow.

He ran through every page but found it recorded only once. As if that would lessen the burgeoning anger that swelled in his throat and stifled his breath. The call, the one call, the only call to that number he could find, had lasted all of sixteen minutes.

Which could mean only one thing.

She had answered. And Watt had spoken to her.

For sixteen minutes, a full sixteen minutes, DS Ronnie Watt had spoken to Maureen Gillian Gilchrist.

Sixteen minutes.

As if they had a mind of their own, his fingers curled like talons and mangled the pages into a crumpled ball. 'You bastard,' he hissed, and closed his eyes and prayed he would do nothing violent when he next saw Watt.

But he could never be sure.

That night came back at him, swirling dark as the blackest smog, settling and clearing until he saw her face, her eyes, the shock still there, still unmistakable and clear, as if the vile event had not happened eight years ago, but only yesterday. He tried to shift her image, but it impinged on his mind like the thickest of syrups that clung to his thoughts and slowed the action of his memory until it seemed he was watching the scene one frame at a time.

She was sitting upright, her back to him, and turned as he reached out to her, her face pale and blank with the rigidity of shock. Then she lifted herself up, her underage buttocks flexing with teenage ease. And he tried to keep from looking at her private parts as she slipped off her partner.

Hey, Andy. What's up?

He remembered looking at Watt's face, puzzling over it for a confusing moment, as if he was looking at someone he had met a long time ago, but could not place when or where.

Then the frames sped up.

Get out.

Dad.

Get out of my house.

Dad.

He turned to Maureen then, turned to confront his fifteen-year-old daughter, her back pressed to the wall as if she had no place to run. One hand covered her pubis, the other her half-developed breasts. Her cheeks glistened with tears. Then as if by *legerdemain*, her clothes were in his hand.

He threw them at her. *Get dressed.*

She caught them, pulled them to her.

He turned on Watt who smiled at him, mouth chewing, arms

folded behind his head, his unprotected erection flat to his belly, still veined and full and glistening with the spoils of his conquest for all to see.

That was the moment Gilchrist snapped.

He remembered stepping forward. He remembered that. He could still see it. And looking down at Watt's smiling face. He remembered that, too. But the next memory he had was of standing upright, chest heaving, lungs burning, wondering why there was so much blood, and why Watt had not tried to fight back.

And here was Watt again. Calling Gilchrist's daughter and talking to her. Talking to her and chatting to her. Chatting to her for sixteen minutes.

Sixteen minutes.

Gilchrist threw the crumpled report onto the passenger seat and thudded into gear. The Merc's tyres cut into the asphalt with a tight squeal. Only once before had his control failed him. And that was against Watt. He had almost lost his job over that incident. But back then, he'd had two children and a wife to consider. None of that mattered any more.

He had heard criminals say they would *swing for the bastard*. Now he knew how they felt.

CHAPTER FOURTEEN

BY THE TIME ST ANDREWS' skyline came into view, Gilchrist had calmed down. Perhaps *calmed down* was not the correct expression. He was thinking more clearly.

The drive through the country roads, overtaking cars and lorries as if he had a will to die, had taken his mind off his vengeful purpose and enabled him to rationalise his thoughts.

What exactly had Watt done?

He had phoned Maureen. That was all. A mature twenty-three-year old, a woman of astute intelligence, feisty, too, if he was honest about it. She was nobody's mug, and never would be. Certainly not with the likes of Watt. Gilchrist knew there came a time in every father's life when he had to let go and trust his children, trust that he had done the best for them, and that they would mature into responsible adults.

And that was what he had to do. Trust Maureen.

But it was almost too much for him.

He dialled her home number. He counted fifteen rings before hanging up and trying again. This time he counted twenty, all the while his mind firing with questions that needed answers. He pulled his Merc off the road and hung up.

Maybe he was jumping to the wrong conclusion.

He had checked Watt's records for Maureen's home number only, not her mobile phone number. He searched his phone's memorised numbers until he found what he was looking for, then retrieved

Coyle's crumpled sheets from the passenger well and flattened them against his thighs.

But his conclusion was not wrong. He found her mobile number on five separate dates and circled them with a pen. The lengths of the calls ranged from twenty-six minutes, to the shortest at two minutes, three weeks ago. Since that call, Watt had not called Maureen on her mobile again.

What did that mean? That Maureen and Watt had an affair that ended? That she wanted nothing more to do with the man? Or was it worse than that? Did it mean that she was calling Watt?

He tried her number once more, but after ten rings slammed the Merc into gear and headed towards St Andrews determined to have it out with Watt. As he neared the Old Course Hotel, all thoughts of choking the truth from Watt were put on hold. Two socos were erecting an Incitent on the other side of the stone wall that bounded the hotel grounds.

Had they found another body part? But no one had called him. As he reached for his mobile phone it rang. He expected it to be the Office, but it was Mackie.

'They said they couldn't reach you.'

Gilchrist depressed the accelerator. Up ahead, the Incitent shivered in the sea breeze, looking out of place, as if it had been blown there from the beach. 'I'm almost with you, Bert. What've you got?'

'The other leg.'

'And a note?'

'Cut into the flesh. Gouged out more like.'

Gilchrist slowed down. He wondered if this note would confirm his theory, or throw doubt on it. If the order was wrong, the cryptic message might not make sense.

'What's the word this time?'

'*Matricide.*'

Gilchrist took a few seconds to go through the letters, then felt something heavy slap over in his gut. *Murder. Massacre. Bludgeon.* And now *Matricide.*

Dear God. He had his message.

'Any idea what it means?' asked Mackie.

'Maybe,' Gilchrist lied, and hung up.

He stared off to the horizon, pressed his mobile phone against his lips. He had known. He had known as soon as he had the third word. And he had failed to act.

Two hands. Two legs. Four body parts. Four notes.

And he saw how the order could not be mistaken.

Left hand, right hand. Left leg, right leg.

The killer was making sure the notes were delivered in a specific order so the message was clear, and using the simplest of codes so that Gilchrist could not fail to work it out. He now knew they would find three more body parts, all the killer would need to send his entire message. But it was worse than that. Much worse. He reasoned that if the killer intended for Gilchrist to solve the puzzle, then by the time Gilchrist did he would be too late to do anything about it.

He turned onto the expanse of grass that separated the Old Course Hotel from the main road. Parked, he tried Maureen again, cursing when it rang out. He tried her mobile phone, but again could not get through. Christ, it was happening. It was really happening.

He punched in the number for Strathclyde Police Headquarters and asked for Dainty.

'DCI Small speaking.' The voice sounded thin, just like the man.

'Pete, it's Andy Gilchrist. I need your help.'

'If I can, Andy.'

'It's Maureen.' He tried to sound calm, but could not control the tiniest of quivers that seemed to catch the back of his throat. 'Can you have someone bring her in?'

A moment's pause, then, 'Care to explain?'

Gilchrist did, and Dainty reassured him that Maureen must be all right, or he would have already heard from PC Russell. But when he hung up, Gilchrist could not rid himself of the gut-sinking feeling that he was too late. It was the answering machine being switched off that worried him. Whenever Maureen was out, her answering machine was always on. It seemed to be how they communicated.

But now it was switched off.

He had failed to go with his instincts, failed to listen to his sixth sense.

And now he was too late. And seventy miles too far north.

But Dainty was a good detective, and a good man, and Gilchrist took comfort from the thought that Dainty would do his best, treat Gilchrist's request as if Maureen were his own daughter. And maybe, just maybe, Gilchrist could do something at this end.

Mackie greeted him with a hardened face and a spare set of coveralls and rubber gloves. Gilchrist pulled them on and entered the SOCO tent.

A faint yellow light spread over the scene, making the leg look as if it was made of plastic. Gilchrist kneeled. *MATRICIDE* was cut along the length of the inner thigh and calf. Although the curves of the letters *R, C* and *D* looked irregular, he thought the word had been formed with some care.

He turned his attention to the leg itself. Amputated at the top of the thigh, again at an angle, again with a clean cut. But this time the cut had been made too high, and a thin strip of pubic hair trimmed the edge like the beginnings of a weak moustache. Gilchrist felt his throat constrict. This was the leg of a striking young woman, someone he had spoken to, laughed with, had a drink with, someone who shared a life with his son with all the youthful aspirations of the future.

What on earth could he tell Jack?

'Same method of amputation,' Mackie mumbled. 'Some sort of saw. See here?' He pointed at the cut through the bone. 'You can see the curved marks on the femur. See? And where it cuts into the skin. Here.' He ran a pointed finger along the edge. 'Not as fine as a cut by a knife.'

Gilchrist nodded.

'I would say a circular saw. We may be looking for a workshop of sorts.'

'Like a home workshop?'

'Could be.'

Gilchrist frowned. He was looking at too wide a target. Anyone could install a workshop in their attic, or garden shed, or God only knew where. He needed to refine it. 'How about the saw marks?' he said. 'Can we tell the size of the blade from the curve?'

'Might do,' said Mackie. 'But I wouldn't want to bank on a high level of accuracy.'

'You might be able to define some diametrical limits.'

'Possible.'

Gilchrist eyed the leg, resisted touching the skin. 'Why the different techniques?' he asked. 'The first two notes were printed. The next two by mutilation.'

'To make us think there's worse to come?' Mackie tried.

Gilchrist grimaced. Mackie had a point. If each body part was presented with a hand-printed note, where were the scare tactics? The purpose was to frighten Gilchrist by letting him solve the cryptic clues so he would know how revenge was being sought. He swallowed the lump in his throat, dabbed at the cold damp sweat on his brow. The killer's tactics were working. Gilchrist knew what the killer had planned, and now he needed a break in his investigation before, before...

Jesus. It didn't bear thinking about.

Think. Damn it. Think.

But his mind seemed to refuse to work.

'This guy's one sick bastard,' he said, and pushed past Mackie, out into the open.

He freed his hair from the coveralls and peeled off the gloves. The air felt cold, carried the tangy taste of kelp. He breathed it in, almost revelled in the light-headedness of the moment. He unzipped the coveralls, removed his phone to try Maureen again, and was about to punch in the number when Mackie said, 'What's wrong, Andy?'

Gilchrist snapped his phone shut and faced Mackie. Deep intelligence hewn from a lifetime of pathology shifted like a shadow behind the old man's eyes.

'You know,' Mackie said to him. 'You know what the killer is saying. Don't you?'

Gilchrist felt his lips tighten. *Did* he know? Did he *really* know? He could be wrong. He hoped to God he *was* wrong. But every nerve in his body told him he was not. He shook his head. 'I'm not sure, Bert,' he said. 'It's just a thought.'

'Share it with me.'

Gilchrist stared off past the hotel, across the fairways to the grass-covered mounds of the dunes where they had sat on the windswept sands drinking ice-cold champagne.

First Chloe. And now...

He faced Mackie. 'I think Maureen's next.'

Mackie returned his stare.

'I think that's what the notes are trying to tell me.'

'Why do you think that?' Mackie's voice resonated deep and calm.

'I could be wrong.'

'I'm listening.' Mackie placed his hand on Gilchrist's shoulder, and squeezed. 'Run it past me.'

'First note, MURDER. First letter, *M*.

'Second note, MASSACRE. Second letter, *A*.

'Third note, BLUDGEON. Third letter, *U*.

'Fourth note, MATRICIDE. Fourth letter, *R*.'

Gilchrist watched the meaning of his words work through the old man's mind.

'M A U R,' Mackie said.

'E E N,' added Gilchrist. 'Three more body parts.' He watched Mackie's head turn to the side and his eyes stare at the tent, as if trying to imagine how he would feel if that leg belonged to his own daughter.

'I don't want anyone to know, Bert.'

Mackie turned back to him. His eyes creased against the sunlight. 'Can I ask why?'

'I want whoever's doing this to think we don't know what's going on.'

'Playing for time?'

Playing for time. What a way to put it. It sounded like a game. But it was no game. And Gilchrist saw then how he had run out of time. But maybe he had it wrong. Maybe he should have had a couple of minders watch her round the clock earlier. He stepped away from Mackie and opened his mobile phone. But he could still not get through.

He tried his cottage.

Three rings and he was there. He could not mention the latest leg to Jack. 'I need to get hold of Maureen,' he said, and tried to sound calm. 'Do you know where she is?'

'Probably with Christopher.'

Gilchrist's hopes soared. 'You have a number for him?'

'Sorry.'

'Home number?'

'No.'

'Address?'

'Never met the guy.'

'You wouldn't happen to know his surname, would you?'

'Sorry.'

'Thanks, Jack. You're a great help.'

'Why don't you try Mo on her mobile?'

'Why didn't I think of that?' he said, and hung up.

He stared at his phone. When he had been Jack's age, had he been as disinterested in family? He saw, as if for the first time, how like Gail Jack was. And Maureen, too. Had he contributed nothing to the gene banks of his children?

He struggled to refocus.

Despite the obvious, he tried Maureen's mobile phone again, once, twice, then her home, counting twenty-two rings before hanging up. What was wrong with her answering machine? Could she have it switched off? And if so, why? Was it broken? What would that mean?

He glanced at his watch. Even if he jumped in his Merc right now, it would take him the best part of an hour and a half to drive to Maureen's. But what would that achieve? And that thought made him realise that he had to place his trust in Dainty. Dainty would call as soon as he found Maureen. In the meantime, Gilchrist would do what he could to move his investigation forward, and pray that he had it all wrong.

'Dear God,' he whispered.

But if his worst fears were realised, even God could not help him.

CHAPTER FIFTEEN

HE CORNERED NANCE at Golf Place.

'Find anything?' he asked.

She opened her notebook to a tabbed page. 'A Mr Fraser Crowley, staying at the Glen Eden Guest House, saw a car race out of Golf Place at around four o'clock this morning.'

'Race out?' he queried.

'Speeding.'

'Details?'

'Not a lot, I'm afraid.'

'Make? Model? Colour? Registration number? What?'

'Hold your horses. The elderly Mr Crowley—'

'*Elderly?*' Gilchrist groaned.

'Fraser is sixty-seven with a mind as sharp as a tack.'

'On first name terms, are we?'

Nance gave a smile. 'He's quite the lad.'

Gilchrist could not drag up a smile. Deep down he was disappointed. The elderly often proved unreliable witnesses and could break down in court under relentless cross-examination. Just how sharp was a tack at sixty-seven? And what did *quite the lad* mean?

'He thought the car was being driven erratically,' Nance continued. 'Then before passing the R&A clubhouse it swerved across the road then sped uphill.'

Gilchrist eyed the lone stone building and tried to visualise the scene. Crowley's account made sense. The car could have crossed the road to permit the driver to throw the package beyond the footpath. Had Crowley witnessed the leg being dumped?

'A Jaguar,' Nance pronounced. 'XJ-12 with silver paintwork.'

Gilchrist faced her. He blinked once. Twice. He had seen a Jaguar, a silver Jaguar. He had seen one just like that. It took him several seconds to remember where. Then he had it. The road-block in Cupar. He had walked past it, paid no attention to its occupants, been more focused on the Vauxhall Astra. Damn. Was it an XJ-12? Was it *the* XJ-12? Was there any visual difference between the body of an XJ-12 and a XJ-6? If so, could the elderly Mr Crowley have noticed it at that time in the morning? And from a hotel room window?

'Where was Crowley when he saw the car?' he asked.

'Martyrs' Monument.'

'At four in the morning?'

'He said he had an upset stomach and couldn't sleep. He was taking a breath of fresh air.'

Martyrs' Monument stood on the hill at the crest of The Scores. Which meant the old man would have been looking down onto Golf Place and seen the XJ-12. But from fifty or sixty yards?

'Where is this Crowley?' Gilchrist asked.

* * *

It took them two hours to find Fraser Crowley down by the rocks that fronted The Scores, kneeling by one of the sea pools, nothing more than puddles of seawater trapped by the receding tide.

The old man looked up as they approached, then stood with barely a grimace. 'Ah,' he said with a grin. 'The lovely Detective Constable Wilson.' He came towards them, stepping over black rocks with the sure-footed agility of a man half his age. Sunlight sparkled in eyes as blue as bleached denim. His teeth were gap-spaced, long and white. 'We meet again,' he said.

'This is DCI Gilchrist,' Nance said. 'My boss.'

Crowley nodded, as if he was a competitor about to post a challenge for Nance's hand. 'A pleasure,' he said.

'You don't wear glasses,' Gilchrist said.

'I'm a retired pilot. My eyesight has always been excellent.'

'The Jaguar,' Gilchrist went on. 'Why did you think it was an XJ-12?'

'From the front grille.'

'Expert on cars, are you?'

'Cars no, Jaguars yes.'

'Own one, do you?'

'I own several. The pride of my fleet is a '73 convertible E-type V12. Rarely drive the thing, of course.'

'Of course.' Gilchrist felt a smile tug at his lips. Crowley looked like one of those individuals with a panache for life, who earned big money, drank fine wine, made love to beautiful women. And drove fast cars. 'It was silver,' he said to Crowley. 'What else can you tell me about it?'

''1988-ish, I'd say. Run down. Not well looked after. Original paint job. Could do with a re-spray.'

'And all this at four o'clock in the morning?'

'Not at all.'

Gilchrist frowned. 'I don't follow.'

'I'd seen it before.'

Nance pressed forward. 'You didn't tell me that.'

'You never asked, dear Nancy.'

'You knew this was a murder investigation.'

'You mentioned nothing of that until you were leaving.'

'Why didn't you say *then*?'

'Then I would have had no reason to come and see your lovely eyes again.'

Nance glanced at Gilchrist. He took over. 'Where exactly had you seen this Jaguar before?'

'Market Street. By the fountain.'

'When?'

'Last Tuesday.'

'You're clear on that?'

'I visit the bank every Tuesday. I saw the Jaguar then.'

'What time was this?'

'Around two o'clock in the afternoon.'

'Did you see the driver?'

'No.'

''88-ish?'

Crowley's eyes creased, and Gilchrist caught an image of the younger man as a dashing pilot. 'About that, I would say.'

'Why would you say that?'

'Because I know Jaguars.'

'Did you see the registration number?'

'I'm hopeless now with numbers,' Crowley said. 'Memory's not as good as it used to be.'

'But you might have seen the number and associated that with a year of registration, then forgotten the number?'

Crowley shook his head.

'We'll run a search on PNC,' Gilchrist said to Nance. 'Every silver Jaguar XJ-12 from '86 through '90.'

Nance scribbled it down.

'Would you recognise it again?' Gilchrist asked.

'Absolutely.'

'When you saw it at that bank, how close were you?'

'Close enough to see the tax disc had expired.'

'Did you note the month?'

'Now you're asking.'

'See anything on any of the seats?'

Crowley shook his head.

'Papers? Documents? Umbrellas? Jackets?'

'Anything?' Nance chipped in.

'I wasn't looking,' Crowley said.

'Spotless, was it?' Gilchrist tried.

'I wouldn't say that.'

'What would you say?'

'Once I realised it was run down, I didn't give it too much

attention. That's a big no-no for a Jaguar enthusiast.' Crowley grimaced. 'Tyres were worn. Blisters of rust on the wheel arches. The whole thing needed a good wash, wax and polish. Inside *and* out. It's a disgrace that a car so majestic could be treated with such disdain.'

'Any stickers? Aerials? That sort of thing?'

'The boot lid had been patch-painted.'

Gilchrist stiffened. 'How could you tell?'

'It was painted with red lead. Poorly, I might add.'

Red lead. An undercoat used as rust prohibitor on metal. Gilchrist remembered the Jaguar in the roadblock, its boot as dark as spilled blood. 'How would a damaged boot be repaired?'

'If it was my own, I'd take the boot lid off. But I tend to go over the top. I'd buff it back to sound metal then repair the damage, fill in the scratches, knock out the dents, that sort of thing. Then I'd buff some more, fill some, buff, fill, buff, fill, on and on. Properly done it's a job of love. Then eight or nine coats of paint, each sanded with wet-and-dry before the next application. That way you bring out the richness and the depth.'

'And you would use red lead?'

'Not necessarily. There are other proprietary materials on the market that are every bit as good.'

'How long do you intend to stay in St Andrews?'

'Until the end of the month.'

'Then?'

'Spend spring in upstate New York with my brother.'

'No Mrs Crowley?'

'She passed away six years ago.'

'I'm sorry,' Gilchrist said, regretting having raised the subject of wives. Time to leave. 'Give your home address and full contact information to DS Wilson,' he added. 'And don't leave town without first letting us know.'

'Is that necessary?'

But Gilchrist had turned away and was walking up the path towards Martyrs' Monument. Crowley's sighting of the Jaguar last Tuesday troubled him. If it was the same Jaguar used to dump the leg, why had it been in town then? On the other hand, why would it not? The killer could have driven up from Glasgow for a number of reasons. And Gilchrist felt something jar at that thought.

The killer knew Gilchrist. Had he driven up to St Andrews to spy on him, gloat over his imminent revenge, maybe even have a pint in the same pub? And another thought hit his mind with a force strong enough to make him catch his breath.

Did the killer also know Watt?

When he thought about it, it seemed odd that on the day Watt returned to St Andrews the hand was discovered. And Watt was one of the first at the scene. Why? First day on the job, first on the scene? Was that coincidence? But Gilchrist did not believe in coincidence. Things happened, but when they happened together they were connected. Believe that simple fact and everything else fell into place.

He now saw the flaw in his earlier rationale and cursed himself for not taking action sooner. The killer had known Gilchrist would solve the cryptic message. It then followed that he would take Maureen before the last body part turned up. Leaving it any later would risk Gilchrist securing her safety. Maureen lived in Glasgow. And the Jaguar would be registered in Glasgow. On that he would bet his life. So why had he taken no action? And how could he have been so stupid? He looked down at the black rocks, at Nance still in conversation with Crowley. He shouted, pointed to Golf Place, then ran.

He ran in that long-legged stride of his that had served him well on cross-country runs at school, and in later years through days of personal training. His gangly build would never permit him to be any kind of sprinter, but he could jog at a steady pace for hours.

He had the Merc's engine started and the gear lever slotted before he closed the door. He floored the pedal, reversed into Golf Place, and skidded to a halt. Nance grabbed the passenger door handle and jumped in. Then he was accelerating up the hill, Nance pulling the door to her, hands searching for the seatbelt.

'Forgot a clean pair of underpants?' she quipped.

Gilchrist turned right, raced across oncoming traffic. Tyres squealed. Horns blared. Two pedestrians stepped back as if the road surface had burned the soles of their feet.

Nance pressed both hands against the dashboard as Gilchrist screeched through the roundabout at Pilmour Links and City Road. 'What's got you so pumped up?' she asked.

'Call the Office and have someone stay with Jack. Check with Beth, too.' Gail was safe, of that he was sure. At home with not long to live, where was the terror in killing her now? Besides, the cryptic clues pointed to only one person. 'Then get hold of Watt. Ask him where the hell he is.'

But Nance could not locate him, and five minutes later she left instructions with the Office to have him call DCI Gilchrist the instant they contacted him.

She shut her mobile phone. 'What now?'

'Start praying.'

'For good brakes?'

Gilchrist grimaced as he overtook three cars. 'That we're not too late.'

CHAPTER SIXTEEN

ON THE OTHER SIDE of Cupar, Dainty called Gilchrist.

'Maureen's slipped us.'

'What about your man—'

'That's another bloody matter,' Dainty growled.

'What happened?'

'Said he followed her from her flat. On her way to work, he assumed. And he lost her. In downtown Glasgow? It beggars fucking belief.'

Gilchrist gritted his teeth. All his senses were screaming at him. *Too damn late. And stupid. So fucking stupid.*

'Do you know where she works?' Dainty asked.

'Let me get back to you,' said Gilchrist, then hung up.

He twisted his hands on the wheel. The problem with Maureen's job was that he did not know where she worked. He'd never had a reason to call her at work, called her only at home or on her mobile phone. Which screamed questions at him.

Why did he not know where she worked? Or what she did for a living?

Wouldn't any normal father know the answer to that simple question? His daughter living away from home was no excuse. Had he failed his family so completely that Maureen could not discuss her life with him? How had his relationship with his children sunk so low? And it struck him then that Jack might know.

He caught him on his mobile phone.

'Hey, Andy. How's it going?'

Jack's upbeat tone surprised Gilchrist, until he caught the hubbub in the background and realised he had to be sitting in a pub.
'Which pub?' he asked.

'You need to quit playing Sherlock Holmes, Andy,' Jack said. 'But
if you must know, it's the Whey Pat.'

The Whey Pat Tavern. The pub in which he and Gail first met.
He had not set foot in that pub since Gail left, as if to do so was a
violation of his memories of her, of his family, of how it used to be
when they were in love, before his career and her infidelity destroyed
what they had.

'Listen, Jack,' he said, 'you don't know where Maureen works,
do you?'

'She changed jobs about six months back. Working in some big-
shot agency in the city centre. Don't ask me where. Got the job
through her latest boyfriend.'

'Chris?'

'That's the one.'

'And you've never met him?' he tried.

'Mo introduced Chloe and me to some punter by the name of
Chris,' he said, and Gilchrist felt surprise at the ease with which
Jack was able to mention Chloe's name until he realised from the
slur in his voice that he had downed a few. 'If he's the boyfriend,
he's an utter plonker. One of those big shots. Wads of cash. Buys
every round. You know the kind. I hated him the instant I set eyes
on his alligator-skin wallet.'

Gilchrist felt himself deflate. Jack knew as little about
Maureen's personal life as Gilchrist did, which only served to com-
pound his feelings of failure. When he had stumbled across Gail's
affair with Harry, all he wanted to do as a father was to convince
Gail to stay with him. *Stay together for the sake of the children.* Is
that not what parents did? But not Gail. At the first moment of
confrontation, she rushed off to Glasgow with Harry and the kids
faster than a skelped cat.

'Mum wouldn't know where Mo works, would she?' Gilchrist asked.

'Not a chance, Andy. Sorry.'

Well, that was that. He closed his phone.

'Problems?' Nance asked.

'No one knows where Maureen is.'

'Maybe she's out shopping, Andy. You know, that thing women like to do.'

Gilchrist tried a smile. But what was the point of faking despair? He should have acted sooner, instead of waiting for the next body part to turn up.

Murder. Massacre.

Even with those two words, he had seen something. He had worked out the two letters, *M* and *A*, and he had known. He had known then. But two letters were not enough of a progression to solve a cryptic clue. And that was his mistake.

He had known, God damn it. He had known.

But had failed to act.

And now he was acting, he was terrified he was too late.

On the unlikely off-chance that Maureen had phoned the Office, he called for his messages. None. Not from Maureen, not from Watt, not from anyone else. He asked for Greaves, but was told he was unavailable. Jesus, he felt as if he was becoming obsolete. He drove on in silence, deep in the pit of his misery.

Maureen lived in a modernised apartment building in Glasgow's Merchant City. Once derelict and soot-covered, the brick and sandstone tenements had been refurbished and converted into low-tech office space and luxury residential apartments.

Gilchrist parked his Roadster on a double yellow line.

He confirmed Maureen's address from his mobile phone, checked the street signs, then dialled both her numbers once more for good luck.

No answer.

He stepped into a grey Glasgow drizzle, upped his collar to ward off the cold. What was it about this place that it always seemed to be raining? He walked towards Maureen's flat, Nance by his side, noting the sand-blasted brick, the pedestrianised streets, the painted bollards.

As if in parallel with his own thoughts, Nance said, 'You never told me your daughter was a high earner.'

'I never knew.' He eyed the fenced trees, the metal gratings, the shining pub sign at the end of the street, all painted, all new. Even the cobbled walkway seemed to glisten in the rain.

'What does she do for a living?'

'Last I heard she was studying to be a physiotherapist,' he said, and puzzled once again over his failure to follow her career. At the entrance door he wondered if he had the wrong address. But the numbers matched. He was about to push it open when he noticed it lay ajar. Just a touch. 'Not as up-market as we thought,' he said, then felt a cold rush as he realised the lock was damaged, the wood splintered where it had been jimmied off.

His peripheral view sensed something to the side, and he turned, caught the jerking movement of a red Mini Cooper pull up at the far end of the street. Something about the driver's look, a furtive glance his way, told Gilchrist he was watching out for someone.

And waiting?

Gilchrist walked towards the car. From that angle he could not read the number plate. He stepped onto the road, and halfway across, the Cooper's engine burst into life with a throaty growl.

'*Nance.*' He started running. 'The number plate.'

Nance surprised him by sprinting ahead.

The Cooper took off, front wheels spinning, and bullied its way down Candleriggs towards Argyle Street. Gilchrist caught up with Nance in time to see the Mini's disappearing tail-end as it zipped from sight. Nance had her mobile phone in her hand.

'Got it.' She poked at the pad of her phone.

'Come on,' said Gilchrist, and jogged towards Maureen's flat. 'I don't like this.' Nance jogged alongside him, and he was surprised by how fit she seemed, how fluid her movement was.

'Run a check on PNC for me,' she ordered into her mobile. 'One of the new Minis.'

'It looked like a Cooper,' he said.

'Mini Cooper,' she repeated. 'Red with a white roof,' and recited the registration number.

Through the entrance door the clamour of running feet echoed off the walls. Maureen's flat was on the top floor, and Gilchrist took the stairs three at a time, Nance so close behind him that he swore he felt the heat of her breath on his neck.

They reached the landing together.

Gilchrist gasped for breath, tried to still the awful pounding in his chest. He thought he kept himself fit, but Nance was barely breathing.

'Is this it?' she asked.

He could only nod.

She gripped the handle. 'Locked.'

For a fleeting moment he thought he had screwed up, that the driver of the Mini was nothing to do with Maureen's flat, that his accomplice or whoever he'd been waiting for was somewhere else on innocent business, that he had it all wrong. Then an image of Maureen as a child crying flashed into his mind, and he remembered promising to do whatever it took to protect her.

He thudded his shoulder to the door.

Solid.

He tried again. It barely budged.

He stood back, lifted his foot, and heeled it hard against the lock.

The door rattled, maybe moved. But not much.

And again.

'Almost there,' Nance said, and kicked at the door in time with Gilchrist.

The lock burst open.

Nance beat him inside.

'Police,' she shouted, and raced down the short hallway.

Gilchrist followed, opened a door on the left. Bedroom. No curtains. No furniture.

Ahead, Nance crashed through the door at the end of the hallway.

'*Police.*'

Gilchrist watched her fall off to her right, then leap backward in a move that seemed to defy the laws of physics. Glass smashed. He rushed to her aid, exploded into the room, and charged at the shape as a foot lifted and caught him a fraction too high to threaten his manhood.

He grunted from the blow, pulled his handcuffs out, whipped them like a chain at a gloved fist that caught him on the chin and snapped his head back. He stumbled, hit the hard edge of the door as his knees cracked the floor. He snatched at the departing figure. His fingers touched fabric, caught it, gripped tight. A black leather boot came at him and buried its toe into his shoulder. It swung again, connected with his chin.

He felt his teeth crack and his grip slip free, and he grunted in despair as long legs strode off and slipped through the door. He pulled himself to his feet, flapped a hand at the wall, missed it, and stumbled across the room. By the time he reached the window and fumbled with the blinds, the figure, a tall man dressed all in black, was running across the cobbled street, phone hard to his ear. At the corner, he waved an outstretched arm as the Mini Cooper pulled level. He opened the door and jumped in as the Cooper sped away.

Gilchrist retreated from the window, relieved to feel his teeth intact. A quick search through the small flat confirmed that Maureen was not at home. He returned to Nance.

She stood with her hand to her stomach. 'Caught me where it would hurt if I was a man,' she grimaced. 'I wasn't expecting it.' She stretched over her shoulder. 'My back hurts.'

'Let me look.'

She surprised him by turning and lifting her blouse. Her skin looked white, her waist slim, her physique more athletic than he imagined. 'See anything?'

He took hold of her blouse and eased it up her back to reveal a black sports bra.

She twisted an arm behind her and tapped with her finger. 'Just about there.'

He eyed an angry welt at the base of her shoulder blade, already darkening to a bruise. 'The skin's not broken,' he said, 'but it looks like it could hurt for a while.' He thumbed the bruise, felt her body jerk. 'Sorry,' he said, and prodded some more.

'Remind me never to come back to your surgery.'

'Nothing's broken,' he said, and noticed a short-legged coffee table twisted askew on the rug, the remains of a glass tumbler in the corner near the stereo set. 'I'd say you hit the corner of the table.' He let her blouse drop, and she surprised him once more by unzipping and tucking it in, giving him a glimpse of black thong underwear.

Then she lifted her hand to his temple. 'You're bleeding.'

He almost pulled away.

'Stop being a baby,' she said.

'Will I live?'

'Regrettably.' Then she stepped back. 'It's just a graze.' She looked around the tidy room and grimaced. 'I'd say we got here before he had time to steal anything.'

'Who said anything about stealing?'

'What do you think he was doing? Choosing furniture?'

'Looking for something.'

Nance raised an eyebrow. 'Looking for something?'

Gilchrist moved through the room, fingered a pile of CDs that lay scattered on a shelf, an eclectic mix of old and new that included Marti Pellow, Elton John, Sade, Nelly Furtado, Lionel Ritchie, Craig David. And he saw in Maureen's collection the wants and longings of a young woman searching for love. He turned away.

'Notice anything?' he asked Nance.

'Like what.'

'The walls.' He looked around the room. 'And the shelves.'

'I'm not sure I'd choose the colour scheme.'

'No photographs,' Gilchrist said.

'Is that odd?'

'Yes,' he said. 'Maureen was a keen photographer. I bought her a camera for her thirteenth birthday. Back then she was going to be a photojournalist.'

'What happened?'

'She met men.'

'Figures.'

It struck Gilchrist then that he had never been invited to Maureen's flat, or introduced to any of her friends. He would meet her in Glasgow on the odd occasion, take her out for a drink and a meal, but she would never invite him back to her home. *You wouldn't want to see it. It's too messy. Getting decorated.* So he never pushed.

Other than an archway into a modern kitchen-dining room, only one other door opened off the living room. It led to the hall-way. The flat was small, probably too small to share, and some-where in the back of his mind he recalled Maureen saying that one day she would have a place of her own, no one to pick up her dirty knickers, tell her what to do, how to run her life. He wondered if this was it.

'It's not too messy,' Nance said.

Gilchrist was not sure if she meant Maureen kept her place tidy, or the intruder had not done much damage. He chose the latter. 'We caught him in the act,' he said. 'But what's odd about the break-in? What do you see?'

'I don't get it.'

He let his silence do the asking.

'This place isn't exactly crawling with people,' she tried. 'Did you notice anybody checking out what all the commotion was? We weren't exactly quiet breaking in here.'

Gilchrist nodded. The apartments were probably owned by young professionals with careers and money, who worked long and hard and socialised harder still. No time for kids. During the day the building would be deserted. But something else did not fit.

'The outside door was jimmied,' he said. 'But the door to Maureen's flat wasn't.'

'So he let himself in?'

'Maybe.'

'With a key?'

'Maybe.'

Nance eyed him. 'Maybe he was an expert lock-picker?'

'So why jimmy the outside door?'

'It takes time to pick a lock. He couldn't risk being seen fiddling with it.'

'So he jimmied it instead?' Gilchrist shook his head. 'I think not.' He scanned the room once more, eyed the CDs, the shelves. Why no photographs? What was he missing?

Nance's mobile rang. She listened to the call, then said, 'The Mini belongs to a Tony Brenton. Lives with his mother in Edinburgh.'

'Right,' said Gilchrist. 'Let's pay him a visit.'

'Won't help,' she replied. 'Yesterday morning he reported it stolen.'

As Gilchrist's mind worked through the rationale, he struggled to keep his emotions in check. The stakes had just been raised. If he had any doubts about the danger Maureen was in, they were dispelled at that moment. The fact that someone would steal a car in Edinburgh to break into a flat in Glasgow put the crime in a different league. He was no longer dealing with local thieves, but with someone much higher up the food chain, someone with money, someone with contacts and power and crews who worked the streets. Someone with the criminal wherewithal to lead Gilchrist by the nose and make sure he would never find his daughter.

Even though this was Maureen's flat, and he was standing on her rug, looking at her sofa and chairs and tables and shelves and CDs, personal effects she had chosen for herself, touched and listened to and sat upon, he did not feel close to her. At that moment he felt farther from her than at any time in his life. He thought he caught a glimpse of what life would be like without Maureen in it.

And it felt lonely and cold and dark.

CHAPTER SEVENTEEN

GILCHRIST CALLED IN FOR a Lookout Request for the Mini Cooper. It was stolen, almost certain to be abandoned, but you could never tell. And he elected not to report the break-in to Dainty, deciding instead to do some investigation of his own first. This was his daughter's home, after all.

The flat had two bedrooms; one unfurnished that smelled of fresh paint and plaster. Surprisingly, he thought, Maureen's room was clean, with the queen-sized bed made. He pulled back the duvet cover and confirmed only one side had been slept in, and felt a surge of guilt flush through him.

Sweaters, jeans, shirts and socks lay folded on open Formica shelves that took up most of one wall. In a fitted cupboard, he found a selection of silk blouses, mostly white, and expensive-looking jackets hanging on wooden coat-hangers. A dozen pairs of shoes sat in formation on the floor. Again, expensive-looking.

One thing continued to trouble him. He knew Maureen had a computer. But other than a double telephone plug in a socket close to the bed, the flat seemed devoid of all things digital. Nance suggested Maureen had a laptop and had it with her, but he thought it odd that they found nothing computer-like; no disks, no software, no electrical leads.

He checked under the bed again, and discovered a couple of deep fitted-drawers either side, which he had mistaken for part of the bed-frame. With the fitted sheets and valance on, the drawers were hidden.

Nance was almost right. Maureen did have a laptop, but not with her. He found it in the fitted drawer next to the headboard end, as well as a CD filing box that held a number of CDs. He removed one of them and read Maureen's scribbled label.

Short Stories

And another one.

Mystery Novels 1 & 2

Gilchrist shook his head, stunned that Maureen would try to write not just one novel, but two, and dismayed by the fact that he knew nothing about her efforts. He flipped through the other CDs and found she had written six mystery novels. Was she published? Was that how she could afford this flat?

Again, the feeling that Maureen was so far removed from his life rushed through him in a warm flush. But this time he saw it was not so much Maureen being out of *his* life, but that *he* was not in *hers*. She wanted little to do with her father. She was growing up, *had* grown up, and wanted to live a life free of parental ties.

He plugged in her laptop, feeling guilty that he was about to violate her privacy.

What right did he have to read her personal writings?

The hard-drive hummed alive. He stared at the screen. If the laptop was password-protected he would have to take it to the experts, the computer geeks who would then have open acess to Maureen's files. They could read her personal correspondence, see that she wrote books, maybe make a joke or two. But did any of that matter? Probably not. What did, was the time it would take to—

The screen flickered.

He held his breath.

The screen blanked, recovered, then settled at Maureen's desktop.

Well, he was in, which pleased and disappointed him. Maureen might be a mature young woman, wise to many things in life, but personal security was not one of them. He clicked on *start*, moved the cursor to—

'My Documents.'

Gilchrist almost jumped.

'That's a good one to try,' said Nance. 'Give it a click.'

Although Nance had no personal interest in Maureen's files, Gilchrist could not rid himself of the feeling of violating Maureen's privacy. He shut the laptop down, and closed the cover. 'I'll go through these later,' he said, and pulled himself to his feet.

'You want me to report the break-in?'

Gilchrist grimaced. Strictly speaking, Maureen's flat was a crime scene. And removing her laptop and CD files was a serious violation of scene of crime protocol. But what would Strathclyde Division find? The people behind the break-in were professionals. Of that, he had no doubt. And SOCOs scouring Maureen's flat from floor to ceiling would uncover nothing. Better that he explained it to Dainty directly, he thought.

'Let's get out of here first.'

But just in case he had it all wrong, he left a note for Maureen to call him on his mobile as soon as she returned.

They drove to Pitt Street, but Dainty was tied up in a major interrogation and could spare only a few minutes, time enough for Gilchrist to tell him about Maureen's flat and the Mini Cooper, but mentioning nothing about the laptop and CDs. Dainty ordered Gilchrist to write a full report, and assigned a scar-faced detective to the case, who introduced himself as Tony and insisted Gilchrist give him a blow by blow account. Once Tony was dealt with, Gilchrist asked for a desk and two phones. The remainder of the day was a mess of phone calls and paperwork.

The Mini Cooper was found abandoned in St Enoch's carpark, doors unlocked, keys in the ignition, and all surfaces wiped clean of fingerprints. And Stan confirmed that, surprisingly, only three criminals had been released within the last year, none of whom could be involved in Chloe's murder. One had died four months ago from a massive heart attack; one was in a hospice waiting to die; and the third was in Portugal lapping up the sun and the booze.

By 8:00 pm they were no farther forward.

'My stomach's rumbling,' said Nance. 'Fancy a bite?'

Gilchrist tried to remember when he had last eaten, and thought a pint and a bite might uplift his spirits and re-energise his sense of detection.

'We could go out for your favourite,' Nance pressed on.

'Which is?'

'A pint of real ale?'

'And a bridie, chips and beans. With HP Sauce?'

'I know just the place.'

* * *

The Horseshoe Bar in Drury Lane – a narrow alley running between West Nile and Renfield Streets – was one of Glasgow's more famous pubs. The bar itself, shaped more like a circle than a horseshoe, had once been recorded in the *Guinness World Records* as the longest bar in Great Britain at one hundred and four feet.

Gilchrist ordered two Eighty-Shilling that came still and creamy with a hint of spillage. He lifted his glass to Nance's, took that first mouthful, cold and smooth, and almost purred with pleasure.

The bar buzzed with the hubbub of a Glasgow evening. A powerful fragrance of second-hand smoke tainted with the faintest aroma of cooked meat filled the air. Gilchrist inhaled, found himself wishing he had never taken that bet. It had been fourteen years now, and was the best thing he'd ever done to maintain his health, other than his runs along the beach, which had become hit-or-miss since Gail left. He eyed the crowd. It felt good to be out, to let his mental powers recover, to force himself to relax if only for an hour or so.

'How did you know about this place?' he asked Nance.

'Spent two years at Strathclyde studying Biology.'

'I never knew that,' which had him thinking that he seemed not to know much about Maureen. Or even Gail. His thoughts darkened as his mind cast up his last image of his ex-wife, teary-eyed and pale, and bitter beyond reason.

'There's a lot you don't know about me,' she said.

Gilchrist was not sure how to take that remark. Nance had a reputation as a bit of a teaser, but had kept all relationships off her own doorstep, so to speak. But the beer was hitting the spot, so he said, 'Like what?'

'What would you like to know?'

'Why give up Biology and join the police?'

She almost sneered. 'Biology gave me up. I lost interest. Spent too much time in places like this. Met the wrong guy. Failed my exams. More or less in that order. Give or take the odd shag or three on the side.'

Gilchrist felt unsure of himself all of a sudden. Nance seemed different, as if being in a bar in Glasgow gave her thoughts of re-enacting her days as a student, guzzling beer and screwing men. She had developed a devil-may-care attitude in the space of one pint, and a hint of sexual mischief sparkled in her eyes. Or maybe the beer was affecting *his* attitude.

He tried to shift his thoughts and eyed the dark décor, the black and white framed pictures, the massive mirrors on the back wall. He read the motif on one of them, thought it looked like a horsewhip twisted into the shape of an s.

'You wouldn't happen to know what that letter s stands for?' he asked.

'I do,' she said. 'Scouller. The original owner. He owned the Horseshoe in the late 1800s. Also another couple of bars named after horsey stuff. The Snaffle Bit was one. And The Spur.'

Gilchrist tipped his beer towards her. 'I'm impressed.'

'Don't be. I have a good memory. That's all.'

He nodded to other initials. 'And JYW?'

'John Whyte, I think. He took over in the early 1900s.' She glanced at him, her pint poised at her lips. 'And no,' she said, 'I don't know what the Y stands for.'

Letters. Gilchrist sipped his pint, again troubled by his thoughts. Letters defied time. A century ago, two pub-owners, John Scouller and John Whyte, immortalised themselves in Glasgow's pub-lore by having their initials imprinted on bar memorabilia. Was that what would happen to Chloe's case? A hundred years from now, would someone browse through police records and come across the words *Murder, Massacre, Bludgeon, Matricide*, then the letters *M, A, U, R*, and ridicule the SIO for his inability to jump-start such an obvious case?

That thought brought with it the need to find out what was on Maureen's laptop. He downed his pint with a rush.

'Hold your horses, Andy,' she said, and had a £20 note in her hand as if from nowhere.

'I'm getting these,' he protested. 'This is my treat.'

'Your treat comes later,' she replied with a wink, and ordered two more pints of Eighty-Shilling.

Gilchrist knew it was a mistake not to leave then. But two pints later, with not too much to eat, they traipsed out into Drury Lane.

As they turned into West Nile Street Nance slipped her arm through his. Gilchrist let her, telling himself it would be rude to pull free. Besides, it was cold. He could feel her body shiver. Their breaths puffed in unison in the damp air. As they crossed St Vincent Street her thigh bumped against his, and he caught her fragrance as she swept her free hand through her hair. And all of a sudden it struck him that without discussing it she seemed to have decided they would spend the night together.

Not so fast, he thought.

He considered driving to St Andrews. But the earlier adrenaline rush from searching for Maureen, plus three pints in under two hours, had left him far from his brightest.

A night in Glasgow would have to do. Besides, he had Maureen's files to go through.

He clicked his remote. The Merc's lights blinked. Like the gentleman he knew he should be, he held the passenger door open as Nance slid inside. He was conscious of her eyes on him as he sat behind the wheel and slipped the key into the ignition.

As he eased into traffic, Nance said, 'Where are you taking me?'

'I'm not sure this is a good idea.'

'No one's forcing you to do what you don't want to.'

'I have a spare key for Jack's flat,' he said. 'It's a bit rough at the edges, but at least it's got two beds.'

'Good,' she said. 'Then that's it settled.'

* * *

Jimmy squeezed Wee Kenny's shoulder.

Wee Kenny looked at the hard hand only inches from his neck.

'You look worried, wee man.'

Wee Kenny shook his head. 'No me, Jimmy.'

'You done a good job there.'

Relief flooded through Wee Kenny in a rush so strong that for one crazy second he thought he was going to piss in his pants. He forced a laugh. 'I done my best, Jimmy. You know I done my best.' He tried to force another laugh, conscious of the fingers digging into his collarbone, but it fell flat.

'It's looking good.'

Wee Kenny eyed the Jaguar's boot lid. He had never spray-painted a car before, and paint rippled like orange peel in parts where he'd sprayed it too thick. But overall, he thought he done a good job.

'It'll be dry for the morra,' he said.

Jimmy took a deep draw of his cigarette. Thin cheeks pulled thinner, and eyes as dark as coal closed for a moment's pleasure. Smoke curled from nostrils thick with hair that leaked into his moustache. Long-nailed fingers picked a sliver of tobacco from thin lips, which he spat to the ground with the tiniest of flicks of his tongue. As he stared into the night, Wee Kenny thought Jimmy's mouth looked like one more scar on a face creased with scars.

Jimmy kept a week-old growth to hide his scars. Black stubble, a quarter of an inch long, hid the worst of them, a jagged welt that ran from the corner of his right lip to the lower jaw, the result of a broken bottle to his face. And Wee Kenny remembered what happened to big Archie Chalmers, the punter who done it to him.

It was years ago. Jimmy was fifteen. Not much more. Archie in his early twenties, a small-time thug making a name for himself as a hard man to be reckoned with. Even though Jimmy still has the stitches in his face, he and his big brother, Bully, goes to see Archie at his home on the fourteenth floor in Red Road. Jimmy stands out of sight while Bully knuckles the door. Archie's mother opens up. Bully smiles and asks for Archie. But when Archie turns up, Bully steps back, Jimmy steps in, open razors slashing up and down, left and right, like a drummer gone wild. The story goes that the slashing was so bad, even Bully almost threw up.

One slash cut Archie's left eyeball in half. Another almost had his nose off. Bully had to stick the head on Jimmy to stop him cutting Archie to death, and ended up with sixteen stitches himself from a cut that opened his palm.

But from that day on, no one messed with the Reid boys. If they did, they got what was coming to them. And then some. Bully and Jimmy lived their own street cred to the letter, a variation of *Don't get mad, get even.*

For Bully and Jimmy it was, *Get mad, then get even.*

But Bully was now in the Bar-L serving twenty years for manslaughter. The charges should have been murder, but even the Procurator Fiscal seemed too afraid to go for the maximum. Being in the Bar-L should have been enough to keep Bully out of the picture, but he was keeping himself busy behind bars, with Jimmy doing his legwork.

Rumour had it that something big was about to break. And Wee Kenny knew better than to ask Jimmy what it was. No way would he ask.

If he did, that would be the end of him.

CHAPTER EIGHTEEN

IT FELT STRANGE BEING in Jack's flat without Jack's presence, as if he was violating his son's personal space. Chloe's paintings hung on the walls, wild and tortured images that he still found troubling. And the flat was filled with other tell-tale signs of Chloe's life with Jack – opened drawers that spilled silk and cotton underwear; wardrobe shelves littered with discarded skirts, blouses, shoes; paperback books open and broken on the floor by a bedside table; the sweet tang of oil paints in the air, almost thick enough to taste. Gilchrist tidied up as best he could, making a mental note to have a word with Dainty about the carelessness of his forensic team, and all the while he worried that he had not heard from Maureen.

He stumbled across Jack's makeshift cocktail cabinet on the bottom shelf of the food cupboard; a Glenfiddich single malt that looked particularly tempting, but contained no more than an inch of whisky, or a ten-year-old Longrow, still in its burgundy gift box, which he remembered gifting to Jack on one of his infrequent visits. He opened the lid to confirm it was almost half-full. Perfect.

He picked up a thick-bottomed tumbler and the ten-year Longrow and stepped down the hall to Jack's bedroom. As he passed the bathroom he heard the rattle of glass and the sound of running water.

'Goodnight,' he called out.

Nance did not reply.

In Jack's bedroom, he poured himself a large one and powered up Maureen's laptop. He remembered Nance's advice and double-clicked *My Documents*. Another screen flashed up with a list of yellow *Folder* icons entitled, *Novels, Letters, Research, Databases,* and the last one, *Spreadsheets*. The toilet flushed, and the bathroom door opened and closed with a quiet double click. A shadow drifted by the gap at the bottom of the door like a spectral image, then vanished as the hall light was switched off. He clicked his bedside lamp off and took a sip of whisky, feeling its fiery warmth work through his system. The only light in the room came from the laptop's screen. He took another sip then clicked on *Letters*.

The screen flashed up a fresh page that contained a list of files with names such as *royalbank–12-01-03, dkerr–29-09-02, smckay –14-07-02*. He double-clicked one to confirm the simple filing system. *jstevens–11-02-03* was a letter to Joyce Stevens dated 11 February 2003. He searched for files containing the title *rwatt*, but found none. He rearranged the lists alphabetically and checked the R's for Ronnie, the W's for Watt, but again came up empty. It pleased him to think that Watt no longer featured in his daughter's life.

By letter, that is.

He tried rearranging the files by date.

The last letter Maureen had written was to the Royal Bank of Scotland in Bath Street, requesting an increase in overdraft facilities from four to eight thousand pounds.

Gilchrist frowned. He seldom borrowed, and at the age of twenty-three would never have dared borrow that much money. Eight thousand pounds? Was Maureen digging deeper into debt? Why would she need that amount of money? A trip to Spain? A down-payment on a car? A new wardrobe? He clicked his way out of the *Letters* folder and into *Novels* to reveal more *Folder* icons named by novel.

He clicked on *Novel 1* to find yet more folders and files that appeared to contain research notes, character traits, synopses, plot ideas, questions, and even one that listed book titles. He clicked on *Correspondence* and spent the following thirty minutes discovering that Maureen had written to over thirty literary agents in London and sent another twenty query letters to agents in the States.

Gilchrist felt as if Maureen was a stranger to him. How long had she wanted to be a novelist? Why had she never mentioned it? Was she published? How many books had she written? And what about her love of photography? Had she given that up?

Years ago he had bought her a second-hand Nikon F3 with an 85mm F1.4 lens, a professional lens for taking portraits, and a 70-135mm zoom. A smile tugged his lips as he recalled the cry of delight that had slipped from her throat in a high-pitched teenaged squeal. He also recalled Gail complaining about the needless waste of money, criticising his decision to buy such a complex camera. He now saw how his marriage had been on the downward spiral, and how he had ignored all the warning signs.

He took another sip of whisky and worked his way out of *Correspondence*, jerked his head to the side as the bedroom door clicked open.

Light from the front lounge cast a faint glow along the hallway, exposing Nance in the doorway. A blanket draped around her shoulders hung almost to the floor. Her feet and ankles were bare. 'I can't sleep,' she said.

'That makes two of us.'

She eased into the room. 'Do you mind?'

Gilchrist tilted his glass to her. 'Like a nip?'

'You rat,' she said. 'Where did that come from?'

He eyed her over a pair of imaginary spectacles, and said in a ridiculous German accent, 'I haf my sourses.'

Nance chuckled and flitted towards him like a shrouded ghost and sat on the edge of the bed. The laptop lay between them like some tech-age chastity belt. She eased the tumbler from his fingers and took a sip.

From the way her lips puckered, Gilchrist could tell she was not a whisky drinker.

'Like it?' he asked.

'The occasional sip.'

He finished the glass and poured another. Three pints and two large measures was not the recipe for feeling great in the morning, but sometimes stuff happened. Besides, alcohol helped his powers of deductive reasoning. Or so he told himself.

'Any luck?' she asked, nodding to the computer. In the faint light, her cheeks looked sunken, her chin square. Her eyes lay hidden in pools of shadow, as if shielding her thoughts from him.

'Most of it appears innocent,' he said. 'Daily correspondence. That sort of thing.'

'Know what you're looking for?'

'Some connection to Ronnie Watt for starters. But I haven't found it yet.'

'You hate him, don't you.'

'Hate's not strong enough.'

'Care to tell me why?'

'Not really.'

Nance reached for the glass again. Her fingers wrapped around his as they clutched the tumbler together. She leaned forward, took a sip, and the blanket fell away, just sufficient for the blue-white light of the computer screen to reveal the round swell of her right breast, the nipple hidden in shadow. 'That tasted better,' she said, and pulled the blanket back around her as if warding off a light chill.

Gilchrist felt something shift deep in his groin. Nance had removed her make-up. In the glow from the laptop her face looked pale and smooth, her eyes dark and large, as if the absence of all things unnatural allowed her own beauty to shine through. But the alcohol, the worry, and the long hours were finally taking their toll, and he felt a wave of sleep fold over him. Or maybe it was Nance prying into his hatred of Watt that had him wanting to end the day.

'I'm done in,' he said, and powered down the laptop.

'Me too.'

'I thought you couldn't sleep.'

The room fell into darkness. Light glowed from the open doorway.

Nance lowered the laptop to the floor, then stood, the blanket hugging her body. She removed the tumbler from his grip and laid it on the bedside table.

'I was enjoying that,' he said.

The blanket slipped to the floor.

Other than the briefest of panties, she stood naked, her body a grey silhouette against the soft light from the hall. Her pubic mound, hidden in shadow, lay level with his face and acted like a magnet to his eyes. He forced himself to look up, and in doing so, scanned the length of her.

Even in the dark, as naked as she was, he could see she was slim and fit. Her pinched waist made her hips look large, her thighs long and lean. She stared off to the side, and he caught a glint in her eyes that told him she was pleased to see her body excited him.

'I'm not sure this is a good idea,' he tried, but his heart wasn't in it.

She leaned down, pulled the cover from his light grip. Her breasts hung as firm as half-melons as she slid in beside him. 'You can tell me to leave anytime.'

Her feet felt as cold as ice against his legs. With a familiarity that surprised him, she turned on her side, threw a leg and an arm over his body, and snuggled in.

'You're all lovely and warm,' she said. She kissed his shoulder, buried her head into the crook of his neck. 'Do you mind if I go to sleep?' she whispered.

'You're quite the woman of contradictions.'

'Is that a yes or a no?'

For an instant, he was confused as to how to respond, then said, 'No. I don't mind if you sleep.'

'Good.' She pulled closer.

Gilchrist felt the lump of her pubis on his thigh, the swell of her breasts on his chest, the warmth of her breath on his neck. He lay still, staring blind-eyed at the ceiling, and wondered what Greaves would do to them if he ever got wind of this.

Within seconds, it seemed, sleep pulled Nance down. He felt her muscles twitch as she faded away. He turned his face to her and brushed his lips through hair as soft as merino. He felt his own fatigue overpower him and pull him down into the dark unconsciousness of troubled sleep.

Then he fell away.

Twisted images of amputated body parts swelled in his mind then manifested into the body of a female. She held her arms out to him. He recognised her, knew she was calling, reaching out to him for help. He tried to fight his way towards her, but failed, trapped by a dead weight that clung to his body as she pulled away from him.

Maureen, he tried to call. *Maureen*.

But she could not hear him.

* * *

Wee Kenny felt a shiver run the length of him.

When Jimmy gave you one of his looks it could turn your legs to jelly.

'What's up?' he asked Jimmy.

Another draw on a roll-your-own held between the tips of thumb and forefinger, eyes creasing from the heat, the dowt flicked away. Then that stare. Always that scary stare.

'Fancy a pint, wee man?'

Wee Kenny almost shook his head. He didn't want to upset Jimmy, but what could he do? 'I'm skint,' he confessed, and cringed as the hand slapped on his shoulder again.

'Consider it payment for painting the car, wee man.'

'You're gonnie buy the beer?'

'A couple of pints for the job you done.'

Wee Kenny smiled, but something was not right. In the four years he'd been Jimmy's gofer, never once had Jimmy bought him a pint. But maybe Jimmy was beginning to appreciate all he done for him.

'You drive, wee man.'

Wee Kenny slid behind the Jaguar's steering wheel. It felt odd sitting there. It had been a while. Even though the Jag was his, and he paid for the petrol, tax, insurance, repairs, and now the paint job to keep Jimmy happy, he had not been allowed to drive it since teaming up with Jimmy.

In the mirror, Wee Kenny watched Jimmy walk around to the passenger side. With a twist of the key the Jaguar started with a roar. He gripped the steering wheel, hands damp with sweat, and for one crazy moment thought of putting the foot down. Then what? Jimmy would come after him. No, he thought. He would do as he had always done. He would do as he was told. That's what gofers were for.

The door opened and Wee Kenny felt the big car lean to the side as Jimmy slipped in. He could feel the presence of the man, the heavy heat from his body. Jimmy wasn't well. Wee Kenny was sure of it. The big man looked rough as fuck some mornings. Wee Kenny winced as the door slammed shut.

'Where to, Jimmy?'

'Just drive.'

Wee Kenny dared a glance. 'Like, just anywhere?'

'Don't make me have to say it again.'

Wee Kenny eased the Jaguar from the derelict warehouse into the unlit streets of the abandoned business park. It was too soon to take the Jag out for a drive. His paint job was too fresh. No sooner had those thoughts crossed his mind when the skies opened, and Wee Kenny knew his paintwork was fucked. He would need to do it all over again.

But no when Jimmy was looking.

He gripped the steering wheel. 'It's pishing it down.'

'Drive, wee man. I'm thirsty.'

'Right, Jimmy. Where to?' He darted a glance. 'I didnae mean that, Jimmy. Slip of the tongue.'

'Just drive, wee man.'

So Wee Kenny drove. He had no idea where to, only that he had to keep going. He did not like the look of Jimmy, the way his eyes seemed to burn, warning him he was in one of his moods. Wee

Kenny had seen Jimmy in one of his moods before, and knew he could be a right cruel bastard.

'Get onto the M80, wee man.'

Wee Kenny did as he was told, pleased that at last Jimmy was giving him directions. That usually meant Jimmy had business to attend to. Not that he ever asked what kind of business, but he had heard about some stuff in the pub a few days earlier. Some punter with their head smashed in. Or their throat cut. Beads of perspiration gathered on Wee Kenny's lips, and he ran a hand behind his neck, surprised to find it damp.

Getting your throat cut must be a right sore way to go, he thought. But Jimmy's business was not deadly that night. He felt sure, because he had not seen Jimmy's weapon, a ten-inch butcher's knife honed to a sharpness finer than a razor.

Wee Kenny drove on in silence, and forty minutes later said, 'Is it much further, Jimmy? It's just that I need to fill it up.'

Jimmy twisted his head and looked out the back. 'No much further, wee man,' then ahead out the windscreen. 'Here it's now. Take this exit on the left.'

Kenny did as he was told. As he pulled up the off-ramp, Jimmy said, 'Right at the top.'

Kenny indicated right.

'Go on for about a mile and you'll come to a bridge. Cross it and take the next left.'

'Sure thing, big man.'

The road narrowed at the bridge, and Wee Kenny peered ahead.

The Jaguar's headlights pierced the night rain, and the skies let loose as he pulled left into a narrow lane that was little more than two wheel ruts overgrown with grass.

Fifty bumpy yards later, they arrived at a closed gate.

'What now, Jimmy?'

'Douse the lights and turn the engine off.'

Wee Kenny did as he was told.

'Give me a hand to open the gate, wee man.'

Wee Kenny stepped into the rain, stumbling through the uncut grass. As he fumbled about in the darkness, he wondered why Jimmy had asked him to switch off the headlights. It would be easier to open the gate if he left the lights on.

'Over here, wee man.'

Wee Kenny stumbled towards Jimmy's lean figure in the shadows.

'The key's down there.'

'What key?'

'The key for the padlock. For fuck sake, wee man, don't annoy me. It's down there. Under a stone. Get it.'

Wee Kenny wondered for a moment how Jimmy knew the key was under a stone, but he stepped past him and pushed his hands into the dripping bushes.

'Whereabouts, Jimmy? It's dark.'

'Here, wee man. Let me show you the way.'

As Wee Kenny stood, a couple of things struck him, one after the other. That it was more painful having your hair grabbed and your head twisted back than it was having your throat cut. And having your throat cut was not sore at all, more like not being able to catch your breath. It was the sound of blood spurting over the bushes that confused him.

'Down you go, wee man,' as a hard hand kept a grip of his hair, and lowered his head to the ground.

The grass felt cold and soaking wet. He tried to lift his hands to feel the slit in his throat, but he had lost all strength, just wanted to close his eyes, go to sleep. He heard the Jaguar's engine roar into life, and for a fleeting moment his world exploded with light. Then that, too, faded, until all that was left was darkness and the sound of rain.

And his own bubbling whimpers.

* * *

Gilchrist wakened with a start.

He lay still for several seconds, confused as to where he was and who he was with. They had turned from each other in their sleep, and he felt a shiver of surprise as his fingers found, then touched, bare skin.

Nance moaned, a soft sound that hinted of consent and compliance, and she turned, rolled her body into his. An arm slid over his chest, a leg over his thighs. He felt the press of her pubis and the heat of her breath as her lips worked up his neck like damp fingers, searching for him.

They found each other.

His body pulled towards her while his mind flew away, as if some sensual part of him had been released from his physical being and was floating, looking down at what was left of him. From somewhere deep in the logical part of his brain he heard a whisper call out to him, a sound that was almost indistinguishable from the rush of blood in his inner ear. Then the whisper took on urgency that ordered him to stop.

He came to with a jolt.

'Nance,' he said. 'I'm—'

'Sshh.' Her finger pressed against his lips. 'You don't have to say a thing.'

'I—'

'Not a thing.' She kissed him then, her lips swollen and soft, like flesh of the sweetest fruit peeling apart. Then she pulled back. 'Would you like me to stop?'

Gilchrist felt his heart bound in his chest like some caged animal. *Yes, I would like you to stop. But make love to me first. Please stop.*

'No,' he said.

'Are you all right?' she whispered.

'Yes.'

That was how he should have answered her first question. *Yes,* he should have said. *Yes, I would like you to stop.* But now it was too late. He felt as if some part of him that had lain dormant for too long had resurfaced in all its sensual libidinous glory. He felt, too, that he was breaking the rules. Not just constabulary rules, but his own unwritten code of ethics that had guided him since his affair with Alyson Baird several years ago. He had made a promise to himself to keep sexual relationships remote from the Office.

'Kiss me again,' she said.

Her lips tasted as moist as mango, and when he opened his mouth her tongue powered inside like some living thing driven to search out every sensual nerve of his being.

Her fingers slid down his chest. His breath caught.

Her hand found him, slid down the base of him, and cupped him in its warm grip. He heard someone groan then recognised his own voice and let himself freefall into the dream.

Was he dreaming?

She seemed to be all around him, in his mouth, against his chest, his thighs. Fingers of the lightest silk slid over him, down and under to hold him, rubbing, stretching, then up again, caressing the head of him. Then she shifted, pulled away from him.

He lay there, confused for a moment as to what he had done wrong, then felt his desire surge to a new high as he heard the soft rustle of her thong being slipped off.

When she returned to him, she slid a leg over his thigh, pulled herself up, and straddled him. Her fingers took hold of him, guided him, and he opened his mouth to afford her one last opportunity to stop.

We shouldn't, his mind whispered.

She set herself down on him and he slid into the depths of her. She eased herself up, as if riding the lazy waves of a Caribbean surf. With each slow mounting, she leaned farther forward, falling closer to him, until her arms reached around his neck and he took hold of her breasts.

Her wetness ran onto his aching sac and down and over the top of his thighs. He took control then, placed his hands on her buttocks, pulled her onto him, her rhythmic surfing more frantic with each rising thrust.

Still, his personal turmoil persisted.

Please stop, he wanted to say. *No, make love to me. Let me make love to you. No. You. Me. Please. No.*

Yes...

His breath caught in his throat, gave out tiny gasps that hardened as she impaled herself onto him again and again. The waves rose and fell, the seas roughened, the swell deepened, falling lower, rising higher, climbing, peaking, then crashing onto the warm shores of their drenched bodies to ebb and flow with a force that almost sucked the heart out of him.

She lay on top of him, her body writhing, squeezing every last ounce of pleasure from the moment. And Gilchrist wanted to thank her for what she had given him, but could not find the words. Instead, he drifted off and dreamed the dream of the dead.

CHAPTER NINETEEN

GILCHRIST THOUGHT HE DETECTED the whisper of rain on glass, but realised it was Nance having a shower. He raised the white-cotton Roman blinds to the pale grey of a Glasgow morning. He tried Maureen's mobile number and let it shunt him to her voice mail before hanging up, then called Dainty's office for an update, only to be told they had uncovered nothing overnight.

The hard unequivocal fact that his daughter was missing hit him like a blow to the gut. A cold sweat came over him, and he lifted his hand to his forehead, surprised to see his fingers tremble. He clenched his fists. He had never felt such helplessness, and he forced his mind to think over the facts, come up with something he was missing, some intangible clue that might lead him to her, or at least give him a start in the right direction.

But what? And how?

He retrieved the laptop from the floor and stirred with impatience as it went through its starting routine. He entered *My Documents* and tried the *Research* folder, then into more subfolders, working his way through one branch, then back out and down another until he came to a group of folders that stopped him. His eyes fixed on one of them.

Topley.

He stared at it. He had heard that name somewhere before. Topley. But where, he could not remember. He clicked it and opened a screen that contained three more folders.

Chris
Kevin
Links

He eyed *Chris*. Maureen's boyfriend?

He opened that folder to a list of Microsoft Word files entitled *chris* followed by the numeric date. He rearranged the icons and established that the last entry was in January, the first almost two years ago.

Two years? According to Jack, Chris was Maureen's latest boyfriend. Had they been dating for two years? Despite the distancing in their relationship, Gilchrist thought he knew Maureen well enough to know that two years was too long for her to keep any romance secret. Ergo, Chris could not be her latest boyfriend. Or could he?

He chose a file at random: *chris-22-11-02*.

The screen popped up with what looked like a Memo.

From: MG
To: CT
Date: 22–11–02
Re: Incoming
As requested, written confirmation has been sought for incoming order expected to arrive within the week.

How harmless was that? It was so harmless it sounded alarm bells.

MG was Maureen. CT was Chris Topley.

But what was the *incoming order*?

He clicked through several other files, but they offered him nothing more. Frustrated, he exited and eyed the *Kevin* folder.

Kevin?

The name niggled at him. He had come across it last year, on a visit to this same flat when he had asked Chloe why her paintings were so wild and tempestuous. She said she had painted that series to work through the sudden death of her friend, Kevin.

But Kevin who? Kevin Topley?

Gilchrist eyed the screen. The likelihood of Chloe's Kevin and Maureen's Kevin being the same person was almost laughable. But the name wouldn't leave him. He clicked the folder icon to another screen listing more folders numbered 1 to 5, and a list of files saved by date.

He tried folder 1.

When it pulled up, he felt his senses kick him alert.

Was this what he was looking for?

He stared at a list of files all entitled *Ronnie* followed by the numeric date. He arranged them by date and read the name of the most recent, less than four weeks ago.

He clicked it open to reveal a letter headed by Maureen's home address, to Ronald Watt at a P.O. box number in Glasgow.

> *Dear Ron,*
> *I'm sorry I haven't written since before Christmas, but I've been busy. Work is hectic. You know how it is. And Chris can be a real slave-master. But you know that, too. I've missed you, and I look forward to seeing you again at Glenorra, if only to say farewell. I'm sorry things haven't worked out between us the way you would have liked, but that's life. You have yours, and I have mine. Let's live and let live. And let bygones be bygones.*
> *Love.*

He was not sure if he was angered by Maureen's feelings for Watt, or embarrassed at reading her personal correspondence. However he felt, it was clear she had resurrected her relationship with Detective Sergeant Ronald Watt, transferred from Fife Constabulary's Crime Management Department to some outpost in the city of Glasgow all those years ago.

And now Watt was back in Fife, and Maureen was seeing him. Again.

Gilchrist seethed. This was betrayal at its worst. Maureen had lost her virginity one month after her fifteenth birthday, and had since renewed her affair with the culprit, a man ten years her senior. Now after eight years, after all that time, she had reneged on the promise she made to her father.

He eyed the letter.

I've missed you.

Missed you? Gilchrist squeezed the bridge of his nose. Jesus, Mo, what were you thinking? How could you have let the man back into your life? He grimaced at the screen.

I'm sorry things haven't worked out between us the way you would have liked.

He read that line again, then once more, and felt his heart grasp onto that slender slice of hope and cling to it. Watt wanted to keep the relationship alive. Not Maureen.

I'm sorry things haven't worked out between us...

...the way you would have liked.

He almost grinned. Maureen had told that bastard it was over.

...let bygones be bygones.

He clenched his jaw. Let bygones by bygones? How could she ever forgive the man, for Christ's sake? After what he had done? And in his mind's eye, Watt pulled himself from bed and staggered to the door, crumpled bed-sheets pressed to his bloodied face.

Gilchrist had moved towards Maureen then.

'*Stay away from me.*'

The words had been screamed. And even now, he flinched at the memory.

He remembered his breath rushing in and out in short hits, as if his body had forgotten how its lungs worked. He was fit, as fit as he'd ever been, but his burst of anger had carried him beyond some physical limit.

'You hit him.'

He stared at her.

'You *hit* him,' she repeated. 'You beat him up.'

'What did you expect?'

'Not that.'

'He deserved it.'

At fifteen, Maureen had the verbal alacrity to argue with her elders as if on an even footing. Rationale and logic were not necessary prerequisites of course, and even Gail had a tough time withstanding the occasional verbal lashing.

'Did he?' was all she said.

It seemed surreal to be talking to his naked daughter, her eyes defiant, her clothes clutched to her body.

'He raped you.'

'He didn't rape me.'

'That's not what it looked like to me.'

'Was I screaming for help?'

'That's not the point.'

'What is the point, then?'

'Having sex with a minor is against the law.'

'Not if I wanted to.'

Gilchrist felt a pain stab his chest. 'It doesn't matter if you wanted to or not. You're fifteen. It's against the law.'

'I don't care what the law—'

'You're *underage*.'

She turned her back to him then, bent down, took hold of her knickers, and he had to divert his gaze from the swell of her vulva. 'So?' she said, as she stepped into them, one leg, two legs, then up. And something about the way she did that reminded him of Gail all those years ago.

'You could be charged,' he tried.

'Charge me.'

Gilchrist remembered feeling stunned by that remark. It seemed such a challenging thing for his daughter to say, as if she was testing his familial loyalty. 'I don't think you understand what—'

'I understand perfectly well, Dad. You hit him. You hit a defenceless man who—'

'He was having sex with a minor for God's sake. That is rape. It is against the law. Can I make it any clearer than that?'

She slipped her bra over her tight bosom. 'Minor?'

'Yes. *Minor*. Now get dressed.' He had turned then, not knowing what to do, what to say. His knuckles were bloodied from battering Watt. The sound of water running in the kitchen had him fighting off the ridiculous urge to apologise to the man. But his dilemma was clear. Charge Watt with rape, and Watt would reciprocate by charging him with assault. And he saw that was why Watt had not fought back. He had been caught breaking the law, could lose his job in a heartbeat, and had egged Gilchrist on simply by smiling at him.

The door clicked.

Gilchrist exited the file.

Nance walked into the bedroom, her hair a glistening mass of blackened curls, a bath-towel around her body. She gave a white smile, and Gilchrist tried to reciprocate.

'What's got you upset?' she asked.

'Maureen's seeing Ronnie Watt.'

'Tell me you're joking.'

He eyed the screen, struck by the sudden thought that he might have jumped to the wrong conclusion. How many Ronnies were there in the world? Were the files nothing to do with Watt, but with some other Ronnie?

Nance slipped the bath-towel from her body and dried her hair as she walked towards him, firm breasts bouncing from the effort. Her pubic hair stood at the joint of her thighs, as trim and tidy as a black exclamation mark. 'What've you got?' she asked.

Gilchrist struggled to concentrate. 'Some correspondence,' he said.

'From Maureen?'

'Yes.'

'To Watt?'

Gilchrist bit his tongue. Even just the thought of Watt contacting his daughter riled him. He should have charged Watt for all he was worth, taken his chances with his own assault charges. Instead he had let Gail talk him out of it.

What would the gossip do, for goodness sake? She's only a child. And there's your career to think about. You might lose your pension. And what about the mortgage? Think about someone other than yourself for once in your life. Damn you to hell if you do this.

So he had not pressed charges, instead worked a deal with the powers that be to have Watt transferred out of St Andrews. Now eight years on, Watt had the audacity to be seeing Maureen behind his back. And was back in St Andrews. It did not bear thinking about—

Gilchrist's mobile rang. He turned from Nance's nudity.

It was Stan. 'Bad news, boss. We got an arm this morning.'

'Left arm?'

'Correct, boss.'

Gilchrist thought the left arm was significant, because whoever was feeding Chloe to him in pieces still needed to keep the sequence in order. Left right, left right. Like marching, he thought, then wondered if that was significant. Was the killer in the military? Was that part of the message?

'Any note?' he asked.

'Yes, boss. Felt-tip pen printed along its length.'

Thank God for small mercies.

'Dismember, boss.'

Dismember. The fifth note. He spelled it in his head to the fifth letter. *E*.

M A U R E. Christ, how clear could it be?

'Who found it?'

'John McAllister. One of the greenkeeping staff. You'll have seen him in the Dunvegan. Found it on Grannie Clark's Wynd on the eighteenth fairway, wrapped in plastic.'

'Close to the boundary fence?'

'About ten yards in.'

'Thrown there?'

'Bert thinks it was placed, boss.'

Gilchrist puzzled over the killer's fascination with the Old Course. But because it was expansive and open to the public it was almost impossible to monitor around the clock. At night, it would be the simplest thing to drop an amputated limb in the passing.

But surely someone somewhere must have seen something.

'Tell me we've got a witness, Stan.'

'Afraid not, boss.'

'Don't we have the place flooded with uniforms?'

'No one saw a thing.'

How the hell could someone drop an arm on a golf course in the middle of the night and not be seen? They were supposed to be patrolling the place, for God's sake.

'Where's Ronnie Watt?' he demanded.

'Haven't seen him yet.'

'When was the last time anyone saw him?' he asked.

'Yesterday morning, boss.'

Yesterday.

Gilchrist's mind crackled with possibilities. Maureen had been corresponding with Watt, ending their affair. Now Watt had gone missing the same day Gilchrist could no longer contact her. Watt displayed the mental characteristics of a psychopath, and was not a good loser. Maureen's letter four weeks ago would have given him time to set things in motion, if that had been his intention. First, Chloe, his son's girlfriend. Second, Maureen, his daughter. Revenge for Gilchrist kicking him out of St Andrews, and for Maureen dumping him? Was that possible? Had the man they chased from her flat been searching for her computer so he could delete any reference to *Ronnie*?

Gilchrist decided to take the beast by the balls. If he had acted on his hunch sooner, Maureen might be safe. Now he could no longer afford to wait. 'Stan,' he ordered. 'Get a warrant for Watt's arrest.'

A pause, then, 'On what charge, boss?'

'On suspicion of murder.'

'Are you sure, boss?'

No, he wanted to say. *No, I'm not sure. But I need to take action.* 'I have evidence that Maureen's been seeing Watt,' he said. 'Now she's missing and so is Watt. I don't believe in coincidences.'

Stan whistled. 'Greaves'll blow a fuse, boss.'

Gilchrist thought it an odd thing for Stan to say, and found himself wondering why Greaves would insist on Watt being on his team in the first place. 'If Greaves has a problem with that, Stan, he can talk to me.'

'Okay, boss.'

Gilchrist hung up.

'I suppose that makes a quickie out of the question.'

Gilchrist glanced at Nance. She had partially dressed and stood in thong knickers. Stubble speckled the tops of her thighs. Her breasts stood proud-nippled, and for one disorienting moment he was back in his bedroom facing a fifteen-year old Maureen.

'Get dressed,' he said, then tried to soften his tone. 'We've got work to do.'

But from the way Nance turned away, he knew he had not pulled it off.

CHAPTER TWENTY

BY MID AFTERNOON, Gilchrist established that Maureen was employed as a marketing representative with the Topley Agency, a company owned and run by Chris Topley, an ex-hard-man from the Gorbals who spent three years in Barlinnie for beating up his neighbour over a pint of beer. According to Dainty, the neighbour committed suicide the week before Topley was to be released. Rumour had it that if the man had not taken his own life, Topley had promised to take it for him.

The Topley Agency was housed on the fourth floor of a glass and steel building that fronted the River Clyde. The reception area was finished in glistening blacks and reds and stainless steel, with bronze statuettes and towering plants that had Gilchrist wondering how much his daughter was earning. The receptionist asked them to wait while she paged Mr Topley. Nance took one of the deep leather chairs that backed onto a tiled wall. Gilchrist remained standing.

Fifteen minutes later, they were ushered through to an office that looked as if it had been designed and furnished by a minimalist. The walls were bare, except for two small black and white photographs in oversized frames. An expansive desk lay devoid of clutter. Gilchrist saw no filing cabinets or anything else that would suggest the room was ever used.

The door clicked.

Gilchrist and Nance turned like a choreographed act.

Despite the expensive dark-blue suit with silver shirt and

matching tie, Chris Topley had failed to lose his bruiser image. According to Dainty, he had earned a reputation as a freelance minder in the late '80s, and as he framed the doorway, it did not take much imagination to picture him booting someone to death in the wet streets of Glasgow.

He stepped into the room. The door closed behind him with a dull thud.

Gilchrist stood a good six inches taller than Topley's squat figure. From that vantage point, Topley's sandy hair, shorn to the bone, looked like roughened wood grain.

'Chris Topley?' Gilchrist tried.

Topley eyed Gilchrist with the look of a businessman not sure if this was an opportunity about to blossom into cash or some past deal come back to haunt him. 'And you are?' His accent was hard Glaswegian softened to a low growl.

'Detective Chief Inspector Andy Gilchrist.' Gilchrist declined to show his warrant card or tell Topley they were from Fife Constabulary. He had the impression that neither point would matter to a man of Topley's background. Instead, he offered his hand.

Topley's grip felt hard and moist, like roughened leather greased smooth. An overpowering fragrance of aftershave hung around him, and his gaze slid off to the side as he eyed Nance from top to toe. By the time he offered her a gold-toothed grin, Gilchrist felt as if she had been stripped and abused before his eyes.

Topley held out his hand to her.

Gilchrist almost smiled when Nance ignored it.

'You have a name?' Topley asked her.

'Yes.'

Topley flashed some more gold, oozing charm like a snake in an alligator pool, and Gilchrist wondered how Maureen could ever have taken up employment with the guy.

'Well well well,' Topley growled. 'Two detectives. I must say I'm honoured. How can I help you?'

Despite the attempt at upper-class wealth, Topley could not rid himself of his city slum upbringing. His face had the hardened look of a street fighter and bore the faded scars of past disputes. A nick on the forehead. A dotted line on the right cheek. Disfigured knuckles on bunched fists.

'Maureen Gilchrist is one of your employees,' said Gilchrist.

Topley seemed to miss the paternal connection. 'A lovely girl,' he said. 'What about her?'

'She's missing.'

'She is?' Topley scrubbed the back of his hand under his chin, the sound like sandpaper on wood. 'Since when?'

Gilchrist tried to work out if Topley was being honest or covering the truth.

Then Topley pointed a finger, and said, 'Now I get it. You're the old man.' He stepped around the polished surface of his desk, and Gilchrist had the distinct impression that few paper trails were left in the company. Topley stood behind his high-backed leather chair, his right arm along the top. In the light from the glass wall, his eyes took on a hunted look, like a guilty man waiting for the damning question.

Gilchrist kept his voice level. 'Do you know where she is?'

'Could do.'

Gilchrist toyed with the idea of walking around the desk and grabbing him by the throat. Topley lowered his arm, his dark suit sliding over his shoulders like an ill-fitting shell. But beneath the silk-clothed carapace flexed the rippled muscles of a tough street-fighter.

'I'm not here to play games,' Gilchrist said. 'Just answer the question.'

'Should I be talking to my solicitor?'

'That's your prerogative.' It was Nance.

Topley smiled. Gold fillings glinted either side of front incisors. 'She speaks,' he said.

'She also arrests,' said Nance.

Topley held out his arms, wrists pressed together. 'Please. It's been a while since I've been handcuffed by someone so pretty.'

And at that moment, Gilchrist knew one thing for certain. Chris Topley was not Maureen's boyfriend. On that fact, he would bet his life. 'We can handcuff you later,' he said, 'but for now we're trying to establish if you can help with our enquiries, when you last saw Maureen, who you last saw her with, where she might be. That sort of thing.'

Topley lowered his arms. He grinned. 'Maureen told me I wouldn't like you.'

The sound of his daughter's name coming from the mouth of an ex-convict sent the chill of horripilation through him. He struggled to control his loathing. 'Why would she say that?'

'Because she cares for you.'

Topley's use of the present tense sent some signal through Gilchrist's system. Maureen was alive? Was that what he was saying? And if so, how did he know?

'As an employee, what does Maureen do?' Nance again.

'She's in marketing.'

'Marketing what?'

'Topley clients.'

'Who are?'

'The rich and the famous.'

'And the infamous?' Gilchrist tried.

'I'm clean,' Topley growled. 'The past is past. This business is legit.'

'Why don't I believe you?'

Topley's eyes flashed, nothing more than a widening of the pupils. But for a fraction of a second Gilchrist caught a glimpse of the wilder version of the man. Then the anger evaporated, and Topley said, 'I couldn't give a monkey's toss what you believe, Mr Gilchrist.'

'Detective Chief Inspector Gilchrist.'

'Oh. Yeah. Right. I forgot. How fucking silly of me.'

'How long has Maureen been employed here?' Nance again.

'Why don't you ask her?'

'If I could, I wouldn't be here asking you.'

Topley inhaled, let it out in a bored rush. 'About a year.'

'The job pay well?'

'Basic of sixty to seventy. Then a bonus that usually doubles it.' He flashed some gold. 'At Christmas.'

'How nice,' Gilchrist quipped. But Maureen earning upwards of a hundred-thousand at the age of twenty-three did not sit well with him. Why had she never told him about this job? Had Gail known? Had Harry? Or Jack?

'When did you last see Maureen?' Nance asked.

Topley turned to the tinted glass panels that ran from floor to ceiling and wall to wall and provided a spectacular overlook of Glasgow's refurbished waterfront. The Clyde slid past like some dirt-caked beast, its murky waters as sluggish as mud, a silent reminder of Glasgow's dark industrial past.

Topley stood with his back to the room, hands clasped behind him so that Gilchrist caught the blue lines of some tattoo on the inside of his left wrist. The twin-tipped tail of a swallow, he thought.

'Two nights ago,' Topley said. 'We went out for a drink after work.'

'Anyone with you?' Nance had her pencil and notebook out as if by sleight of hand.

'No.'

'Just the two of you?'

'Yes.'

'Like on a date?'

'I wouldn't put it that way.'

'What way would you put it?' Gilchrist interrupted.

'Two friends having a drink.'

The emphasis on *friends* rankled Gilchrist, but he nodded to Nance to continue.

'Anyone see you?' she asked.

'See us?' Topley shrugged his shoulders. 'Of course they saw us. We weren't hiding.'

'Who saw you?'

'Other than everyone in the pub?'

'At work, I mean.'

'Most of the office staff.'

'You make a habit of going out for a drink with your employees?'

'Just the good-looking ones.'

Gilchrist tightened his lips, thought it better to let Nance get on with it.

Nance seemed to sense his discomfort. 'Where did you and Maureen go?' she asked.

'Had a glass of wine in Arta.'

'Where's that?'

'Not far from where she lives.'

'You know where she lives, do you?'

Topley chuckled. 'Of course I do. I own the place.'

'She rents it from you?'

'In a way.'

'What kind of a way?'

'The flat comes with the job. It's a perk.'

'Any other perks come with the job?'

Topley turned at that question. His eyes creased in a knowing smile. 'Depends on how hard-working my staff are. How far up the ladder they want to climb.' He flicked an ophidian glance at Gilchrist. 'Know what I mean?'

Nance scribbled hard into her notebook as if trying to lead Gilchrist away from the trap. But it was no use. 'No,' he said. 'Why don't you tell me?'

Topley turned to the window again, and Gilchrist sensed the man was not as tough as he liked people to think. 'She does stuff for me,' Topley went on.

'What sort of stuff?' Gilchrist pressed.

'Stuff stuff.'

'Illegal stuff stuff?'

Topley shook his head, gave a dry chuckle. 'She told me about you.'

'Why would she do that? She expecting me to visit you some time?'

Silence.

'What else did she say about me?'

Topley turned then, and any thoughts Gilchrist might have had of the man losing his hardness evaporated. 'That you're a fucking cunt,' he said. 'And a wanker. A fucking wanker.' He smiled. 'That's what she said about you.'

'Those her exact words?' Gilchrist asked. 'Fucking cunt? Fucking wanker? She say that, did she?'

'More or less.'

'So, she never said those words. Not exactly,' he added.

'If it makes you happy, those were her exact words.'

Gilchrist almost smiled. In all the time he had known Maureen, the use of that single word, *cunt*, had never passed her lips. It was the one word she despised more than any other.

'So,' he continued, 'after Arta, where did you go?'

Topley tilted his chin up, as if to look at Gilchrist down the length of his flattened nose. 'Babbity Bowster.'

'How do you spell that?' Nance asked.

'Any way you like, sweetheart.'

Nance shook her head, scribbled in her notebook.

'What did you have to drink there?' Gilchrist asked.

'More wine.'

'A glass?'

'A bottle.'

'Or two?'

'Probably.'

'Pay by cash?'

'How else.'

How else indeed?

'Maureen likes her wine,' Topley continued, as if warming to the idea of being interrogated. 'It loosens her up, if you catch my drift.'

Gilchrist ignored the taunt. 'What kind of wine?' he asked. 'House? White? Red?'

'Red.'

'Red?'

'Yeah. Red. I'm sure you've heard of it.'

Got you, you plonker. Gilchrist knew Topley was lying. He had no doubt Maureen frequented those pubs. They were both within walking distance of her home. But why would Topley lie?

Or was he just stringing them along for the hell of it? 'Two bottles of red between the two of you?' he went on.

'We might have left the second one unfinished.'

'Might?'

'Yeah. I think we did.'

'A red wine? Like a Cabernet?'

'Yeah. That's the one. Cabernet.'

'Sauvignon?'

'Yeah. Cabernet Sauvignon.'

'Did you have a meal?'

'No. We drank.'

'More red wine?'

'Gin.'

Maureen liked the occasional gin and tonic, so Topley was telling him a mixture of lies and truth. 'Then what?' Gilchrist asked.

'We went back to her place and fucked each other senseless.'

Nance giggled, God bless her. She shook her head, slapped her notebook shut. 'In your dreams, big boy.'

Topley seemed not to have heard. He glared at Gilchrist, his eyes like blue burning beads. 'She likes it up the arse. Hard and fast. She swears when she's getting fucked. Did you know that? She swears like a trooper. Fuck me harder, Chris baby, she says. Go on. Deeper. Harder. Fuck me. Fuck me.' Topley stopped his billy-goat thrusts then, and lowered his arms. He ran the back of his hand across his lips, as if out of breath.

Gilchrist smiled. 'Finished?'

Topley frowned.

'Would you like me to charge you with obstructing a criminal investigation?'

'I'm obstructing nothing. You're asking questions. I'm giving answers.'

'You're lying.'

'Prove it.'

'Maureen doesn't drink red wine.'

'Do what?'

'Red wine makes her sick.' Gilchrist turned, stepped towards the door.

'Maybe it was white, then.'

'Maybe you weren't even with her.'

Topley's face deadpanned.

'Thanks for your time,' Gilchrist said. 'I've enjoyed myself.' He gripped the door handle, then hesitated. 'By the way, if I were you I'd make sure my books were in order.'

'I'm legit.'

'You'd better be,' said Gilchrist, and raised his wrist. 'Because in about twenty-four hours this place is going to be crawling with inspectors from the Inland Revenue and Her Majesty's Customs and Excise. Wouldn't you say, Nance?'

Nance shook her head. 'Wouldn't think it would take them that long.'

'Bye,' said Gilchrist, and opened the door. 'Oh. And one other thing.' He turned to Topley, pleased in some cruel way to see his fists bunching. 'Maureen's never liked it up the arse. She prefers to be on top.'

Topley unclenched his fists, then closed them in a white-knuckled crush.

Gilchrist pulled the door shut. His stomach churned. He should not have mentioned Maureen, but he had caught an image of her turning, dismounting from Watt, and the words had slipped from his lips before he could stop himself.

Outside, Nance said, 'He's lying through his back teeth. There's no way Maureen would let him touch her with a barge pole. And what's with the gold fillings? Did you see them?' She shivered her shoulders.

Gilchrist shrugged.

'Was it true about the red wine?'

Gilchrist nodded.

'So, what's he up to?'

Gilchrist could not answer her. Topley's hatred had been revealed to him with such intensity that he felt the man had to be holding some grudge. But why? He had never met Topley before. He might have served time in Barlinnie, but as far as Gilchrist was aware their paths had never crossed. Why would Maureen become involved with someone like that? Was Topley just a philandering employer who took advantage of his position? Or was there more to it?

Gilchrist did not know.

He knew only that Maureen was in grave danger.

CHAPTER TWENTY-ONE

GILCHRIST WAS ABOUT TO step into Babbity Bowster when his phone rang. It was Dick.

'That mobile number you asked me to do a reverse check on,' Dick said. 'It's listed to a Peggy Linnet.'

'Got an address?'

'That's where it starts to get complicated. According to the company's records she lives in Dundee. In one of those high-rise flats. But the council has it belonging to a Jerry McPhail, who works as an engineer in Saudi—'

'And he hasn't been in the country for months, right?'

'First time.'

'Renting it out?'

'Maybe.'

'Can you have someone in the Office check it out for me, Dick? Let's try to find this Peggy Linnet.'

'Will do.'

Gilchrist hung up. Who was Peggy Linnet? And why did Watt call her? The calls were too short and at such unusual times of the day and night for her to be his lover. Or was she?

Inside at the bar, Gilchrist removed a passport-sized photo from his wallet. A young woman, fiercely attractive, with the fire of defiance burning her dark-brown eyes, looked as if she was daring the camera to take her picture.

He held it out to Nance. 'Maureen with her hair short.'

'She has your eyes,' she said. 'But she looks angry.'

'She has Gail's temperament.'

'Ouch.'

Gilchrist held the photograph out to the barman. 'Have you seen this woman in here recently?' he asked.

The barman looked too young to be pulling pints, more like a teenager stunned to find himself freed of his mother's apron strings. Clotted hair spiked his head. Angry pimples flared on his cheeks. He glanced at the photograph. 'I'm only part-time.'

'That's not what I asked,' Gilchrist growled. 'Take a good look.'

The barman eyed the photo, shook his head.

'What about the others?'

The barman turned to a guy stacking glasses, and shouted, 'Hey, Brian. Someone wants to speak to you.'

Brian slid the last of the glasses onto the shelf and walked out from behind the bar, drying his hands on his apron. A silver ring in his left eyebrow looked tarnished. Everything else about him seemed fresh. He stared at the photograph and nodded. 'She's a regular.'

'Define *regular*,' Gilchrist said.

'Comes in every other day, or so. Mostly early, doesn't stay long.'

'Like after work?'

'Yes.'

'Alone?'

'Not always. Sometimes she's with someone.'

'Male? Female?'

'Both.'

Gilchrist exhaled. He was getting nowhere, confirming only what he already knew, that Maureen had the occasional after-work drink in Babbity Bowster, one of her local pubs, sometimes by herself, sometimes with a work associate, male or female.

'When did you last see her?' he asked Brian.

'Couldn't say.'

'Last night?'

Brian shook her head. 'I wasn't on last night.'

'Have a guess.'

'Last week, maybe.'

'But not since?'

Brian shrugged. 'She could have been here and I wouldn't necessarily have noticed.' He stared at Gilchrist for several long seconds,
then said, 'Look, I'm sorry. I get paid to work here. Not eye the talent.
When this place gets busy, it's heaving. Know what I'm saying?'

Gilchrist was about to slip the photograph back into his wallet,
when he said, 'Do you know Chris Topley?'

'Yeah, I know Chris Topley. Who doesn't around here?'

'How would you describe him?'

'Mr Big-Shot. Spends cash like it's going out of fashion.'

'Wealthy, is he?'

'He's loaded. And I mean *loaded*.'

'And?'

'And he shows off in front of his friends. Know what I'm
saying? Fancies himself as the brain of Britain, too. Always giving
his opinion about this and that. But he's as thick as shite. Don't tell
him I said that.'

'Did you ever see him with Maureen?'

'With who?'

'The girl in the photograph.'

'I thought you didn't know her name.'

'I didn't say that.'

Brian eyed Gilchrist, as if seeing him for the first time and
working out if he could trust him or not.

'He's her father,' Nance said.

'And she's missing,' Gilchrist added. 'Did you ever see her with
Chris Topley?'

Beads of sweat glistened on Brian's forehead. He blinked once,
twice, as if his brain was having trouble sorting the question. Or
coming up with an evasive answer.

Nance removed her hand from her pocket and flashed her
warrant card.

'You're police?'

'Yes.'

'What's this about?'

'Why don't you let us ask the questions?'

'Is she in trouble?'

'You're not listening.'

'Am I in trouble?'

'Why would you say that?'

Brian's lips tightened.

'She's missing,' Gilchrist said.

'That's why we're asking the questions,' Nance followed.

'Look,' Brian said. 'I only know Topley because he comes in here now and again. He's Mr Big around here. His friends come and go. You don't see them for months on end, then in they come all grins and cash and fancy cars. Know what I'm saying?'

'From out of town?' Nance tried.

Brian sneered. 'From Barlinnie, more like.'

'You know that for a fact.'

'That's the pub scoop.'

Brian ran the back of his hand under his nose, then sniffed. And that simple action let Gilchrist know what Brian's problem was. He took drugs. And Topley supplied him.

'Did Maureen ever take drugs?' he asked Brian.

Brian tried to hide his surprise at the *non sequitur*, but failed. 'No,' he said.

'I thought you didn't know Maureen.' It was Nance.

'I don't.'

'But you know she doesn't take drugs?'

'Yeah.'

'You sure about that?'

'I'm sure.'

Gilchrist and Nance said nothing, just waited for Brian to continue. It worked.

'She doesn't look the kind,' he continued. 'Know what I'm saying?'

'What kind does she look like?' Nance again.

'She's classy,' Brian said, risking a glance at Gilchrist. 'She's way above the likes of Topley and his hangers-on.'

Hearing those words sent pride surging through Gilchrist. Maureen did not do drugs and was perceived as not only classy but someone who would not associate with the wrong kind of guys. Which did not explain why she was employed by the Topley Agency. Was it for money? Over a hundred thousand pounds a year kind of money? Plus a flat as a perk for doing *stuff* for Topley? Surely she could not know about his criminal past. And once again, Gilchrist felt as if so much water had passed under the bridge of his daughter's life that he was left standing high and dry on the banks of his memories.

'Look,' said Brian. 'I've got work to do.'

'You never answered the question,' Gilchrist said.

'What question?'

'Did you ever see Chris Topley with Maureen?'

Brian dabbed the back of his hand under his nose, then shook his head. 'Can't say that I did.' He eyed Gilchrist. 'Look, I'm telling the truth. He's not her type, that's all.'

Gilchrist wondered why he had not thought of asking the question until then. 'How about Ronnie?'

'Ronnie?'

Gilchrist waited.

'Ronnie Watt?'

Gilchrist tried to hide his surprise. 'Did you ever see her with Ronnie Watt?'

Brian nodded. 'Once or twice.'

'Twice? Once?'

'Several times, then.'

'Like they were regular boyfriend girlfriend?'

'Not really.'

'Why not really?'

'They didn't look close, like. They argued.'

'Argued? About what?'

'How would I know? I work the bar.'

'You couldn't hear them?'

'No.'

'So how do you know they argued?'

Brian shrugged. 'She looked unhappy. Like she didn't want to be in his company. And one time she just got up and left him sitting there. Know what I'm saying?'

Gilchrist almost smiled. *Fuck you, Ronnie*, flitted through his mind, followed by, *That's my girl.*

'And?' Nance again.

'And what?'

'And did you ever see Ronnie Watt with Chris Topley?'

Gilchrist almost smiled. Nance was beginning to make jumps in logic on her own, jumps that could catch someone cold. Himself included. He stared at Brian, expecting him to shrug the question off.

'Once or twice,' Brian said.

What? 'When?' snapped Gilchrist.

Brian took a step back, held up his hands. 'Hey, man. Steady on. What's your problem?'

Gilchrist realised he was breathing hard. The whole thing with Maureen and Watt was getting to him. And now a link to Topley. He struggled to keep his voice level. 'My problem,' he growled, 'is that my daughter's missing and she's got herself involved with scum of the earth like Topley and Watt.'

Tight-lipped, Brian stared at him.

'Do you know what Topley and Watt talk about?'

Brian shook his head.

'Think about it,' Gilchrist said, and returned Maureen's photograph to his wallet. 'And when you've worked it out,' he handed a business card to Brian, 'give me a call.'

Outside, the sky had darkened. Swollen clouds hugged the skyline, low and dark like the ceiling of some dingy nightclub. The city was about to experience a *thunderplump*, as his mother used to say.

'Let's try Arta.'

But after showing Maureen's photograph around the place, they were left none the wiser. She might have been seen. She might not. She looked familiar. But then again, did not. As they stepped back outside, Gilchrist pulled his phone from his jacket and searched its memory. He found the number he was looking for.

It rang four times before being answered.

Gilchrist said, 'Terry Leighton, please.'

'This is he.'

'DCI Gilchrist. You did some work for me last year.'

A pause, then 'Oh, yes, I remember now. How can I help you?'

'I have a laptop I'd like you to take a look at. I want you to print out every file in it.'

'*Every* file?'

'Is that a problem?'

'Well, some files simply aren't printable. Well, they can be printed, but they're mostly computer code. I'm not quite sure what you mean.'

'I'm not looking for those files. Just your common or garden Microsoft Word files.'

'Oh, yes, I see. That should be quite easy.' A pause, then, 'When do you need them?'

'Will you be at home this evening?'

'Well, I, I...'

'Good. See you this evening.' He hung up before Leighton could object.

'What a pity we're heading back to St Andrews,' Nance said.

'Why's that?'

'I was looking forward to another treat.'

From the questioning look in her dark eyes, Gilchrist realised she was being serious. Why would she want to get involved with someone like him? He was twenty years her senior, drank too much, spent too many hours at the Office, and seemed incapable of sustaining any relationship with the opposite sex.

She lifted her hand to his face. 'You look sad,' she said. 'And vulnerable. Not like the fearsome crime-buster of legendary fame.'

'Who writes that stuff, anyway?' he said. 'Come on,' he growled. 'We have work to do.'

Nance shoved her hands in her pockets and strode alongside. 'You know, Andy, you can be a real bastard at times.'

'I've been called worse.'

'I wonder why.'

Gilchrist grabbed her by the arm.

She stopped, frozen in mid-step, glaring at him until he released his grip.

'I'm sorry,' he said to her. 'I didn't mean it that way. I guess I'm not used to it.'

'Used to what?'

'A woman showing some affection.'

Anger danced behind her eyes, as if she was preparing to launch an invective onslaught. Then she shook her head. 'You're an easy man to like, Andy. But a difficult man to get to know.'

'You got to know me last night,' he tried.

'Fleetingly.'

He was not sure how to take that remark. Was she letting him know he had been too selfish? Could he be blamed for that? It had been a while. Almost a year. And with Chloe's murder and Maureen's disappearance, he supposed it was a wonder he'd been aroused at all. He felt something touch his hand, and looked down to see Nance's fingers entwine with his.

'Come on,' she said. 'We really do have work to do.'

He let her lead him back to Maureen's.

CHAPTER TWENTY-TWO

GILCHRIST WALKED THROUGH each of the rooms, his fingers dragging along the top of the sofa, the tassels of her plumped-up cushions, around the edge of a book-shelf. He wondered what Maureen had last done in this house, where she had last walked, and he breathed in the flat's newness, searching for her vestigial fragrance, only to be overpowered by the smell of paint and emulsion that haunted the air like a poltergeist.

In the bathroom, he lifted a bright-red box of perfume. It had never been opened. Had she been given this as a gift? A half-full atomiser of another, almost empty, shared the same glass shelf, all the fragrances Maureen seemed to possess. Not like Gail who collected perfumes and lotions the way others collected stamps.

His mind offered an image of Maureen as a child, on the floor in the master bedroom, Gail's vermilion silk scarf around her neck, an opened bottle of *eau de parfum* dripping into her hands. Gail had stepped into the bedroom at that moment and let out a shriek, and Maureen toppled the bottle in her fright, and splashed it over her fingers that she then dabbed at her eyes. It had taken Gilchrist two hours of soaking and bathing Maureen's eyes with lukewarm water before she stopped crying.

He eased the cabinet door shut, as if closing an opening to his past. Maureen was missing, and moping around her flat was not going to uncover any more clues.

He drove to Strathclyde Police Headquarters, 'H' Division in Pitt Street, where he pulled in an old favour by having Dainty put out another appeal on national television for information regarding Maureen. Dainty was all hard handshakes and curt commands, with nothing being too much for the search of an associate's daughter, not even a follow up call with Chris Topley, which Dainty seemed pleased to offer.

'It'll keep the bastard on his toes, let him know we've got our eyes on him.'

'Getting too big for his boots?' Gilchrist asked.

'That's one way of putting it.'

The appeal was set for the evening news, targeted for Glasgow and the surrounding areas. Gilchrist watched it with Nance in a bar off Charing Cross. He asked the bartender to turn the sound up, and found himself holding his breath when Maureen's face filled the screen. But no one seemed to take any notice, not even when the announcer said, 'Any person knowing the whereabouts of Maureen Gillian Gilchrist, twenty-three, slim-built, five ten, shoulder-length dark hair, last seen having a drink in Babbity Bowster in Glasgow's Merchant City several nights ago should contact Strathclyde Police.' A number was given for callers to use with complete anonymity.

Gilchrist pushed his unfinished pint across the bar and stomped out.

On the drive back to St Andrews, he called Jack. He sounded upbeat, which had Gilchrist worrying that he was on drugs to help manage his pain and his life. Maureen had not called, as expected, but he took advantage of Jack's cavalier mood and asked if he would call Mum, find out when she last spoke to Maureen.

Ten minutes later Jack called back.

'Mum was asleep, but Harry says they haven't spoken to Maureen since last week.'

'Did he mention the news? We put out an appeal.'

'He never said a word, Andy.'

Gilchrist felt his lips tighten. This was his and Gail's daughter,

Jack's sister, Harry's step-daughter, for crying out loud, and no one seemed to know anything about—

'I tried Jenny again, on the off-chance. But she hasn't heard from her either.'

'Jenny?'

'Jenny Colvin. A friend of Chloe's.'

At the mention of Chloe's name, Gilchrist felt his lips purse. He had not told Jack about the left arm. Now was not the time to bring it up.

'Did Jenny say when she last saw Chloe?' he asked.

'Last year. Way before Christmas. We would sometimes go out with her.'

'You and Chloe?'

'And sometimes Maureen, too.'

Gilchrist pressed the phone to his ear. 'I didn't know you and Maureen went out together.'

'Not often. Maureen's got her own circle of friends.'

'How about boyfriends? Did you meet any of them?'

'That's how I met Chloe.'

Things always seemed confused with Jack. 'What do you mean?'

'Jenny's boyfriend knew Kevin.'

Kevin. Chloe's boyfriend before Jack. Out of nothing comes something. 'I'm listening,' he pried.

'Jenny used to go out with Roddie. Roddie knew Kevin. We went to a party in the south side. I was with Sheila. Chloe was with Kevin. That's where we met. Me and Chloe...'

Gilchrist could not fail to catch the saddening in Jack's tone. 'Sounds a bit like musical chairs,' he joked.

'Yeah.'

Gilchrist stared through the windscreen. Twin beams speared the wet darkness. Windscreen wipers swept back the drizzle. He felt powerless to lift Jack's spirits and now regretted having called. He needed to end it before Jack asked about the investigation.

'Before I go,' he said. 'Whose house was the party in?'

'Kevin's.'

It was a long shot, but worth a try. 'You wouldn't know where Glenorra is?'

'Who?'

'I thought not. Did Maureen ever mention Glenorra to you?'

'Not that I remember.'

Gilchrist sensed the conversation was about to turn to Chloe. 'Listen, Jack, I've got to go.'

'Yeah.' And with that, Jack hung up.

Gilchrist sat his mobile phone in the centre console. What the hell was he doing? Have a chat with Dad and ruin your day? When was the last time he had spoken to Jack without picking his brain?

'Do you ever feel you're losing control?' he said to Nance.

Nance placed her hand on his thigh and squeezed. 'You give the impression of always being in control.'

He eyed the road ahead. Always in control? Of what? His family? His career? His life? That was a laugh. He felt as if he was hanging on by his fingernails while the stallion of life galloped off like some untamed beast. And Nance's hand on his thigh had his thoughts reverting to other problems. Beth.

He and Beth had resurrected their affair after Beth's attack, the worst possible time. And now their affair was over, even before it had been consummated, Beth still needed help. Should he not be helping Beth rather than getting involved with someone at work? If Greaves found out, he would—

'Penny for your thoughts.'

Gilchrist gave a defeated shrug.

'Don't worry,' she said. 'No one'll find out about last night.'

Gilchrist eased the Merc through a sweeping corner. 'And here was me thinking I was the one with the sixth sense.'

'I can read you like a book, Andy.'

'What am I thinking right now?'

'About how much you enjoyed last night, but don't know how to tell me you don't want it to continue.' Her hand gave a quick squeeze, and he glanced at her, but she was staring out the side, into the darkness of the passing fields.

'It's not that I don't want it to continue,' he said. 'It's... I'm not sure I'm ready for another relationship.'

'You're being presumptuous, don't you think?'

'In what way?'

'That I would want us to have a relationship.'

'Isn't that what this is about?'

'This?'

Gilchrist twisted his hands on the steering wheel. Why do women have the ability to turn the simplest of comments into the most damning of statements? 'Well, isn't it?' It was all he could think to say.

Nance eyed the road ahead.

'I'm sorry,' he tried.

'For what?'

'For being presumptuous.'

'I'm sorry, too,' she said, 'for making you sweat.'

'Who's sweating?'

She laughed, a long chuckle that let him know the air was cleared. 'I think that's what I've always liked about you,' she said. 'Your honesty.'

'It's nice to know someone thinks I'm telling the truth.'

'Aren't you?'

It seemed as if their convoluted conversation was some form of verbal foreplay. And he found himself wanting to move on. 'So, tell me. What *are* you looking for?'

'In a man?'

'In a relationship.'

Nance turned her head to the side window again. Beyond, the countryside passed by unseen, like grey shadows shifting through the night. She stared out the window for what seemed like a full minute, and Gilchrist was thinking he had somehow offended her, when she said, 'Affection,' then added, 'And kindness.'

'Anything else?'

'And sex.'

'That sounds undemanding enough.'

'Especially the sex?'

'The affection.'

Nance slapped his thigh. 'You smarmy bugger.'

'What about trust?' he asked.

'Kindness covers trust. If you're kind to someone, you wouldn't want to do anything to upset them. Therefore you can be trusted.'

'Touché.'

'Is it a deal?'

A deal? Gilchrist was on the verge of reiterating the bit about presumption, when he heard her chuckle. With women, he could never be unkind, which he supposed satisfied one of the criteria. 'Let me think about it,' he tried.

Nance shook her head. 'Men and commitment,' she said. 'Never the twain shall meet.'

'That sounds like a quote.'

'It is.'

'Who said it?'

'Detective Sergeant Nancy Wilson.'

Gilchrist gave a chuckle of his own. 'I thought you didn't want commitment.'

'Only to affection, kindness, and sex.'

'That's all?'

'The rest will follow.'

'The rest of what?'

'You'll have to be affectionate and kind to find out.'

'What about the sex?'

'You've already passed that test.'

Gilchrist stared at the road ahead as an odd tranquillity settled over him. Nance was under his skin. She was under his skin from the moment she entered his bedroom last night. She had known he would not say no. And he had known that, too. But he could also see she had the ability to control him *sans* sex, twiddle him around her tongue with barely a flicker.

As they drove towards St Andrews, he wondered if that was how he had behaved with Gail. Back then had he been as malleable? Was that why his marriage had failed? How was it possible to be so wrapped up in a career, that other more important issues slipped by? Was that the reason Maureen had drifted away from him? Had he spent too much time concentrating on issues of lesser import?

Family mattered. Family had always mattered.

Jack mattered. Maureen mattered. He just had not paid enough attention to that basic tenet. God, he prayed he was not too late to change that.

Maureen meant so much to him, he would die for her.

And he realised that without his children in his life he was dead anyway.

CHAPTER TWENTY-THREE

GILCHRIST ABANDONED HIS ROADSTER half-on and half-off the pavement, then walked along the gravel lane, sidestepping puddles that shone in the still night like mirrors.

They found Leighton's terraced house at the end of the lane, bordered by a six-foot stone wall draped in branches of clematis as twisted as shrivelled veins. A brass coach-lamp, polished like new, hung by a gleaming door. Tiny flies, tricked into life by the warmth of the sheltered spot, orbited the lamp like minuscule satellites. In the lambent light the windows glistened spotless.

The doorbell chimed from deep within.

Ten seconds later the door opened with a sticky slap.

Leighton looked down on them, a crimson cravat stuffed into the neck of a starched white cotton shirt. Black trousers covered enormous thighs joined together at the knees, it seemed, and a shiny black leather belt with a silver buckle circled a fifty-plus waist. Suede slippers spoiled the look of lord and master.

'You're late,' he said.

'Traffic,' Gilchrist offered.

'We had to cancel our dinner reservation.'

'Sorry.' Gilchrist held up Maureen's computer. 'This is the laptop I mentioned. And some CDs.' He pushed the lot into Leighton's pudgy hands. 'I haven't looked at all of them, but I think they're mostly manuscripts.'

'What kind of manuscripts?'

'Novels.'

Leighton scowled. 'Do you want me to print out novels?'

Gilchrist pulled a folded A4 sheet from his jacket pocket, on which he had printed the names of some files. 'You'll find this useful to start with,' he said.

Leighton took it from him without looking at it. 'It would speed things up if I printed everything in draft format,' he said. 'Would that do?'

'As long as it's legible.'

'We haven't discussed payment,' Leighton said. 'I would propose hourly, plus moderate expenses. Paper, printer cartridges, delivery. That sort of thing.'

'Don't bother with delivery. Call me when it's ready. I'll pick it up.'

'I'm assuming you need this as soon as?'

'I'd be grateful.'

'I'll see what I can do,' Leighton said, then followed with, 'Why me?'

It was Gilchrist's turn to frown. 'What do you mean?'

'Fife Constabulary has its own computer experts. Why not use them?'

Gilchrist nodded to the laptop. 'Some of the files may be personal in nature.'

Nance stepped in. 'What DCI Gilchrist is omitting to tell you, Mr Leighton, is that the laptop belongs to his daughter. He doesn't want anyone at the Office to read his daughter's private writings.'

Leighton gave Nance's words some thought, then said, 'How old is she?'

'Early twenties.'

'Do you have her permission to—'

'She's missing,' Gilchrist interrupted. 'That's what this is all about. What her laptop contains might help us locate her and solve an ongoing murder investigation.'

Leighton's eyes widened. 'The body part case?'

Gilchrist nodded, disappointed that it had to take the notoriety of a murder enquiry to arouse interest.

Leighton pulled the laptop to his chest, as if it now belonged to him, with all its untold secrets. 'I'll call you tomorrow.'

The lane slipped into darkness as the door closed.

When they reached the Mercedes, Nance said, 'Where to?'

'It's almost ten o'clock.' Gilchrist pressed the remote. 'I've got an early rise and a busy day ahead of me. If you'd like, I could drop you off.'

'Trying to get rid of me?'

'Jack's at my place,' he said. 'It's not a good idea.'

'There's that presumption again.'

Gilchrist drove through the back streets in silence and pulled to a halt in front of a row of three-storey terraced apartments. Parked cars lined both sides of the street.

Nance gripped the door handle. 'You needn't worry,' she said. 'Your secret's safe.'

In the dim light, he thought she might not see his smile, so he said, 'Thanks,' and before he could stop himself added, 'for last night.'

She seemed to hesitate, as if reconsidering whether to stay or leave. 'No ties,' she said at length. 'No commitment. Just affection, kindness, and the occasional session. That way no one gets hurt. How does that sound?'

Impractical? Impossible? 'Impressive,' he said.

She chuckled and stepped into the night. A cold breeze brushed his face. Before he could say, 'Goodnight,' she had closed the passenger door.

She crossed the street, slipped between two cars, and skipped up a short flight of steps to her front door. The key must have been in her hand, or the door unlocked, for she seemed to vanish from sight without missing a beat or giving a backward glance.

He pushed into gear and eased away.

His thoughts hammered back to Maureen as he accelerated down the hill by Abbey Walk on his way to Crail. It was his help-lessness that hit him the hardest, the fact that he could do nothing to ensure her safety. Where was she? Was she all right? Jesus, he didn't even know if she was alive or...

She was alive.

She had to be. He had to believe that.

He had to, because he would not let her die.

He reached Castle Street and parked the Roadster facing downhill, a latent hang-up from past experience with bad starter motors. The rain had stayed off, but the wind had risen, carrying with it an icy chill off the sea. By the time he reached Fisherman's Cottage he brushed off the cold with a shiver.

Inside, the heat hit him. The thermostat had been adjusted to thirty. When Dad was paying, cost did not enter the equation. A goal-scoring roar came from a half-opened door along the hallway. When he entered the front room, Jack twisted in his seat. Even from one glance, Gilchrist could tell he was well on his way.

'Hi, Andy. Didn't hear you come in.'

'I wonder why.'

Jack pointed the remote at the TV. The noise dropped.

'What're you watching?'

'Liverpool and Man U. Giggs's been booked.'

'Good game?'

'Seen better.' Jack settled back into his chair, held up a glass of whisky, and swirled it about. 'I'm afraid your Johnny Walker's taken a beating.'

'The Black?'

'Of course.'

It pleased Gilchrist in some paternal way that Jack drank his whisky. Jack's life as a freelance artist-slash-sculptor was not the highest paying, and he could not hold a grudge if his only son overindulged when he visited. However, demolishing the better part of a bottle of Johnny Walker Black did not provide the opportunity for a sober face-to-face. He decided not to mention Maureen's flat or his disappointment over their appeal on the news.

Defeated, he said, 'I'm for a Sam Adams.'

'I'll join you.'

'That took a lot of persuasion.'

'You know me,' Jack said. 'I'm fussy about what I drink. It's got to be liquid.'

Even though he had heard Jack cough out that phrase a thousand times, he smiled. It always irritated Maureen, and an image of her frowning at Jack entered his mind with such clarity that he caught his breath. He coughed, cleared his throat. 'Frosted glass?'

'By the neck'll do.'

Gilchrist strode to the dining room where his black and silver drinks trolley sat. It held his entire collection of spirits and liqueurs. He picked up a crystal tumbler, blew into it to clear the dust, then slipped a bottle of Dewars under his arm and walked into the kitchen.

The television was off *Mute*, and Gilchrist closed the hatch. The previous owner had done away with the door between the kitchen and the front room. Several other ill-advised modifications enabled Gilchrist to buy the cottage at a knock-down price with the intention that one day he would make improvements of his own, when he had the time and the money. But for the last five years he had lived in the cottage just as he had bought it.

When Gail left, Gilchrist had stayed in the family home for almost eighteen months. But with the children gone the place lost its heart, no longer a home, but just somewhere in which to sleep. He replaced none of the furniture or changed the wallpaper or colour scheme, and felt as if his life was stagnating until he woke up one Sunday morning to find a woman in his bed, a friend of a friend who had taken pity on him the previous drunken night.

'Are you just moving in?' she had asked him.

'No,' he had told her. 'I'm just moving out.'

Decision made, he bought Fisherman's Cottage the following month, put the family home on the market and left St Andrews. Crail sat on the coast ten miles south, and the lengthened commute was negligible. The only downside, as it turned out, was that he could not spend as long in the pub after work. But now and again he took a taxi, which cost a fortune.

He removed two bottles of Sam Adams from the fridge and was struck with a sudden memory of Beth. He wondered what she was doing. In bed? With or without her valium? He still cared for her, but there was only so much he could do, even less when she seemed hell-bent on refusing medical assistance.

He removed a handful of ice-cubes from the freezer and popped them into the crystal tumbler, then splashed a good measure of Dewars into it. On impulse, he picked up the kitchen phone and dialled Beth's number. The man's voice took him by surprise.

'I was calling for Beth,' he said.

Muffled scraping told him the phone was being passed over.

A few seconds later Beth said, 'Yes?'

He tried to sound chirpy. 'Hi. How are you?'

A pause, then, 'Why are you calling?'

Disappointment slumped to the pit of his stomach. He had not known what to expect, but downright disinterest had not entered his mind. 'I'm sorry,' he said. 'I didn't mean to interrupt—'

'You're not interrupting anything, Andy. Nothing's going on. That was Steve, Cindy's boyfriend. We're discussing Spain.' Another pause, then more forceful, 'I don't know why I have to explain this to you.'

'That's not what I—'

'Look, Andy. I need time by myself. Away from here. Away from everything. Can't you understand that?'

Gilchrist caught the shiver in her voice, and knew she was still a long way from being well. His calling at that time of night was doing her no favours. 'Yes I do,' he said. 'I hope it works out for you in Spain, Beth. And I'm here if you ever need anything. Just call. Any time. All right?'

She hung up.

Gilchrist held onto the phone for several seconds before replacing it. Any thoughts he might have had of maintaining their relationship evaporated. Beth was going ahead with her plans to sell her shop and leave St Andrews, and he could do nothing about it. Helpless, was how he felt. He swallowed the Dewars in one hit.

Back in the sitting room, he handed Jack his Sam Adams and took a seat opposite the fireplace. The microbrew tasted cold and soothed the fire in his throat. He wondered if he was coming down with some bug, or just burning out. He was getting too old for all this shit. He tried to redirect his thoughts from Beth by asking

Jack, 'How long do you intend to stay? I mean, stay as long as you like. It's great that you're here.'

Jack tipped his Sam Adams at him. 'Cheers. But I'm not sure how long. I'm kind of keen to start on something new.'

Gilchrist nodded. Jack had inherited the trait from Gail that when she was unhappy she worked harder. Maureen was the same. Not that Gilchrist could put in more hours even if he tried. 'How was Harry?' he asked.

'The usual.'

'Which is?'

'Bit of a diddy.'

Gilchrist frowned. 'You don't like him?'

'He's all right. He looks after Mum.'

Somehow hearing how Harry and Gail interacted did not sit right with Gilchrist. He had never fully understood why he had been so upset about their break-up. Had it been the loss of his kids to another man? Or the mental image of Gail making love to Harry? Or was it because he thought he still loved her, even after all she had done? Their marriage had died years before the split. He could not deny that. So what was his problem?

As he sipped his beer and watched the football, the heat and alcohol took their toll. Within minutes he was asleep, dreaming of wakening up in a coffin, finding he was sharing it with someone, a woman who turned out to be Maureen. Except that it wasn't Maureen, but Chloe with her body parts stitched together.

He woke up sweating to a dark room and black television screen and an empty chair vacated by Jack. By the time he pulled himself to bed, he would be back on his feet in less than three hours.

CHAPTER TWENTY-FOUR

BY 11:00 THE FOLLOWING MORNING no one had heard from Watt. Gilchrist checked with Bowers who confirmed Watt had signed out of the crime scene at 7:12, which was the last record anyone had of him. And it puzzled Gilchrist why Greaves continued to side with the man.

'What do you think you're playing at?' Greaves blasted. 'A warrant for Watt's arrest for murder? What in the name of God's gotten into you, man?'

'For *suspicion* of murder,' Gilchrist corrected.

'Cut the pedantics, Andy. It's not on.'

'Why did you assign Watt to me?'

Greaves' anger dissipated to annoyance. 'I thought we'd been over this already.'

'I never asked for Watt. He wasn't needed.'

'That's for me to decide. Not you.'

'And now he's vanished off the face of the earth?'

'Oh, do come along, Andy.'

Gilchrist pushed his fingers through his hair. He had come up against Greaves in this mood before, once when he had argued the case for extra compensation for the Office staff. He had lost then. And he was losing now. Then it struck him like a slap to the head, and he wondered why he had not thought of it earlier. 'You know where he is.'

Greaves' lips tightened.

'It's out of your hands. Isn't it?'

'Don't push it, Andy.'

'Push what, Tom?' Gilchrist stepped closer. But Greaves stood six-two and was not a man to be intimidated. 'My son's girlfriend has been murdered and is being fed to me in bits. Not to you. Not to anyone else. But to me. Her left arm was found yesterday.' From the look on Greaves' face Gilchrist thought he had just told him some news. 'Now my own daughter's missing and I'm terrified she's going to be served up to me in bits as well.'

Greaves' eyes narrowed, showing in their reflection the tiniest glimmer of compassion.

'And Watt does a runner at the same time? Tell me why I shouldn't put out a warrant for his arrest.'

Greaves took a deep breath. 'Very well, Andy,' he said, and returned to his seat.

Gilchrist waited while Greaves stared hard at his desk, as if gathering his thoughts.

Then Greaves looked up. 'Ronnie's with Strathclyde Drug Squad,' he said. 'I can't give you any details, for the simple reason that I don't know. My remit was to find him a position in this Division and make it look as if he was back with Fife Constabulary.'

'That doesn't explain why you assigned him to me.'

Greaves sneered. 'It was a perfect arrangement.'

'Perfect? What are you talking about?'

Greaves gave a tiny smirk. 'You hate the man. Can't say I blame you. So, I knew you would do your damnedest to keep him out the picture.'

'I don't follow.'

'Oh, do come along, Andy. It's a bit late in the day to play dumb.'

Gilchrist wondered why he had never noticed until that moment the cruelty reflected in Greaves' eyes. He had seen him in argumentative action before, stripping the fabric of another man's ego to ribbons with his tongue, as sharp and cutting as thirty lashes with a bullwhip. He thought Greaves had been flexing the muscles of seniority back then. Now, he was not so sure. Then some twisted rationale shifted deep in Gilchrist's mind, and he thought he saw an answer, and wondered if Greaves could really be that devious.

'You knew I would keep Watt busy,' he said. 'You knew I would bury him in the investigation, have him go off on his own, and by doing so, give him a means by which he could carry out his Drug Squad business.'

Greaves gave a tight smile.

Something was missing. How could Watt vanish for days then come back all smiles and chewing gum and expect to keep his cover intact? Then it struck him. 'Something's about to break. And Watt's not coming back. Is he?'

Greaves glared at him.

Gilchrist pressed on. 'Did you know Watt was seeing Maureen in Glasgow?'

Greaves stiffened. 'No.'

'Does that not make you suspicious?'

'Of what?'

'Now who's acting dumb?'

'Watch that tongue of yours.'

'I don't believe in coincidences, Tom.' Gilchrist struggled to keep his voice steady. 'If I ever find out that Watt is in any way involved with the disappearance of my daughter, I swear to God, Tom, I'll hold you personally responsible for interfering with my investigation.'

'I'll pretend I didn't hear that.'

'Don't pretend. Pray.' And with that, Gilchrist strode from Greaves' office.

Outside on North Street he thrust his hands into his pockets. His outburst had drained him. He felt emptied, devoid of emotion, beyond anger. He imagined Greaves on the phone with ACC McVicar, demanding his resignation. McVicar had stood up for Gilchrist in the past, but there were only so many rules a man could break, and his final threat to Greaves might have broken the lot.

He headed towards the Old Course. Watt's involvement with Maureen was key to the case. But how? Maybe Dainty knew someone in the Drug Squad who might know where Watt was. But even then, the chances of Gilchrist being made privy to an ongoing drug operation ranged from zero to one-hundred below.

Further evidence of Watt's treachery struck him as he reached the Dunvegan and turned into Golf Place. Greaves had said something he should have known nothing about. *You hate the man. Can't say I blame you.* Which meant he knew about the incident with Maureen, and only one person could have told him.

At the Old Course he walked down The Links, the road that paralleled the eighteenth fairway. The wind hit him, chilling and stiff, carrying with it the smell of the open sea. He took Grannie Clark's Wynd, the strip of asphalt that crossed the eighteenth and first, then veered off and walked across the course itself, oblivious to the golfers.

Why the Old Course? Why were its fairways and bunkers and environs being used as the depository for amputated body parts? Was the course itself significant? Or was it being used simply to gather media attention? He reached the Road Hole Bunker by the seventeenth green then kicked his feet through the long grass that bordered the fairway's length. The Old Course seemed such an important part of the killer's plan that he felt an almost irresistible need to walk the links. Or maybe his sixth sense was telling him the next body part was about to be delivered and this was where it would be found.

He continued alongside the sixteenth. From there, the course ran all the way out to the Eden Estuary. He plodded on in his solitary search, criss-crossing the dunes like some game-dog, groping as far as he could into gorse bushes that cluttered the rough. He had to dislodge himself from a bristling clump off the fourteenth fairway to answer his phone.

The rush of Jack's voice had him pressing his mobile tight to his ear.

'Harry's just called.'

Gilchrist eyed the distant town. Grey buildings overlooked a black sea. Harry calling Jack was not good. His gaze wandered the horizon while he waited to be told about Gail.

'Why didn't you tell me about Maureen?'

The question almost threw Gilchrist. But he recovered with, 'It's early days, and I didn't—'

'Early days? What the hell's that supposed to mean? Harry told me there's an appeal for any information on Maureen's whereabouts out on the news. That sounds late to me.'

Late. Were they? Were they now too late to save Maureen?

'I'm sorry, Jack. I didn't want to say anything until I knew for sure.'

The fight seemed to go out of Jack as the stark meaning of Gilchrist's words filtered through his system to their logical conclusion. 'Don't tell me,' Jack whispered. 'Don't tell me Mo's next.'

'I hope not,' Gilchrist said, but before he could offer anything more, Jack hung up.

Gilchrist folded his mobile phone and eyed the expanse of grass and gorse that lay before him like some undulating sea. How could he go on with this? How could he search for Chloe when his own daughter was missing? But he knew that the answer to Maureen's disappearance would be delivered to him through the remaining parts of Chloe's body.

So he hung his head and struggled on.

By the time he stood on the twelfth tee he had found nothing new. But he did not feel disappointed, instead felt oddly satisfied at having ruled out blanket areas of overgrown grass and impenetrable gorse. The walk had warmed him and, as he faced the wind, beads of sweat chilled on his brow. Overhead, clouds tumbled by like windblown cotton. The tide was out and the sands of the Eden Estuary lay before him, flat and damp and uninviting as mud. He decided to cut across the Jubilee and over the New Course onto the West Sands and walk back to town along the beach.

He set off at a brisk pace.

As he ducked through the wire fence that bordered the links, his mobile phone rang.

'No luck,' said Dick without introduction. 'Peggy Linnet is one of three students who rent the flat from McPhail. The number belongs to her ex-boyfriend who used her address for billing purposes.'

'Got a name?'

'Joe.'

'Joe who?'

'That's the problem. She only ever knew him as Joe.'

'How long had she been going out with the guy?'

'Three months.'

'And she never knew his name?'

'Looks like it.'

'Are they covering for him?'

'Don't think so. Apparently he was a nasty piece of work. Drank too much. Argued all the time. Left without paying his share of the rent. Peggy says she keeps getting his bills and keeps sending them back. They would all gladly shop him if they could.'

'Description?'

'Slim. Dark hair. Five-eight. Thirty-something going on fifty. Smokes. Rolls his own. Brought up in Glasgow. Rough as they come.'

Gilchrist dug his thumb and forefinger into his eyes. That description would fit any one of a thousand Glaswegians. 'Keep at it, Dick,' he said, even though he felt it was probably useless.

He now knew Watt had called someone by the name of Joe. If that was indeed his name. And it looked like the only way to find Joe was to find Watt himself.

Which brought him back to the beginning.

He slid down a worn path between two dunes. The West Sands stretched before him, copper and gold bordered by the dark waters of the North Sea. Multi-coloured kites of reds, yellows, blues, dipped and swooped then soared high, held fast on the winds by invisible leashes. Grass-covered dunes lined the back of the beach, like some unkempt lawn that hid neater fairways and greens.

In the distance he noticed a crowd gathering and wondered if a busload of day-trippers had offloaded and spilled onto the sands, or if someone was having a party, a student perhaps, celebrating God only knew what excuse for a drunken orgy.

By the time he figured out what it was, his feet were pounding the hard sands at the water's edge, his breath coming at him in hard hits. He heard his own harsh whimper burst from his mouth with the certain knowledge that after a few more minutes he would have only one more body part to find.

And then...

'Dear God, no.'

CHAPTER TWENTY-FIVE

GILCHRIST ORDERED EVERYONE TO, 'Step back. Police. Step back.'

And louder. '*Sir*. Back from the body.'

He had used the word *body*, even though it was not a complete body, but a somewhat limbless torso. As he stood by the white thing that lay before him like a lump of bloodless meat, his lungs seemed unable to pull in sufficient air. He stumbled to his knees. Seawater soaked through his trousers. His fingers clawed the cold damp sand.

He stared at the thing, the white thing, the headless torso with one arm and no hand, which shifted on the sands with each incoming wave. Ruddied pockmarks dotted the skin where gulls and other seabirds had pecked through.

He brushed sand from the flat swell of the stomach, revealing what looked like a black stain about an inch or so above the belly-button. He cupped seawater in his hands and sprinkled it over the torso. As rivulets of sand ran from the flesh, a tiny love-heart swam into view. If he still harboured any doubts, they vanished at that instant. He was looking at Chloe, at the hacked-off torso of his son's girlfriend.

He pushed himself to his feet, brushed his hands on his thighs and despite himself could not take his eyes off the blackened nipples of Chloe's small breasts. It struck him then that her nakedness was exposed for all to see, and he swept his arm and snapped, 'Go on. Get out of here. What are you looking at?'

With hesitant reluctance the crowd backed up.

Gilchrist slapped his mobile to his ear. He ordered the socos and gave directions, but it was not until he closed his mobile phone and stared at the blonde pubic mound that lay between twin circles of butchered meat that he realised something was missing.

Curiosity overpowered his revulsion. He kneeled again, eyed the stomach, studied the tiny love-heart. The finest of blond hairs, dried by the sun, stood proud, as if refusing to give up life. His gaze shifted over the nippled humps then on to bony shoulders made all the more narrow by the missing left arm, down across a rippled ribcage to a wasp-like waist that made Chloe's torso seem strangely thin and frail. The gulls had not done too much damage. Open pits around the upper chest looked more like unhealed sores than carrion food-spots. Clots of sand clung to her skin. Except for the tattoo and the peck-holes the torso was unblemished and glistened damp in patches as white as fresh alabaster.

But of the note, Gilchrist found nothing.

A wave rushed the shore and a hacked thigh bumped against his arm before he could move. He choked back a cry. He thought he had seen enough brutal sights in his life to make him think he was inured to the horror of it all, but he found himself fighting off the sudden urge to throw up.

He tried to convince himself it was the personal nature of the torso that was making him gag, but he saw with a clarity that stunned him that it was more than that. For once, he was on the receiving end, the relative of a murder victim, the person left to cope with death. How heartless he must have appeared to relatives of victims over the years. No amount of whispered condolences or words of kindness could ever salve the loss, replace the emptiness, the feeling of violation that threatened to erupt in a primal scream for justice.

He took a deep breath, forced himself to think about the task at hand, to see this as just another murder. And that thought stopped him. *Just* another murder? Dear God, how had he ever let himself become this cold? He gripped Chloe's right arm and pulled her up and over, surprised by how light she felt. Her torso slapped onto the sand, and a muted gasp rushed from the crowd as they took another step back.

He had his note. His sixth note. Gouged into the back with V-shaped cuts deep enough to show bone.

BUTCHER.

And the sixth letter. *E.*

It could be no clearer now.

M A U R E E

His daughter was next. And she was missing.

* * *

'Hey.'

Gilchrist pressed his phone to his ear, stared across the Eden Estuary. 'Jack,' he said.

'Hey, Andy, listen, I'm sorry about earlier. I just—'

'Jack.'

A pause, then, 'It's Chloe, isn't it?'

Gilchrist eyed the limbless torso still being jostled inland on the swelling tide. A temporary cordon of yellow tape was strung out farther up the beach. Uniformed policemen were interviewing onlookers from a dwindling crowd.

'Tell it to me straight, Andy.'

Straight? What could he say? He stepped away as two SOCOs in white coveralls lifted the torso onto a stretcher and carried it dripping with seawater to the back of their van. Mackie would examine it at Ninewells.

'I'm sorry, Jack. It's Chloe,' he said. 'That's all I can tell you.'

'Jesus,' Jack hissed, and from that one word Gilchrist could almost feel Jack's anger. 'Bastard,' he said. 'How could anyone do this? How could he do this? How could he?'

Gilchrist wondered if he had made a mistake, if he should have spoken to Jack face-to-face rather than over the phone. He had handled his marriage all wrong, the break-up, too. And now he was handling his son wrong.

'Jack. Listen,' he cut in, and waited while Jack quietened. 'There's nothing you can do. But we will solve this. I promise you that.' He hoped his words were helping. Jack's silence made him think they might. And he tried to force all thoughts of failing from his mind. But you could never tell with a murder enquiry.

'Where are you?' he asked.

'Down by the harbour.'

Gilchrist caught an image of Jack as a boy facing the sea, Gilchrist by his side.

'It's where we walked,' Jack said. 'Chloe loved the sea. Did she tell you that?'

He was about to say yes, then realised that Jack needed to air his grief. 'No,' he said. 'She didn't.'

'Chloe had some thing about not being able to paint the sea. Something about it being too wild and beautiful. *The sea represents life in its perpetual evolution*, she once said. She refused to paint seascapes because she thought she could never capture its beauty in stillness. You had to see it moving to appreciate its true beauty.' A rush of breath, then, 'I tell you, Andy, Chloe was something else. She was special, man.'

'I know she was.' It was all he could think to say. He turned as the SOCO van roared into life and eased along the sands. A young police-woman, Jane Crosbie, he thought, was rolling in the yellow tape, her lips pressed tight in reverent silence. Already Chloe's torso on the beach was being assigned to history. Onlookers drifted away.

'I feel like, you know...' Jack let out a rush of breath. 'I feel helpless, Andy. Just out-and-out helpless.'

Like father like son, he thought.

'Do you, uh, do you need me to do anything?'

Gilchrist knew what Jack was saying. But how could he ask his son to identify a torso? That could push him over the edge of what-ever limit he had reached. 'No,' he said, and thought he caught a sigh of relief. Or maybe it was the rush of surf. Then the harsh reality of it hit him. No matter how bad it was, he had to force his investigation forward.

'You haven't heard from Maureen yet, have you?' Jack asked.

That single question told Gilchrist that Jack was now in denial. First his girlfriend, then his sister. It was too much to ask anyone to handle emotionally.

'You really don't think anything's happened to her. Do you?'

No, Gilchrist wanted to say. *I don't think. I know*. But Jack did not need to hear him say his sister was next to be hacked to pieces. 'I'm sure there's a simple explanation,' he tried. 'You know Mo. She's probably gone away for a few days.'

'Remember she ran off to Spain for a month without telling you or Mum?' Jack went on, cheering up. 'You went ballistic, man. Through the roof.' He chuckled. 'Maybe she's gone there again. Do you think?'

Gilchrist kept the deception alive. Having Jack do something was better than him doing nothing. 'Maybe,' he said, and tried to sound convincing. 'Why don't you look into that, Jack? Call a few friends. Find out if they know anything.'

'Yeah. I'll do that.'

'And when you get hold of her,' Gilchrist said, 'give her an earful and tell her to call her old Dad.'

Jack forced a chuckle down the line. 'Will do, Andy.'

By nightfall Gilchrist had not heard from Maureen.

But he had not expected to.

* * *

Maureen startled at the scraping sound.

Someone was outside.

She heard it again.

A key? A knife?

She peered into the darkness, but saw only the shape of the door and the curtained window of the hut she was in. She struggled to move, but the knots bit into her skin, brought tears to her eyes again.

She fought back the nip of tears, bit down hard on the gag, and breathed through her nose. She had worried about the gag, worried that if her nose blocked she would be unable to breathe. It had happened once, two nights ago, and she had passed out from lack of air. But she wakened later, her nasal passageways clear again.

Another scrape.

A key that time. No doubt about it.

The door opened and in the dim greyness she could make out the dark silhouette of his figure. She felt wetness spread between her legs, and tears well at her inability to contain her fear. The warm smell of urine lifted off the wooden floorboards.

She felt the floorboards shiver from the heels of his boots, smelled the stale tobacco that clung to his body like his personal scent. Although she had never liked that smell, it gave a welcome respite from the stench of defecation that had filled her senses for days.

The door closed and the lock turned with a heavy click.

An explosion of light hit her like a blow to the head.

She squeezed her eyes shut.

'Fuck sake,' the voice growled. 'It's fucking honking in here.'

Footsteps thudded across the floorboards. A tremor took hold of her then.

Don't let him touch me. Don't let him come near me.

The footsteps stopped. Without opening her eyes she knew he was standing in front of her. She heard a rustle of cloth, jacket rubbing jeans, perhaps, the sound of a bottle being opened.

She eased her eyes open, squinted against the hard light of a handheld torch.

He squatted no more than three feet from her, his filthy moustache thick and dark over lips as tight and narrow as a scar. He smiled a slow smile that exposed uneven teeth, cracked and yellowed, then held a plastic bottle out to her. All of a sudden she felt the dryness in her throat, the heavy weight of a thick tongue as she tried to speak through the gag but failed.

'Want some?' he said.

She shifted herself on the floor, felt the damp squelch of her own defecation as it squeezed thick in the folds of her underwear.

She eyed the bottled water, tried to say yes, but managed only a groan from behind the gag.

'Want me to take that off?'

She closed her eyes in a long blink.

Please, take it off. Please. I won't do anything. I promise.

She held her breath as he tilted the bottle to her upturned face and dribbled water onto her gag. She worked her tongue, sucked at the damp cool liquid.

'More?'

But the bottle tilted upright with the quick shift of a hand.

He waved it in front of her, teasing. 'Some more?' Then he grinned at her, his eyes dark and feral, his hand lowering to his zip. 'This first,' he said.

She turned her head to the side, closed her eyes.

I can't, I can't. Don't make me do this. I can't.

She heard his zip being pulled down, some rustling, a grunt.

Hard fingers dug into her hair, twisted her head to face him, face it.

'Open your eyes.'

She whimpered.

'*Open* them.'

She started to cry then, her breath rushing in and out of her nasal passages, short sharp blasts that made her think she might pass out. She had read somewhere that hyperventilation resulted in fainting. She shortened her breaths, prayed she would pass out.

The grip tightened. She whined from the pain.

'Open them, bitch. Open your eyes.'

Quick breaths. Fast and hard.

She felt herself falling.

I'm going, I'm going.

'Open them, you fucking bitch.'

Please God. Don't let him. Not again. I'll spew and choke. I know I will. I know it.

He was close. She could tell by the way his breath rasped, the way his grip clutched and scratched her hair. She had looked once.

She had opened her eyes the first time he had done it, seen how his face twisted into an ugly grimace as he climaxed.

Dear God. He's coming. He's coming.

She clenched her lips, squeezed her eyes, heard him groan as sperm hit her forehead in a long warm squirt. Another over her cheek. And one more, followed by a relaxing of his grip, then drips like warm syrup that oozed down her cheek and threatened to slide behind the gag and over her lips. She lowered her head, felt his sperm slither over her chin and drip free.

She had not done as he had asked. She had not opened her eyes, and she knew he would give her no water. Which was now what she wanted.

Without water, she would die.

Please God, let me die. Just let me die.

CHAPTER TWENTY-SIX

BUT SHE DID NOT DIE.

Instead, she was photographed.

He took the Polaroid prints into the other room, through the door to the side, from where she heard the hard metallic click of a staple gun. He came back and looked down at her, and she tried to stare him out. But a sliver of sperm slipped into the corner of her right eye, and she closed it, losing the effect of her short-lived resistance.

'Get up.'

She shuffled on the floor, hoped he would see how impossible it was, then cut back her cry as he grabbed her by the hair and pulled her upright.

'I said get up.'

She tried to stand, she truly did, but her legs gave out. She shook her head, hard and fast, felt the slime by her eye drip free. Then she looked up at him and gagged a scream as a knife flashed in front of her.

She whimpered as the blade pressed against her calf, then watched in silent disbelief as it sliced through the cords around her ankles. She tried to turn as he walked behind her, but a heavy boot against her shoulder forced her face against the wall as the rope that had held her hands behind her back for the last three days and kept her captive to an iron ring on the wall, was cut. Another slice, this time at the back of her neck, and the gag slipped loose.

She gulped in lungfuls of air, sucked it in with opened mouth, lolling her tongue like a panting dog.

'Get up.'

She pulled her hands from behind her back and grimaced from a pain that burned like fire in her shoulders. She gripped the loose gag. Her fingers felt thick and stiff, as if they belonged to someone else. She used the gag to wipe sperm from her eyes and face, then tried to twist into a sitting position, but slumped to the floor. Her head hit the floorboards, but she felt no pain, only a numbing sense of relief at being able to move her arms, her legs, breathe unrestricted.

'Don't make me have to say it again.'

'Water.' But the voice that cracked from her dried throat did not sound like her own.

He held the bottle out.

She grabbed it, forced herself upright, ignoring the clotty dampness at her rump, and drank. Long glorious gulps of cool clean water that overflowed from her mouth and spilled down her chin. She coughed, almost choked, took another mouthful then remembered reading somewhere that too much water after a time without could make you sick.

'For the last time,' he snarled, 'get up.'

Maureen pressed a hand to the floor and rolled over onto her knees. A bit wobbly, but already the benefit of fluids in her system was doing wonders for her strength and her morale. She wondered for one crazy moment if she could make a run for it, but as she pushed herself upright, she knew she would not manage ten feet without being caught.

She flapped a hand at the wall and steadied herself. For a frightening moment her peripheral vision darkened, and faintness swept through her. Then vanished. She held her head as high as she could, and said, 'I'm up.'

'Strip.'

'Fuck off.' Her tongue and lips were still not working the way they should, but it felt good cursing.

He leaned to the side, opened a holdall that she had not noticed until then, reached inside, and removed a handful of crumpled clothes. He dropped them onto the floor.

'Now take off your fucking clothes and get into these.'

'In case it's escaped your attention,' she growled, 'I'm covered in shit.'

Without taking his eyes off her, he backed up to the door and stepped outside. He reappeared with a garden hose in his hands. 'We can do this in there or out here. I really don't give a fuck.'

Maureen blinked, fighting back tears of hope. Was she being set free? It seemed impossible. But he was giving her clean clothes, offering her a wash. Why?

'Outside,' she whispered.

'Strip first,' he said. 'Then outside.'

She could smell sweet fresh air that wafted into the hut in a chilling breeze. If she did as she was told, she could be washed and wearing clean clothes and underwear in a few minutes. That thought alone was almost enough to make her move. She thought she caught the sound of traffic, somewhere off in the distance, the scent of cooked meat on the wind, and felt her stomach knot with hunger. When had she last eaten? Three days ago? She was weak, did not have the strength to fight back or make a sustained run for it.

Even if she knew where to run to.

She made her decision.

She crossed her arms, flinched with the pain of flexing stiffened muscles, grimaced from the sight of her bloodied and bruised wrists, and tugged her top up and over and dropped it to the floor. Undid her zip at the side, let her skirt fall off her. She choked at the sight of her inner thighs, coated with faeces and glistening damp from fresh urine. She had become inured to the stench, but against the fresh air the rancid guff hit her with renewed strength.

Hands behind her back, off with her bra.

Oh, God. Just do it.

Thumbs hooked in her panties, dropped to the floor.

She fought back a choke of disgust and staggered outside into the fresh night air.

Cold water hit her with a shock that took her breath from her. She gasped, turned away, felt the jet hit her backside, and she faced him again, to hide her mess from him. Her hands slid over her body, her upper thighs, her behind, her filth washing through her fingers like wet mud.

'Do you have any soap?' she tried.

'Where the fuck d'you think you're at? The fucking Hilton? Get on with it before I switch it off.'

She swept her hands over her skin, rubbing and brushing.

The jet stopped.

'I'm not clean,' she pleaded, then shielded her face as a blast hit her again.

'Fucking hurry up then.'

When she pushed her hands through her hair the jet stopped.

She stood shivering from the cold, watching dark eyes study her nakedness.

'Get the clothes.'

She stepped back into the hut and the fetid air almost choked her. She pressed her hand over her nose, amazed that she had breathed in the vile stench of that confined space for so long. She picked up the bundle and rushed outside into the fresh air.

He stood on a slabbed path that slipped between bushes at the back of a bungalow that looked vaguely familiar. She assumed that had to be the way out, because he was blocking her escape route. But in the darkness she could not be sure, and she could not stop the tremor that now gripped her limbs with a spasmodic shiver. Running was out of the question.

She tugged at the clothing. 'Do you have a towel?'

'Get the fuck dressed before I change my mind.'

She separated the bundle to find it consisted of only two articles, a skirt and a sweater.

'There's no underwear,' she said.

He turned his head, gobbed off to the side.

She turned her back to him and slipped on the skirt. It felt tight, too tight to fasten at the waist. But it was long and black and woollen soft. She pulled on the top, a black woollen sweater, thin at the elbows, with cuffs frayed and stained with paint. It felt tight around her boobs, but she felt warmth seep through her system, despite being wet.

Then a hand gripped her hair, twisted her head, and she gasped as the cold steel of a blade pressed against her throat. 'One squeak and I'll slit you from ear to fucking ear.' Breath as stale as cigarette ash warmed her face. 'Now start walking.'

She was pushed and prodded along the slabbed pathway, through the bushes to the dark hulk of a car she recognised as a BMW. The boot was already open.

'Get in.'

'You're hurting me.'

'Get the fuck in.'

At least he was not going to gag her, or tie her hands and feet. She lifted one leg over the rim, then the other, and ducked just in time as the boot lid slammed shut. She listened to the sound of footsteps fading, and imagined him returning to the shed to put out the light and lock the door. Cover their tracks? Why would he do that if she was being set free? And if she was being freed, why would he lock her in the boot of his car?

Oh, God, I'm wrong, I'm wrong. He's going to kill me.

But her rationale insisted he would not have had her clean herself if he was going to kill her. Confused, she lay on her back, pleased to feel her thighs clear of the clotted tackiness of the last few days. But the cold shower had not rid her skin of the smell of defecation that clung to her like smoke to clothing.

She turned to the side, fumbled in the darkness, knowing that in some cars you could access the rear seats through the boot. But the darkness was total and the carpeted boot-space solid. She lay still. What was going on? Where had he gone? Was she to be freed? *Dear God, tell me he's going to let me go. Tell me he's not going to do any more of that to me...*

But the truth settled inside her like an anchor sinking into dark waters, pulling all hope down with it. She would not be set free. She had seen his face and known he was not the type to let witnesses to his sadistic crimes roam the streets. *He's going to kill me. He's going to take me away somewhere and slit my throat.* Her eyes strained into the darkness. She had never been scared of the dark before, but as she lay there in the black silence she felt the warm sting of tears in her eyes—

Footsteps.

She held her breath as they stopped at the back of the BMW. The lock popped, and she shielded her face as the boot lid opened.

It was him again. Smiling. Something in his hand.

He leaned into the boot, placed it by her face.

'Look after this,' he said.

She stared at it.

Horror seared her throat in a voiceless scream.

She scrambled away from it, pushed herself back, felt her head hit metal, her legs kick like a trapped swimmer, her arms flail the air for some way out.

The boot lid slammed with a thud.

She screamed then. A primal scream that reflected the terror she had seen in Chloe's sightless eyes.

* * *

Gilchrist wakened with a start.

He had been dreaming, more nightmare than dream.

Maureen had been talking to him, speaking in a language he knew but could not place. As he listened to her he realised she was speaking the language of the dead. He had reached for her, tried to say, *I'll help you.* But with every step she seemed to fade away, so that when he grabbed her she was nothing more than a ghost, a sliver of a shadow that danced in the mirror of his imagination, weak and faint as the vaguest remnants of his oldest dream.

That was when he came to.

He tried to still the jackhammer pounding in his chest, pulled himself upright, T-shirt clinging to his skin like damp cloth. He glanced at his radio clock.

3:33.

He breathed in, almost sobbed. *Dear God, tell me this isn't happening. Tell me that if I had never joined the force Maureen's life would not now be in danger.* His head slumped into his hands and he choked back a sob. He clenched his jaw and looked up. *Get a grip, Andy. You have to get on with it. Sitting around moping won't solve a damn thing.* But how was he supposed to think when his daughter was next in line to be served up to him in bits?

He staggered through to the bathroom and turned on the shower, scrubbed himself with soap as if he wanted to rip his skin off his bones. The daily routine of an early morning shower usually brought his thoughts into focus, but ten minutes later he stepped from the cubicle none the wiser.

He pulled on a pair of blue denims and a Timberland shirt, the one he had bought in Lake George three years ago on holiday with Beth, which brought memories flooding back in a surge of despair. Beth was far from well and needed help, and for one confusing moment he thought of asking Doctor Buchanan to make a house call. But he decided it would be best if he gave her time to settle in Spain, then contacted her through Cindy. Just to be sure she was all right.

In his kitchen he poured a glass of orange juice and distilled water, then checked with the Office. But Watt had not called, and no one had heard from him. What had he expected?

Again, his sixth sense was niggling him, telling him that Watt's disappearance was tied up with Chloe and Maureen somehow. But how, he could not say. He tried Dainty on his mobile phone, but it rang out. He got through to the Pitt Street Office but was told Dainty would not be in until eight. He asked for a home number but the receptionist declined to give it out. He next called Directory Enquiries for Strathclyde Police Drug Squad, but when he asked for Watt he was surprised to be told they had no record of a Ronnie Watt, Ron Watt, Ronald Watt, or any variation of that name, either at Detective Sergeant or Constable level.

Gilchrist almost cursed as he hung up.

What the hell was going on?

He had nothing. He thought for a moment. Not quite nothing. For out of nothing comes something. He had learned that Watt, whoever he was working for, must have pulled one over on Greaves. Was that possible? Watt would be transferred to Fife only on written authority. So, either Watt had faked the transfer, or Greaves was in on it. Or Gilchrist could be pissing against the wrong tree, of course.

He checked his watch. He would make one more call.

'This is DCI Gilchrist,' he said. 'How much have you printed?'

'Mr Gilchrist?' grumbled Leighton. 'Do you know it's five o'clock in the morning?'

'You said you would call.'

A pause, then, 'I've been quite busy working on them,' he said, more apology than excuse.

'I'll be there in twenty minutes. Give me what you've got.'

He pulled on his black leather jacket and stepped out into a cold east coast morning.

Today he would find his daughter.

Even if he had to die doing so.

CHAPTER TWENTY-SEVEN

'IT'S COLD. CAN I COME IN?'

Leighton scowled. 'Through there,' and pointed to a door at the end of the narrow hallway. 'I don't like being wakened at this time of the morning.'

'Neither do I.'

Gilchrist brushed past and opened the door as directed. Heavy velvet curtains blanked out a window to the side. The room had about it the strange redolence of furniture polish and warm dust. In the centre stood an oak-panelled dining table with folded leaves, reminiscent of the one his grandmother used to have. Several reams of printed paper stacked the table's polished surface, bound by rubber bands. On a coffee table by the curtains, Maureen's laptop sat hooked to an HP DeskJet printer. Two opened boxes of copier paper squatted on the carpet.

'Is this it?' Gilchrist asked.

'As much as I've printed thus far.'

He picked up the top half-dozen sheets, miscellaneous letters, each with Maureen's name and her old address in Glasgow's West End as her letterhead. He noted the first one, to a firm of solicitors, McBain, McBride & Crawford, with offices in the city centre, about some failed repair to a leaking gutter, and a damning complaint about the incompetence of the contractor. Another to the Royal Bank of Scotland complaining about a £30 charge for returning a cheque. He noted the date. Two years ago. Maureen was now allegedly earning in excess of £100,000 a year with Chris Topley, but two years ago she was struggling to pay the bills.

Gilchrist flipped through more pages. Leighton had printed them in chronological order and divided them into piles by year. A single sheet listed the file names in each stack.

'Is there much more to print?' he asked.

Leighton let out a high laugh. 'That's only one day's printing. My ink-jet's quick, ten pages a minute, quicker on draft, so you'll see I've put in quite a bit of time already.'

Gilchrist thought of repeating his question before realising Leighton was hinting at payment. He removed his wallet, and said, 'How much?'

'Twenty an hour. Plus expenses.'

'You mentioned that already,' Gilchrist said. 'Ten hours cover it so far?'

Leighton didn't hesitate. 'That should just about do it. Yes. Quite.'

Gilchrist knew he was being ripped off, but peeled ten twenties from his wallet and passed them to Leighton. He slipped out another two. 'That cover your expenses so far?'

Leighton almost smiled. 'Quite.'

Gilchrist picked up one of the copier paper boxes, tipped it upside down, and let an unopened ream fall onto the carpet. 'Mind if I use this?' he asked, and walked to the table without waiting for Leighton's answer. He slotted the printed pages into the box. 'How soon until you print the rest?'

Leighton shrugged. 'Novels, too?'

'The lot.'

'In that case I'd say you're looking at the best part of several days.'

Gilchrist shook his head. 'Too long.'

'I can only print out as fast as my printer will allow.'

'Get another one,' snapped Gilchrist. 'Get two. Three. I don't care.' He moved to the door, the box under his arm. 'There's an extra two hundred quid in it if you have them all printed out by tonight.'

Leighton puffed out his chest. 'I'll need to rent some printers. I'm not sure, I, eh...'

'I'm paying your expenses,' Gilchrist countered.

'Well in that case, yes, quite.'

'Tonight. Seven o'clock.'

'That doesn't give me much time. Make it eight?'

'Eight it is,' said Gilchrist. It made no difference. He would return at seven regardless. 'You'd better get on with it,' he said, then strode down the hall.

* * *

The BMW drew to a halt.

Its engine purred in the quiet of some deserted spot. Maureen knew it was deserted, because the sound of traffic had stopped fifteen minutes earlier, after which she had bumped and rolled around in the boot from too many tight turns. They had to be in the countryside somewhere. But even if she knew how far they had travelled, she did not know the starting point, or in which direction they had come.

They could be anywhere. Maybe not even in Scotland.

The engine died.

She lay silent, listening to the sounds of the door opening, closing, then footsteps crunching the length of the car. The foot-steps stopped.

The boot lid popped open.

Before she had time to move, fingers as tight as talons grabbed her by the hair.

'Don't even think about it.'

She let herself be pulled upright. 'You're hurting me.'

'Too bad.'

'I'll scream.'

'Scream all you like—'

She screamed—

A blow to the side of her head sent her slamming into the dark confines of the boot. She lay still, disoriented, tried to gather her thoughts. Was she being freed? Was that why she was not allowed to scream?

Warm breath by her ear. 'I won't hurt you if you do as you're told.' A pause, then, 'Is that clear?'

'Fuck off.'

He gobbed off to the side. 'If you want to see your old man again, you'd better do as you're told.'

Maureen felt the oddest mixture of hope and fear surge through her in a confusing wave. If she did as she was told, she would see her father again. But why mention her father, not her mother? Did he know her mother was ill? If he knew that, what else did he know?

'Sign this.'

She peered up. The sky was still dark, but she caught the high-pitched chatter of birdsong. A blackbird? A starling? Did that mean it was morning, not night? She had no idea how to answer that simple question.

A beam of light pierced the darkness, and she glimpsed the back of Chloe's head in the corner of the boot. When the BMW had driven off, Chloe's head had rolled into her. She had screamed then, pushed the thing away, hating the feel of Chloe's hair on her bare skin, and just managing to keep down the vomit that threatened to erupt from her throat. She must have jammed it into a hole or something, for the head had not moved for the rest of the journey.

'Here.'

She stared at a pen and a rough-edged piece of paper.

'Sign.'

'Why?'

'Don't play the silly cunt with me.' He dropped the pen and paper into the boot then picked up Chloe's head. He pushed it towards her. Maureen screamed and buried her face in her hands. 'If you don't want that to happen to you, you'd better sign.'

Once more, hope soared within her.

If she signed, would he let her go? She peered out from behind her hands. Chloe's head was gone. She picked up the pen and paper and noticed something printed on it.

'What's it say?'

The beam of light shivered across the paper.

'Vengeance? What's that supposed to mean?'

'Just sign the fucking thing?'

'You'll let me go then?'

'I won't slit your throat, bitch.'

Maureen stared at the lantern jaw made all the more gaunt by several days' growth, at a thick moustache yellowed from too much tobacco smoke. Where was his knife? Was it in the car? Could she run for it? But once again that thought flew from her mind like smoke in a tornado. She would not stand a chance. But if he was not going to let her go, what could she do? Sit and wait for him to kill her?

She turned to the note and pretended to have difficulty holding the pen. But between looking up at him, then down at the pen, she took the opportunity to glance past him to the bushes by the wall. It was morning. She could tell by the way the sky was lightening.

If she ran, could she hide? Were they miles from nowhere?

'What the fuck's up?'

'I can't get it to work,' she said, and looked beyond him. And that was when she saw it, when she knew he had no intention of letting her live. She felt the warm release of urine, and a tremor took hold of her hands. She almost dropped the pen. 'Please,' she whimpered. 'Please let me go.'

His face darkened. 'Aw, fuck you, you bitch, you've pissed in the boot of my car. I ought to slit your fucking throat for that. Get out.'

She tried to pull herself to her feet, but her legs gave way. She did not even have the strength to scream as he hauled her out by her hair.

She slumped onto gravelled asphalt.

'Now sign that fucking paper or I swear to God I'll rip your fucking head off.' He spat off to the side, a thick glob of phlegm that anger had released from his throat.

Maureen tried to make sense of the single word through the blur of her tears.

VENGEANCE.

What did it mean? But it was pointless asking. She was going to be killed, no matter what she did. Maybe by signing she could leave some message to her parents, let them know she had remained defiant to the last. She almost laughed at the thought. How could she even think she had been defiant when she wet herself with every spurt of fear?

She gripped the pen and signed beneath that single word.

Mo, she wrote. That was all.

She held the pen and paper out to him.

He took it, folded it, stuffed it into his pocket.

She sat there, saying nothing as he reached behind him. He was going for his knife.

That was where he kept it. In a leather sheath on his back.

She stared at the bushes, or what she had mistaken for bushes. Now morning was dawning, she could make out the old stone wall and the headstones behind it. She looked to her left, her right, as the strangest thought coursed through her mind.

A cemetery seemed such an appropriate place in which to be killed.

* * *

'Andy. It's Pete Small. You tried to reach me?'

Gilchrist pushed away from his desk and stood. He dug his thumb and forefinger into his eyes and stretched his back. 'Ronnie Watt,' he said. 'He's not one of yours. Is he?'

'You know I can't talk about that, Andy. Is that why you called?'

Gilchrist did not fail to catch the anger in Dainty's voice. The man might be small in stature, but that did little to lessen his presence. Dainty's tongue on the loose had torn many a larger man down to size. 'There used to be a time when we worked hand in hand.'

'Don't play with words, Andy. You know the rules.'

Gilchrist looked at the letters on his desk. He'd been reading his way through them for the last four hours, but had come up with nothing startling. He fingered one. 'Watt knows Chris Topley. Did you know that?'

'Yes.'

'They were seen having a drink together. Does that not interest you?'

'I've had the odd pint with a criminal or two. So has half the force. It's how we keep in contact with the underworld.'

Gilchrist almost smiled at Dainty's old-fashioned way with words. 'Where did Topley get the money to start his business?' he asked.

'Topley's clean. We've checked him out. He might have an eponymous agency, but it's part of a larger holding group. Some international company with too much money.'

'Does it have a name?'

'Can't remember. W-something-something-Holdings International. It puts up the money.'

'Can you find out?'

'Can do.'

'And where it's based?'

'Can do. Why?'

He had no clear idea why his interest was piqued, other than his sixth sense was telling him something did not ring true. A holding company? Why? But yet again, why not?

'Just a hunch,' he said.

'Let me get back to you on that,' Dainty said.

'Thanks.'

'One other thing, Andy.'

Gilchrist caught the bite in the voice. 'I'm all ears.'

'A body was found in a deserted farm lane on the outskirts of Castlecary.'

'Where's that?'

'Off the M80 on the way to Stirling. The body was that of a male. In his early thirties. Throat cut. Being treated as murder, obviously.'

'Anyone we know?'

'Kenneth Finnigan.'

'Never heard of him.'

'Wee Kenny to his friends. But for the last two or three years was employed as Jimmy Reid's gofer.'

Jimmy Reid? Why was Dainty telling him this? Reid? Then he felt the hairs on the nape of his neck rise. 'Bully's brother?' he said.

'The one and only.'

Jesus. 'What does Jimmy have to say about it?'

'Jimmy's shot the crow. We raided his house in Castlemilk this morning, but he's packed up and left. Spain, probably. Has a villa there. We've already been onto the airlines and the Spanish police.'

Gilchrist could tell from Dainty's tone that Jimmy's disappearance was not the crux of the matter. 'What aren't you telling me?' he asked.

'Wee Kenny's car was discovered twenty miles away, burned to a shell.'

'A Jaguar,' Gilchrist said.

'Right first time.'

'How badly burned?'

'Nothing left of it.'

Gilchrist knew they would not be able to tell from the paintwork if the boot of the Jaguar had been patch-painted. But they might from the metalwork. 'The boot,' he said. 'Any damage done to it?'

Dainty chuckled. 'You don't miss a thing, do you?'

And neither do you, Gilchrist thought.

'Repaired pockmarks were found on the boot. Forensics tell me they look like bullet holes. Six in total. Which might suggest an old-fashioned revolver.'

'For an old-fashioned gangland war.'

'Could be. Jimmy was involved in some turf war about eight years ago.'

'About the time Bully was put behind bars?'

'Some time after that. Rumour had it he was looking after the family business.'

Bully had been sent down for manslaughter. Twenty years, with no chance of parole. Was it possible he was still pulling the strings from behind bars?

'Bully's still in prison, right?' Gilchrist asked.

'The Bar-L. The one and only.'

'He's not getting out any time soon, is he?'

'He's hired one of the top legal firms in town.'

'Meaning?'

'They're pushing to have him out in maybe two years.'

'You're joking.'

'Afraid not.'

The Jaguar. Burned to a cinder. Kenny Finnigan. Dead in a farm lane. Ronnie Watt. Disappeared. Maureen. Vanished. Jimmy Reid. Gone to Spain. And Bully. Getting out in two years. Did it all add up to something Gilchrist should be able to see? He hated to hear himself say it, but only one person was available to him. 'I need to talk to Bully,' he said. 'Can you set it up for me?'

'This afternoon do?'

'Perfect,' he said, and closed his mobile.

Gilchrist had once believed, even prayed, that he would never have to face hatred like Bully's again. Now he had arranged to meet the psycho. He shook his head. Billy Reid, aka Bully to friends and family. Jesus. Of all the people. Don't tell me Bully is involved with Maureen's disappearance. Dear God, anyone but Bully.

But he knew Bully was involved.

He did not need his sixth sense to tell him that.

For eight years he had dreaded this day coming.

Now it had, he prayed he was up to the task.

CHAPTER TWENTY-EIGHT

GILCHRIST REMEMBERED IT as if it were yesterday.

He closed his eyes, saw Bully's face, saw the spittle splutter from Bully's twisted mouth as he was led away, handcuffed, screaming a vindictive diatribe that had Sheriff MacFarlane thumping his gavel with the energy of a piecework blacksmith.

Fuck you, Gilchrist. Fuck you. I'm going to have you for this. D'you hear, you fucking cunt? You'll regret this, Gilchrist. To your dying fucking day you're going to regret this. D'you hear?

Gilchrist heard all right. He turned away as Bully was led from the dock, and had since wondered if he had shown some weakness. Should he have stared the man out? Should he have smiled and mouthed *Goodbye?* He could still see the anger in the crazed eyes, still hear the echo of his threats in the canyons of his mind.

Gilchrist pulled his Roadster into the car park that fronted the dark stone monolith of Glasgow's Barlinnie Prison. He had not set foot in the building for over ten years, when he had visited a petty crook by the name of Donnie Crawford who was serving twenty years for murder. Accompanied by Donnie's court-appointed solicitor, Gilchrist asked specific questions that in the end had proven Donnie's innocence. He remained proud of his efforts that day. Donnie joined the Army six months later and ended his life of crime before it started in earnest. The last Gilchrist heard, Donnie had married and was now the father of two young daughters.

But Bully was a different animal altogether, *animal* being the operative word. Bully was beyond salvation. And had been ever since the murderous age of ten.

After signing in, Gilchrist was escorted through a series of steel-barred doors, along a corridor with breezeblock walls painted prison-grey, and into a square room furnished with one table and two chairs opposite each other.

He sat.

The sour smell of urine filled his senses. He found his hands patting his pockets for his cigarettes, recalling that when he first came across Bully he had been smoking thirty a day. By God, he could be doing with one right now. He took several deep breaths and tried to focus on why he was there.

He was there for Maureen. And for Chloe.

If Bully was indeed involved, Gilchrist might be able to glean something from him, some tiny detail that might lead him to Maureen. Bully had always thought he was above the law, and that cockiness had been his downfall in the past, and could be again.

The door opened.

Gilchrist looked up.

There stood Bully, six-foot-one of him, street-fighter-thin and prison-hard. He paused at the doorway before being pushed into the room, arms and legs shackled. The guard pulled out a key and manacled the chains to a metal ring on the floor.

'Sit.'

Bully sat. Sweat glistened on his brow. The whites of his eyes were tainted yellow, and Gilchrist could tell from that first glance that Bully was not well. The guard stood with his back to the door, and Gilchrist found himself surprised by an odd reluctance to lock eyes with Bully. Even after eight years.

Bully broke the verbal standoff. 'I've been expecting you.' His voice echoed off the block walls, deep and thick with the guttural accent of a Glasgow hard man grown old.

Gilchrist tried to show no reaction. But it was almost too much. He forced himself to focus on his hands on the table. He wanted to give Bully the impression that his words had slipped over his head.

But he had heard. And he understood.

I've been expecting you. Why?

Because I knew you would work out who was behind Chloe's death and Maureen's disappearance?

Gilchrist looked up.

After eight years, he stared at eyes that sparkled with the pleasure of anticipated revenge. 'Why?' was all he said.

Bully chuckled.

Gilchrist leaned closer, caught the sour scent of sweat from pock-marked skin, the stale stench of garlic from twisted lips. He struggled with the deduction of his rationale. It screamed at him, telling him that Bully must know. But did he know? Or did Gilchrist have it all wrong? He forced himself to control his voice. 'I'll ask you again. Why were you expecting me?'

Bully stopped chuckling. His eyes flickered with a crazed look, leaving Gilchrist in no doubt that Bully had not lost his appetite to maim and kill.

'You think I know where your daughter is,' Bully said.

'Who told you she was missing?'

'Word gets around.'

'And do you know?'

'That's for you to find out.'

'I'm not here to play games.'

'You're free to leave.'

'You don't want me to leave.'

'I'm not stopping you.'

Gilchrist felt the tiniest of tremors take over his left leg. He pressed his heel to the floor. But he recognised the symptoms. Fear. Of all the criminals he had come up against, Bully was the only one who scared him. All of a sudden he was not sure he could tackle him about his daughter. But, Jesus, he had come this far.

'What's wrong, Mr Gilchrist? Are you thinking playing games might not be such a bad idea?' Bully laughed, a dry chuckle that sounded forced.

'Where is she?'

'I don't like that game.'

'Where is she?'

'Don't you want to play?'

'*Where is she?*'

Bully's face deadpanned. 'Do you think I'd tell *you?*'

'So you know.'

'*Hah.*' The word was barked. Spittle formed at the corners of thin lips. 'You're not a stupid man, Mr Gilchrist. But you're coming across as one.'

'Where is she?'

'Where is who?'

'My daughter.'

'I haven't the fucking foggiest.'

'I don't believe you.'

'I don't give two fucks what you believe.'

'So why were you expecting me?'

Bully seemed lost for words at the snap question, but Gilchrist wanted to keep the momentum going.

'What's to stop me having you charged as an accomplice in murder?'

'Because you'd never fucking prove it.'

No denial. Was that as good as a confession? Gilchrist leaned across the table. 'Don't bank on it,' he snarled.

'In case you haven't noticed,' Bully said. 'I'm inside.'

'You are indeed.' Gilchrist smiled.

Bully glared at him. 'I told you I'd get even with you.'

'No you didn't.' Gilchrist shook his head. 'You said I'd *regret* it.'

Bully looked confused for a short moment, then revealed white teeth that looked at odds with the hard-man image. 'You always were a cocky cunt.'

Gilchrist pushed his chair back. 'Well now's your chance to make me regret it.'

Bully cocked his head to the side. 'Look at you,' he said. 'The best of gear. What'd the leather jacket sting you? Four hundred? Five? More? Yeah, I bet it was more. And the shirt.' Bully tutted. 'You're spoiling the image without a tie.'

'You're spoiling my day, Bully. And talking shite.'

Bully seemed unfazed. 'You must be worth a few bob.'

Gilchrist struggled to hold Bully's eyes. Was he hinting at ransom money? But money was not the object of Bully's exercise. Getting even was. By hitting Gilchrist where it hurt the most. Not his pocket. But his family.

'And look at poor old me,' Bully continued. 'Dressed in the best of prison rags.' He glanced down at himself, then up at Gilchrist. Anger shifted like ripples in his ruminating jaw. 'You put me here.'

'You put yourself here,' Gilchrist snapped back. 'If you hadn't massacred that family, you and I would never have met.'

'I'm innocent.'

'Sure you are.'

'They were asking for it.'

'What's your point?'

'You wanted to see me.'

'And you've been expecting me. Why?'

Bully stared at the table, as if giving Gilchrist's words some thought. Then he looked up. 'D'you know what pleasures I have in life now?'

'No. But I'm sure you're going to tell me.'

'Writing.'

'Sold anything to the *Beano* yet?'

'You're so funny, Mr Gilchrist. You know that?'

'I don't see you laughing.'

Bully tried a grin, but his eyes seemed sucked dry of pleasure. 'I could fuck your life like that,' he said, and snapped his fingers with a hard flick.

Gilchrist stood. 'You're wasting my time, Bully.'

'Got things to do? More criminals to put away?'

Gilchrist nodded to the guard who moved towards Bully.

'Missing your *princess*?' Bully hissed.

Ice fingered Gilchrist's spine. He raised his hand to the guard. 'What did you say?'

Bully side-nodded. 'Get rid of the monkey.'

They had discussed this possibility; Gilchrist and Bully being left alone in the same room. The Prison Director had not liked it. But Gilchrist had insisted. He gave a tiny nod, and the guard stepped from the room.

'I'll be right outside if you need me, sir.'

Gilchrist waited until the door was closed before he said, 'Talk. Or I'm walking out that door and you're never going to hear from me again.'

'D'you know what?' Bully said. 'You're a brainy bastard.'

'What's your point?'

'You're smart.'

Gilchrist had no idea where this was going, so he waited.

'But I'm smarter. I'm smarter than you. I'm smarter than ape-face out there. I'm smarter than the whole fucking lot of you piled together.'

Gilchrist said nothing. He sensed Bully was leading the conversation to what he wanted to talk about, what game he wanted Gilchrist to play.

'Wee, sleekit, cowerin, timorous beastie,' hissed Bully, and smiled a cruel smile that darkened his face and warned Gilchrist to beware. 'Oh what a panic's in thy breastie.'

Cowering? Timorous? Panic? Was that Bully's game? Was he trying to sew the seed of fear into Gilchrist's mind? If so, he needn't bother. Fear was already well and truly stitched where Bully was concerned. Gilchrist resisted the urge to shift in his chair. 'Didn't know you were a Burns aficionado,' he tried.

Bully chuckled. 'You shitting yourself yet?'

Not quite. 'What's your point?'

'His knife see rustic Labour dight, an' cut you up wi' ready sleight, trenching your gushing entrails bright.'

Gilchrist had been to enough Burns Suppers to know Bully was reciting from 'To a Haggis'. But the reference to gushing entrails had him worried. He tried to redirect the flow with, 'You're talking in riddles.'

'I'm talking in poems, Mr Gilchrist. Father of Jack. Protector of Maureen. *Poems*.' Bully tapped the side of his head. 'It's what makes me smarter than the rest of the bozos in here. Poems.'

Gilchrist pressed on. 'Why did you ask if I was missing my princess?'

'That's what you called Maureen. When she was young. Your little princess.'

Gilchrist felt his breath leave him. Hearing Maureen's name being uttered from the mouth of a convicted murderer hit some point deep inside him. How had Bully known Maureen was his princess? She was five when he called her that. *Time to go to bed, my little princess.* Then he would lift her up and carry her upstairs.

'Inhuman man! Curse on thy barb'rous art, and blasted be thy murderin eye.'

The words sounded like Burns, but they were unfamiliar to Gilchrist.

'May never pity soothe thee with a sigh, nor ever pleasure glad thy cruel heart.'

More unfamiliar verses, but he could not fail to catch the emphasis on *cruel.* Was Bully talking about himself, or suggesting something else? And why say these words after mentioning Maureen's name? *Inhuman man!* That would certainly describe Bully.

As if reading Gilchrist's confusion, Bully said, 'Do you know what's good about being in this place?'

'You not being outside.'

Bully narrowed his eyes. 'You always were a cheeky bastard, Gilchrist. But you know that. And I'm too long in the tooth to rise to your petty baiting now.' He shook his head. 'Honesty,' he said. 'That's what you get when you're in here. Honesty.'

Gilchrist felt his eyebrows lift. He could not think of a more dishonest bunch of souls than those incarcerated behind the stone walls of Barlinnie prison. 'Now you really have lost me,' he said.

Bully chuckled, a hacking cackle that seemed to come from somewhere deep inside his lungs. 'No one tells lies in here,' he said. 'Why should they? They've got nothing to lie for. Not like the world you live in.'

'So what are you telling me? That you've seen the error of your ways?'

Something dark shifted behind Bully's eyes. 'Three lawyers' tongues turned inside out,' he growled, 'wi' lies seamed like a beggar's clout. Three priests' hearts, rotten, black as muck, lay stinking, vile in every neuk.' Bully's lips parted in a tight smile. 'Even back in Burns' day, lawyers and priests were still the same lying fucking shites they are today.'

'And your point is?'

'I would have thought a brainy bastard like you would be able to work it out.'

Work what out? The verses? The reference to lawyers and priests? The lies? The truth? What? But what Gilchrist thought he had worked out, was that Bully was behind Maureen's disappearance. Of that he was almost certain.

'Where is she?' he demanded.

Bully seemed to let Gilchrist's question hang between them. Then he glanced at the door, and Gilchrist felt his hopes soar at the improbable off-chance that Bully was about to tell him. Then his look returned, dark and hard and gleaming with victory.

'Oh princess, by thy watchtower be, it is the wished, the trysted hour. Those smiles and glances let me see, that makes the miser's treasure poor,' and with an abruptness that had Gilchrist on full alert, Bully pushed back and stood. He raised his hands, shackles jangling in the dank room, then brought them down on the table with such force that Gilchrist was sure he must have cracked several bones.

The guard burst in. '*You. Sit.*'

Bully held out his hands, and Gilchrist saw the disfigured fingers of crushed joints.

'Take me,' Bully said to the guard, then shuffled forward, body stooped, as if the act of smashing his hands had drained him of all energy. At the door, he halted. 'Vengeance, Mr Gilchrist. You put me away. Eight years ago. And through every second of every minute of every hour of every one of those eight years, vengeance has kept me going.'

Gilchrist saw how Bully's eyes were glazed not from illness, but from drugs. Was he having dope smuggled in? Was that possible? Or was he being prescribed medication by the prison doctor? But he also saw that Bully was not going to offer more. How could he let him walk away without revealing where Maureen was? He had to give it one last shot.

'Maureen's done nothing to harm you,' he tried. 'Let her go.' It was useless to negotiate with a psychopath, he knew that, but he tried anyway. 'Please,' he added. 'What's she ever done to you?'

Bully eyed him for a full ten seconds before saying, 'The wind blew as twad blawn its last. The rattling showers rose on the blast. The speedy gleams the darkness swallowed. Loud, deep and lang the thunder bellowed. That night, a child might understand, the Deil had business on his hand, Mr Gilchrist.' Then Bully tilted his head and let out an ear-piercing howl like a demented wolf.

Even the guard looked taken aback.

Gilchrist stared at the man, knowing he was being toyed with, knowing Bully was taking the greatest of pleasures from the knowledge that he was in control. Another howl raised the hairs on Gilchrist's neck, followed by a crazed laugh that cut to the heart of his soul.

Then Bully stepped into the corridor.

The door closed with a metallic clang.

Gilchrist sat stunned for several seconds, listening to the sound of Bully's laughter and wolf-howls fade, until all that was left was the silent echo of prison life. He pulled open his jacket and switched off his micro-cassette recorder. He wound it back, hit *PLAY*, and listened to Bully's demented howling fill the tiny room.

He recognised some of the words, excerpts from poems by Robert Burns. But what did they mean? Nothing? Something? Was Bully giving him more clues? Or just playing with him? That would be his style.

On the way out, Gilchrist checked with the prison doctor who confirmed Bully was not on medication.

'What about his health?'

'In the pink.'

'Any sweats, yellow eyes, that sort of thing?'

'We have the occasional viral infection passing through the prison population. Much like the real world. According to my records, Mr Reid has not had any serious illness for five years.'

'And five years ago, what happened?'

'The flu.' A twist of the head, like a puzzled dog. 'I'm sorry to disappoint you, Inspector, but I'm afraid Mr Reid has enjoyed, and continues to enjoy, excellent health.'

Driving back to St Andrews, Gilchrist let his thoughts run their convoluted course.

Bully was not being prescribed medication. So, was he having drugs smuggled in? Hard to do, but not impossible. Gilchrist could not say. But one thing he did know, was that Bully was a devious twisted psychopath, as clever as they came. And his gibberish had to mean something. Of that, Gilchrist was certain.

But what?

And if he found out, could he save Maureen?

* * *

Maureen gasped from a stab of pain at the nape of her neck. That was where he had hit her, knocked her unconscious. Since coming to, she spent the last thirty minutes kicking the wooden door that was the only exit from her chamber. Her efforts had resulted only in bruised and bloodied bare heels.

Her mouth was gagged with duct tape that ran around the back of her head and pulled her hair tight. In the dusty air of the tiny chamber, the tape made breathing difficult. Pain throbbed through her head in sickening waves. Behind the gag, her tongue felt hard and dry. It seemed that every joint in her body ached, and she wondered how long she had been out.

She wriggled onto her rump, shuffled across the concrete floor until her back hit the stone wall. She pulled her knees into her chest. Her ankles were bound with the same duct tape as her gag. Behind her back, her hands were, too.

As best she could work out in the pitch darkness, the chamber was no more than six feet square. The ceiling was low, barely high enough to allow her to sit. The air tasted thick and dusty, and she wondered if she would die from lack of oxygen.

She began to cry again. She knew by the way the duct tape was wound four or five times around her limbs that she was not meant to escape.

And she knew, too, that he was not coming back.

She was alone. All alone. No water. No food.

She was going to die. This chamber was to be her final resting place. And it pained her to think that no one would find her, no one would ever visit her once she was gone.

No one would know.

The tears came then, racking sobs that threatened to steal the air from her lungs. Thoughts of all the things she had done wrong in her life, the indifference she had shown her parents, the cruel comments she had made to her father, the disregard she had shown her brother, the recklessness she had developed in later life, swirled around her mind in waves that threatened to drown her. Oddly, it was the thought of dying that stopped her crying. She sniffed. She was not dead yet.

She would not lie down and die. She would not let that happen.

She wriggled to the door, turned her back to it, felt her fingers fumble over the rough edge of the concrete wall, found a bit that was chipped, its edge almost sharp enough to cut.

She gritted her teeth, pressed the tape to the wall.

She would not die. She would not let him win.

She rubbed her wrists up and down.

Up and down.

CHAPTER TWENTY-NINE

JACK LOOKED UP AT GILCHRIST. 'That's scary, man. What the hell does it mean?'

Gilchrist shook his head. He had asked that question a hundred times. *What the hell does it mean?* And a hundred times he had come up with the same answer. *I don't know.*

Had Bully been teasing him into thinking he was giving him clues, knowing it meant nothing? Now that would be Bully, devious and cruel to the point of mental sickness. But Bully had said something that told Gilchrist he was testing him.

You're a brainy bastard. You're smart.

Followed by the *coup de grâce.*

But I'm smarter. Smarter than the whole fucking lot of you piled together. That's what Bully was telling Gilchrist, that he would never find Maureen. Not in a year. Not in a hundred years. Not now, not ever. And why not?

Because *I'm smarter.*

And because Bully believed he was smarter, he had left clues. Gilchrist was certain of that. If Bully's recitals had not been intended as clues, then what the hell did they mean?

Which brought him full circle.

He fingered the recorder. 'Let's go through it again.'

Jack seemed to have come to terms with the reality of Maureen's disappearance, and had offered to help in any way he could. Trying to decipher Bully's madness was as good a way as any. He cocked his head, hand poised with pencil. Bully's voice whispered at them in its metallic timbre. Jack hit the button, scribbled on his notepad.

'Wee, sleekit, cowerin, timorous beastie,' he said. 'That's the start of 'To a Mouse'. Right?'

'Right.'

He clicked the recorder on, then off again, and scribbled some more. 'Which one's that from?'

"To a Haggis'.'

'The start?'

'Fair fa' your honest sonsie face.'

'What?'

'That's the opening line of 'To a Haggis'.'

'Yeah, well, whatever. Listen, Andy. We'll check it out. If we can't make any sense of it, maybe the clues are in the following lines, or something.'

Gilchrist raised his eyebrows at Jack's train of thought. Why had he not thought of that? Perhaps the clues, if they were indeed clues, were in the number of the verse within the poem. Or in the date the poem was written. Or in the number of words in the verse. Or in any other millions of different ways a nutcase like Bully could screw with your brain. No, he thought, Bully had wanted his body-part clues to be worked out, so that Gilchrist would come to him. He would want to toy with Gilchrist again, so whatever clues he was giving needed to be tricky, not impossible, which had him wondering for the hundredth time if they really were clues—

'And this one?'

'Don't know.'

Another click of the recorder. 'How about this?'

"Tam O'Shanter',' Gilchrist said.

When Jack had all the verses down, he read them out, line after line. Then he handed them over. 'Any clearer?'

Gilchrist felt his lips tighten as he studied the verses. No, God damn it. It was not any clearer. It was less clear. And what if the clues were in the following verses? That would be typical Bully.

Plant the seed. Then grow the wrong crop. But that would be too complicated. And again he felt certain that whatever Bully was trying to tell him had to be in these verses. And with that thought, his gaze settled on *Oh princess, by thy watchtower be*. He mouthed the line, the first verse Bully recited after Gilchrist demanded to know where Maureen was. Was the secret to her disappearance hidden within that single line? He read it again. But again came up with nothing. He shook his head.

'I could search the Internet,' Jack said.

'Please do.'

'Just one thing, Andy.'

'What's that?'

'You don't have a computer.'

Gilchrist blinked. For God's sake. He'd never had a computer at home because he used one at the Office. Damn it. He reached for his mobile phone, punched in the number, and got through in seconds.

'Nance,' he said. 'Where are you?'

'At the other end of this line.'

'I need assistance.'

Serious now. 'Shoot.'

'Can you get onto the Internet and download Robert Burns' poems 'To a Mouse', 'To a Haggis', and 'Tam O'Shanter'.'

'Can I ask why?'

'It's important.'

'I gathered that.'

He caught some rustling in the background. 'And also the poem that contains the verse *Oh princess, by thy watchtower be*. And the one that contains the verse...' He read from the list. '*Inhuman man! Curse on thy barb'rous art.*'

"The Wounded Hare'?'

'What?'

'*Inhuman man!* It's the opening line of 'The Wounded Hare'.'

Wounded hare? Was Bully trying to scare him into believing Maureen was wounded, or physically harmed? 'Does it die?' he asked, and regretted the whisper of desperation in his voice.

But Nance seemed not to have noticed. 'The hare? Not that I remember. More like it was *about* to die.'

Gilchrist felt his breath leave him. That was it. Bully was telling him Maureen was about to die and there was bugger all he could do to prevent it—

'Hang on. Let me look it up.'

'You on the Internet?'

'Yep,' she said. 'Ah, here we are. The second verse is, *Go live poor wand'rer of the wood and field!*'

Go live? Hope swelled for a moment—

'*The bitter little that of life remains.*'

Something slumped deep in the pit of Gilchrist's stomach. There, he had it. The hare will die. So will Maureen. And just as Bully planned, Gilchrist could do nothing to stop it.

'I'm sorry, Andy,' Nance whispered, as if realising why Gilchrist had asked. 'Is it to do with Maureen?'

'Afraid so.'

'We'll find her, Andy. We have to.'

Gilchrist felt the first hint of a smile in days pull his lips, and puzzled at how close he felt to Nance. She seemed to have the ability to put him at ease with barely a murmur. 'Can you read out the entire poem?' he said, 'so I can write it down.'

She did, and when he hung up he read it from start to finish, returning to *Ah, helpless nurslings, who will now provide that life a mother only can bestow?*

He felt his lips tighten, his eyes nip. Would Maureen ever become a mother? Would she ever survive to have children of her own? He read the poem again, but came up with nothing new. Did he have it all wrong? Was there really a clue in the words? Or was Bully just setting him off on the wrong track?

He read it again. Just innocent words. But his sixth sense was stirring.

Bully had been expecting him. Which meant that Bully's scheme of revenge was working to plan. The notes on Chloe's body parts. Sent to Gilchrist. No one else. From which Bully knew that

Gilchrist would work out Maureen was next. But were these lines now Bully's clue for Gilchrist to save Maureen?

They had to be. Why else would Bully have recited them?

So what was he missing? It had to be something obvious. He would stake his life on it. Then he realised he could read these verses until he was blue in the face, and nothing new would come to him. He needed help.

He dialled Nance's number again.

'This is becoming a habit I could enjoy,' she said.

'Do you know if Hammie's still around?' he asked her. 'I need him to decipher some of this stuff.'

'I'm a detective. Not a psychic. Care to explain?'

Gilchrist gave her a quick rundown of his meeting with Bully, asked her to write down the lines Bully had recited, then said, 'Maybe Hammie can make some sense of them. He was one of the best cryptologists I ever worked with.'

'He's now retired,' she said. 'And I believe he's moved from the area. If it's a cryptologist you're looking for, I can contact Hector Wallace in Edinburgh—'

'Let's try Hammie first. I've worked with him before.'

'I'll get back to you.'

'Tonight, Nance. I need it tonight.' He hung up and turned to Jack.

'You look knackered, Andy. Why don't you give it a break? I'm going to think about it over a pint,' he said. 'Like to join me?'

Gilchrist slipped the verses into his pocket and eyed the pile of Maureen's letters on his corner table. 'I'd love to,' he said. 'But I can't.'

'Anything else I can do to help?'

Gilchrist shook his head. 'Have a pint for me.'

With Jack gone, he sifted through Maureen's letters. He had no idea what he was looking for, then realised he had forgotten to collect the rest from Leighton. But even if he had them in front of him there was nothing more he could do. He had only one pair of hands, one pair of eyes. He glanced at his watch. 22:09. In less than two hours, Maureen would have been missing for one more day, and he was no further forward. Dear God. He pressed on with reading her letters, but half an hour later took a break to call Nance.

'Any luck tracking down Hammie?' he asked her.

'He's still in Scotland. Just.'

'Meaning?'

'That he's moved to the Borders.'

'Shit.'

'I've got him working on it, though.'

'How did you manage that?'

'I recited the verses over the phone. That was what you wanted, right?'

'Of course.' It took Gilchrist a full two seconds to realise the folly of his thinking. He'd had it in his mind that he needed to hand-deliver the verses to Hammie. Jack was right. He really was knack-ered. Maybe a few hours kip would have him thinking straight. Nance's voice came at him as if from a distance. 'What's that?' he said.

'I was asking if you've eaten.' He paused long enough for her to say, 'Why don't I nip down to the chippie and bring you out your favourite?'

'It's really no—'

'I'm on my way.' The line went dead.

Gilchrist closed his mobile then reached for the top letter on the next pile.

A note to Tracy. Never heard of her. He eyed the date. Two years ago. Then the address. West End of Glasgow. He fingered others, reading, but not reading, scanning for key words that caught his attention. He felt tired and wondered if he should have gone to the pub with Jack. One pint would not have—

He pulled the letter close, frowned at the addressee's name.

Kevin Topley. Chris Topley's brother?

Then the address. Christ.

He grabbed his mobile, punched in Nance's number. 'Where are you?'

'PM's.'

'Stay there. I'm on my way.'

It was a long shot, but a shot nevertheless. On the way to his car he dialled Dainty's mobile phone. It was answered on the first ring.

'Small speaking.'

'Dainty. It's Andy. Can you get a hostage team together at short notice?'

'Is this to do with Maureen?'

'It is.'

'You know where she is?'

Gilchrist wanted to hold back, say he was not sure, but instead heard his voice say, 'Yes. I do.'

CHAPTER THIRTY

NANCE WAS WAITING for him as he squealed to a stop at PM's fish and chip shop.

She managed to pull the door shut as he floored the pedal. 'I'd like to eat this from the wrapper,' she said. 'Not off the back window.'

'Sorry,' he said, and powered the Roadster down North Street.

'Open wide.' Nance slipped a piece of battered cod into his mouth, did the same with a couple of chips then waited until they cleared the town and were accelerating into the dark tunnel of the country road before saying, 'Care to tell me where we're going?'

'Glenorra.'

'Ah, Glenorra. I've always wanted to go there. You should have told me sooner and I would have packed my bikini.' She popped another piece of fish into his mouth. 'Haven't brought my passport. Is that a problem?'

'Very funny.'

'So, where is Glenorra?'

'The question should be, *what* is Glenorra?'

'Sorry, Andy. But you have me at a disadvantage here.'

'It's Kevin Topley's home address.'

Nance mouthed an *ah-hah*. 'Mr big-shot Chris's brother. That Kevin Topley?'

'The very one.'

'And?'

'And Chloe had a boyfriend called Kevin.'

'The same Kevin?'

'I think so.'

'But you don't know?'

'No.'

'Okay,' said Nance. 'Anything else I should know?'

'Chloe's Kevin's dead. And Dainty confirmed that Chris Topley lost his brother a few years back.'

'Okay,' she said. 'How old was he?'

'Early thirties. From a drug overdose, according to Dainty. Before Chloe met Jack, she had a flat in the south side of Glasgow. Her relationship with Kevin was in the south side also. She frequented pubs there. They both did. That's where Jack met her.'

'In a pub?'

'At a party. But I'm sure drink was involved, if that's what you're implying.'

'Must run in the family.' She slid another piece of fish into his mouth.

Five minutes later Nance scrunched up the wrapping. 'Where can I put this?'

'Not outside.'

'Of course.' She dropped the wrapper on the floor and nudged it into the depths of the footwell with her foot.

'Here.' Gilchrist held out a cloth. 'For your fingers.'

'A gentleman to the end.' She cleaned her hands, held up the cloth. 'Floor, too?'

'What can I tell you?'

Nance dropped the cloth between her legs. 'So, what's so special about Glenorra?'

'It's the place where Maureen said she and Watt should meet. In a letter she wrote to him.'

'So you're telling me we're driving to the late Kevin Topley's house to do...' She faced him. 'What exactly?'

'I think Maureen might be there.' He gripped the steering wheel. 'I can't just sit back and do nothing,' he snapped. 'Talk to me. What am I missing? What the hell do Robert Burns' poems have to do with anything?'

'Are you sure this Bully guy isn't jerking your chain?'

'Therein lies the problem.'

'Do you have Maureen's letter?'

He pulled it from his pocket and handed it to her.

'What's all this?'

'The verses recited by Bully.'

Nance pulled the visor down and switched on the mirror-light. 'This letter's three years old.'

'Correct.'

'Dear Kevin. Thanks for the party. Larry and I really enjoyed ourselves. Who's Larry?'

'One of Maureen's conquests?'

Nance read on. 'It's a thank-you letter.'

'So?'

'The only questions this raises are, has Maureen never heard of thank-you cards? And why would she not write it by hand?'

'She's a wannabe novelist. Maybe sitting at her computer is easier.' He shrugged. 'Maybe she's lost her handwriting skills. I don't know. Does it matter?'

Nance turned her attention to the sheet of verses. 'Does any of this mean anything to you?'

'Just the reference to princess, which was what I called Maureen as a child.'

'And Bully knew that?'

Gilchrist twisted the steering wheel. 'That's what worries me. I don't like it.'

She studied the lines. 'How accurate are these?'

'I taped our meeting. Why?'

'I'm not sure,' she said, and removed a piece of paper from her own pocket. 'I did a search on first lines only, and variations of that first line, thinking that perhaps Bully had got them wrong, maybe forgot the words.'

Gilchrist shook his head. 'Bully thinks he's smart. Smarter than me. Smarter than you. Smarter than all of us. It's a characteristic trait of a psychopath.' He overtook a group of cars indicating to turn left. 'He's playing some kind of game,' he went on. 'Bully was expecting me. It's the first thing he said. *Don't you want to play?* He said that, too. Read it out again,' he ordered. 'The verses about the princess.'

'Oh princess, by thy watchtower be, it is the wished the trysted hour,' she said, then added, 'but do you know what I didn't do?'

'What's that?'

'I didn't do a search on the second lines, only the first.'

'You think it's important?'

'Could be. As far as I could find out Robert Burns never used the word *princess* or *watchtower* in any of his poems.'

Ice chilled Gilchrist's spine. Was this Bully's clue? Had he made up these words and slipped them into a Burns' poem? Princess, for Maureen. And watchtower for...? For what? And a thought struck him. 'What if that line is not from a poem by Burns?' he said.

Nance shook her head. 'The search would have picked it up no matter who wrote it. That line does not appear in anything written by anyone.'

Gilchrist let the logic of Nance's words sift their way through his mind, as a frisson of excitement brushed the nape of his neck. It had to be Bully's clue. Why else would he say these words? But he had recited a number of other verses. Were there more clues in these? Or had Bully just thrown them in as some kind of verbal smokescreen—

'And do you know what else I didn't do?' Nance said. 'I didn't do a search for any of the other lines.'

'Call Jack,' he ordered, 'and tell him to do that, and get him to call back the instant he finds something.' He gripped the steering wheel. 'Maureen's alive,' he whispered. 'She's alive. I know it.'

As he accelerated into the night, he prayed he was right.

And that he would not be too late.

* * *

The cold hurt.

It bit through her skin, wormed deep into her core, dug into the marrow of her bones. She drew her legs into her chest, wrapped her arms around them, tried to stop the shivering. But the air cut through her woollen skirt and top as if she was naked. She had read that the human body could stand low temperatures as long as its core did not drop below a certain level.

But she could not remember what that level was.

Her breath rasped in grunts that hurt. The pain in her chest was greater than the pain in her bruised and bloodied wrists. Her efforts to cut through the duct tape had caused the skin to rub off from the inside of her forearms, leaving deep gashes into raw flesh. She had ignored the pain, just kept driving her arms up and down. But when she did finally manage to rip the tape off, the sight of her torn skin almost had her fainting.

With her arms freed, she ripped the tape from her mouth, then her legs. Only then did she realise the seriousness of her predicament. She thumped the wooden door, appalled by its strength. She fingered the hinges, dark and rough with rust. She eyed the keyhole, but saw nothing in the darkness of her tiny tomb. A small gap at the bottom allowed her to slip her fingers under. But she felt only the dustiness of cold concrete.

She shouted long and hard, then screamed with all her strength until the back of her throat hurt. She thumped the door again and again until she could no longer stand the pain in her fists. She scraped at the stone around the hinges until her fingernails bled.

Then the cold hit her.

Her chamber felt as cold as a morgue. Which was what this stone tomb was about to become. She saw that now. Her stone chamber, her cold prison, her final resting place. Her own personal sarcophagus. Only, no one would pay her a visit.

Because no one would know where she was.

* * *

Gilchrist pulled his Roadster onto the pavement.

From the activity around the house he knew they were too late. A SOCO van, with its door open to reveal an array of equipment, sat on the pavement as if abandoned.

He found Dainty in coveralls, phone pressed to his ear. When he saw Gilchrist, he slapped his phone shut.

They gripped hands in grim silence.

Gilchrist held his breath, waiting for Dainty to tell him Maureen's corpse had been found, that his daughter was dead, that he had been too late to save her.

'Maureen was here,' Dainty said. 'But we're too late.'

Gilchrist felt his breath leave him, the power to stand almost desert him. 'Too late?'

'She's been moved.'

'Moved?'

'We found a shed at the back of the bungalow.'

Gilchrist stepped past, but Dainty gripped his arm.

'It's not pretty, Andy.'

'I need to see.'

Dainty squeezed his lips together as if reaching some difficult decision, then said, 'You have coveralls?'

Gilchrist nodded.

'Put them on.'

The back garden looked like a film set. Dragonlights lit the scene like the stage of some play. An unkempt beech hedge pushed branches over a slabbed pathway overgrown with weeds. Beyond, a light shone from an opened doorway of a building at the bottom of the garden.

Together, they stepped down the pathway to a wooden outhouse as large as a garage. SOCOs shuffled in silence, tagging and bagging. Someone was pouring a milky looking substance onto the ground, making a cast.

'We found a bare footprint,' Dainty said. 'Over there. The grass is covered in shite. We think it's human.'

Gilchrist followed Dainty in silence. His tongue felt hard, his mouth dry, as if he had lost the ability to produce saliva. He stopped on the threshold, gripped the doorframe, held on for support. The stench almost had him backing up.

In the near corner, discarded underwear lay knotted and thick with faecal matter. Close by, a bra, a skirt, a white blouse, dirty and bloodied. But no shoes. Gilchrist ordered his memory to call up an image of Maureen. Was the blouse hers? The skirt, too? But it was useless. He forced himself to analyse the facts as if he was looking at the crime scene of a stranger. He stared at bloodied smears on the floor and walls. Was that Maureen's blood? And he found himself wondering if Maureen had suffered any pain. A chain fetter lay coiled on the floor, next to a stain that had him gritting his teeth. The chain ran up the wall to an iron ring bolted to the wood near waist height.

Dainty's voice snapped him back.

'Through here.'

Gilchrist followed.

He entered another room, not much larger than the one with the metal shackles. The air was thick enough to taste, a cloying stench of fat and meat that stuck to the tongue, a rich fleshy smell that reminded him of the butcher's shop on Market Street. A table as thick as a workbench lined one wall. He narrowed his eyes as he took in the instruments of torture; the circular saw with its twelve-inch blade that Mackie had calculated, three hacksaws, blades dark with blood or rust. The bench was scarred with a history of cuts and scrapes clogged with dried blood. Bits of flesh or skin lay curled on the clatty surface like tiny scraps, and Gilchrist wondered if they would find slivers of fingernails embedded in the sides. Beneath the table, the floorboards lay stained black. Flies stirred from the mess with a noisy rush.

To his side, dull wooden walls were brightened with a display of stapled photographs. The stapler sat on a shelf next to an ash-tray filled with stubs and ash. They should be able to extract DNA from the stubs.

He stepped towards the wall, felt his breath catch.

He stared at the closest image, the one that caught his eye. Chloe's white face. Pale eyes stared at him with the vacant look of the dead. It took Gilchrist a full second to realise that the slime on her lips was sperm. Another to the side. Chloe on the floor, on her back. Naked. Breasts as flat as a child's. *Mons veneris* lined with a pathetic strip of blonde hair that did little to hide the mouth of her vagina.

Around her ankles, Gilchrist recognised the shackles.

He peered closer. Was that the toe of a boot?

Closer still. It was.

'There's two of them,' he said to Dainty.

Dainty pressed in beside him.

Gilchrist pointed at the image. 'Can we get an enhancement on that boot?'

'Can do.'

'What do you think, Nance?' he asked, and saw from her grim look that the worst was yet to come. A glance at Dainty revealed he knew that, too.

Nance glanced to the side.

Gilchrist did likewise, his eyes settling on a collection of no more than six prints, grouped together, and cleaner than the others. Even from where he stood, he recognised Maureen. Her bloodied blouse, the abandoned garment in the adjacent room, reflected the glare of the flashlight. Her bare legs looked thinner than he remembered.

'Don't touch,' Dainty snapped.

Gilchrist had to force himself from ripping the lot from the wall. The photographs could provide clues, could be used as evidence, dusted for prints, analysed for age. But who had taken them? And when? And how long since Maureen had lain chained to the wall?

Gilchrist tried to study the images with professional detachment. He was a DCI with Fife Constabulary, in charge of a murder investigation. The fact that the victim was known to him should be of little significance. It had to be. So that his powers of detection remained uninhibited, his sense of reasoning unimpeded, his—

'I'm sorry, Andy.' It was Dainty.

Gilchrist stared at the images the same way he had stared at the images of a hundred dead bodies before. He felt an odd sense of satisfaction that Maureen had been alive at the time of taking the photographs. But he had seen that red-rimmed look of fear locked in the eyes of too many victims for him to be mistaken. Maureen had known she was going to die.

He felt his lips tighten as he struggled to comprehend the sperm splattered on her forehead, dripping from her chin, creeping into her eyes. He tried to see past that, focus on what any normal detective would. He struggled to reason the facts like an impartial investigator. But it was no use.

He pressed his hand to his mouth, bit down on his knuckles, struggled to fight off the agony. Tears came at him in gasping sobs, and a fire that he had not felt since he had been bullied with a leather strap at the age of twelve rose from somewhere deep within him and emerged in a choked curse. Dainty's hand gripped his shoulder.

He shook it off, thudded from the shed into the cold morning air, past the socos, the flickering camera, the murmuring voices, and strode down the slabbed path.

He was going to have Bully.

He was going to have him with his bare hands.

He was going to tear him limb from limb.

If Maureen's body was served up to him in bits, he would kill Bully.

By Christ, he promised himself that treat.

CHAPTER THIRTY-ONE

IT TOOK THE REALISATION that Glenorra had to be the key to finding Maureen, it *just had to be*, to force Gilchrist back to the crime scene, force him to concentrate on the evidence.

'Our best guess is that she was taken from here within the last twenty-four hours,' Dainty said. 'Her underwear may help determine exactly when. We'll need to run DNA tests.' He eyed Gilchrist. 'Could you give a blood sample?'

'Of course.'

Dainty nodded.

Gilchrist read the pain in Dainty's eyes. He tried to focus on his hardened features and struggled to fight off the images of his daughter, flickering memories that seemed to dance in his mind's eye like some faulty video.

He knew how Dainty was thinking, how he would feel if it was his own daughter's life on the line, how he could ask the unanswerable question. How could any father be asked to carry out his professional duties as if the victim was not related to him? It would be too much for Dainty. Gilchrist saw that.

And he saw, too, that it was too much for himself.

He stepped into a kitchen commandeered by Dainty's investigation team. Muddled voices and the crackle of radio static filled the air. He pushed past the hubbub through an open doorway into the relative quiet of the hall. He forced himself to concentrate, fight his way back into his investigation. If he had any hope of saving Maureen, he had to think.

Think, God damn it. Think.

Topley. Glenorra. Bully.

How were they connected?

Had Chloe visited Glenorra when she dated Kevin Topley? Had she walked along this hallway, stepped into that kitchen? And Maureen, too? She had been at Topley's party. Had she once stood on this same spot, maybe even eyed the same rooms? Had she ever been here with Chris Topley? Gilchrist doubted that. The house had been in a state of disrepair for too many years.

Gilchrist looked around him, at cobwebbed cornicing, at a dusty balustrade that led up a staircase of bare floorboards to an upper hallway that seemed to swim with motes of dust. Once-white wallpaper hung from the stairwell in dried strips, like flaking skin peeled from flesh. Why had the house been allowed to fall into such a state? Who now owned it?

And why here? Why hack Chloe to pieces here? Why keep Maureen chained in the garden shed? Why leave evidence on your own doorstep?

To Gilchrist, it made no sense. If he was going to kill someone, the last place he would do it was somewhere that could be traced back to him. Was Bully trying to make it look as if Chris Topley was involved in Chloe's murder?

Chris Topley had shared a cell with Bully. Gilchrist had established that fact. And Chris Topley had employed Maureen, which Gilchrist still could not get his head around. Chloe had dated Kevin Topley then dumped him for Jack. Was that part of a twisted plot dreamed up by Bully in the stark cells of Barlinnie prison? To set Gilchrist's son up with his cellmate's brother's ex? Then kill her?

It seemed too complex by far. Or was it?

Gilchrist stepped from the hall into a darkened lounge. Heavy floral curtains were still drawn over bay windows. He pulled them apart. Light slid into the room on dusty beams. Another day was dawning. Would he find Maureen alive by the end of this day? Or was she already dead? He clenched his jaw, tried to bury that thought, and peered out the window.

Glenorra stood at the end of a narrow road lined by mature trees. The footpath opposite was edged by a privet hedge, behind which an open field rose into the daybreak gloom. No more than fifty yards to his left, the grey hulk of the only neighbouring house seemed to manifest in the lightening skies.

Who lived there? Had they seen anything? Heard anything?

Outside, nothing stirred.

He faced the room.

The floor was still carpeted. Why had no one lifted it? Was someone expecting to come back and live here? He scanned the room, worked out the positions of removed furniture from the impressions left on the carpet pile.

A three-seater once stood over there, its back to the hall, flanked by two chairs, one by the door, the other close to the corner. Some heavy piece of furniture had lined the back wall, leaving a sharp rut as deep as a cut. A bookcase, perhaps. Light patches on the flocked wallpaper were ghostly reminders of removed pictures. What had these pictures shown?

Upstairs, the same questions worried away at him. Why this house? Why here? Why use the garden shed to hack up a murder victim, and why keep another one captive? But the house stood in a tranquil country setting, so why not?

On the ceiling, in an oversized cupboard off the upper landing, he found the entrance hatch to the attic. He reached up and pulled it down to reveal a sliding ladder. He waggled it to the floor then clambered up the wooden treads.

He stood with his head and shoulders in the confines of the attic. In the darkness the air smelled dry and musty and warmer than the rest of the house. His fingers found a light-switch close to the entrance hatch, but the electricity had been disconnected. He called for a torch. Two minutes later, Nance obliged.

'See anything?' she asked.

'Not yet.'

Gilchrist ran the beam around the attic space. What was he looking for?

From the undisturbed dust around the entrance hatch, he guessed no one had been in the attic for years. The space was small, the angle of the ceiling restrictive to someone his height. Planks of wood ran at right angles across the beams, creating a floored area about ten by ten. Beyond that, rafters ran into the dusty darkness like ship's ribbing.

Two old suitcases lay one on top of the other. From the hollow sound they made when he tapped them, he could tell they contained nothing. He pushed them, just to make sure. They shifted with ease. Four tea-chests lined one edge of the attic flooring. He pulled himself up and over the rim and into the attic.

Nance scrambled in after him. 'Looking for anything in particular?' she asked.

'Just sniffing.' From the top of the chest, he removed an item wrapped in newspaper. He unravelled it to uncover a bone-china teacup. He was not an expert in antiques but had a feeling he was holding something of value. 'Why leave this stuff here?' He shone his torch across the broadsheet. '*The Herald*,' he said. 'January '93.'

Nance dug her hand into the adjacent tea-chest. 'You think the house has been deserted that long?'

'We can have it checked out.' The rest of the tea-chest revealed more crockery, but nothing of any real interest. 'Is this stuff expensive?' he asked Nance.

'You're asking the wrong person. My grannie wanted to leave me her china set and got all upset when I told her I didn't want it. I prefer Mikasa.'

'Whatever.'

'Oh, shit.'

Gilchrist shone the torch at her.

'Is this what I think it is?'

Gilchrist trained the beam on an urn that shone with the sheen of polished copper. Although it had been wrapped in newspaper, he caught the green stain of verdigris around the rim of the base.

'Betsy Cunningham Topley,' he said. 'Born fifth of June, 1912.

Died first December 1997.' He looked at Nance. 'Topley's mother?' The date on the paper in which the urn had been wrapped suggested that the house had been cleared shortly after her passing.

'But why keep her here?' Nance asked.

Gilchrist had no answer for that. His own parents were dead, and their funerals had been carried out in accordance with their wishes. Both had been cremated, and their ashes interred in a small plot in the local cemetery. It sometimes embarrassed Gilchrist to think how seldom he visited.

The attic revealed nothing else of interest. More bone-china, an assortment of leather-bound books, mostly classics, small brass ornaments with the tell-tale curvature of Middle Eastern origin, which had him wondering if Topley Senior had worked overseas.

He left the attic hatch open, the access ladder down, and had Nance notify the crime scene manager. Not that the stuff in the attic was relevant, he supposed.

In the back garden, the SOCOs were still combing the grounds. The dawn light flickered with the staccato flare of the police photographer's flashlight.

'Has anyone interviewed the neighbours?' he asked Dainty.

'Not yet.'

Gilchrist knew he was out of his jurisdiction. But he also had a sense that Dainty was overwhelmed with the mass of evidence being gathered. 'Do you mind if I do?' he asked.

Dainty punched at the pad on his mobile phone. 'Make sure you give me a typed report,' he said, then turned away to make the call.

The street surface was littered with small potholes that glistened black with rainwater. A heavy dew painted the front lawn in a transparent white. He caught movement behind an upper curtain as he and Nance approached the house, a smallholding with roughcast walls in dire need of paint. He glanced at his watch. 6:15. Then at the nameplate on the door. Hutchison. He rang the doorbell.

It took no more than five seconds for the door to crack open. An elderly woman with white hair as wild as candy floss faced them.

A blue housecoat stained from overuse covered a pink nightgown. Worn slippers warmed blue-veined feet as white as porcelain.

'Mrs Hutchison?' Gilchrist asked.

'Yes?'

'We're with the police. May we come in?'

She glanced along the street. 'Is it to do with the Topley's old house?' she asked.

'It is.'

'Well, thank goodness. You'd better come in.'

Gilchrist followed her tiny frame down a dark hall and into a dull kitchen that needed gutted. Cupboard doors hung from hinges long past their sell-by date. Woodchip wallpaper was painted deep yellow, but the alcove above the oven was black with grease. A white lace tablecloth covered a small plastic table in the centre of the room.

'Would you like some tea? I always have a pot brewing.'

'That would be nice,' Nance said.

'Do you live alone?' Gilchrist tried.

'For the last eleven years.'

'I'm sorry to hear that.'

'Cancer done it. That's what took my Tom. Lung cancer. I told him to give up the smoking. But he never listened.' She smiled, an odd crinkling of her lined face. 'It's what I liked most about him,' she went on. 'That he took no one's advice but his own. I wanted to marry an independent sort of man. And Tom was independent if nothing else. Milk, love?'

Nance nodded. Gilchrist did likewise.

She handed Gilchrist a chipped cup with tea like melted Caramac and speckles of soured milk spinning in it like dandruff. He took a polite sip through closed lips, then said, 'Why were you so pleased to invite us in?'

'The old Topley house,' she said. 'Been empty for years, so it has, then all of a sudden it's like Sauchiehall Street.'

'You've seen someone go into it?' Nance asked.

'In and out, in and out. You'd think they'd no home to go to.'

'They?'

'Two of them. Like tinkers. Scruffy they was.' She shivered, as if fending off a cold draft. 'Tom hated tinkers. I remember once we were in Margate for the Fair Fortnight and we had just—'

'Did you call the police?' Gilchrist interrupted.

'Oh, dear, no. I don't like to. I try to mind my own business.'

Gilchrist gave a tight smile. 'Could you describe them?'

'The tinkers?'

'The two people who go in and out.'

'Well, let me see.' She gave Gilchrist's question some thought then shook her head. 'My eyesight isn't what it used to be, you know. I need a new prescription.' She scanned the kitchen with a worried frown. 'Where on earth did I put my glasses?'

'Tall small? Fat thin? Male female?'

'Oh,' she said. 'One was tall and gangly.' She screwed up her face. 'I've never liked that in a man. The other was small. With short legs. Like Tom.'

'Two men?' It was Nance.

'Of course, love.'

'Could you tell us what they were doing?'

'Doing, love?'

'Were they carrying anything?'

'I don't think so. They were just going in and out.'

'In and out?'

'Making a nuisance of themselves.'

'In what way?'

'Slamming car doors. My sight might not be as good as it used to be. But there's nothing wrong with my hearing.'

'And when did all this going in and out take place?'

'Only last week.'

'And before that?'

She shook her head. 'Oh, dear. Not for a while.'

'Did they come by car?' Nance asked.

'Yes, love. A car.'

Gilchrist was sure he was about to waste his breath, but he asked anyway. 'Did you get the number plate? The make of car?'

'Goodness gracious me. No. Tom was the one for the cars. Not me. He always used to say he would buy me a big car so he could drive me to the shops.'

'Can you remember the colour?'

'Shiny. Like metal.'

Gilchrist remembered the silver Jaguar with the paint repair on the boot. 'Silver, perhaps?'

'Yes. I think so.'

'Did it have any scratches or dents? Blotches of paint a different colour?'

'Oh, dear. I couldn't say. I've no idea about that.'

'Did you ever see anyone else with them?'

'I don't think so. No.'

Gilchrist and Nance continued to grill Mrs Hutchison in a gentle round-about fashion, getting nowhere, learning nothing, until Gilchrist asked about Topley Senior.

'He was a strange one.' She twisted her lips as if she had just bitten into the core of a rotten apple.

'Why do you say that?' Nance asked.

'He was just strange. That's why. And a loud drunk. I never did like a man who drank too much. Singing and shouting all those religious songs. But Betsy was nice. I don't think John done her any harm. But I never understood why she went and married him.'

Gilchrist had learned over the years that some of the best information was acquired by listening, not asking. He glanced at Nance, pleased to see she was thinking the same.

Together, they waited.

'I think it was the children that done her in in the end.'

'Done her in?'

'Wore her out.' She shook her head. 'A disappointment to her, they was.'

'What can you tell us about the children?'

'Two boys. But that was two too many, if you ask me. And poor Betsy. She lost their first child, you know. A girl. She died at birth. She's buried in the family plot in Maryhill. Betsy used to place flowers by her grave every year. November the eighth.'

'You have a good memory, Mrs Hutchison.'

'I used to. I remember it well because it was three days after Guy Fawkes.' She smiled. 'Remember remember, the fifth of November.'

'What were the two boys like?'

Her smile evaporated. 'Horrible, they was.'

That would certainly describe Maureen's boss, Gilchrist thought. 'In what way?' he asked.

'Cheeky, cheeky, cheeky. They used to break the heads off my roses. And when they kicked their football into my garden, they would just come in and pick it up. They never once asked permission.' She bit into the apple again. 'Horrible.'

'And what about John, their father? Did you see much of him?'

'No. He died from a heart attack.'

'When would that be?'

'Ten years ago.'

'You remember it, do you?'

'It was the year after Tom. But Tom had been ill for a while.'

'I'm sorry to hear that,' said Gilchrist.

'It was so sad when Betsy passed away.' Her face seemed to fail her then, as if the muscles had died. 'I went to John's funeral. But I didn't go to hers. Never even got a chance to pay my last respects.'

'Why not?' Nance asked.

'They didn't want me to.'

'Who didn't want you to?'

'The boys.'

'Kevin and Chris?'

'Not so much Kevin. But that Chris. Horrible, he was. He swore at me.'

'Why?'

'Called me an old cow. It was terrible what he done.'

'What did he do?'

'Betsy wanted John to be laid to rest in the family plot, you know. The one in Maryhill. But he wouldn't have none of it, that Chris. He had John buried somewhere else. Betsy was in a terrible state about it. But she could never stand up to those boys. And when she died, I couldn't believe it. They had her cremated at Daldowie.'

Tears welled in rheumy eyes. 'Betsy didn't want that. She wanted the family to be laid to rest together.'

Gilchrist decided not to mention the urn in the attic. 'Do you know why he did that?' he asked.

She shook her head, tears close to the surface.

'Where's John buried?'

'In a cemetery in his home town.'

'Where's that?'

'Kirkintilloch.'

Gilchrist had never heard of the place, but made a mental note to check with Dainty. Not that it mattered, he supposed, but he said, 'Do you know which cemetery?'

'I remember it well,' she said. 'The Auld Aisle. I remember thinking it was an appropriate name for a cemetery.' Then she frowned. 'But I never understood why there.'

'I thought you said Kirkintilloch was his home town.'

'But that was years ago. When he was a little boy. Betsy told me. They moved to Milngavie at first, then bought the house up the road. All his family are buried in Maryhill. His mother and father. His brother, too. And little Betty.'

Gilchrist watched reminiscence cross her face then fade to a look of loss. For her own family, or her past, he could not say. He reached inside his jacket, felt his lips tighten as he held out Maureen's photograph. 'Have you ever seen this woman before?'

The old lady looked around her, and without a word Nance walked to the window ledge and picked up a pair of spectacles. 'Are these what you're looking for?'

'Yes, dear. Where on earth did you find them?' She slid them over her ears then peered long-armed at the photograph. 'What a beautiful face,' she said. 'Such lovely eyes. Tom always wanted a girl. It's funny that, don't you think? Tom wanting a girl. Not a boy. Most men want boys.'

'Have you seen her before?' Nance nudged.

She shook her head.

Gilchrist then showed her a photograph of Chloe.

'She reminds me of Aggie.'

'Aggie?'

'My sister. Such lovely eyes. I miss her, you know.'

Gilchrist retrieved the photographs and pushed himself to his feet. 'You've been very helpful, Mrs Hutchison.'

'Stay for another cup of tea,' she said. 'Please?'

'I'm sorry. We really must be going.'

At the door the old lady said, 'My, that was a strange kerfuffle last night.'

'Pardon?'

'Last night. With that car parked outside. I thought he was up to no good.'

'He? Can you describe him?'

'It was too dark, dear. But I think it might have been the tall skinny one.' She bit into the apple again.

Gilchrist's mobile rang, and he excused himself to take the call.

'What time last night?' Nance asked.

'After midnight. When I looked out a little later, the car was gone.'

'Was it the same silver-coloured car?'

'I don't think so. It looked darker. I'm not very good with cars. If Tom was here, he would've been able to tell you.'

'Don't worry,' Nance said. 'And thanks for the tea.'

When she turned she could tell from the look on Gilchrist's face that the last body part had turned up. She ran after him as he jogged towards the Mercedes, and caught up as he jumped into the driver's seat.

'It's Chloe,' he said, and jerked the ignition.

The engine started with a hard roar that had two police constables looking their way. But he did not shift into gear, just sat there, eyes glazed, staring straight ahead.

After thirty seconds of silence, Nance leaned over and switched off the engine.

'What's wrong, Andy?'

Gilchrist looked away. 'I haven't the faintest idea where Maureen is,' he whispered. 'I hear her voice in my head. She's calling out to me. I close my eyes and I see her. But I can't reach her. I can't help her. I feel helpless. Impotent.'

'You said it was Chloe.'

He faced her. 'They found her head.'

'Jesus,' whispered Nance.

'The final word is *vengeance*.'

'So it *is* Bully.'

'Oh, it's Bully all right. Just in case we couldn't work it out he had Maureen sign it.'

'Sign what?'

'A note. Stuffed into Chloe's mouth.'

He covered his face with his hands. His eyes burned. But he refused to cry. He had to be strong. He had to see it through. Not for himself. But for Maureen.

He had to save Maureen.

'The bastard had Maureen sign it. *Mo*,' he gasped.

Then the tears flowed.

CHAPTER THIRTY-TWO

'I'M SORRY, JACK,' Gilchrist said, 'but Chloe's body won't be released until Bert's done.'

Jack stared out the windscreen. He had listened in abject silence as Gilchrist brought him up to date with the investigation. With Chloe's head, the last body part had surfaced, but Gilchrist mentioned nothing of Maureen's note.

Deep in the misery of his own thoughts, he had driven through the back streets of St Andrews. Jack had confirmed that Bully's bastardised line was the opening line of Robert Burns's poem 'Mary Morison'. Instead of, *Oh Mary, at thy window be*, Bully had changed it to, *Oh princess, by thy watchtower be*, which left Gilchrist in no doubt that Bully was responsible for Maureen's disappearance. But neither he nor Jack could come up with any reason for the change from window to watchtower.

He pulled the Roadster off the road and switched off the engine.

'Where's this?' Jack said. 'Some new pub?'

At that angle and with that frown Jack's eyes had an uncanny similarity to Gail's. It surprised Gilchrist that he had never noticed until then. 'You offered to help,' he said.

Jack shrugged. 'Sure.'

Gilchrist opened the door. 'Come on. I'll show you.'

Leighton looked tired. His jowls shivered with irritation. 'It's taken me quite a bit longer than I thought it would,' he grumbled. 'Even with three printers. But I've finished it now.' He lumbered down the hallway and into the front room.

Gilchrist and Jack followed.

Five stacks of printed paper stood on the carpet.

'I had quite a difficult time accessing one of the folders,' Leighton said.

'Which one?'

'Novel Three.'

Gilchrist frowned. 'How many novel folders were there?'

'Four. All of them contained the same sub-folders relating to pages written, research, synopsis, and with each of these sub-folders were a series of sub-sub-folders. Not in every sub-folder, mind you.'

'It sounds complicated,' Jack said.

'Quite. But it was more troublesome than complicated.'

'What was the access problem?' Gilchrist asked.

'I kept receiving some obscure error message. Which made no sense. In the end, I copied the file to a rewriteable CD then accessed it from my F-Drive only. Don't ask.'

'I won't,' said Gilchrist. 'But when you finally accessed it, what was in the folder?'

'I had no time to read the files. As soon as I accessed them, I printed them out.'

Intrigued, Gilchrist eyed the piles. 'Which one gave you all the trouble?'

Leighton showed him.

Gilchrist thanked him, and said, 'Send me the bill.'

That seemed to please Leighton, for he smiled and tugged at his belt.

Gilchrist felt certain that Leighton had read more than he was letting on. But it didn't matter. What did was that he had all of Maureen's files printed out. Maybe he would find something that would give him a clue to her whereabouts.

Driving back to Crail he explained to Jack, 'I'd like you to go through Maureen's stuff. Put a post-it at any that reference Watt,

Glenorra, Topley, and anyone or anything else that you don't understand, or that seems suspicious.'

'I was dreading you asking me to do that,' Jack said.

'You did offer.'

'Yeah, I suppose I did.'

* * *

Gilchrist did not find Maureen alive by the end of that day.

Nor by the end of the next.

Strathclyde's forensic teams confirmed that the discarded clothes belonged to Maureen. Blood, bone and skin tissue recovered from the butcher's bench confirmed that Chloe had been dismembered in the shed. Chris Topley, registered owner of Glenorra, was grilled in person by Dainty for four hours, but denied being within ten miles of the house. Alibis were presented and checked, and Topley walked away as clean as a laundered suit.

Bully was interrogated in Barlinnie by Strathclyde's top negotiators for ten straight hours. They even hinted at the possibility of a deal. *Just tell us what you know, where you've instructed the body to be hidden, and we'll look to get you a pardon.*

But Bully said, 'It couldn't have happened to a nicer bastard. He had it coming,' after which he refused to utter another word. And for ten straight hours, he just sat there and smiled at them.

By the morning of the following day Gilchrist had come to realise that no one was supposed to find Maureen. That was Bully's revenge. It mattered not that he had murdered an entire family of six, including a five-year-old child, in their holiday caravan. Like most psychopaths, Bully had no conscience, moral or ethical, no sense of remorse or compassion, was incapable of understanding his wrongs, took no responsibility for his actions, and therefore could suffer no emotional consequences for his misdeeds.

It was now clear to Gilchrist what Bully had planned.

To frighten him into believing Maureen was about to be served up to him in bits, and that if he acted quickly, solved the clues, then he might be able to ride in on his white stallion and save his princess.

But Gilchrist had not reckoned on Bully's trump card. Bully had never planned to hack Maureen into pieces. No, Bully's plan was much worse. Bully intended to have her kidnapped and killed, then her body buried where it would never be found. For Bully was living in his own private hell, not knowing if he would ever live to see the day he would be freed. And to even the score, the man responsible for locking him away would live out the remainder of his life, never knowing if his daughter was dead or alive, and fearing that she had suffered a death of excruciating pain. The worst possible hell.

Gilchrist thought of interrogating Bully once more. But doing so would let Bully see Gilchrist's pain, and give him another opportunity to taunt him with his secret knowledge of Maureen. So, he decided against it.

Hammie could offer nothing more than Gilchrist already knew. Bully's reference to Burns' words contained nothing mystical. The message was clear for all to see in Bully's bastardised line.

Oh princess, by thy watchtower be.

According to Hammie, Bully was telling Gilchrist he knew where Maureen was, and even if you tried to torture the truth out of him, his lips would be sealed until the day he died. And the use of the poem 'Mary Morison' was significant as it was generally understood that the Mary Morison in Burns' poem was Alison Begbie whom Burns dated when he was in his early twenties, but who refused to marry him. The significance being that where Burns had failed in his quest for a wife, so too would Gilchrist fail in his search for his daughter.

The other verses were simply smokescreen.

Gilchrist had a different opinion. He remained convinced that Bully had given him a clue, was playing a game, strong in his own misguided belief that he was much smarter than everyone else, including Gilchrist. And if Gilchrist was right, Bully's ego would be his downfall. That was the flaw in Bully's plan.

So, he went to see Chris Topley again.

Nance came with him.

Topley entered the conference room in a suit that looked like silver shards of herring-bone. It glittered like foil when he walked by the window and stood on the opposite side of an oval light-wood desk. He gave Gilchrist a gold-toothed smile. 'Nice one,' he said.

'Nice what?'

'Leather jacket. It suits you.'

'Wish I could say the same about your suit,' Nance said.

Topley smiled at her. 'Want me to throw you out now? Or fuck you later?'

'Try throwing me out now.'

Topley widened his gold smile. 'Maybe we'll just fuck later.'

'You wouldn't get past Go.'

Topley lowered his eyes and stared at Nance's crotch.

'Now we've got the foreplay out of the way,' Gilchrist said, 'I'd like to ask a few more questions.'

Topley lifted his prurient gaze. 'I don't feel like answering any questions today.'

'Like us to arrest you instead?'

'I'd be interested to hear the charge.'

'Attempted rape.' Nance again.

'Do what?'

Nance stepped forward. She stood a couple of inches taller than Topley. 'Believe me,' she snarled, 'my story will stick. If DCI Gilchrist hadn't arrived in the nick of time and pulled you off me, I do believe you might have scored.'

'You wouldn't fucking dare.'

'You'd better fucking believe it. Now answer the nice man's questions, or you're going back to your cage in the Bar-L zoo.'

'Maybe I should call my solicitor.'

'That's your prerogative,' Gilchrist said. 'But we can be out of here in a few minutes, or we can take the long road. Your choice.'

'I'm clean. Let's have it. Anything to get rid of you lot,' Topley sneered.

'You shared a cell with Bully Reid,' Gilchrist said.

'So?'

'For how long?'

'About a year.'

'I heard eighteen months.'

'If you know the answer, why ask the question?'

'To make sure you're telling no lies.' Gilchrist caught a flush of anger wash across the hard face. 'What did you and Bully talk about?'

'Are you joking or what? How the fuck would I remember what we talked about?"

'Try.'

'It was a while ago.'

Gilchrist moved closer to the table. 'Did Bully ever mention my name?'

'Don't fucking flatter yourself.'

'Did he ever mention my daughter's name?'

'No.'

'Don't lie to me. I don't like it.'

Topley narrowed his eyes. 'He never mentioned your daughter's name.'

'Did he mention any woman's name?'

'Sure he did. But I can't remember them all.'

'But you remember he didn't mention Maureen.'

'That's right.'

'How did Maureen get a job with your company?'

'Replied to an ad. The same way every other bit of skirt gets a job here.'

'I thought some of them had a horizontal interview,' Nance chipped in.

Topley chuckled, his eyes flashing. 'Want to apply?'

'Maureen's a compulsive saver,' Gilchrist pressed on. 'She's kept every bit of paper she's ever read, every letter she's ever received, written, or just thought of. And that includes job advertisements.' He was lying now, just winging it, but sometimes you have to push. 'We never found an ad for your firm in her papers. So, I'll ask you for the last time. How did she get the job?'

'Word of mouth.'

'Whose mouth?'

'Now you really are pushing the boat out.'

'Do you know something?' Nance said. 'I'm hoping you don't answer the question, because I can't wait to face you in court.'

Topley glared at Gilchrist. 'Ronnie Watt,' he said.

Ronnie Watt? The name stung like a slap to the face. Gilchrist struggled to keep his tone level. 'What did Ronnie say exactly?'

Topley smirked. 'Said he was going out with a tidy bit of stuff, right classy looking, tight tits with nipples out to here, the kind punters love to rub their cocks over. Nice legs, too. And a muff so fine you could floss your teeth with it.'

Gilchrist ignored the taunt. 'And?'

'And she'd do anything to get a job.'

'So you hired her.'

'After the interview.' Topley flashed some gold at Nance. 'If you get my meaning.'

'When was this?'

'About a year ago.'

'By which time you'd been out of prison, what, a year, give or take a month or two?'

'Yeah.'

'Keep in contact with Bully, do you?'

'What for?'

'That's why I'm asking.'

'No.'

'Spoken to him since?'

'No.'

'Written to him?'

'No.'

'Contacted him in any way?'

'No.'

'Not even one visit, one letter, one call, to let Bully know you'd hired Detective Chief Inspector Gilchrist's daughter?'

Topley turned to face the window, placed his hands behind his back, revealing a swallow tattooed on the inside of his left wrist. 'You're fucking fishing.'

'I take it that's a *Yes*.'

Topley faced Gilchrist again. 'N – O.' He etched the air with a pointed finger. 'In huge big baby letters.'

'What about Bully's brother?'

'What about him?'

'Talk to him?'

'Jimmy's a nutter. Bad for business. Know what I'm saying?' He hooked both thumbs under the lapel of his suit and hitched it up.

'So who's your go-between?' Gilchrist asked.

'Do what?'

'Your go-between,' Nance chipped in. 'You know? The idiot who runs between you and Bully.'

'Like I said, you're fishing.'

'How about Glenorra?' Nance asked.

Topley's eyes narrowed. An arm searched for the back of his chair and rested against it in an air of casual indifference. But he would never pass an audition.

'We know you own it.' Gilchrist again. 'So be careful how you answer the question.'

'What question?'

'Was it ever Kevin's?' Gilchrist asked.

'We used to have a half-share each.'

'After your mother died?'

'Yeah.'

'Then what?'

'Kevin died.'

'And left Glenorra to you?'

'Yeah.'

'So it's all yours?'

'You deaf or what?'

'And the hut at the back?' Nance said.

'What about it?'

'You own that, too, do you?'

'Yeah.' A bit unsure.

'When were you last at Glenorra?'

'What the fuck's going on? I've explained all of this to that tiny little fucker—'

'Just answer the lady's question, will you. There's a good boy.'

A sniff. A tightening of his grip on the back of the chair. 'About a year ago.'

'Never been back since?'

'No.'

'You still got a key to the hut?'

Topley shrugged. 'Could do. It's been a while.'

'Ever get another one cut?'

'What for?'

'Ever lend it to anyone?'

'Like I said, what for?'

'Why don't you let us ask the questions?'

Topley shifted his shoulders. 'I never got a key cut and I never lent one out. That fucking good enough for you?'

Gilchrist smiled. 'Book him,' he said to Nance.

'Here. Hold on a fucking minute. Book me for what?'

'Accessory to murder.'

'Do what?'

'You heard.'

'You can't just come in here and fucking—'

'Oh yes I can sonny Jim, oh yes I can.' Gilchrist leaned across the conference table, glared hard into Topley's tight eyes with a hatred that worried him. How much more of this could he take before he flipped? How many more lies could he listen to before he took the law into his own hands?

He pulled back. 'Book him,' he said again.

Nance stepped forward.

'She warned me about you, she did,' Topley complained. 'Said you were a right evil fucker.'

Gilchrist almost pushed Nance back on her heels, moved so close to Topley that he could see minuscule beads of sweat on the flattened nose. It would be so easy to wrap his fingers around his short neck and press his thumbs into the windpipe. '*Evil?*' he growled. 'You don't know the meaning of the word. You're nothing but a crook pretending to be straight.'

Topley's eyes blazed. A chair bumped against the table.

'*Andy.*'

Gilchrist blinked, once, twice, as Topley's face twisted into an ugly grimace.

But Topley's hatred could never light a flame next to his own.

CHAPTER THIRTY-THREE

WEAK NOW.

Too weak to sit.

She rolled over and her head cracked against the concrete floor. But she felt no pain.

She felt nothing. The pain had disappeared. The cold, too.

She fought off the urge to close her eyes, but the lids fell, and she felt her body wallow in the slow motion of the moment, as if she was lying in a warm bed, or a hammock on the beach, the Caribbean, St Maarten, where she and Larry spent a whole week, a lifetime ago. She was there again, and she smiled, turned her face to the sun, felt its rays on her face, her lips, tried to move her tongue over them. But it felt too thick, too heavy. Too dry.

Thirsty. So thirsty.

But it's late now. Time to go to bed.

To sleep. Close my eyes and just...

...sleep.

So tired...

Just want to lay my head on the pillow, pull the sheets over my warm skin, and fall asleep. Overhead, the ceiling fan swirls. Even with my eyes closed, I can see it.

Turning and turning. But it makes no sound.

It seems not to stir the air.

So tired...

* * *

'I really must object, Inspector. My client has rights—'

'And my daughter has rights, too. She has the right to marry, the right to be a wife, a mother, have children, the right to live her life and grow old.' Gilchrist slammed a clenched fist onto the table, splashing water from a polystyrene cup. He glared across the grey desk at Topley's narrowing eyes. 'And so help me to God I'll have it out of you before the end of the day.'

Jerry Foster looked as if his black pin-striped suit was about to burst open. He wiped a thick-fingered hand over his lips. 'That's all very well, Inspector, but my client has repeatedly said that he knows nothing of your daughter's disappearance.'

'Your client's *lying*.'

Foster turned to Topley. 'Are you lying?'

'On my mother's grave.'

Foster looked at Gilchrist. 'On his mother's grave.'

'His mother doesn't have a grave.'

Foster's forehead creased into fatty folds.

Gilchrist said, 'Her ashes are in an urn—'

'You've been snooping—'

'—in the attic.'

'I beg your pardon,' Foster blurted.

'Ask him.'

'I don't think that's anything to do—'

'Your client's lying. Now ask him.'

'As I said—'

'*Ask him*.' Gilchrist pulled himself upright, surprised to find he had almost crossed the desk.

Foster pushed his chair back with pudgy fingers. Sweat glistened on his balled face. 'I don't intend to have my client sit through—'

Gilchrist slapped the desk, leaned forward so his face was inches from Topley's. 'Why did you have your mother cremated?' he shouted. 'Why not have her buried with her husband? Why not grant an old lady her dying wish?'

Topley grinned.

Gilchrist stood. 'I'm having a coffee.' He glared at Foster. 'And when I come back I expect your client to be more forthcoming.'

Foster fingered the knot in his tie.

At the coffee machine Gilchrist felt something touch his elbow. He turned. 'What?'

Nance tried a weak smile. 'I've never seen you like this before, Andy.'

'I've never had a daughter missing before.'

'Go easy. Will you?'

'Milk and sugar?'

Nance strutted off, her legs as stiff as a mannequin's.

Gilchrist sipped his coffee. Too hot, too bitter. He felt the start of a headache and wondered if it was all too much for him. Was Nance right? Was he behaving in a manner unbefitting a DCI? But how the hell was he supposed to behave when that bastard smiled and whispered in his solicitor's ear? And Dainty had taken some persuading before agreeing to provide him an interview room. And Greaves, too, he had blown a fuse. Why all the fuss about jurisdiction and protocol? Could no one see the connection? In despair, he patted his pockets for his cigarettes, and held back a curse. Jesus. Habits were hard to beat. Habits were things that made men behave like boys. Habits could—

Not habits. *Agreements.*

Silent compliance? Between Topley and Bully?

Was that it? Had Topley been compliant? Had he agreed to do as Bully asked, so he could score a few more Brownie points for his hero?

The possibility seemed that simple he wondered why he had not thought of it sooner. Dainty had told him of Topley's early life with Bully, of how he had to prove his worth by fighting for him. Topley had been one of the tougher kids, a teenager who thought nothing of slicing off an opponent's ear so he could drop it at his master's feet, a token of his worthiness.

And of Bully, Gilchrist knew about his parents, a father who ran away from a beaten life and a beaten wife, leaving her to raise eight children on her own. Six girls and two baby boys. Bully and Jimmy. What little money she mustered came from doing turns in tenement closes. But take the money first, always the money first.

And once she had the money, it didn't matter what they did to her. It was mostly over in a few minutes. She groomed her daughters for prostitution so that when Maggie, the oldest, reached twelve, money started to come in. Not flood in, mind you, but having enough food to put on the table was no longer a worry. Bully was only seven when Maggie and two other sisters ran off to London. He never saw or heard from them again, and that seemed to be the start of Bully's hatred of all things feminine.

Had Bully's misogyny rubbed off on Topley?

Bully had been serving time when his mother passed away, and turned down a day on the outside to attend her funeral, a cremation at Daldowie. Which struck Gilchrist. Daldowie was the same crematorium where Topley had his mother cremated against her wishes.

Was that the connection? A crematorium? And why Daldowie?

The closest crematorium to Glenorra was Maryhill. Not Daldowie. If the city of Glasgow was a circle, Daldowie was more or less diametrically opposite Maryhill, south-east versus north-west. So why would Topley have his mother cremated in Daldowie?

Because Bully told him to?

In Bully's world, he was considered a leader. Everyone else was a follower – sheep herded to the cliff edge and ordered to jump. Or rob. Or murder.

Bully the leader, the man of words, the poet.

Oh princess, by thy watchtower be.

And it came to Gilchrist with a clarity that stunned him, how they had all ignored the one word that told them *where*, how he had not thought of it until now.

How could he have been so stupid?

He threw his coffee away and stepped inside.

He asked a young sergeant at the front desk to check out something for him as a matter of urgency, and the instant, the absolute *instant* he had the result, to let him know.

'I'll be in Interview Room Two. Just say yes or no.'

Gilchrist almost exploded into the room.

Topley stiffened, mouth frozen in the act of a whisper to Foster.

Gilchrist stepped past Nance, swept around the desk, and hauled Topley to his feet.

Foster pushed his chair back. 'This is—'

'*Shut up.*'

The chair hit the floor with a hard clatter.

'I have to warn you that—'

'And I'm warning you,' Gilchrist turned on Foster, 'that if you are in any way responsible for letting this piece of shite keep information from me that could save my daughter's life then I'll hold you personally responsible.'

'You can't do—'

'Do you have children?'

Foster's lips tightened. His throat bobbled.

Gilchrist secured his grip on Topley's suit lapels, pulled the man's muscled bulk up and over so the tips of their noses almost touched. Topley's arms dangled by his side, as if to tell Gilchrist that he knew he would not dare hit him. How wrong could he be?

'Why is your father buried in the Auld Aisle Cemetery?' Gilchrist hissed.

'Buried where?'

'You heard. The Auld Aisle Cemetery. Why?'

'Why not?'

'The rest of his family's not buried there.'

'So?'

'So why only him?' Gilchrist felt Topley shrug, a tight shuffling of shoulder muscles that had Gilchrist toying with the idea of throwing him to the floor. 'Did Bully tell you to do that?'

'Bully?'

'Yeah. Bully. You know, the guy who pulls the strings of puppets like you.'

'Fuck you.'

'Oh I'm just about to fuck *you* don't you worry about that.' He thrust Topley back onto his seat, turned to Foster. 'I'm upping the charges.'

'On what grounds?'

'For pissing me off sort of grounds. Okay?'

'This is outrageous. I'll be filing a complaint—'

'File what the hell you like.'

Foster's bloated face paled. Drooping jowls shivered. Sweat glistened on swollen lips like beads of water.

Gilchrist faced Topley. 'I'm charging you, Christopher Topley, as an accessory in the murder of Maureen Gillian Gilchrist—'

'This is preposterous, utterly outrageous, a violation of my client's rights.' Foster's colour had returned along with his power of speech. Anger danced like madness in button eyes. 'Murder? What murder? Maureen Gilchrist isn't...' He halted then, like a hunter realising he was about to set off his own baited trap.

'Maureen Gilchrist isn't dead?' Gilchrist said. 'Is that what you wanted to say? She isn't dead?' He could feel his eyes blaze. 'You forgot to add, *Yet.*'

Foster looked all of a sudden as if law was something he no longer wanted to practise.

'You're a loopy one, that's for sure,' Topley quipped.

'Loopy or not. You're going to jail.' Gilchrist leaned down, fought off the almost overpowering urge to head-butt the man. That close he could almost smell the fear. Topley's silvery suit looked out of place, as if he'd turned up at the wrong fancy-dress party. 'And d'you know what Bully's going to do to you when you get back inside?'

Topley's eyes flickered.

That got your attention, thought Gilchrist.

'Me and Bully are mates.'

'You think so?'

'Yeah.'

'I thought you hadn't spoken to him in a year.'

'Yeah, well, mates is mates.'

'Bully's not well. He's ill.'

'Says who?'

'Says me. I saw him.'

'Yeah, I heard.'

Gilchrist pushed back. He had him. He felt cheered by Topley's slip up. 'You heard?' he said. 'Thought you didn't keep in touch.'

'Yeah, well, someone in the pub told me.'

'Got that, Nance?' Gilchrist shouted over his shoulder. 'Someone in the pub told him.' He eyed Topley. 'Which pub?'

'Can't remember.'

'Which someone?'

'Can't remember.'

Gilchrist looked at Nance and nodded to the door. She frowned and stepped from the room, leaving the three of them. Topley ran his hand across his top lip, and Gilchrist leaned closer, almost kissed a scarred ear. 'Just you and me,' he whispered.

Topley frowned, but said nothing as Gilchrist walked away and stood with his back to the far wall, arms crossed.

It took Topley several slow seconds to turn to his solicitor. 'Beat it, Jer.'

'I beg your pardon.'

'Go on. Skedaddle.'

'I must advise against—'

'And don't bill me for your fucking time, you useless twat. It's a fucking crime what you lot charge. We're through. Got that?'

Foster slid his papers into an opened briefcase, spilling them off the desk. His bag snapped shut with a metallic click. He eased his bulk upright, lumbered splay-footed to the door, and squeezed himself from the room.

Topley pushed his seat back, stretched his arms behind his neck. 'Fucking wanker.'

Gilchrist sat down, eyed the micro-cassette recorder that lay between them on the desk, and clicked it off. 'Ready?' he asked.

'You expect me to trust you?'

Gilchrist hoped Topley would detect the sincerity in his whispered words. 'I only want to find my daughter.'

'What if I don't trust you?'

'It's your choice. But I can help you.'

Topley pressed his elbows on the desk. 'Or?'

'Or it's back inside.' Gilchrist lowered his voice to that of a co-conspirator. 'And believe me, I'll trump up the charges so much that you'll make Peter Manuel look like a virgin choirboy.' He smiled. 'Ready?'

CHAPTER THIRTY-FOUR

IS THIS WHAT DEATH is like?

No sound. No feeling. No movement.

Just stillness. Like dreaming. Like floating on air.

Across the stone floor, the wall is tilted at an angle that seems to defy gravity. I try to sit up, move my neck, and I think the wall moves. It is no more than two feet from me, and I reach out to it, to touch its roughened surface.

But my arm won't move. Why won't it move?

I try to twiddle my fingers but feel nothing.

Not even the pull of my lips as I smile.

I have died. I am already dead. That is why I feel nothing, hear nothing, can move nothing. Because I am dead.

Something escapes my lips, an indecipherable sound that I have difficulty placing until I recognise it as my own voice, weak and pleading. A sob.

Not dead. But alive.

And cold. It's so cold. So cold again. Freezing.

I pull my legs up, lock my knees against my chest.

So cold. Why is it so cold?

* * *

'Bully's got it in for you,' Topley said to Gilchrist.

'Tell me something I don't know.'

'He hates you so much, he's forgotten why.'

'Tell me what he said about Maureen.'

Topley pushed back, levelled his head, stared hard into Gilchrist's eyes. 'I don't know a thing about that. And that's the truth.'

Gilchrist felt a nip in his gut. Did he have it wrong? 'What about Ronnie Watt?' he asked. 'Did he ever talk to you about Bully?'

'Not a chance.'

Gilchrist was not sure he believed that answer. But for the time being it would have to do. 'How do you know Ronnie?'

'Does a bit of stuff for us.'

'Us?'

'My company.'

'What kind of stuff?'

'Stuff stuff.'

Now where had he heard that before? 'Did you know Watt's with Strathclyde Drug Squad?'

Topley's eyebrows raised. 'You're joking. Right?'

Gilchrist eyed Topley. Ham actor of the century. Maybe even the universe. 'Why did Bully want your father buried in the Auld Aisle?'

'Who says he did?'

'Me.'

Topley paused, as if deciding whether or not to continue lying, then shook his head. 'I don't know.'

Gilchrist laid his hands on the metal table. 'You're pulling my plonker.'

'I don't know, I'm telling you. I don't know why the fuck he wanted the old man buried there. All right?'

'But you did as he asked.'

'Yeah.'

'Why?'

'What the fuck's that supposed to mean?'

'He was *your* old man. Why let Bully become involved?'

'Why not?'

Gilchrist moved closer. 'You scared of Bully?'

Topley twisted his neck, as if stretching tight muscles. 'I can look after myself.'

'That's not what I asked.'

Topley sniffed, wiped the back of his hand under his nose. 'No.'

'Why did you not tell Bully to bugger off?'

'What the fuck did I care? I mean, the old man's stiff as a parrot. What the fuck difference does it make? He's gone. Out of it. Food for the worms.'

'It made a difference to your mother.'

'Fuck me. What the fuck is this? You'll be pulling the old violin out any minute.'

'She cared.'

'Yeah, well, she's gone where she doesn't need to care any more.'

'Ashes in the attic?'

Topley looked off to the side, as if trying to avoid Gilchrist's eyes. But Gilchrist was having none of it. He narrowed the gap, fingered the micro-cassette recorder.

'Did Bully tell you *not* to bury her beside your father?'

'Fuck you.'

'Did you ever ask yourself why?'

Topley's flattened nose flared with anger.

Gilchrist sat back. He was missing something. He was certain of it. But what, he was not sure. Did it matter that Bully had ordered Topley to bury his father in some cemetery far from the family plot? And then not bury his mother there? Why would Bully do that? Or was Gilchrist just toddling up the wrong track, beating around the wrong bush? He could not say. All he knew was that his sixth sense was telling him to keep pounding, keep thudding his head against the door, and it would eventually crack open. But he also knew from the heavy-lidded look in Topley's eyes that some impasse had been reached. According to Mrs Hutchison it had been ten years, but Gilchrist was interested in hearing how Topley would answer.

'When did your father die?' he asked.

'Fuck sake. How would I know? It was years ago.'

'Twenty?'

'Not as long as that.'

'Ten?'

'Yeah. About that. How the fuck would I know?'

'Were you in Barlinnie when he died?'

'Fuck you. No. I had a good job back then.'

'I thought you liked your father.'

'A bad tempered drunk, is what the old fucker was.'

'Ever hit you?'

'That'd be the fucking day.'

'How about Kevin? Your father hit him?'

'Kevin would have nailed him to the door.'

Gilchrist frowned. Nothing seemed to fit. He had met Jack's girlfriend, and what had struck him about Chloe was her sensitivity, her artist's gentleness, her philosophy that life was to be lived and all God's creatures had that right, too. He remembered her straining to open a window to let a fly escape, and telling him that cats were the cruellest animals on earth, responsible for the decline in the bird population. Yet Kevin Topley had been her boyfriend before Jack. It seemed improbable. But there was Maureen, too, his daughter, an employee of the likes of Topley. What the hell was the world coming to? Or more to the point, what the hell was he missing?

The door opened.

Gilchrist spun round.

The detective almost backed off. 'Sorry, sir. You did tell me to let you know.'

'Well?'

'Yes. Sir.'

Gilchrist succeeded in maintaining his composure in front of Topley. 'Thank you,' he said, and watched the door close. He almost pushed his chair back and stood, but he wanted to ask Topley one more question. He leaned forward. 'When was the last time you visited your father?'

'You're fucking loopy. You know that?'

'When was the last time you visited his grave?'

Topley shrugged.

'You've never visited it. Have you?'

Topley almost smiled. 'Like I said. He's dead as a parrot. What's the fucking point?'

Gilchrist felt a flush of disappointment course through him. Would anyone visit his own grave after he was dead? Had he made any impact on the world, left anything of any significance behind him? At those thoughts, the futility of it all seemed insurmountable. The world was filled with villains much worse than Topley, individuals who tortured, murdered, without pity or compassion of any kind, the cruellest of human beings who took everything and gave nothing. And after trying to extract bits of information from Topley, Gilchrist now felt like a dog that had been scraping for a meatless bone in the wrong hole.

'You're free to go,' he whispered.

'I didn't know I'd been arrested.'

'Don't push it.' Gilchrist pushed his hand through his hair. His fingers tined the thinning spot at the back of his crown. He clenched his teeth at the memory of Maureen teasing him about his balding patch. *Don't worry, Dad. I'll still love you when you're bald.* Dear God, what would he give to hear her say those words again?

He waited until the sound of Topley's footfalls faded down the hall before he stepped from the room. 'Do you know how to get to Kirkintilloch?' he asked Nance.

'Not yet.'

'Could you do something else for me when you're at it?'

'What's that?'

'Get on to the Auld Aisle and find the exact location of John Topley's grave.'

* * *

Gilchrist pulled his Roadster through the old gateway of the Auld Aisle Cemetery. The cemetery's watchtower stood at the edge of the oldest part of the cemetery. Beyond the wall, rusting cages huddled over gravesites with tilted headstones weathered smooth.

Gilchrist stopped at the foot of the stone stairwell and jumped out. A chill wind swept in from the north. He upped the collar of his leather jacket. From behind, high in the bared branches of a towering oak, a colony of crows watched his movement with black-eyed disinterest. He walked to the foot of the watchtower's staircase, the stone of each tread curved from age. How many shoes had marched up that short flight? What had it been like for these guards to carry out round the clock shifts to protect the dead? He had once read an article that dispelled the truth about the efficiency of watchtower guards. They were often bought, and grave-robbing had not declined, but been carried out with more care.

He eyed the abandoned structure.

The base of the watchtower had an arched passage through it, the entrance to the original cemetery. Was this where he would find Maureen?

'Andy?'

Nance reached out and touched his hand. Her skin felt soft and warm.

She glanced up at the watchtower. 'Let me do this.'

Gilchrist almost nodded, then grabbed the walled stairwell. The stone felt cold on his fingers, but he found he could not rush, instead took the steps one at a time, his heart heavy with the prospect of what he dreaded he would find when he reached the top.

His breath puffed in the cold wind.

He reached the top step and faced the door.

It looked hard, worn, convict-proof, designed no doubt to protect the watchtower guards from the unlikely onslaught of overeager grave-robbers. He resisted the urge to call out her name, instead pressed the side of his head against the wind-dried surface.

He heard nothing.

He gripped the rusted door handle, gave a hard tug.

Locked.

He slapped his hand against the wood, afraid to call out in case she could not answer. He slapped again, thudded the heel of his hand against the door. Nothing. He heeled the door again. 'Anyone?' he shouted.

He gave a start when Nance joined him.

'Stand back.' She leaned her upper torso back, kicked out with the heel of her foot.

The door rattled.

She kicked again.

On the fourth kick, the wood by the lock splintered.

Gilchrist stepped forward, gripped the handle, thudded his shoulder to the door, once, twice. Then the lock gave out with a sharp crack, and he stumbled into the dark interior.

Empty.

Nance stepped in, a tight silhouette against the back-light from the opened door.

Oh princess, by thy watchtower be.

Gilchrist ran his hand through his hair. He pirouetted in the stone chamber, saw nothing but bare walls and boarded over window openings, then stepped back outside.

Bully had him beaten. It had all been a hoax—

'*Andy.*'

But he was already out the empty watchtower and tearing down the steps. He ran around the base like a demented lunatic, slapping his hands against the cold stone, hoping, praying he would find some secret door, some window, some opening that would validate his desperate theory that Bully had Maureen interred in some long-forgotten chamber.

But the watchtower had no such opening.

He pressed the flats of his hands to the cold stone walls and hung his head. It took him several seconds to realise Nance was not with him. He saw movement from the corner of his eye, down by the gate to the cemetery extension, and caught up with her as she strode along a gravel path lined both sides by worn memorials. Headstones, darkened with age, spilled down the cemetery slopes to the Bothlyn Burn.

He tugged at her elbow.

'Go back to the car,' she said.

'I need to see for myself.'

'We don't know for certain, Andy.'

'No,' he whispered. It was all he could hope for.

Nance handed him a folded sheet of paper. He took it, tried to read the directions, but found his mind blank, his sense of logic numbed. Silent, he strode beside her, let her show him the way.

They found John Topley's grave in the newest part of the cemetery, an area that seemed brightened by shiny headstones of glossy grey and bituminous black, footed by wreaths that sprinkled the grass with pinks, reds, yellows, whites, like the leftovers from some garden party.

Topley's grave was marked by a flat black headstone with an empty pewter flower-holder at its head. Shorn grass grew as tough as reeds around it. Gilchrist read the chiselled epitaph.

Gone, but not forgotten.

How meaningless words could be.

At the base of the memorial, he noticed slices in the turf where the grass had been lifted and relaid. He checked the chiselled words once more. John Topley had died at the age of sixty-two, ten years earlier, yet the turf that fronted his headstone had only recently been relaid.

He scrubbed the sole of his shoe against the adjacent memorial, scraped off a crust of caked mud that had hardened on the black marble, and saw that the turf must have lain against that headstone when it was lifted.

Gilchrist now knew there was no hope.

He pulled out his mobile phone. 'Dainty,' he said. 'I need authorisation to exhume a coffin.' He listened to Dainty fire meaningless questions at him, then heard his own voice say, 'I think we might have found her.'

CHAPTER THIRTY-FIVE

IT TOOK LESS THAN two hours to uncover the coffin. As Gilchrist had expected, it was not buried deep. Bully's men would have had little time in the space of a single night to bury it, and a shallow grave at least ensured it was out of sight. But the fact it was a coffin at all puzzled Gilchrist.

Why would Bully go to that bother, or expense? Why not wrap Maureen's body in plastic sheeting, the same sheeting in which Chloe's left leg had been wrapped? It made no sense to him. Or maybe it did.

Would lugging a coffin into a graveyard in the middle of the night raise less suspicion? Or maybe they used a hearse. Or maybe Bully had known not to trust his men, that they would not follow his instructions to the letter and might bury the body in a grave shallow enough for some feral dog to dig up. A coffin would at least offer the cadaver some protection.

But Gilchrist's rationale was confused, muddled. Something did not fit. The finish on the coffin looked scratched and worn, as if it had been in the ground for years, rather than days. One of the SOCOs unscrewed the brass holders and prepared to open the lid. Gilchrist glanced at Nance and caught the glitter of tears in the late afternoon sun.

Gloved hands gripped the coffin lid.

Gilchrist stopped breathing.

The lid was lifted and placed on the grass.

'Fucking hell.'

'What's this then?'

'*Don't touch.*'

Dainty stepped forward, head bowed, as if defeated, and Gilchrist saw from Nance's glance and furrowed brow that she was as puzzled as Dainty. The others, too.

'There must be millions here,' Dainty gasped. 'Bloody hell. A fucking fortune is what it is.'

Gilchrist looked into the opened coffin, at tight bundles packed like icing sugar wrapped in clear polythene, the same material as that around the left leg, he would bet, crammed into the confines of a coffin stripped of silk and padding to make more room.

Dainty scratched his head. 'I think our Mr Topley's got a lot of answering to do. Wouldn't you say?'

Gilchrist should have been relieved that Maureen's body was not in the coffin, but it surprised him to feel a sense of disappointment course through him. If Maureen had been buried there, then he had found her, could have tried to live with the horror of it all. But now she was still out there, somewhere, tied up, dead, buried, hacked to pieces, or God only knew what, her body planted for him to find, or not find, at Bully's dictate.

He now saw why Topley's mother's ashes were in the attic. The coffin was used for the temporary storage of drugs. How long had it been going on? It had to have started after John Topley's death, but before Betsy's, which was why Bully had instructed Topley not to bury his mother here. The gravediggers would have unearthed an unrecorded coffin, and Bully's hidey-hole would be lost, along with his millions in drugs.

Gilchrist held out his hand. 'Gloves.'

The nearest SOCO offered him a pair.

Gilchrist pulled them on and leaned into the coffin. He gripped one bundle by the corner and eased it out. He set it to the side, then did the same with two others. But he knew Bully would not have risked contaminating the consignment by storing it with Maureen's body. Six packets later he knew he was right. He slipped off the gloves.

'What do you think?' Dainty asked.

'When does Bully get out of Barlinnie?'

'Two, three years, give or take six months or so. Why?'

'He must have known,' Gilchrist said.

'Known what?'

'That he would be prime suspect in Maureen's death.'

'Come on, Andy, the guy's behind bars—'

'So what—'

'He's in a top security prison—'

'I know it's him—'

'You can't prove a—'

'I *will*,' Gilchrist snarled. 'Believe me, I will.'

'You'll have a tough time.' Dainty's eyes flared for a moment, then saddened, like those of a doctor to a dying patient. 'His brief's Rory Ingles.'

'And who is Rory Ingles?'

'Solicitor to the mob. And the likes of Bully.'

'So?'

'So he's never lost a case.'

'And he costs a ton of money.' Gilchrist glanced at the coffin. Three socos were dusting it for prints, but he knew they were wasting their time. 'There's Bully's legal nest-egg for the next thirty years.'

Dainty breathed out with a rush. 'So this is nothing to do with Topley, is what you're telling me.' His voice sounded calm as if tempering surprise.

'It's Bully's—'

'Give it up, Andy,' Dainty snapped. 'You've got Bully on the bloody brain.' His mobile phone rang at that moment, and he seemed relieved to turn away.

Gilchrist struggled with a surge of anger that had his face flushing. He turned, almost bumped into Nance.

'I don't know what to tell you,' she said.

Gilchrist ignored her and walked onto an asphalt path that led to the older part of the cemetery. Bully could not have anticipated the discovery of his cache. That was a huge plus in Gilchrist's favour. Or was it? Once Bully found out, he would go berserk. Then how could he ever force Bully to confess to what he had done with

Maureen? They had almost caught them at Glenorra. But Bully had been one step ahead.

Why?

Why had Maureen been moved?

Maybe that was the question he should be asking.

Not *where* had she been moved to? But *why* had she been moved?

Why that night? Why not two nights ago? Or three? Why that specific night?

Because by Gilchrist arranging to interview Bully in Barlinnie, Bully would have known he was getting close, that he was putting all the cryptic clues together. And Gilchrist saw then the reason for the cryptic clues. Not to lead to Maureen, but to ensure that Gilchrist would suspect Bully and arrange to meet him. So that Bully could gloat.

Was that it? Was Bully only a red herring?

Were the answers with Bully's brother, Jimmy, who had not been seen for two weeks? Was Maureen's body moved the same night Wee Kenny was murdered? Was Jimmy already living it up in Spain, soaking up the sun, setting up the villa for Bully's release in three years, maybe less, with Rory Ingles, solicitor for the rich and infamous?

Jesus Christ. There is the law. And then there is justice.

And never the twain shall meet.

Gilchrist opened his copy of Bully's lyrics. He read that line again. He knew Bully. He had spent almost twelve months trying to bomb-proof the case against him for murder. He had come to know the man as well as he would his own brother, his history as well as he knew his own. So what was he missing?

Oh princess, by thy watchtower be.

Gilchrist crumpled the paper into the ball of his fist, his mind playing that single line over and over.

Oh princess, by thy watchtower be.

He eyed Topley's grave. The SOCOs were loading bags of drugs into their van. Off to the side, some forty feet from the others, Nance was standing by a headstone.

He walked towards her.

She surprised him by saying, 'Joe Reid. Bully's father's grave.'

Gilchrist almost smiled. Nance was showing a side that pleased him. She was willing to take the initiative, and in the process of locating John Topley's grave, had found Bully's father's, too. He read the inscription.

The honest man, though e'er sae poor
Is king o' men for a' that.

Gilchrist recognised the words from Burns's poem 'A Man's a Man for A' That', and marvelled once more at how meaningless words could be. Whoever ordered that inscription could not have known Bully's father. But again, he puzzled over the reference to Burns.

'What's Bully's attraction to all things Burns?' he asked Nance.

'Maybe it was drummed into him school?'

'Did he go to school?' Gilchrist lifted his head. From that location, beyond the wall of the oldest part of the cemetery, he could just make out the spire of the watchtower.

His mobile rang. He flipped it open, started walking towards the tower.

'Hey, Andy.'

Gilchrist could tell from the tone of Jack's voice that he was upset. Was the grim reality of Chloe's death and Maureen's disappearance only now hitting him?

'What's up?' he asked.

'It's Maureen.'

Gilchrist's throat seemed to clamp. 'I'm listening,' he whispered.

'I went through the print-outs like you told me to, and I found something. I tried to check it out before I called, just in case I'd got it wrong. But I got nowhere.'

'Back up, Jack. You're losing me.'

'It's her job, Andy.'

'With the Topley Company?'

'The Topley Company's just eyewash.'

'Are you saying she's employed by someone else?'

'Exactly.'

'Who?'

'The police.'

Something thudded into Gilchrist's chest.

'I mean, who would've believed it? There's no contract or anything. Just two letters, the first confirming she would be available for employment, the second confirming the terms of their verbal agreement.'

Verbal agreement? 'Who are the letters addressed to?'

'DI Ronald Watt. You know him?'

Detective Inspector. Watt had lied to Maureen about his position, probably lied to her about the job, and in the end put her life in danger.

'It says here it was hand delivered,' Jack added.

How else? Watt would not have wanted any correspondence mailed to his office. That would have blown his scheme. Which was why her flat had been broken into, to destroy all evidence of their connection.

Gilchrist stared at the sky. In as noncommittal a tone as he could muster, he asked, 'Which Division was she working for?'

'Strathclyde. And get this. The Drug Squad.'

Gilchrist stopped walking. He turned to look at Topley's grave, at the plastic bags that were piling up in the SOCO van. All of a sudden, a whole new line of reasoning opened up. 'Don't let anyone else see these letters, Jack. You got that?'

'I hear you.'

Gilchrist obtained Topley's number through Directory Enquiries and was kept waiting almost ten minutes. By the time Topley picked up, Gilchrist was ready to crush his balls with his bare hands.

'Who was Maureen working for?' he growled.

'Mr Gilchrist. Nice to hear from you—'

'*Who?*'

'If that lovely daughter of yours doesn't show her tits around here any time soon, she won't be working for me any longer. Know what I'm saying?'

'Did you know she worked for Watt?'

'Can't say that I did.'

Although the words were spoken with conviction, Gilchrist thought he caught the tiniest of hesitations in the delivery. Was Topley surprised by the question? Or lying? Gilchrist decided to go for it. 'In about thirty seconds,' he said, 'Bully's going to be told you grassed on him to the Drug Squad.'

'That supposed to scare me, or what?'

Gilchrist eyed the socos. The plastic bags were stacking higher. Just how much cocaine did a coffin hold? 'This afternoon,' he said, 'we found about thirty million pounds worth of cocaine. All wrapped up in neat little bundles.'

'Who's a lucky Detective Inspector then?'

'We found it buried in your old man's grave.'

A pause, then, 'I know fuck all about that.'

'But you know Maureen worked with Watt.'

'No chance. I swear. On my mother's grave.'

Gilchrist could almost hear Topley sweating. 'How do I contact Watt?'

'You're asking the wrong bloke. Try calling Strathclyde HQ.'

'So you knew Watt's with the police?'

Another pause. Another lie on its way?

'You lot are a dead giveaway.'

'And you know where he is?'

'Like I told you—'

'Don't lie to me,' Gilchrist snapped. He felt his heart thump in his chest. He struggled to regain composure. 'Why don't you just tell me how *you* contact him?' He listened to the digital ether fill the line, and an image of Topley trying to manufacture his next lie manifested in his mind.

'He'll know it's come from me,' Topley said.

Gilchrist crushed the phone against his ear. Did Topley really know how to reach Watt? 'Your choice,' Gilchrist said. 'Bully or Watt. I really don't care.'

'Look. If I tell you, you've got to help me.'

'Keep talking.'

'We have a deal?'

'You're in no position to bargain,' Gilchrist said. 'Just cough it out, and I'll see what I can do.'

It took so long for Topley to answer, that Gilchrist thought he had lost the connection. When Topley's voice came back at him, it growled low and guttural, letting him know there could be no compromise. 'You didn't hear this from me. All right?'

'All right.'

A pause, then, 'He drinks in the Dreel Tavern.'

Gilchrist knew the east coast. 'Anstruther?'

'Most nights between nine and ten.'

'Who does he meet? I need a name.'

'I don't know. I swear. I asked once. I did. But Watt trusts no one. He's a fucking psycho. You know what he's like.'

Gilchrist almost nodded. *Fucking psycho* was an apt description. 'I don't believe you.'

'Believe what the fuck you like.'

'How's about I believe that if I offer you up to Bully he's going to have you at his leisure?'

'We had a deal.'

'No name, no deal.'

'Fuck you, Gilchrist.'

'No,' he snarled. 'Fuck Watt. I need a name.' Silence filled the line. Gilchrist pressed on. 'Give me a name, and it'll go no further. You have my word.'

It took a full ten seconds before Topley said, 'Bootsie.'

'Come again?'

'Real name's Joe Cobbler. Everyone calls him Bootsie.'

Bootsie. Joe Cobbler. Joe. The same Joe who stole Peggy Linnet's phone?

'Got an address?' Gilchrist said.

Surprisingly, Topley had.

CHAPTER THIRTY-SIX

IT IS NIGHT AGAIN.

How many nights is that now?

I've lost count. But I can tell by the coldness. It is so bitter I no longer shiver. I think my body is turning to ice. I can no longer feel my feet. My fingers are stiff. My eyes are heavy. But I am afraid to close them in case I will never wake up. I have to stay awake.

For one more day.

It is getting darker now. Around me it seems to be clouding over. Like dark fog taking over my sight.

I have to hold on. For one more day.

Just one. Then one more.

But I'm so weak, so tired, I don't know how many more days I can hold on. How many more minutes.

I don't know. I don't know...

...how long...

...I can...

...hold...

* * *

Gilchrist almost didn't recognise Watt. He had lost weight, and his sunken face displayed stubble that had not yet reached the curled stage. Another week and he would have a full beard.

He waited until Watt wrapped his fingers around his pint before he joined him.

'Mine's an Eighty.'

Give Watt his due, he never so much as flinched. 'An Eighty over here,' he nodded to the barman. 'Pubs in St Andrews shut, are they?'

'You tricked Maureen,' Gilchrist growled. 'You tricked her into thinking she was working undercover for the police.'

Watt shook his head. 'Where do you get off?'

'Oh I'm staying on to the bitter end you'd better believe it.'

Although Gilchrist had not raised his voice, Watt picked up on the change in mood. He took a sip of his beer. 'If you must know,' he said, 'Maureen approached me and begged me to hire her.'

The word *begged* did not conjure up an image of Maureen in Gilchrist's mind. He slapped a hand onto Watt's forearm with a force that splashed beer over the wooden bar top and stopped the barman from pulling his pint. 'She's missing,' he hissed. 'And you know who's behind it. You've known all along. But made no attempt to stop it. Why?'

Watt scowled at Gilchrist's hand until he released his grip. 'Crap like that can get a lad like you hurt.'

'Are you denying it?'

'What do *you* think?'

Bootsie or Watt? One of them was lying. But who?

Gilchrist searched his mind for some other way to crack Watt's façade. 'Bootsie isn't coming tonight,' he tried.

'Who?'

'The Bootsie you used to phone first thing in the morning and last thing at night.' He waited. '*That* Bootsie.'

Watt took another sip of beer. 'Fifty quid says you never had a warrant to pull my mobile phone records.'

Gilchrist realised his attempts to call the number on Watt's records had succeeded only in scaring Watt off. 'You knew someone was onto you,' he said, 'but you couldn't risk hanging around to find out who it was. So you did a runner.'

Watt smiled.

'But life goes on, so instead of calling Bootsie morning noon and night you meet him here.'

'If you say so.'

'Bootsie says so.'

Watt sipped his beer like a lonely man.

'And Bootsie also says you've been sniffing around the east coast waiting for some drug shipment from Europe. That's why you finagled a reassignment to Fife. To keep your finger on the pulse. Putting you back with me was Greaves' idea of giving you grief.'

'In his dreams.'

'But there is no drug shipment.'

Watt's eyes seemed to dull over then, and he shifted his stance so that he faced Gilchrist. 'Says Bootsie? Bootsie knows the square root of fuck all.'

'This didn't come from Bootsie.'

Watt narrowed his eyes. 'You always were a right cocky bastard.'

Gilchrist struggled to hide his anxiety. Watt was giving off the wrong signals. Did he have it wrong? He had spent thirty minutes interrogating Bootsie, having to cut it short to catch Watt before he left the Dreel. Had Bootsie told him a rat's nest of lies just to get rid of him? Nance was still interrogating Bootsie, trying to squeeze what she could from him, and Gilchrist found himself wishing she was with him at the Dreel, helping him pierce a way through Watt's deception.

Gilchrist shook his head. 'It took me a while to piece the bits together,' he said. 'Maureen, Topley, Bully, Jimmy, you. Bit of a Chinese puzzle, really. It was the drug shipment that helped me work it out.'

'And here was me thinking you were good at puzzles.'

Despite himself, Gilchrist felt his lips tighten. He had still not worked out the puzzle of where Maureen was. Bootsie had not been able to help them either. The speed with which Bootsie had broken down had surprised Gilchrist, as if the man had just been waiting for any excuse to let it flow. Which had Gilchrist thinking something must have happened in Bootsie's life. But what, he had no idea.

'How's this for a puzzle?' he said to Watt. 'How about I charge you as an accessory to murder?'

Watt smiled. He really smiled. And Gilchrist struggled to keep from launching himself at the man. 'The Lone fucking Ranger,' Watt growled. 'That's you. You always get your man.' He chewed imaginary gum, and something in the glint in his eye told Gilchrist the worst was yet to come. 'That's why Maureen hated you.' Watt's teeth flashed a victorious grin. 'The most successful Detective Chief Inspector in the history of Fife Constabulary, but an abject failure as a father.'

Something cold washed over Gilchrist then, as if Watt's words were spoken through a cloud of ice that chilled him to the bone. He found himself looking away.

He knew he had failed. Failed as a father, failed as a husband. Perhaps if he had been there for his children they would not have left him to live with their mother, without so much as a backward glance, a wave, a smile. In his mind's eye he watched the door open, the empty hallway appear before him, and a slump-shouldered figure step inside, into a new life, all alone.

But Maureen *hated* him?

Gilchrist almost shook his head. *Hate* was too strong a word. No, it was *Watt* who hated him. And with that thought he saw it was time to turn the screws.

'Bootsie's ready to tell all,' he said.

'Fuck Bootsie. One wrong word from him and I'll put him away for life.'

'Funny. That's what Bootsie said about you.'

Watt's jaw ruminated, and Gilchrist knew his words had hit home at last. Then Watt picked up his pint, downed it, and turned from the bar.

Gilchrist grabbed his arm. 'Don't even think about it,' he said. 'Bootsie's safe and sound. Leave now and the next time you see him will be from behind bars. Not his. *Yours.*'

Watt tugged his arm free.

Gilchrist could almost see Watt's mind working, trying to figure out what Gilchrist had over him. But in reality, he had little to fear. Gilchrist needed Watt to fill the gaps in his puzzle. He could not let Watt leave. Not just yet.

He turned to the bartender. 'Same again,' and waited until a glass was shoved under the tap before he said, 'Talk to me, Ronnie. Will you? For Maureen's sake.'

Gilchrist thought he understood Watt's dilemma. Some part of him liked Maureen, but nothing could ever come of their relationship because of the past. And behind Gilchrist's back Watt had tried to resurrect their affair by tricking Maureen into working for him. Now she was missing and might never be found, Watt could deny it, talk his way out of it, lie himself clear. But Gilchrist suspected Watt was up to his neck in unofficial police work, straddling the fine line between working inside or outside the law.

It would probably not take much to put him away.

And Watt knew that.

'If Maureen dies,' Gilchrist whispered, 'I'll make it my life's mission to make sure you never see this side of a prison wall as long as you live. You got that?'

Watt held Gilchrist's gaze for several long seconds.

Then nodded.

CHAPTER THIRTY-SEVEN

'DO YOU KNOW WHERE SHE IS?' Gilchrist asked, and watched the sad shadow of truth shift behind Watt's eyes.

'I don't think even Bootsie knows.'

Gilchrist felt his jaw clench. Nance had asked Bootsie the same question and been given the same answer. 'Who does?' he tried.

Watt took a sip of his fresh pint. 'That body they found?'

'What about it?'

'Bootsie says it's Wee Kenny.'

Gilchrist remembered Dainty mentioning Wee Kenny, but he frowned, hoping to give Watt the impression that the name meant nothing to him. Sometimes the way to get answers was not to ask questions.

'Bootsie used to live in Glasgow,' Watt went on. 'Left to start a new life. But some losers never change.'

'Bootsie moved,' Gilchrist added. 'But kept in contact with old friends. Is that it?'

'And with Bootsie gone, the job was vacant.'

'What job?'

'Jimmy Reid's gofer.'

The connection. Jimmy Reid. Bully's brother.

Watt rested his elbow on the bar, shifted his body so that he faced Gilchrist. 'What's this about there being no drug shipment?'

The question threw Gilchrist, but he was not ready to give anything out. 'Why the east coast?' he asked.

'A hunch.'

'You're beginning to sound like me.'

'The famous Gilchrist sixth sense?' Watt shook his head. 'Just putting two and two together.'

Gilchrist waited.

'Jimmy's ill,' Watt continued.

'Flu? Cold?'

'Cancer.'

Gilchrist felt a flush warm his face. His mind leapt to Gail, and he had to blink, once, twice, three times, to clear the image. 'Terminal?' he asked.

'Word is he's got less than six months.'

'So he'll be dead and buried by the time Bully's out.'

Watt nodded. 'All his life he's lived in Bully's shadow. Even with Bully inside Jimmy still played second fiddle. But he can't wait for Bully to come out. It'll be too late by then. Jimmy wants to reap the benefits of a life of crime before he dies.' Watt took a sip of beer. 'He'd been coming up this way several times a week. I figured he was getting ready to handle one final shipment.'

Now it made some sense. Watt had been working under the assumption that Jimmy's visits to St Andrews were solely for setting up that final shipment. Being in the Drug Squad, Watt knew about Bully and Jimmy's drug supply business. But he had it wrong. The final shipment had already arrived, hidden in a coffin in the Auld Aisle cemetery where it would remain until either Bully got out of Barlinnie, or Jimmy shifted it before he died. 'And you added two and two,' Gilchrist said. *And got five,* he thought.

'I had a hunch.'

'What hunch?'

'Jimmy had Kenny's Jag re-sprayed.'

An image of a rust-coloured boot lid seared Gilchrist's mind. But cars got re-sprayed, sold, or just disappeared. If Jimmy had been so afraid of his Jaguar having been seen at the stop-and-search in Cupar he could have sold it, lost it, or done any number of things with it. But it was found burned to a shell. 'Meaning?' he asked Watt.

'Meaning, why would he do that when he's shutting down the family business?'

Gilchrist frowned. When he put Bully behind bars eight years ago, he had dug into the Reid family business. Drug supply and extortion in the back streets of darkest Glasgow. The business was small-time, west-side only, until Bully took it into his mind to go on a killing spree. 'You sure about that?' he asked Watt.

'No doubt about it. Bully's out in two, maybe less. Rumour has it his feet won't hit the streets of Glasgow. Jimmy's made three trips to the Spanish mainland this year alone.'

Gilchrist clenched his jaw. Why had he not known that? 'Setting up his retirement villa?' he asked. 'For him and Bully?' Watt nodded, sipped his beer. Gilchrist had never liked Watt, had hated him for the best part of eight years, but found himself warming to him in a professional way. Gilchrist worked from his own hunches. Watt was doing the same. But too many pieces were still missing.

According to Bootsie he had told Watt when and where each body part was going to turn up, thus alerting Watt to Jimmy Reid's visits to St Andrews so he could keep his eye on him. What Gilchrist could not rationalise was the fact that Watt had known Jimmy Reid was involved in Chloe's murder, but had turned a blind eye to it for greater personal rewards, such as the discovery of the drug shipment.

'How did Bootsie know when Jimmy was going to make a trip to St Andrews?'

'Wee Kenny.'

Gilchrist frowned. 'Jimmy's gofer was grassing on him?'

'Without realising it. Wee Kenny told Bootsie that Jimmy was about to hit pay dirt. Big time. And Bully's putting it about in the Bar-L that he's getting out and going to retire to Spain a wealthy man. I've been keeping my eye on Jimmy for some time. He's a right bad bastard. Some say he's even worse than Bully.'

Gilchrist nodded. It was beginning to make sense. With Jimmy dying from cancer, the key was the next six months. For Bully to get even with Gilchrist, what better way than to have Jimmy take care of it while he was still in prison? What did it matter to Jimmy if he killed a few more? But where was Jimmy at that moment? In Spain? Hiding in Scotland? Waiting for the final shipment to come in?

'You still haven't told me why you think there's no drug shipment,' Watt said.

Gilchrist decided to tell him. 'We found it.'

Watt stilled, then his eyes creased. 'You're a joker all right. I'll give you that.'

'No joke.' Gilchrist puzzled at the look of distress that passed like a shadow over Watt's face. 'It never was at sea,' he added.

Watt's jaw froze in mid-chew. 'Where?'

'The Auld Aisle Cemetery. Where Bully's old man's buried. Topley's, too.'

'You found it?'

Gilchrist almost failed to hide his surprise. Had Watt known about the shallow grave, about the coffin filled with cellophane-packed drugs? 'All thirty million of it,' he said.

Watt stared at him for several silent seconds, then placed his glass on the bartop with practiced calm. Then he faced Gilchrist. 'Two years,' he hissed. 'Two years we've had our eye on that.'

'On what?'

'Don't fuck around with me, Andy. Two years. Do you understand what I'm saying? Two years of watching and waiting for the right moment.'

For once Gilchrist's sense of logic left him. 'What're you telling me?'

'You don't get it, do you?'

Gilchrist almost shook his head. No, he didn't.

'The drug shipment was never *coming* from Europe. It was *going* to Europe.'

Now Gilchrist understood. John Topley's grave in the Auld Aisle Cemetery was being used as a holding spot.

'For the last two years I've been monitoring the European connection.' The muscles on Watt's jaw rippled across his face like a wave. 'Two years flushed down the toilet,' he growled, 'all because of you and your fucking daughter.'

Gilchrist hit him then, a straight fingered punch to the solar plexus that had Watt gritting his teeth and gasping for breath. He caught the bartender's alarmed look, but Nance stepped to the bar behind Watt and held up her warrant card. Gilchrist had failed to notice her entrance, and wondered for one confusing moment what she had done with Bootsie.

'Mine's a pint of Eighty,' she ordered.

The barman seemed relieved to oblige.

Watt straightened himself, tried to act as if nothing was hurting. But from the grey sheen around his eyes, Gilchrist knew he was struggling. He pressed on. 'So, with Jimmy's visits to St Andrews you thought the shipment was about to be moved.'

Watt nodded. 'Through Topley's company.'

Part of a larger holding group. Some international company with too much money.

'And you had Maureen spy on Topley and report back to you with all the details.'

Watt almost smiled.

'Damn you to hell,' Gilchrist growled. 'You put Maureen's life at risk, you pompous prick. And all for what?' He paused, stunned by the strength of his voice and an anger that choked his throat and threatened to take his breath away. For sixpence, he could rip Watt's heart from his chest with his bare hands. 'Did you not think of telling her the danger she was in?' he went on. 'Did you not think of anything other than your own egotistical needs?'

Watt turned on Gilchrist. 'I tried,' he shouted. 'I tried to get her out. But she was having none of it.'

'Oh, no,' Gilchrist snapped. 'You're not getting off as easily as that.'

'She refused to meet with me. She didn't want to talk to me, didn't want to see me. What the hell could I do? I ended up pleading with her on the phone.'

'When?'

'About a week ago.'

The sixteen minute call to Maureen's home number. 'And?'

'She said she thought something was about to break.'

'Damn it, Ronnie. You should have got her away from Topley.'

'You still don't get it.' Watt's eyes burned. 'It was Maureen who terminated our arrangement. Told me to fuck off. In about as many words.' He shook his head. 'I tried to warn her. But you know what's she's like. She wouldn't listen.'

Gilchrist knew there was more than a hint of truth to what Watt was saying. At times, Maureen could be like her mother. Stubborn beyond reason.

Watt tried a laugh, but coughed instead. 'She wanted to write crime novels.' He shook his head. 'Wanted firsthand experience of scenes of crime and police procedures.'

Jesus. All Maureen had to do was ask her father. Could she not have done that? Was he so far out of her life that she couldn't even ask him for help? He forced his mind to keep on track, keep the pressure on Watt. 'But you still needed someone on the inside,' he said. 'So, you let her walk into the lion's den.'

'She jumped at it.'

'Didn't she know about Topley's criminal background?'

'She's a bit like you,' Watt said. 'It didn't take her long to work it out.'

'But she never worked you out, did she?'

Watt tried a smile, but his lips seemed not to work. He took another sip of beer then pushed it away and covered his eyes, digging and grinding with his fingers and thumb as if trying to obliterate some visual memory.

It took Gilchrist a full ten seconds to realise Watt was struggling to hold back his tears. He glanced at Nance. She looked as puzzled. He gave Watt a moment of silence before saying, 'What am I missing, Ronnie?'

Watt came to, stared at his pint. 'The hours were long. Which was part of the cover. No one would notice her working late at the office, digging up shit on the guy.' He shook his head, lifted his beer. 'I thought she was safe.'

Gilchrist waited.

'She was good at it,' he said. 'Oh she was a charmer all right.

A great actress. You know that? She had them all fooled. Topley never knew a thing. Not a fucking thing.'

'Well somebody did,' Gilchrist said.

His words seemed to stop Watt's thought process. Or perhaps deepen it. Watt's eyes focused on the glass. Thick fingers rubbed the surface as if cleaning a part that reminded him of his own muddied thoughts.

'I loved your daughter,' he said.

Gilchrist caught the past tense.

Watt shook his head. 'I'll always wonder,' he went on, 'if I could have done something more to prevent her being killed.'

CHAPTER THIRTY-EIGHT

GILCHRIST GRABBED WATT'S ARM. 'What do you mean?'

'Maureen's gone, Andy. Bully's closing shop, tying up loose ends. No one's ever going to find her body. *Ever*.' He tugged his arm free and turned to his glass. 'She's gone, Andy. I'm sorry,' he whispered.

Gilchrist thought he kept his emotions in check, but was not sure. His stomach burned as if the beer was acid. Something flashed in his mind's eye, an image of Watt's bloodied face, Maureen's tortured grimace, her lips pulling back in a silent curse. She hated him then, at that instant, at the moment of his discovery, at their being caught. Had she died with those thoughts?

He pushed away from Watt and stepped from the bar.

'Andy.'

Nance's voice came at him from a distance. Fingers gripped his arm, tight as talons. He looked down, then up, then off to a picture on the wall, the window. Darkness outside. Another night. One more night without Maureen. Was she dead? Was Maureen really dead?

The hand tugged. 'Andy.' Fingers on his chin, turning his face.

'She's gone, Nance,' he whispered.

'You can't be sure.' Her eyes fired up. 'You can't give up, Andy. Not now.'

'No,' he said. 'I've lost her.' The sound of his own voice seemed to puzzle him. Was it as simple as that? Had he lost her? Or had she let him go? But he loved Maureen. He loved his daughter. But daughters fell out with their fathers, held grudges for days, weeks, months, could even hate their fathers.

Had Maureen hated *her* father?

How could she? When he sat her on his knee and pretended they were on a runaway horse together, he remembered how she had giggled and squealed and wrapped her arms around his neck. How could she hate him?

'Come on, Andy. Sit down.'

His arm tugged. His feet lifted.

The bench seat thudded hard against his back.

The wooden table glistened with spillage, the ashtray grey with burned dust. He pulled out his wallet. 'Here,' he said, 'get me a whisky. A large one.'

'You need rest,' Nance said to him.

'What for, Nance? What the hell for?' He struggled to his feet. Hard hands pulled him down. He slumped back onto the bench seat.

'Look at you,' she said. 'You're dead on your feet.'

Dead on your feet. The irony of it brought a grin to his face. You had to be alive to be dead on your feet. 'Good one, Nance. Good one.'

She frowned again, as if not understanding. But what was there not to understand? Maureen was dead. And he had let it happen. Right under his nose, he had let it happen. He had ignored the warning signs, the notes, the cryptic clues, the crystal clear messages from Bully. Jesus, how could he—

'*Andy.*' She tugged his sleeve. 'Look at me.'

He eyed her.

'Don't listen to a word Watt says. He knows nothing, Andy. Nothing. Do you hear? Bootsie doesn't trust him.'

'Where's Bootsie now?'

'In hiding.'

'I know that. But where?'

Nance glanced at Watt as if to make sure he was out of earshot, then said, 'It doesn't matter, Andy.'

Gilchrist stared at her. He could tell from the fire in her eyes that she no longer trusted him. Is that how it all begins? A little bit of distrust? A bit more, until all of a sudden the ground opens up and hell swallows you whole?

Trust? Who knew what the fuck trust was any more.

He stood, the move so sudden that Nance gaped up at him.

He gave a twisted smirk. 'I'm having a drink.'

'Getting drunk's not the answer, Andy.'

'D'you know what, Nance?'

She looked at him, and he saw uncertainty flicker in her eyes. She had never seen him this unhinged before. He knew that. And he was scaring her. If he wasn't so fucked up he would be scaring himself.

'I'm not looking for any more answers,' he said. 'I've had it up to here with answers. I'm through with being lied to every minute of every day. So do you know what I'm going to do?' But his question was not meant to be answered. 'I'm going to get drunk. That's what I'm going to do. If it's all right with you, of course.'

Nance lowered her eyes as he brushed past her.

He reached the bar and opened his wallet. He fingered a twenty, was about to remove it when it struck him what Nance had said. Had he misheard? Had he misunderstood?

He returned to the corner and leaned down to her, so close that his lips were almost kissing her right ear. 'Bootsie doesn't trust Watt?' he said.

Without looking at him, Nance smiled.

'What's Bootsie holding back?'

'Topley's mother.'

'What about her?'

'And Wee Kenny's mother.'

'Yes?'

'Were sisters.'

Gilchrist slumped into the bench seat and stared at her. For the life of him he could not figure it out. 'And?'

'Which makes them cousins.'

Gilchrist frowned. Maybe Nance was correct. Maybe he really was dead on his feet. 'I'm listening.'

'And family,' Nance added.

Gilchrist narrowed his eyes. *Family. Now* he thought he understood. He placed his hands flat on the table. 'And Topley knows Wee Kenny's dead?'

Nance nodded.

'But he doesn't know how or who?'

'He knows how. He suspects who.'

Now he had it. 'Jimmy Reid.'

Nance smiled.

'Which means..?' Gilchrist held Nance's dancing eyes.

'Any allegiance Topley had with Jimmy and Bully,' she said, 'has just gone out the window.'

'A new turf war?'

'And then some.'

Gilchrist smiled, but only for a moment. Something was missing. 'When did Topley find out it was Jimmy?' he asked.

'Oh...' Nance glanced at her watch. '...I'd say about ten minutes ago.'

* * *

Despite the tiredness and the alcohol Gilchrist felt wide awake. As he gunned the Merc through the night, his mind sparked questions at him like a crazed crackerjack.

Who would launder a coffin-load of drugs?

Chris Topley, perhaps? Cleaner of all things dirty, with his above-board Topley Company, shuffling money through offshore banks, business ventures, legal acquisitions, not to mention his own personal cut.

Why bury the drugs in Topley's grave? Why not hide them in Bully's father's grave?

Because if the drug cache was ever found, it would be a simple case for Bully to deny all knowledge. And a difficult case for anyone to prove otherwise. Topley would be blamed. Was he not the first person Dainty pointed to when the coffin was uncovered?

And will Bully be freed in two years?

Maybe even earlier. He's up for parole in three months. With his shit-hot solicitor, Bully could be walking the beaches of Spain by the end of the year.

Had Jimmy killed on Bully's orders? Would he do that?

You bet he would.

Why would Jimmy kill Wee Kenny?

Because Wee Kenny knew about Jimmy's involvement in Chloe and Maureen's murders. Maybe Jimmy even knew Wee Kenny had grassed on him to Bootsie. And Jimmy trusted no one. Alive, that is.

Why risk killing three people in the space of a month?

Because Jimmy's dying, with six months to live. That's why he's buying property in Spain now, why he's closing shop, why he's clearing the decks.

But Bully and Jimmy had made a fatal mistake. They had not known Wee Kenny and Topley were cousins, had not known they were family. And family changes everything.

Which was where the solution lay.

Gilchrist and Nance reached Glasgow city centre before midnight, slipped off the M8 at Charing Cross, and powered onto Sauchiehall Street. The one-way systems had Gilchrist swearing under his breath, but Nance shouted directions.

'Right at the next light.'

Gilchrist obliged, throwing the Merc into a tight right.

'Through the next one and left at the one after that.'

The Merc's engine roared as Gilchrist floored the pedal.

But it had been almost five years since Nance lived in Glasgow, and twice they took a wrong turn, negotiating an alternative route with more than the odd curse word.

They reached Babbity Bowster at five to midnight.

The barman told them Topley had been in earlier, but had left with several others.

'How about finding out where he went.'

The barman looked at them, dumb with confusion.

'Ask someone,' snapped Gilchrist. 'Hey. You.'

A young girl with dirty-blonde hair in a loose ponytail almost jumped. The barman said something to her which Gilchrist failed to catch. But she shook her head, and without further prompting the barman stepped from the bar and returned a few minutes later with, 'He left with a bevy of women, heading for Truffles.'

'What's that?'

'The Truffle Club. In Drury Lane.'

The street name tripped Gilchrist up. He had heard it before, but Nance beat him to it. 'Opposite the Horseshoe,' she said.

It cost ten pounds each to enter.

Gilchrist stepped up a carpeted stairway to an upper level that glowed blue and red from the strip club's disco lighting. He thought of walking through the place and looking for Topley, but the aroma of the bar was too much for him, and he ordered a half for himself and a gin and tonic for Nance. He passed over a twenty then faced the open floor.

Men in dull suits and sharp ties sat at tables in small groups. Some eyed the dancer on the stage, others drooled at bare breasts presented to them table-side. Notes were palmed with the legerdemain of men trained in marital deceit, and by the time their drinks came up Gilchrist had counted eighty pounds being disposed of at the table closest to him.

'He's over there,' Nance said, nodding to a table near the corner of the stage.

Topley looked drunk, not happy, and proffered money into girls' hands with the disinterest of a financial glutton. A glass of something clear was thrown back and the empty tumbler returned to the table with a smack that Gilchrist heard above the ambient din. They did not have long before Topley would be beyond talking. If he was not there already.

Gilchrist threw back his whisky and said, 'Let's go.'

Topley did not notice them until Gilchrist squeezed his shoulder. A muscled man seated opposite slid a hand into his inside suit pocket. Nance whispered something in his ear, and the man's hand slipped to his knee.

Topley let out a guffaw then threw a pile of notes, all twenties, onto the table. 'A hundred quid for you, darling, if you pop them out for us. Go on. Let's have a goggle at those lovely tits of yours. What d'you say, Ray?' He nodded to the man opposite. 'Fancy pushing your fat cock into that little lot?'

Topley struggled to pull himself upright then flopped back as if the simple act was beyond him. He laughed again. 'Here,' he said to Nance, and unfolded his wallet. He frowned as he rummaged inside it. 'I thought I had a fifty in here.' Then he looked up with a dazed smile. 'Only hundreds.' A single note flew from his hand and fluttered to the floor. 'Tell you what, darling. I'll make it two hundred. How's that? Just for a peek.' He raised his hands to the air as if a gun had been placed to his skull. 'I won't even try to touch them. House rules. There you go. How fair can a man get?'

Nance picked up the money, and for one confusing moment Gilchrist thought she was going to strip off her blouse and do as Topley ordered. But she leaned forward, money held out, and said to Topley's spinning eyes, 'Should you not be giving this to Wee Kenny's mother?'

Topley's face flattened. His eyes died. He lowered his hands, placed them on the table as if to prove he was unarmed.

Gilchrist readied himself to step in.

'Or do I get to keep it,' Nance pressed on, 'if I tell you where Jimmy Reid's at?'

Gilchrist knew she was bluffing. But it was lovely to watch the effect of her words worm through the drunken fuzz of Topley's mind. Then Topley raised one hand, and Gilchrist realised with a spurt of surprise that four bouncers stood behind them.

CHAPTER THIRTY-NINE

GILCHRIST FROZE. Nance stood as stiff as a puppet.

It felt as if the world was waiting for Topley to lower his hand. Even the music seemed silenced, the dancers stilled.

'Tell the heavies to vanish,' Gilchrist tried.

Topley sat motionless.

Gilchrist felt his muscles tense and wondered if Nance would take out the man to her side, or if she would expect Gilchrist to do that. Or maybe both of them would be frog-marched from the club and deposited into Drury Lane.

Then, as if kick-started into action, Topley's head jerked to the side with a drunken nod and the man called Ray pushed his chair back and stood.

Gilchrist sensed the space behind him clear. A gang of five men in suits as dark as their slicked-back hair trundled to the bar where they eyed Topley's table like a pack of dogs just itching to crunch their teeth through meat and bone.

Gilchrist took Ray's seat. It felt warm.

Nance pulled up the chair beside him.

Topley tried a smile, but some part of his nervous system was not working the way it should. On the stage by Topley's left shoulder a blonde in a thong, with breasts the colour of milky coffee, stretched into a backward crab on her hands and feet then rolled onto the stage floor. A group of men at the table to Gilchrist's left huddled in conversation, oblivious to the torsioned nudity by their side. The group seated at the table to his right ordered drinks. The blonde skipped to the middle of the stage, breasts bouncing like water-filled balloons.

'You're a persistent bitch,' Topley said to Nance.

'Nasty's my middle name.'

Topley gave a gold-tooth grin then shoved the notes over to her. 'Go on, take it,' he said. 'You can owe me a blow-job.'

'You don't get it, do you?'

'Not yet,' Topley said, and grinned. 'Maybe later?'

Gilchrist felt his eyebrows lift as Nance picked up the money. Then he smiled as she tapped the notes together like a pack of cards, ripped them in two, once, then again, and let the pieces flutter from her fingers onto the table.

Topley chuckled. But Gilchrist could see he was fooling no one, and worried that some part of the man's psyche was about to crack and the bouncers would be called with the flicker of an irritated eyebrow. He tried to distract Topley's annoyance by leaning forward.

Topley turned dead eyes Gilchrist's way. In the shifting light, colours danced in time with the music, casting shadows that made Topley's face look as beaten as a boxer's.

Gilchrist did not want to raise his voice, but felt he had no choice. 'You never told me,' he shouted over the music.

'Told you what?'

'About your mother being Wee Kenny's aunt.'

'So?'

'So you want to get even with Jimmy?' It was Nance.

'What's it to you?' Topley snarled.

'Tell us,' she added.

'Tell you?' He chuckled. 'Tell you what, darling?'

'How to fuck Bully.'

Topley pulled himself off his chair and pressed his chest against the table. 'You don't look like you need a lesson in fucking anyone, darling.'

Nance exhaled, shook her head. 'Why don't you be a good dog and give it up?'

Like a referee, Gilchrist stepped in. 'We know you're getting ready to take on a big shipment,' he said to Topley.

Topley turned the full heat of his leaden glare onto Gilchrist. Half-shut eyelids narrowed. Fingers balled into bruised-knuckle fists. If anything was going to happen, it would happen in the next few seconds.

'What the fuck're you talking about?'

'Drugs,' Gilchrist said. 'Isn't that what you do?'

Topley stared at him, then glanced beyond Gilchrist's shoulder. Had he just called his team over? Gilchrist felt himself readying for the thump of muscled hands.

'You're walking on thin ice, Mr Gilchrist. You're talking about things that people like you do not talk to people like me about.'

Gilchrist sensed it was now only a matter of time until Topley's bodyguards threw them out. 'I'm not interested in your grubby little empire,' he said. 'I want to find my daughter.'

Topley's half-shut eyes almost opened. 'Sounds like you're looking to make some other deal.'

'I'm not interested in how you make your money.'

'Well, you see, Mr Gilchrist. This may come as a surprise to you and your pretty sidekick with the big tits.' He reached forward, gathered in the torn notes, then held them up to Gilchrist's face. 'But I *am* interested in making money. Lots of it.' He balled his hand, crushed the notes, then deposited them into his pocket.

Gilchrist waited.

Topley sat back. 'What's in it for me?'

'I won't press charges.'

Topley guffawed, head back, eyes to the ceiling.

A waitress came to the table, carrying a tray on which stood a bottle of champagne and three crystal flutes. She placed a glass in front of each of them and without a word topped them with fizzing champagne. As she left the table, Topley palmed her a single note. Another hundred, Gilchrist thought.

'Charge me with what?' Topley growled.

'Let's not go through that again.' It was Nance. 'Why don't you just cough up or shut up?' Nance grabbed her crystal glass and took a sip. 'Not bad,' she said.

'Dom Perignon,' Topley purred.

'I prefer Moet.'

'I'll have a crate sent to your home.' Topley gave a wry grin. 'All I need is your address, darling.'

'And if I give it to you?'

'Two crates of Moet would be delivered to your doorstep.' Topley placed his hand to his chest. 'With all my love.'

'Who would do the delivering?'

'Whoever you want, darling.'

'And would the delivery boy be expected to stay and help me polish off a bottle or two?'

Topley leaned forward, puzzled by the change in Nance's attitude. Gilchrist's ears were perked, too. 'Whatever you like, darling, could be arranged.' Topley reached across the table, and Nance surprised Gilchrist by taking hold of his hand.

'Someone once told me,' she said, 'that men with money make the best lovers, because they can have all the toys they want, but can't buy a woman's love.' She squeezed Topley's hand. 'So, tell me, Chris. Just how much money do you have?'

'More than enough.'

'More than enough to keep a girl happy?'

'More than enough to keep a girl *very* happy.'

'Even someone who's difficult to please?'

'*Especially* someone who's difficult to please.'

Nance leaned lower. Her breasts swelled against the table. 'I'll make a deal.'

Topley seemed to hold his breath.

Nance had his full attention. Gilchrist's too.

'Do you have a good memory?' she asked Topley.

'Why?'

She released Topley's hand, then lifted her glass of champagne and pressed it to her lips. Over the rim, she eyed him. 'I'll say my address once.' She took a sip. Her eyes seemed to glitter with cheekiness. 'And it'll be up to you to remember it.'

Topley's lips twisted in a smirk of victory.

'But first,' she said, and returned her glass to the table. 'You have to answer some questions.'

'How can I trust you?'

This time Nance smirked. 'You can't.'

Topley frowned and smiled at the same time, and Gilchrist caught the street cruelty of the man. Topley could kick another man to death then hand his widow money at the funeral. Gilchrist had heard how Topley as a teenager had taken a boy's kitten from him then beaten the young kid half to death. When asked why he had taken the kitten, he said he had not wanted to see it get hurt. Enigmatic cruelty seemed to be his trademark.

'All right,' Topley said. 'I'll play along.' He swallowed his champagne with barely a breath, then snapped his fingers over his head. Within seconds a bouncer as large as a lock forward stood at his side.

Gilchrist felt himself shift in his seat.

'Another bottle of this stuff,' Topley ordered.

The bouncer retreated.

'Right, darling.' Topley reclined in his chair with a crack of his knuckles, as if settling in for the evening. A dancer pirouetted like an ice-skater on the stage behind him, her arms almost clipping his shoulder, her body close enough for Gilchrist to smell her perfume. Topley grinned. 'You were saying?'

Nance rested her arms on the table, one hand over the other, as if to keep them from Topley's reach. 'You spent eighteen months in Barlinnie,' she said.

'Don't tell me you hold that against me.'

'And you shared a cell with Bully Reid.'

'Had to share with someone, darling. Bully's better than some. He's not into plugging holes, if you get my meaning.'

'Bully mentioned Maureen's name.' Not a question.

Topley paused, as if trying to work out if Nance was telling or asking, and if he gave the wrong answer had he blown any chance of being told her address. As Gilchrist watched the thought process work across Topley's hard features, he realised with a spurt of disbelief that the man's brain was too far gone on drink and drugs to see Nance's scheming for what it was. He really thought he had a chance at getting a leg over. Amazing.

Topley nodded. 'He did.'

'What did he say about her?' Nance asked.

'Are you sure you want to hear this?'

'I want to hear all of it.'

Gilchrist felt a shiver tingle his spine. The thought of a convicted criminal talking about his daughter meant only one thing. Bully had been driven by revenge for years.

Topley glanced at Gilchrist then grinned at Nance. 'He told me how he'd love to tie her father down, nail him to the floor, like, then fuck her in front of him.'

'Anything else?'

'Then he said he would make her watch while he did him in.' Topley shook his head. 'He's a bit sick that way, is Bully. A fucking nutter.'

'Charming, is he?'

'Charming isn't what Bully's about, darling.'

They sat tight-lipped while another waitress placed three more champagne flutes on the table and topped them up. Liquid frothed over the rims and puddled on the tablecloth. Topley ignored her as she retreated.

To Gilchrist's side, a table-dancer straddled the thigh of a bleary-eyed businessman and bunched her breasts together, nipples as large and flat as saucers.

'He'd never seen Maureen, though,' Nance said. 'Right?'

'He had a photograph of her.'

Gilchrist almost jolted. 'Where did he get that?'

Topley shrugged. 'You'd be surprised what you can get inside. Nude books. Porno videos. The real thing if you know who to ask and have the dosh to pay for it. A photo of your favourite Detective Inspector's daughter is a piece of piss to these guys.'

'Would he still have the photograph?' Gilchrist asked.

Topley grinned. 'He wanked that much over it, it would have dissolved into spunk by now.'

Nance shook her head, and Gilchrist could tell she was having a tough time keeping her tongue in place. 'What else did he say about my daughter?' he tried.

'That she was the way to get back at you for putting him inside, the way to make you suffer for what you did to him.'

Gilchrist bristled. Being beaten up by Bully was something he could handle. It would not be the first time he had taken a thrashing at the hands of some thug. But having his family threatened was a different matter. He struggled to relax, took a sip of champagne. It tasted sweet. He gulped a mouthful.

Topley chuckled. 'It's not Maureen's fault. Bully had it in for you. I can tell you that much.'

Gilchrist thudded his glass to the table. The champagne bubbled and fizzed. Just the way he felt. 'Other than shooting his load over Maureen's photo and nailing me to the floor,' he growled, 'did he ever tell you how he would make me suffer?'

'Can't say that he did.'

Something in the way Topley quipped the denial told Gilchrist he was lying.

'Or when he planned to do it?' Nance added.

'No.'

'He wouldn't want to do in someone the instant he came out of prison, would he?' Nance continued. 'He'd be straight back inside.'

'Bully's not scared of prison.'

'But he likes his freedom.'

'We all do.'

'Did he tell you he wanted his brother, Jimmy, to do it?'

'No.'

'So, he told you nothing?'

'About that subject. Yes. He told me nothing.'

Nance sat back. Gilchrist leaned forward. 'How about Robert Burns?'

Topley seemed puzzled by the question.

Gilchrist helped him out. 'What's Bully's obsession with Robert Burns?' he asked.

'Never knew he had one.'

'Come off it,' Gilchrist snapped. 'He's got an epitaph on his father's grave that's a direct quote from Burns. And he did nothing but quote to me from Burns. He even rewrote one of his opening lines. *Oh princess, by thy watchtower be.*'

At first he thought the change on Topley's face was anger, then realised something was working through the man's mind. He glanced at Nance and saw she had seen it, too.

'You've remembered something,' Nance said.

Topley seemed puzzled, as if surprised to find himself seated at the table with two detectives. Then he looked at her. 'Bully read a lot of stuff. Jimmy would bring it in for him. Books. Tapes. CDs. He was always writing poems. He let me read some of them.'

Bully as a poet did not fit Gilchrist's image of the man. 'Can you remember what any of them were about?' he asked.

Topley shook his head. 'Mostly about killing and raping and stuff like that.'

Now they were getting back on track.

'But he did mention a watchtower,' Topley added.

Gilchrist pulled himself forward. The bulging breasts on display over Topley's shoulder shifted from his peripheral vision. 'I'm listening,' he said.

'Once. About a week before I got out.'

Gilchrist held his breath.

'Said I should keep my eyes and ears open. That one of those days I was going to read about a killing. The watchtower killing, he told me.'

'Were those his exact words?' Nance again.

'Can't remember. Bully ranted on about a lot of stuff. His mind

was getting fucked with the drink and drugs and revenge and stuff.'
Topley fixed a dead-eyed stare on Gilchrist. 'Told me you were going
to rue the day you ever had a daughter. I remember that much.
Remember thinking the two were linked. You know? Watchtower
killing. Your daughter. Because he said he would send you a blank
postcard and you would know it was from him.'

'Why would I know?'

'Because it would have a watchtower on it.'

'What kind of watchtower?' Nance asked.

'Like the old watchtowers in cemeteries.'

Gilchrist felt his blood turn to ice. He'd been right all along. But
was he right about the Auld Aisle? Then a thought hit him, and he
wondered if he was stretching his rationale too far.

'Did he ever tell you what he would do with the body?' he
asked Topley.

Topley frowned. 'What body? Bully wasn't going to kill her. He
wanted to bury her alive. That's what he told me. He wanted you
to know he had buried her alive.'

Gilchrist struggled to control his emotions. It seemed as if every
molecule of muscle and fibre and sinew in his body was about to
coil in, then unfold in fury against Bully.

'And he said something else I thought was odd,' Topley added. 'I'd
never given it another thought. Not one. Not until you mentioned
watchtower.'

Gilchrist sat motionless.

'He said he had it all planned, that it was all ready, just waiting
for her, as soon as he emptied it.'

'Emptied it?' Nance asked. 'The watchtower?'

'The coffin.'

Gilchrist stiffened. All his senses seemed alive, as if his mind
and body were acting as one. He heard the breathing of the dancer
as she writhed her sexual dance to his side, the soft shuffle of her
shoes as she turned and shifted across the stage. The music seemed
clearer, too, as if the instruments were whispering in his ear.

Buried alive. The coffin was ready. Those were the key words.

'This drug shipment,' Gilchrist said. 'When was it to be moved?'

Topley's face deadpanned, as if his dreams of sex with a full-chested policewoman had just evaporated. 'I thought we agreed not to talk about that.'

Gilchrist leaned closer. 'I'm not interested in your drug-worshipping empire,' he growled, and prayed Topley would believe him. He would get down on his knees and beg if that was what it would take. 'Was it soon?' he asked. 'Were the drugs to be moved in the next couple of days?'

Topley turned away, offered his heavy-lidded gaze to Nance.

'St Andrews,' she said. '100 North Street.'

Gilchrist held his breath. Would Topley recognise the address of the police station?

Topley's lips parted in victory.

Got you. 'She could still be alive,' Gilchrist urged.

'Rumour has it something was going to happen tomorrow,' Topley whispered, then glanced left and right, as if to ensure no one was listening. 'But I wouldn't know about that, of course.'

'Of course.'

'Tomorrow night.'

Gilchrist pushed his chair back and stood. The coffin. They were not supposed to have found it. But they had. Which could mean only one thing.

Maureen was no longer going to be buried alive.

She was going to be killed.

CHAPTER FORTY

GILCHRIST ENTERED THE Auld Aisle Cemetery from Woodilee Road. He swung into the small car park then accelerated through the iron gate, sending it crashing to the side. He raced along asphalt pathways wide enough to accommodate a hearse or two. Headstones passed in a shadowed blur. In the darkness, he could not tell exactly where he was, but when he thought he was close enough, he veered onto the grass verge.

He left the engine running, the lights on, and stepped into the silence of the cemetery.

His feet slipped on the damp grass as he crossed beds of graves. Nance reached him by the time he stood at Topley's.

'She's here,' he said to her. 'I know it. I feel it. She's here, Nance.' Nance stared into the darkness.

Gilchrist lifted the strip of yellow police tape and bent under it. He pulled back the tarpaulin that covered the excavated pit of Topley's grave. The drug-laden coffin was gone, but the SOCOs had left the excavation open for the cemetery staff to repair.

Gilchrist jumped into the grave. He stood waist deep. He stamped his feet on the bottom, but the soil was firm. The coffin containing the body of John Topley would be a couple of feet beneath him. He kicked the sides of the grave, but they were untouched, solid.

Nance eyed him from a safe distance, as if watching the antics of a madman.

Gilchrist pulled himself from the pit. 'She's here, Nance. I know it. She's here.' He brushed soil from his clothes and scanned the dark shadows.

'*Maureen?*'

Nance shuffled her feet.

'*Maureen?*' Gilchrist cupped his hands to his mouth. '*Maureen?*'

'Andy.'

Gilchrist faced her. His breath panted in the cold air. He had tried to explain his thinking on the drive from the city. But she seemed unconvinced. Did she not understand? Maureen was here. *Here*. In this cemetery. She had to be. That's what Bully had been telling him. It was simple.

'The coffin,' he said.

'I know. You told me.'

'That's why they moved her from Glenorra. To bring her here. Closer to the coffin.' He lifted the yellow tape, stepped across the grass, marched along the asphalt pathway. '*Maureen?*'

Nance followed.

The moon broke through the clouds and cast a ghostly glow across the cemetery. Headstones stood like silent bodyguards ready to slay whoever soiled their owners' graves. A cold wind stirred in the passing, like the chilled breath of wraiths wakened by his calling.

'*Maureen?*'

Nance followed him through the opening in the stone wall that separated the old cemetery from the new. The headstones seemed larger, more ominous, the sky darker, too, as the moon settled behind a shifting band of clouds. She pulled her collar around her neck and caught up with him.

'*Maureen?*'

'Why bring Maureen here?' she asked.

'It's closer to the coffin.'

'I know that. But why here? Why not keep her in a house somewhere, and when they empty the coffin bring her then?'

'Why move her at all?' he replied. 'Have you asked yourself that?'

'The neighbours were becoming suspicious? They didn't want

to keep her in one place for any length of time? The hut in the back was becoming a liability? How would I know?'

'And from one house to another house?' Gilchrist shook his head.

'Maybe she's in a house nearby,' Nance offered.

'Maybe.' Gilchrist marched on.

'You could be wrong, Andy.'

Gilchrist stopped. 'I'm not wrong,' he snapped. 'I know I'm not. I feel it here. Right here.' He thumped his chest with a force that should have stopped his heart. 'Bully might be a murdering psychopath, but he's not stupid. He had it planned. The coffin was ready. That's what Topley said. Maybe Bully's getting out in two years. Maybe sooner. Who knows? But with Jimmy dying, he couldn't wait any longer. He needed Jimmy to do his dirty work. So he started the ball rolling.'

'That's all very well,' she said. 'But—'

'No buts.' Gilchrist gripped her arms. 'Help me, Nance. Help me find Maureen.'

'Okay. Okay, Andy.' She stared at him. 'Okay.'

Gilchrist released his grip. He could tell from the tone of her voice and the tightness in her lips that he was scaring her. If she did not want to help him he would find Maureen by himself. He walked up the hill towards the oldest part of the cemetery.

He reached the old gate and pushed through. The watchtower stood like a miniature cathedral, an eerie grey in the moonlight. He strode towards it, reached its steps, and bounded up them two at a time.

She was here. She had to be. Not buried. Not yet. But alive. Bully wanted her alive.

He cupped his hands. '*Maureen?*' The sound of his voice settled over the graveyard. High in the branches behind him, he heard the flutter of wings, the harsh caw of a crow. He cupped again. '*Maureen?*'

Nance stood at the bottom of the stone stairwell.

Oh princess, by thy watchtower be.

Oh princess...

Bully's words that told him who.

...by thy watchtower.

And where.

He gripped the cold stone. His breath clouded the night air. Jesus, it was so cold. Who could survive in cold like this? Was he already too late? But Bully had not wanted her dead. He had wanted her alive.

To bury her.

He cupped his hands, shouted again. '*Maureen?*'

Princess. Watchtower.

Watchtower was the key.

...by thy watchtower.

She was here. By the watchtower—

He stopped, frozen by a sudden thought that blew into his mind.

The poem. 'Mary Morison'. Why had he not given that any thought?

Why that poem? Why not some other poem?

Had Bully left clues in the other verses? But they had not been changed.

Again, his mind screamed at him to challenge the logic.

He removed the crumpled sheet from his pocket, flattened it as best he could, and tried to read it from the light of the moon. Movement by his side startled him.

'Here,' Nance said, and held out a set of keys.

'What's this?'

She fingered the keyring. A weak light lit up the page.

He read out the verses. 'Oh princess, by thy watchtower be, it is the wished, the trysted hour. Those smiles and glances let me see, that makes the miser's treasure poor.' And underneath the first line, the original words printed in Jack's sprawling hand.

It took Gilchrist a full five seconds to realise what he had missed, what they had all missed, the one word that Bully had slipped in unnoticed. Until now.

He read the original line. 'Oh Mary, at thy window be.'

He read it again. 'Christ,' he whispered.

–At. Not *by.*

It meant something. It had to. Why else would Bully have changed it?

He scanned the other lines, his gaze settling, then fixing on the words *...and glances let me see...*

See.

Let me see. By thy watchtower.

At thy watchtower. *By* thy watchtower. Did it matter?

Let me see. Was that the key? What could he see from the top of the watchtower? He peered into the darkness, over the oldest part of the cemetery for which the watchtower was built. He could see the frames of iron cages and lonely headstones that guarded graves targeted by nineteenth-century grave robbers on their nightly plunders—

He caught his breath. Was that it?

Nightly plunders. The graves were robbed at night.

When the guards were in the watchtower.

...let me see...

At night? From the watchtower?

What could he see from where he stood?

He scanned the graveyard, kept his focus on the wall within view, the headstones closest to him. But he could see nothing in which a body could be kept until the coffin was ready. He turned to the gate, the main entrance to the original cemetery, next to the caretaker's house—

Christ. The house. It was derelict. Why had he not noticed before?

He rushed down the steps and reached the front windows. A metal grille of sorts had been installed over them. He gripped one of them, but it was solid. He turned to the front door and shouldered it.

Solid, too.

He stepped around the side, down a narrow alley that bordered the cemetery, and reached the back door. The air smelled of dampness and rotten leaves.

He gripped the door handle.

'What are you doing?'

Nance's voice jolted him. 'She's here,' he said.

'Andy, I think you need to consider what you're doing.'

Gilchrist shouldered the door. The frame splintered.

'*Andy.*'

He shouldered it again.

The door burst open. The shattered frame clattered to the floor as Gilchrist stumbled into a dank hallway of bare boards and blistered walls.

'*Maureen?*' He ran into the first room, an empty room to the right. '*Are you here?*' He heard Nance repeat Maureen's name from another room, pleased she had put her doubts behind her, if only for the time being. He kicked something on the floor, almost tripped, but in the dark could tell only that it was low and wooden. A coffee table? A packing box?

The next room yielded the same result. His shouts echoed off the walls. 'Maureen? Can you hear me?'

He tried another room.

Nothing.

Nance almost bumped into him in the centre of what Gilchrist took to be the living room. The realisation that he had failed locked his breath in his throat. He felt a stab of pain in his chest, and wondered for one frightening moment if he was going to black out.

'Andy?'

'It's...' He spun around, stared at the dark walls, the boarded windows. 'It's...' *It's useless*, he wanted to say. He spun on his heels. Around him only walls, stark and bare and black as night. It was useless. He saw that now. He was too late. *Too late.* He cupped his hands, screamed at the top of his voice. '*Maureen?*'

'She's not here, Andy.'

The strength in Nance's voice hit him. 'Maureen,' he whispered to her. 'Dear God, Maureen,' then covered his mouth with his hands, felt his breath rush through his fingers, warm and wet. Jesus, how could he be so wrong? Why had he let himself believe in the slimmest of hopes?

Nance tugged his sleeve.

He shook her hand free. 'No.' He stepped to the side. '*Maureen?*

Maureen?' His breath came at him in gulping waves that hit his lungs in sobs. He stepped to the door, felt his legs give out.

'Andy?'

He grunted as his knees hit the floor. He pressed his hands to his face, fought back the cutting bile in his throat, felt Nance's hand on his shoulder, her fingers flex. He said nothing as she stood beside him.

'Andy.'

He shook his head, opened his eyes. 'I can't lose her,' he gasped. 'I can't, Nance. I just, I can't...'

Nance's fingers tightened.

He looked to the floor, heard her shoes shuffle, except...

Except...

Nance had not moved.

Gilchrist gripped her hand, lifted it from his shoulder.

'What is it, Andy?'

He looked to his left. 'Did you hear that?'

'Hear what?'

'Sshh.' He tilted his head to the side. 'Listen.' He had gained his night-sight, but in the darkness all he saw were shapes.

Nothing moved.

He eyed the darkness to his right, to his left, twisted his head over his shoulder as—

Another shuffle.

He stared to his right, to the packing box on the floor.

A shuffle. But not a shuffle. More like...

A scrape? From what?

A mouse? A rat? Something else?

Nance had heard it, too. He knew from the stiffness in her posture, the way her body turned to the wooden crate on the floor.

'*Maureen?*'

Silence.

'*Maureen? Can you hear me?*'

Another scrape.

Nance beat him to it. She thudded the box out the way and was scrabbling at the floor, tugging the carpet, peeling the damp material back. He thought she was ripping it into shreds, until he realised a rectangular piece had been cut from it. He gripped a corner, pulled it back—

'Bully warned me about you.'

Gilchrist felt his body turn to ice, his blood to water. If he'd had anything in his stomach he would have dropped the lot there and then.

Light exploded in his brain like a kick to the teeth.

He had time only to cover his eyes and turn away from the boot coming his way, managed to pull back far enough so that it caught him only a glancing blow on his ear. He roared as pain shot through him, and rolled into the darkness, hand pressed hard to the side of his head, half expecting to feel a bloody mess where his ear had once been, but it was still intact.

A beam of light chased him as he dived to the side, felt the thud of something heavy and sharp shiver the floorboards by his head. A deep curse, a guttural scream, then a flurry of light around the room as the flashlight clattered to the floor.

Gilchrist lunged for it, felt the wind of something brush his ear, the hard metallic clatter on the wall behind him. He picked up the flashlight, trapped the shape of two figures in its beam, caught Nance beneath a raised arm, a sharp point—

He threw the flashlight.

The room flickered as wild as lightning then fell into darkness with a grunt as the flashlight bounced off bone. He heard the thud as the body hit the floor and had time only to dive at where he thought the figure had fallen.

Cuffs out. 'You're under arrest,' he shouted, then the hard clip of metal as he slipped them over a bony wrist.

A grunt, then, 'Fuck you,' and a fist as hard as stone hit him on the jaw.

His head jerked to the side and he almost lost his grip on the cuffs as another hammer blow hit the side of his head. In the blind darkness and the close struggle Gilchrist knew he could never trap the man's free arm long enough to cuff it, so he clipped the cuffs to his own wrist. 'Got you, you bastard.'

He felt himself dragged to his feet by the figure at his side, surprised by the animal strength of the man. He fought to grab the loose
arm as it hit him on the neck in a poorly aimed rabbit punch, and felt
his breath leave him as a knee came up between his legs. He smelled
the stale tobacco stink of the man, felt the roughness of stubble, the
wet spray of spittle as the voice by his ear cursed and spat.

But cuffed together, the man was going nowhere.

Arms as thin and strong as steel ropes wormed their way
around his ribcage.

Gilchrist tucked his left foot behind a leg and pushed forward.

They hit the floor like a loaded sack.

He heard the air go out of the man, but before he could overpower him a hand slapped onto his face, and fingers as hard and
sharp as steel claws dug into his skin.

Light again. A dancing beam.

'You're under arrest.' Nance's voice, high, unsteady.

'Fuck off.'

A roar, a grunt, and before Gilchrist could move, the man had
rolled on top of him, then over, body twisted to the wall.

The dancing flashlight caught the blade of the hunting knife at
the same instant as Gilchrist saw Jimmy Reid's fingers fold around
the hilt and the knife rear into the darkness above his head.

'No,' he shouted, and caught the grim smile of victory as the
blade flashed down at him.

CHAPTER FORTY-ONE

THE KNIFE THUDDED INTO FLESH.

But not Gilchrist's.

He heard Nance gasp, felt her body go limp, and realised she had dived at Reid and taken the blow meant for him.

Fire flashed through his mind.

Reid shifted his weight.

Nance's body tumbled off, and Gilchrist knew Reid had pulled the knife from her back. No time to think.

Only to move.

And move *now*.

He gripped his cuffed wrist tight with his free hand, pulled his legs up and rolled heels over head.

He heard a grunt of pain, a hard gasp of surprise. He tightened his grip, rolled in toward Reid, felt the pain as his own elbow twisted, the strain on his wrist as the metal cuff bit deep into his skin. His contorted move had Reid at a disadvantage. But he still needed to move quickly.

He shifted his weight, pulled himself to his knees, felt Reid's body try to resist as he shoved his arm up his back.

Reid gasped, 'My arm.'

Gilchrist pushed higher.

'My arm,' Reid roared.

Gilchrist heard the dry crunch of gristle tearing and the high-pitched scream like a pig being burned, then felt the strength leave Reid's arm.

On automatic now, Gilchrist unclipped the cuff from his own wrist, pulled Reid's other arm behind his back, clicked the wrists together. He pushed away, brushed the floor with his hands, found what he was looking for, and turned it on.

A beam of light shot out from his hand.

A quick flash at Reid to show him lying on his stomach, face twisted in pain, arms behind his back, the hunting knife with its serrated edge within easy reach.

Gilchrist kicked it to the corner.

He found Nance six feet away, on her front, her right shoulder a bloodied mess. But she was moving, pulling herself forward like some dying animal.

He kneeled beside her, placed the flashlight on the floor, eased her jacket from her shoulder. 'Don't move,' he ordered.

'I wasn't planning to,' she whispered.

He grimaced at her humour, but could tell she was hurting. He pushed his fingers through the bloodied cut in her blouse and ripped the material apart. In the flashlight's beam, the wound was deep and wide, as if the blade had plunged into the skin and been tugged back. But he saw, too, that it had not cut any major blood vessels, and that her sports bra was helping to hold the flesh together, keep the wound tight.

He pulled off his leather jacket, gripped his shirt, and almost tore it from his body. Shirt in his teeth, he ripped off a sleeve and whipped it under her arm and around and over her shoulder. And again. He tied a quick knot. Could be better, he thought, but it would help staunch the flow.

From behind, he heard a grunt.

Reid had twisted onto his side, his body long and lean, crawling out of the shadows like an alligator from a night swamp. From the way he was shifting, Gilchrist knew he was trying to find his feet.

Not so fast.

Gilchrist took one step, two, and booted him in the face. Reid grunted and slumped against the floor. Gilchrist stomped down hard on Reid's torn shoulder and almost flinched from the animal roar. 'Stay put,' he growled, then retrieved the flashlight and shone it at the spot on the centre of the floor.

The patch in the carpet had been cut and stitched like a proper opening. He could make out the shape of the trapdoor, but no handle. He found Reid's knife in the corner of the room and used it to jemmy the trapdoor open.

He pulled the wooden frame up and off and threw it to the side, stuck his head into the dusty underfloor space. He danced the beam beneath the floor, almost cried out in anguish as it flickered over four bare walls.

He pulled himself upright, felt anger shimmer behind his eyes like heat from rock. He shone the flashlight into Reid's eyes. 'What have you done with her?' he shouted, and saw from their puzzled reflection that he was missing something.

Back under the floor.

This time he saw it.

What he had taken at first glance to be a solid wall was a piece of sheetrock cut to fit the space and jammed in to stay upright. He lowered himself through the opening, bent double in the tight space, and pulled the sheetrock back.

He faced a small door. It was padlocked.

He thudded the heel of his fist against it. '*Maureen?*' He held his breath but heard nothing. He gripped the padlock and tugged. Nothing. He gripped tighter, tugged again. The hasp was secure. He thumped the door. '*Maureen?*' And again. But the wood was solid. Out with the knife, thudded down and behind the metal hasp, in as hard as he could, then pulled.

He grunted with effort, but the knife slipped free.

Down again. Harder that time. He tugged, felt the hasp pull from the wood, the screws or nails or whatever was holding it in draw out from the rough grain.

Slipped again. Damn it.

Another stab. Missed. Again. Got it that time.

He gritted his teeth, pulled hard, held it, pulled harder—

The hasp ripped off with splintering wood.

He opened the door, shone his flashlight in, saw her body curled in a foetal position, not moving, and knew from the way she was lying with one arm out to the door that he was too late. He scrambled through the opening, his voice coming in whimpers he failed to recognise as his own.

He reached her, lifted her, cradled her in his arms, and watched in horror as her head lolled back and eyes as lifeless as death stared at nothing.

Oh, dear God, dear God.

No...

CHAPTER FORTY-TWO

THE SMELL OF URINE still hung in the cold room.

Gilchrist tugged the collar of his leather jacket then glanced at his watch. 11:27. He removed her photograph from his pocket, the same one he passed around in his search for her. Dark eyes smiled at him, filled with the youthful promise of life. He rubbed his thumb across her face and startled as the door opened.

A guard pushed at Bully as he shuffled in.

Gilchrist thought Bully had aged, as if a few more days in jail had added several years to the man. Bully scowled as the guard shoved him onto his seat and shackled his legs to the floor, then stood with his back to the door as if to block any escape attempt. Bully looked up at Gilchrist and his face broke into a cruel smile.

'My oh my,' he said. 'How the mighty have fallen.'

Gilchrist did not move.

'What've you been up to? Playing on the motorway?'

Gilchrist knew he looked a mess. His left cheek was swollen and bruised. Common sense told him he would need to have it x-rayed. His leather jacket was slashed at the sleeve where Jimmy Reid had plunged his knife but failed to cut flesh. Underneath, his one-sleeved shirt was missing four buttons and stained with a mixture of his and Nance's blood. The knees of his jeans were caked with dirt. Without a word he placed Maureen's photograph on the table, as if laying down a trump card, then stepped away and pressed his back against the opposite wall.

Bully glanced at the photo. 'What's this?' he asked.

'You masturbate to my daughter.'

Bully blinked, as slow as a reptile.

'You masturbate to my princess.'

Bully tried a smile, but whatever thoughts were trying to fire through his brain were not igniting. 'Your princess?' he said, and coughed out a laugh. 'I hear your princess is a good ride.'

Gilchrist pushed off the wall and paced the short length of the room, eyes to the floor, away from Bully, always away, he thought, and felt wonder at the fear the man was able to instil in him. He reached the wall, turned, and paced back.

'We've been in contact with the Spanish authorities,' he said to the floor. 'We've suggested that it would be appropriate to impound your villas.' He glanced at Bully. 'They do that for drug associated crimes these days. Did you know that?'

The chains rattled.

He concentrated on the floor, did not want Bully to read anything from his eyes, to see how he scared him, even now. He heard the chains clatter as Bully shuffled in his seat.

'We've also been in contact with your solicitor,' he added. 'Rory Ingles.'

'You'll be hearing from Rory,' Bully growled.

'Word on the street is that you think you're getting out in two years.'

'Sooner, now you lot are fucking it up.'

Gilchrist kept pacing, forced a smile to his face. 'I'm not here to argue that point.'

'What the fuck're you here for then? To give me new wanking material?'

Gilchrist stepped to the table with a speed that almost had Bully tensing. He grabbed the photograph. 'You could do yourself a favour,' he said, and held it up for Bully to leer at. 'And confess.'

'To what?'

'That you ordered Chloe's murder. My daughter's, too. That you devised the whole scheme, the body parts, the notes, the kidnapping, all to satisfy your sick psychopathic needs.'

Bully grinned, almost with relief it seemed, as if pleased to find himself back in control. 'Not a fucking clue what you're on about,' he said.

'That's a pity.' Gilchrist slipped Maureen's photograph into his pocket, safe from Bully's lecherous eyes. He started pacing again. 'We'll just have to let Jimmy tell us, then. Won't we?'

Bully hawked phlegm from the back of his throat. 'In your dreams, big man.'

'No dreams,' Gilchrist said. 'Try nightmares.' He gave Bully a passing glance. 'Yours.'

Bully smiled, an odd look that settled somewhere between confusion and anger. 'Jimmy'll tell you fuck all.'

'How do you know he hasn't told us everything already?'

'Even if there was something to tell,' Bully sneered, 'which there isn't. Jimmy knows what'd happen to him when I get out.'

Gilchrist stopped. He faced Bully. 'Don't you mean *if* you get out?'

Bully's eyes tightened. His lips pursed. Sweat dotted his upper lip. 'Wait 'til I talk to Rory.'

'Won't do you any good.'

Bully's eyes flickered, as if he knew something was going on but could not figure it out. 'You're at it,' he said.

'Oh, Rory'll be talking to you,' Gilchrist said. 'He'll be talking to you all right. But it won't be about getting out in two years. More like breaking the news that you'll be spending the rest of your life in prison.' He eyed the walls, faced the slit-window. 'In this miserable hell-hole. Without the remotest chance of parole.'

'What the fuck're you on about?'

Gilchrist leaned forward. That close, he could smell the prison stench of the man. If confinement and desperation had a scent, that was what he was smelling. 'Oh princess, by thy watchtower be,' he growled. 'That's what you said.'

Bully gave a smile of victory. 'You worked it out yet?'

Gilchrist wanted Bully to think he had the upper hand. He wanted him to hold onto that belief for as long as possible, so that when he eventually told him the pain would be all the greater. For a moment he wondered if he had become as cruel as Bully, if something had snapped in his neural system and changed him. But what Bully had done to Chloe, to Maureen, defied the laws of morality and all sense of conscience. And Gilchrist knew he could never be that cruel.

'Confess,' he said to Bully. 'Tell me how you commanded your brother to kill two women for you.'

Bully smiled. 'After I talk to Rory. Maybe I'll think about it. How does that sound?'

'I'll give you one last chance.'

Bully chuckled. 'You crack me up, Gilchrist. You know that? You just fucking crack me up.'

'We found the coffin.'

Bully froze. Something dark shifted behind his feral eyes. Disbelief, perhaps. Or rising vitriol.

'And your secret stash.'

Bully worked his jaw. From the look in his eyes he could have been chewing nails.

'Street rates put it at around thirty million, give or take a million or two.'

Bully strained forward.

'We've got Jimmy, too.'

The chain clattered as Bully shifted his feet. 'You're at it, Gilchrist. You're fucking at it. I know you.'

'Do you?'

Bully seemed to let Gilchrist's question hang in the air for a few seconds, then growled, 'Jimmy's told you fuck all. I know Jimmy. He'd tell the fuzz to fuck off.'

'Oh, and Maureen, too,' Gilchrist added. 'We found her.'

Bully tried a tight grin. 'Now I know you're at it.'

Gilchrist returned to his place on the opposite wall and pressed his back to it again. He stared at the pockmarked face, at demonic eyes that glared at him with madness, and felt a gut-sickening hatred simmer and boil and fill him with an almost irresistible desire to pull Bully across the table and bludgeon him to death with his bare hands. He fought against the moment, felt it pass, then in his softest voice said, 'Maureen is in Stobhill Hospital.'

The chains rattled. Bully clenched his fists.

Gilchrist felt his lips pull into a grin, then onto a heartfelt smile that tugged at his mouth and reached his eyes and made him want to laugh. 'Despite what you had that psycho brother of yours do to her,' he said, 'to my daughter, to my princess.' He narrowed his eyes. 'She survived.' *Barely*, he thought. *Severely weakened. But alive, thank God. Alive.* 'She's alive and well and expected to make a full recovery.'

'Lies,' hissed Bully. 'It's all lies.'

Gilchrist slipped his hand into his inside jacket pocket and removed a folder of photographs. 'Jimmy's no longer afraid of you.'

'I'll kill that bastard if he says a word.'

'And do you know why Jimmy's not afraid of you?'

Bully's knuckles whitened. Spittle foamed at the corners of his mouth. 'Jimmy knows he'll be dead fucking meat.'

For a moment Gilchrist wondered if Bully knew that Jimmy had terminal cancer, or even if he cared. 'Because Rory Ingles, your brief, your high-paid big-shot solicitor, on first-name terms, has now been hired by your brother, Jimmy.'

'*Lies*.' Clenched fists crashed onto the table. 'Fucking *lies*.' Bully reached for Gilchrist, but his fettered legs held him back.

Gilchrist threw the folder of photographs onto the table. It split open. Coloured images spilled out, sliding across the metal surface like a discarded pack of cards.

Bully glared at them.

'Taken early this morning,' Gilchrist said. 'At police headquarters in Pitt Street. Take a good look,' he said, and watched Bully finger through them. 'That one is Rory talking to Jimmy,' he added, 'convincing him his best chance for a deal is to turn Queen's evidence.'

'Lies,' Bully hissed at the images. 'Fucking lies.'

'And here was me thinking the camera never lies.'

Bully looked up. Anger danced like madness in eyes that burned. 'Fuck you, Gilchrist.' He slammed his fists to the table, swept the photographs to the floor. 'Fuck you. It's lies. All of it. It's *lies. Fucking lies.*'

Gilchrist felt his lips pull into the tiniest of smiles. He nodded to the guard who turned and opened the door.

A short man with a balding head and thickening waist walked in and faced Bully across the table. His pin-striped suit looked pristine next to Gilchrist's dishevelled figure.

'William Thomson Reid,' he said in a voice that sounded bored, 'I am charging you with complicity in the murder of Chloe Fullerton, and conspiracy to abduct and murder Maureen Gillian Gilchrist. Charges will also be brought against you for drug related offences...'

As Bully was read his rights Gilchrist stared at him and hoped Bully could read from his eyes the hatred that pulsed beneath his skin in time with the steady beat of his heart. And as he watched the reality of Bully's dilemma settle into his twisted mind, Gilchrist came to realise that he was no longer afraid of the man, as if some road that had stretched out in front of him, once dark and ominous, now lay cleared to the horizon where he could see the safety of his own future.

It took three guards to haul Bully back to his cell, all the while struggling against his shackles and screaming like a demented lunatic. Gilchrist pressed his back to the wall and closed his eyes, let the verbal diatribe vanish over his head.

I'll have you, Gilchrist, d'you hear? I'll fucking have you. I'm not through with you. The fucking lot of you are in for it now. You'd better believe it. You listening to me?

You're dead, Gilchrist.

You're fucking dead.

When all that was left was the echo of Bully's voice and the smell of stale urine, Gilchrist opened his eyes, pulled the mini-cassette recorder from his pocket, and switched it off. He had not been altogether honest about Jimmy turning Queen's evidence, but Bully's murderous threats against him would go a long way to convincing Jimmy to cooperate.

Gilchrist felt tired, and his body ached. He clawed his fingers through his hair, surprised by how dry and grimy it felt. He needed a long hot shower, but first he needed to make another visit.

* * *

He found her still in Intensive Care, hooked up to a plethora of plastic tubes and full bottles and bags on wheeled stands. Surprisingly, he thought, she was awake. Well, her eyes were open, and swam in and out of focus as he approached.

He sat beside her, took hold of her hand. She tried to smile at him, but the effort seemed too much. Feeble fingers entwined around his then squeezed, and he felt his eyes well as her cracked lips formed, 'I'm sorry, Dad.'

He leaned forward, pressed his lips to her damp cheek, not sure if the tears he tasted were from her eyes or his own.

'So am I,' he whispered. 'So am I,' then buried his face into the pillow beside her and let his tears flow.

CHAPTER FORTY-THREE

Two weeks later

JACK SURPRISED GILCHRIST.

Throughout Chloe's funeral, he stood upright and tight-lipped, blue eyes as clear as the sky through the crematory's stained-glass windows. Gilchrist, on the other hand, had to swallow the lump in his throat when commitment prayers were read and the velvet curtains closed on Chloe's coffin.

The mournful sound of some unfamiliar hymn swelled from the organ as Chloe's parents strode down the aisle together, not holding hands, her mother's face tired and defeated, her father's tight and bitter. They did not wait at the entrance to accept condolences from friends and mourners, but hurried down the steps into a glistening black limousine that laid twin contrails of white exhaust in the still April air.

In the car park, Jack surprised Gilchrist again.

'I'm giving up sculpting,' he said.

The unimaginable thought of Jack not working at what he lived for hit Gilchrist like a blow to the gut. 'Is that what you want to do?' he asked.

Jack shrugged, breathed in the cold air. 'I've finally realised I'm no good at it, that my ideas are not original, that I've nothing to say that has not been said before.'

'But your work...'

'I'm going to concentrate on oils instead.'

'So you're not getting a job,' Gilchrist said, then shook his head with a chuckle. 'Sorry. I didn't mean it the way it sounded.'

Jack seemed unfazed by Gilchrist's gaffe. He stared off to the dark walls of the crematorium. 'Chloe always liked my stuff,' he said. 'She thought I was a better artist than sculptor.' He almost smiled. 'I wish I'd listened to her. Now I feel it's the least I can do for her. For her memory.'

Gilchrist could only nod.

'She bequeathed me all of her canvases,' he continued. 'Her parents' solicitors have already challenged my right to have them.'

Gilchrist did not like the sound of that. 'Do you know why?' he asked.

'Money.' Jack's gaze locked on his father's. 'Can you believe that? They want to sell her paintings. For *money*.' He scowled. 'They never supported her, you know. They never called to ask how she was getting on, or asked about her work. In the end, Chloe just closed the door on them. It upset her.'

'I'm sorry.' It was all Gilchrist could think to say.

Jack shook his head, as if the apology was unnecessary. 'I've had a word with a friend who's eager to exhibit Chloe's work. None of her paintings will be up for sale, of course, but she's encouraged me to exhibit some work of my own. Oils and stuff. So I'll see how it goes.'

Gilchrist gripped Jack's shoulder and squeezed. 'That's great news,' he said. 'I'll be rooting for you.'

They stepped off to the side as a stream of cars fled the crematorium grounds. When the final car had passed, Gilchrist shielded his eyes from a burst of sunlight as he stared at the solitary figure at the far end of the car park, just about the last person he expected to see. The day was overflowing with surprises, he thought.

'Excuse me,' he said to Jack. 'Back in a tick.'

He shoved his hands deep into his coat pockets and strode across the car park. As he approached, he thought the beard suited Watt. It hid most of his face.

Watt offered his hand.

Gilchrist ignored it. 'Didn't expect to see you here,' he said.

'Thought I'd pay my respects.'

'You knew Chloe?'

'We met way back. When she dated Kevin.'

'Kevin Topley?'

Watt nodded. 'She knew nothing of Kevin's background, of course. Didn't know he was dealing drugs. Just let herself be lured by his masculine charm. Kevin could be like that.'

'Like his brother, Chris, you mean.'

Watt shook his head. 'Different animal altogether,' he said, then seemed to sense Gilchrist's unasked question. He smiled, as if in reassurance. 'Maureen and Topley were never an item. It was just a story put around to give Maureen cover and a bit of credibility about the office. It gave her access to places that might otherwise have been closed.'

'And Topley went along with that?'

'Topley was on a tightrope, walking the fine line between keeping Bully and his mob happy, and his plans to become Glasgow's Mr Big. He's a pro, so he knew how to handle everyone.'

'Including you?'

'Including me.'

'And if he, how do I say it, stepped off the tightrope on the wrong side?'

'He would lose it all. The business. The money. The underworld respect he craved. Topley lives in a bit of a fantasy world. Sees himself as Glasgow's next Mr Big.'

'And he works for you?'

'Indirectly.'

'Meaning?'

'Keeps his ear to the ground. That sort of thing.'

'Your informer, you mean?'

'I prefer to use the word, *insider*.'

'Don't try to blind me with semantics, Ronnie. I'm too old for that.' Gilchrist shuffled his shoulders. 'Did you never worry that Topley might take a dislike to being ordered about and try to snuff you from the picture? He has the pull.'

Watt smirked. 'Then he would be taken out. I told him that.'

'And he believed you?'

'He believed me.'

Something in the way Watt uttered the words had Gilchrist working through the rationale. Watt would have Topley killed if he did not toe the line? Was that what he was telling him? Things might be different down in Glasgow, but Gilchrist was pretty sure that Strathclyde Police would not entertain their officers threatening the lives of any citizens, good or bad.

And then he thought he saw it.

'Kevin's death was no accident,' he said. 'Was it?'

Watt shrugged. 'Some said he was getting too big for his boots. That Chris wanted to move in, take over. Who knows?'

'Chris had Kevin killed?'

Watt faked a smile.

And at that instant Gilchrist saw Watt for what he really was. 'Not Chris,' he said. 'But you. To let Topley know the same thing could happen to him. If he ever misbehaved.'

Watt narrowed his eyes.

'And just to be on the safe side you did the same to Chloe.'

Watt's eyes flashed. 'Don't push it, Andy. I would never harm a woman. And you know it.'

'Chris Topley?'

'Jimmy Reid. But we'll never know for sure.'

Gilchrist nodded. Bully had ordered Jimmy to kill Chloe, probably because he could never be sure how much she knew of Kevin Topley's drug business and its connection to his own. It seemed as good an answer as any.

He eyed the crematorium gardens, settling on the skeletal branches of some vine or clematis, and felt a surge of sadness flow through him. Chloe would never see another flower bloom, another tree blossom, never enjoy the simplest pleasures of life. Her death seemed such a waste, such a needless act of cruelty. Someone other than the Reid brothers should pay.

'Chris Topley's not being charged,' he snarled. 'Why?'

Watt shrugged. 'Bigger fish to catch.'

'Don't tell me you're letting him off the hook.'

Watt shook his head. 'Topley doesn't know it yet, but he is the hook. And the bait.' Watt chewed his imaginary gum and shuffled his shoulders. 'He'll get what's coming to him in the end. I promise you. But we need to keep the status quo for a few more months.'

Now Gilchrist was beginning to understand. Strathclyde's reaction to Watt's almost criminal activities had him baffled up until that moment. The answer seemed so simple he wondered why it had taken him so long to figure it out.

Watt was not with Strathclyde. He never had been. Watt was some undercover agent battling the influx of drugs to the country. 'I never believed your assignment to the London Met was for real,' Gilchrist said. 'That's cover, too.'

'You're always digging, Andy. Always looking for a reason. You never give up.'

'I heard a rumour that MI5 and 6 had combined to bust some European drug cartel. Is that the reason you're moving to London?'

Watt stared off beyond the crematorium. 'It's time to move on,' he whispered. 'There's nothing here for me.'

Gilchrist needed more. 'Define nothing,' he said.

Something in the way Watt returned Gilchrist's look told him he was about to hear the truth. 'You know what I mean,' Watt said.

'Nothing with Maureen?'

'Yes.'

Gilchrist tightened his lips and nodded.

Watt eyed him for several long seconds, then removed a hand from his pocket and offered it to Gilchrist.

This time Gilchrist took it.

'I'll miss her,' Watt said. 'Another time, another place, perhaps.'

'I'll make sure she never visits London.'

Watt chuckled, shook his head. 'She wants to write about you. She admires you. Did you know that?'

Admire was not the word Gilchrist would have thought of.

'Don't lose her again.'

Gilchrist tightened his lips and watched Watt walk away. He waited until Watt's car slipped behind a copse of trees before he turned away. Watt's words echoed in his mind.

Don't lose her again.

It seemed such an odd thing for Watt to say. But the truth of the matter was that he *had* lost Maureen, he had lost *both* his children. He faced the opposite end of the car park.

Jack stood with his backside against the boot of his car.

Gilchrist felt a smile tug his lips. No, he thought. I won't lose her again. I won't lose either of them again.

He pulled his collar up and strode towards his son.